FIREFIGHT!

Far away, I could hear a firefight. Somehow, I realized it was not far away at all, but was a fight between my patrol and the Viet Cong. I knew I had to get up, to do something to help out, to lead them back out of there, but my arms and legs wouldn't move.

Someone grabbed my useless arm and began to drag me through the brush. I thought, it's one of the guys: they came for me. Then a grenade hit near by, and my rescuer fell over and began to kick. Each kick hit my arm or my hand, and by the time his corpse had stopped twitching, I knew that he was wearing sandals.

The ringing in my ear swelled into a roar, and I lay there on the wet earth and wondered if I was dying....

MEKONG!

JAMES R. REEVES

Copyright © 1983 by Roger M. Reeves

All rights reserved under International and Pan-American Copyright Conventions. Published in the United States by Ballantine Books, a division of Random House, Inc., New York, and simultaneously in Canada by Random House of Canada Limited, Toronto.

Library of Congress Catalog Card Number: 83-90717

ISBN 0-345-31453-3

Manufactured in the United States of America

BALLANTINE BOOKS • NEW YORK

Library of Congress Catolog Card Number: 83–91241

ISBN 0-345-31453-0

Manufactured in the United States of America

First Edition: April 1984

PREFACE

This story is an adaptation of the Vietnam experience of former SEAL James C. Taylor of Harrison, Arkansas, and is as true to the actual events as possible. We chose to present the story through the medium of fiction to avoid difficulties with classified information and to avoid invading the privacy of those whose names and characters would be included in a nonfiction narrative: the survivors of SEAL Team One and Boat Support Unit One . . . or their widows and children. Therefore, all names have been changed, and all characters except the main character are wholly fictitious. Any resemblance to actual persons living or dead is purely fortuitous. To produce a more effective story the locations of many of the actions have been changed, dimly recollected conversations have been embellished, and incidents that occurred on different dates have been combined. In no instance have the exploits of the SEALs been exaggerated, however.

The opinions and emotions concerning Jane Fonda and other antiwar activists expressed by the characters in this story are those recollected by Mr. Taylor and are similar to those expressed by other Vietnam veterans.

CHAPTER 1

Even after we landed at Tan Son Nhut, I thought it would be at least another day before I got to a combat zone. I looked around at that city and I thought, this is crazy—they've got modern buildings here, running water, electricity, people all over the place doing business—there can't be a war going on here. Not a jungle war.

But when that patrol boat backed away from the dock, and the gunners cocked their weapons with a loud snap, I suddenly realized I didn't have a day. Or even an hour. My time had come.

The patrol boat backed slowly away from the pier, perhaps fifty meters into the channel of the Saigon River, before it swung around. Whether we were headed upstream or down, I couldn't tell: There was no perceptible current in the oily brown water. If it wasn't for patrol boats and motor launches bustling around the harbor, the water would have been as smooth as glass. Even wakes and bow waves seemed to languish in the brutal afternoon sun. I could feel its heat pressing against the skin of my arms and my back, and to make matters worse, the water reflected it like a mirror, so I was getting baked from above and below. Waves of humid heat dancing over the channel made the river look as if it was steaming. My clothes were already soaked, and sweat trickled down the crack of my ass.

Lieutenant Commander Gray, standing beside the coxswain den, turned to shout to us over the throb of the engines.

"Here we go! We'll be there in an hour!"

The coxswain opened up the throttles, and the throaty rumble of the two big engines suddenly became a roar. The PBR—Patrol Boat, River, in official Navy terms— surged forward and came up out of the water. We were off, planing down the winding channel out into the Mekong Delta. I was hazy about exactly where we were going. . . . All I knew was that a barge, anchored about sixty miles from Saigon out in Dinh Tuong Province somewhere, was going to be my home for a long time to come.

We were out of the harbor area in minutes, and all traces of Saigon were quickly disappearing behind us. The jumble of buildings and huts gave way to acres of incredibly green flat fields—rice paddies, I realized, the first I'd ever seen. Then the patches of trees between the paddies began to get larger and appeared more frequently. Finally there were just scattered paddies in a mass of jungle, a few ratty huts, and no roads.

This is a fine mess you got yourself into this time, Tyler, I thought. You join the Navy to keep your butt out of the boonies and now here you are, in the thickest of them. This is no place for an old Ozark country boy. You ought to be back in Arkansas slopping the hogs.

For a moment, I felt a flash of anger. My life up to

now had been one of progressively poorer and poorer choices, and it was easy to blame the system, and the people in the system, for everything that had happened ...almost everything. Having to sell the farm after Dad died, the threat of being drafted and sent to Vietnam, and later, just the threat of being shipped out to Vietnam, had pushed me into making choices I wouldn't have made otherwise. In each case, there hadn't been much to choose from in the way of alternatives. It was almost as if everything had been mapped out in advance, for the sole purpose of getting me to Vietnam. It was enough to make you believe in predestination.

First, of course, there was Dad's death. I blamed myself for that. But then there was that damned fat banker, with his sly grin, telling us that with Dad dead, he had to foreclose on our loan. He said it was obvious that a widow and two teenaged boys couldn't run a hog farm, though everybody in the county knew we'd been doing all the work for two years anyway. We knew he was just going to keep the farm for himself, to add to the thousand or so acres he owned already, so we sold it to an old moonshiner from Searcy County for enough to pay off the loan and buy a little place in town for Mom.

Next there was the draft board, spouting all that shit about duty, honor, and country. My own relatives weren't much better. They kept telling me, "Now, J. E., ye know what folks around here think about deserters and draft dodgers—ye'd never be able ta live around here agin." I knew they just wanted to get my trouble-making ass out of town. They hoped I'd get blown away in Vietnam, and not be back to bother them anymore. So to spite them I joined the Navy.

The Navy put me in the Coastal River Squadron, the damned riverboat Navy—and told me I was going to 'Nam as soon as small boat training was over. At the same time Walter Cronkite was saying the war would be over inside

of a year. I had only a few more weeks of small boat
training to go when I found out about SEAL and UDT
training. That lasted a full year, so volunteering for the
SEa Air Land or Underwater Demolition Teams seemed
like an ideal way out of going over to 'Nam. How the hell
could they use frogmen in a jungle war, anyway? So what
if SEALs were Navy Special Forces? After BUDS they
sent SEALs to special warfare school—the war would be
over before I was through training.

BUDS—Basic Underwater Demolition School—was
hell on earth, or so I thought until Hell Week. It is about
the most intensive training that any outfit goes through.
You store your dress blues and whites, because you always wear greens and combat boots. You run from the
time you get up until you go to bed, and you get up early
and go to bed late. They want you in condition before
you start learning anything about diving, or explosives,
or hand-to-hand combat. You run two miles along the
beaches in the morning before breakfast, and after
breakfast your physical training starts! You run two more
miles just to warm up, and then there's calisthenics, and
then you start running the obstacle course. They had barrels and logs to run through, and walls and ropes to climb,
and you had to crawl under barbed wire while you had
your uniform and hat on. You were one of "Daddy's little
tadpoles," and you'd better run everywhere you went—
because if that instructor caught you not running, you'd
be up all night long running . . . and usually he'd slap the
hell out of you for good measure. And you stand at attention . . . if he hits you hard enough to knock you down,
you'd better hit the ground at attention! After four weeks
of that comes Hell Week, when things REALLY get tough.
I'd never realized that you could be so tired and miser-
able, so shitty and dirty and uncomfortable, and still be
able to keep going so long and so hard. They had a little
ship's bell there, and any time you decided you wanted

out, all you had to do was walk over and yank the rope on that bell. Some guys rang it even after Hell Week was over. But every time I thought about it, every time I thought I couldn't swim any further, or felt like I couldn't crawl another foot or run another step, I thought about Vietnam, and dying, and how the war was going to be over before I finished all my training. Walter Cronkite said so. I thought about how smart I was going to look then, and somehow I kept on going.

BUDS wasn't all physical training. There were classes on wilderness survival, weaponry, hand-to-hand combat, and swimming. They taught you all about the different kinds of SCUBA gear—we called it Underwater Breathing Apparatus, Mark Something-or-another—and how and when to use it. There were demonstration dives, and practice dives with some part of your gear rigged to malfunction so you had to go through the proper drill to repair it while underwater. Then they taught you the way to approach a ship or a beach or a pier while remaining concealed. You practiced dropping into the water from a speeding boat and then being picked up by one. You learned to set explosives underwater or on shore. It all seemed to be calculated to exhaust your mind as well as your body.

Once, we ran a little amphibious exercise where we landed on the beach and bivouacked there until dawn. We all knew it was about time for Hell Week, but we didn't make the connection between that and this exercise until it was well under way. Right at midnight a howling mob of "enemy" descended on us, firing submachine guns loaded with blanks and throwing M-80 firecrackers. We dispersed and regrouped at the designated rendezvous point only to be sent out on a mission. I was sent with three other guys to steal a camera out of an officer's desk on the amphibious base. We got there only to find that the base security had been alerted about our coming in.

We got the camera, all right, but when we got back to the rendezvous point it was almost dawn, and the instructors immediately formed us up and ran us twelve miles down the beach. Then they told us to take ten and eat some C-rations, but before two minutes were up one instructor ran in blowing a whistle and we hustled back up the beach. It was like that all day. They didn't give you time to sit down or eat, and hardly time to take a swig from your canteen. That night there was another exercise. We had to plan and execute an attack on a defended position they'd set up. Dawn broke without my ever having taken even a nap, and they formed us up and ran us down the beach again to where a landing boat had come ashore. There they issued us swim fins, had us strip down to our trunks, and loaded us onto the boat, which then took us about five miles offshore. We went over the side and swam back to the beach. They had check points every quarter-mile or so, and it was a good thing, too, because several guys got cramps and had to be fished out. I felt sorry for them. They either had to drop out or go through all that again.

The week continued in the same pattern. We had to slip past instructors hiding along our infiltration routes, plan and conduct more assaults, run the obstacle course, ambush another team sent on an infiltration mission, and swim in to a defended beach to set explosives. Never did they let us sit down or sleep for more than ten minutes. By the end of the week we were all physically and men-tally exhausted. The final exercise was a seven-mile swim. One guy was so determined to make it he wouldn't let on when he got cramps. He drowned.

We had been tested on everything they had taught us, on our physical conditioning, and on our will to stay with it. If you made it through Hell Week, they knew you had the will and the self-discipline to accomplish any mission they might assign to you, or die trying. Hell Week is the graduation exercise for the Underwater Demolition Teams.

It's just the start for SEALs. After Hell Week comes eighteen weeks of learning to use all kinds of weapons and explosives, a form of hand-to-hand combat called *hwarang do*, advanced diving techniques and underwater demolitions, parachute training, how to enter the water or the jungle from a helicopter, and other specialized skills. After that there is even more advanced training: the Special Warfare School, where we learned the techniques of guerilla and counterguerilla warfare, and of psychological warfare, and about jungle botany and advanced survival. They taught us how to snipe and how to set and detect booby traps. There were classes in espionage and intelligence. Of course, the physical training didn't stop, or even slack off. It got tougher. We ran at least fifteen miles every day, up and down the beaches, and they took us out to San Clemente Island to swim against the riptides.

There was a class called Political Orientation, where they told us about the governments of North and South Vietnam and fed us a lot of political indoctrination so subtly that you didn't even realize they were working on your mind until later, perhaps months later. They wanted to make sure that you had the right political motivation to go along with your elite skills and determination to complete your mission. They didn't want you suddenly turning and using those skills and that determination against your own people. Like a lot of the training, indoctrination ensured that you would do what they told you to do, when they told you to do it, and in the way they wanted it done.

Then, after a year of training, the ax fell. Orders came to ship out to Vietnam. The SEAL forces were being built up to cover the withdrawal of the regular troops.

It'd just never gotten through to me that I would really have to go. Obviously the war was going to be over soon. The Marines had landed and the situation was well in

hand. They'd already started withdrawing troops. Anyway, the cavalry always comes riding in at the last minute
to save the day, doesn't it? But, of course, the cavalry is
made up of poor dumb fuckers who never thought their
time would come. Welcome to the cavalry, Tyler.

I looked around at the other six men in the PBR. The
coxswain and the gunner in the bow were riverboat sailors. I'd been told their names, but I couldn't remember
them now. Beside the coxswain was a middle-aged man
of slight build, with a small, oval face and fine brown hair
that was beginning to thin on top. He wore a baseball cap
pushed far back on his head, and a cigarette was stuck
behind his ear the way some people carry a pencil. He
had been waiting when we got off the plane at Tan Son
Nhut, and after we had sorted out our seabags, he called
off the names of the men who were with him. He was
Lieutenant Commander John Gray, commander of the
outfit I was now attached to, Boat Support Unit One. He
had introduced himself to us by his first name, shaken
our hands, and chatted with us like one of the guys on
the drive down to the harbor. He had pointed out a lot
of the sights to us, and places we needed to know . . . bars,
whorehouses, and cutthroat gambling dens; where to get
the best marijuana; and the clump of woods near the airport where the sniper hung out—he was such a piss-poor
shot, the MPs left him alone, figuring if they nabbed him
he might be replaced with someone dangerous. I had decided before we got to the docks that Lieutenant Commander Gray was a number one dude, even if he was an
officer.

The other three men had come over with me from San
Diego. All of them were SEALs, too. The guy manning
the twenty millimeter was starting his second tour. I'd
gotten to know him in San Diego while we were waiting
to ship out. He was a chief petty officer and also a Cher-
okee Indian, so, inevitably, he was known as the Chief.

He didn't really mind, he said. The Mackintoshes had been chiefs among the Cherokees for generations. I figured that if he did mind, he could have done plenty about it: He was bigger than any other SEAL I ever saw. He had a long torso and a barrel chest and broad shoulders, and he leaned forward a little when he stood so that he always seemed about to topple over on you. If he ever did, he'd crush you—he must have weighed two hundred and forty or fifty pounds. He had arms like some men's thighs, a broad swarthy face with a network of fine scars around the eyes and cheeks, and a broken nose with a collapsed bridge—mementos from years on a Navy boxing team. And he had black, *black* eyes that seemed to just absorb you when he looked at you hard. I didn't doubt that he could see every bent blade of grass and every broken twig on the shore a hundred meters away, then tell you how many Viet Cong had passed that way, how long ago, and how long it had been since they'd eaten, and if one of them was worrying about his wife. It was kinda comforting to have him back there on that twenty.

Brewster and Ivy League I'd gone through SEAL training with. Ivy League's real name was Terrence Hartford III. Brewster wanted to call him Terry the Turd, but I stuck him with the nickname Ivy League. It meant he was something of a jock, but still from a background of wealth and education that was foreign to most of us. His parents owned a shipping outfit, and the men in his family had always served in the fleet Navy. He went to one of those eastern schools that only rich kids and the token poor can go to, and lettered on the swimming team. Of course, he'd been in the Navy ROTC, but he wasn't an officer. He'd either partied too much, or maybe he wasn't quite bright enough to hack it and he'd flunked out.... Anyway, without a degree, he didn't qualify as an officer, but he still had that commitment to the Navy. He was a terrific swimmer, and he did well in BUDS, but I always had a few doubts about him. He was too refined for the kind of gross, harsh conditions we were going to have to endure. He was sort of like a pair of fine dress slacks worn out to the hay field . . . tough enough to stand a certain amount of abuse, but just not coarse enough to last when things really got rough and dirty.

Brewster was a complete contrast to Ivy League. If Ivy League was like a pair of dress slacks, Brewster was patched coveralls. Where Ivy League was tall and lean and well muscled, Brewster was so stocky and solid that he sometimes seemed almost as wide as he was tall. And where Ivy League was blond and good-looking, Brewster was swarthy, with coarse features, a wide nose, and heavy blue jowls. He was an ex–coal miner from Kentucky, and had only a ninth-grade education. His daddy had been killed in the mines, and he was raised poor. The other kids had always laughed at him, because he'd carried his lunch to school in an old lard can, and he always had raggedy-assed clothes and hand-me-down, wore-out shoes. He was always fighting. When he was old enough, he quit school and went to work in the mines. Like me, he joined the Navy to keep from being drafted into the Army. The Navy gave him the pitch about UDTs and the SEALs, like they do every boot, and he liked the idea of being the best and the toughest. In fact, that "best and toughest" business sort of went to his head, and he did his damnedest to live up to it.

Brewster saw me looking at him and flipped me a finger. He was like that: He'd bluster and bully and threaten, and cover up his real feelings—someone might find out that he had a weakness and take advantage of it. I knew him well enough to know that he was as nervous and worried as I was.

Brewster was about the only real friend I'd made in the service. Back before I'd volunteered for SEALs, during basic and while I was training for the riverboats up at Mare Island, there'd not been anybody you could depend on, anybody that wouldn't cut your throat for a few dollars or a bag of grass. Brewster and I had gone through UDT training, Hell Week, and Special Warfare School together, and both of us had learned that the other guy could be counted on. None of this closer-than-brothers shit, just a degree of tolerance for each other, a certain amount of mutual respect of the "Hey, this guy's almost as good as I am" variety. I knew that if I'd cover his ass, he'd cover mine, like when we went bar hopping in San Diego. Brewster and I bar hopped a lot together in San Diego, and there were a lot of fights. Many of them he started. . . . Others he just got us into.

Sometimes he'd go up to the biggest and meanest-looking mother in the place and say, "Hey, that little feller over there jist said he was gonna whup yer ass!" And he'd point back at me. But he'd always join in.

It was still oppressively muggy and hot, but there are few places on a PBR where you can get away from the spray, and the combination of spray and the twenty-five-knot breeze cooled me down considerably. We roared on downriver, bearing to the right whenever the channel split. Hell, this isn't too bad, I thought. It's about like a summer day on the lake back home . . . hot and humid, but what the hell. I lived through eighteen summers of heat and humidity, and dug ditches and slopped hogs and hauled hay in it. It's got to get a lot hotter than this to get me down.

I think that was the first positive thought I'd had since we'd left the States, twenty-two hours before.

Everybody had a different reaction when the big DC-10 took off for Pearl Harbor. Some whooped and hollered and laughed and said corney things like "stick your head between your legs and kiss your ass good-bye." Others just sat there and looked out the windows at the coast of California like they might never see it again. The Chief had been quiet. I guess he was thinking about the family he'd just left behind in San Diego. Brewster had been quiet, too: He went right to sleep. Ivy League watched the ocean for a long time—maybe he was wishing he was in the fleet Navy—but after a while he joined in the B.S.ing with the other guys. I tried to keep talking myself, but every once in a while I'd start to thinking about Vietnam and death, or home and my family. Then I'd go back to talking, bullshitting, kidding, telling fuck jokes, anything to keep from thinking. Sometimes, I just looked at a guy's face and wondered what he was thinking and feeling. I wondered how many would make it back, and what shape they'd be in if they did. Some of the guys had baby faces, and some had hard or tough or mean-looking faces. Some looked like they belonged in a classroom, teaching school, or behind a desk, adding up figures. Others looked as if they were fresh off the farm or just out of the mines.

Brewster snored away, his mouth open as usual. He'd shaved before we left the barrack to go to the airport, but already his beard was showing blue around his jowls, as though coal dust was still ground into his pores. The Chief scowled out the window at the ocean—it was hard to picture him at home with a wife and kids, or out on the reservation in Oklahoma; he'd been a sailor too long, and had a salt air about him even now. There were quite a few brown faces, a few black faces, and a few "yellow" ones. Most of the white ones were so tanned that you couldn't tell them from the naturally brown ones.

When we landed at Pearl Harbor, a lieutenant stood up and said, "We'll be here three hours. That's enough time to get drunk, get laid, or go over the hill, if you're so minded. This will be your last chance to do any of those things for a while, so you'd better take advantage of it. Just be back in three hours, unless you decide to desert."

Of course, almost everybody headed for the bars. About

eight of us went off together. We found a large place, fairly close to the base, crowded with fleet sailors, grunts, and Aussies on R and R. (Why didn't they send them back to Australia? It would have been closer and cheaper.) We split up then, and Brewster, the Chief, and I found empty barstools beside some guys from the Marine Force Recon. On the other side, beside me, were some of the Aussies. The Recons were on their way to stateside, having finished their tours. They filled us in on the troop withdrawals that had been going on for some time, and Charley's reaction to them, which was to move in where the troops were pulled out. The Recons thought we'd be doing a lot of search-and-destroy missions, because that's what they had been doing. The Aussies were in high spirits. Apparently they had seen some pretty hot action, and had done pretty well against Charley—at least, to hear them tell it. They had a pretty low opinion of the U.S. Army, so I gathered, and even the regular Marines. They seemed to think pretty highly of the SEALs and the Marine Recons, though. Maybe because a mixed dozen of us were sitting right beside them. We were getting along just fine until some adolescent little Coast Guard shit climbed up on a table and announced that he could whip any fuckin' Limey in the house. I guess I just looked at him with my mouth open. Somebody yelled, "That kid's been watchin' too many war movies!" Just then some Limey pulled the kid off the table and proceeded to stomp his face into the hardwood floor. The Aussies beside me made a dive for some soldiers at a table nearby. I looked at the Chief and Brewster, and to my surprise Brewster said, "Let's get the shit outta here!" So we dropped down to our hands and knees and crawled toward the door. People kept stepping on my fingers and stumbling over me, but I made it almost to the door before someone had to "help" me stand up. Someone else tried to knock me back down. I took care of the two of them easily enough—

they were both regular Army—and just then the rest of our group joined us, and we made a wedge and fought our way to the door. We got out just in time—the M.P.'s were arriving.

At least Brewster hadn't started that one.

When we assembled for the next leg of the flight, everyone was there, but they were all loop-legged as hell. They kept yellin' "Whooya! Whooya!" back and forth, and quieted down only long enough for the roll call. Then we got on the plane. When it took off, I felt like I was leaving something behind in Hawaii. There was a great cold lump that came into my stomach, and the cold air out of the plane's air conditioning system felt like the chill of the grave. It seemed like I could smell death.

Brewster saw me staring out the window and said, "What the shit, Tyler—we asked for it, didn't we? So we got no kick comin', do we?" I had to admit he was right.

Now the PBR motored out of the river channel into a narrow inlet that turned out to be the mouth of a canal. We cruised at slightly reduced speed, weaving in and out among small one- or two-man fishing sampans. The levees of the canal were built up here and there with houses, and occasionally some trees grew on them, but usually there was a trail or road, and paddies stretching away as far as I could see beyond them. Most of the paddies were flooded. They steamed in the afternoon sun and made it impossible to see details very far.

When we came once again to a river, it seemed to be at floodtide. The paddies on both sides were covered with water, and the channel of the river was marked only by strips of trees that grew along the banks and a few scattered clusters of houses raised up on stilts. There was a strong current here, but the channel was wide and made long, looping bends. The coxswain opened the throttle and the little boat lifted right up out of the water and planed along the surface. I heard the Lieutenant Commander shouting, and saw that he was waving for me to come over to the coxswain den. He had a map on a clipboard and showed it to all of us new guys. He pointed with a pencil to a river channel on the map. "This is the My Tho channel of the Mekong River," he shouted. "We're just upstream from My Tho. The barge is another forty-five minutes ahead." He had to shout to be heard over the roar of the engines and the rush of the wind.

There was a lot of air and river activity just after we turned into the main river channel, but it died out as we got farther away from My Tho.

The radio had not been silent since we pulled away from the pier. Radio traffic was heavy around Saigon, but none of it was directed to us. Now it crackled with call signs and a message. The Lieutenant Commander called for a repeat, and I leaned away from the gunwale to get my ears out of the wind so that I could hear the call, too.

"Delta Six—Bravo One. We are drawing sniper fire at [garble]. Can you back us up? Over."

"Say again your location, Bravo One. Over," he added as an afterthought.

"Delta Six—Bravo One. Our location is: Kilometer 7, Nhi My River, in Sector R-12. Did you copy that? Over."

"Bravo One—Delta Six. Roger, we copy. We'll back you up. Our ETA five minutes. Do you have him spotted? Over."

"Affirmative, Delta Six. Near the head of the inlet, running like hell. We are pursuing. Over."

"Negative, negative, Bravo One. Smells like a trap. Stay out of that inlet. Wait for your backup. Over."

"Roger, Six."

The coxswain pushed the throttle further forward, and the PBR leaped ahead even faster. The gunner in the bow glanced back, and the Lieutenant Commander signaled something to him with his fingers, ending up with one hand fully spread. ETA five minutes.

I felt like puking. No shit. I was really scared.

I'd wondered since I got orders to ship out how long it would be before I saw action, how long before I was shot at, or shot at someone. How long before I killed someone. Or how long before someone ki... *don't* think about that, Tyler, I told myself. But I couldn't help it. I looked around at the fiberglass hull of that little boat, and it sure didn't offer much protection. I didn't even have a weapon to fire back with.

It occurred to me then that if we took much fire, my seabag and all my junk were likely to get shot to shit. That irritated the hell out of me for a minute, until I realized just how dumb it was. What a stupid fuckin' thing to be worried about, I thought to myself—you're about to get your butt blown away, and you're worried about holes in your shorts. It was such a ridiculous thought I almost had to laugh.

I glanced over at Brewster. The stupid fucker was grinnin' like a 'possum in a persimmon tree. I shot him a finger.

We rounded a point at high speed and there was another boat ahead. The radio crackled to life again. I tried to make myself fit behind a case of C-rations.

"Delta Six—Bravo One. We've lost him."

"Bravo One—Delta Six. Roger. We have you in sight. Make a sweep through the inlet anyway."

The other PBR swept down into the inlet and back out again, about fifty meters from the shore, while we orbited near the mouth. They drew no fire, although the gunners threw a few rounds into the bush were they'd seen their sniper. I caught the Lieutenant Commander's eye, and he cocked his head slightly. Well, better luck next time, he seemed to be saying. I thought it was pretty damned good luck this time.

Brewster sat with his elbow on the gunwale and his chin in his hand. He looked bored.

We broke away from the other boat, leaving it to continue its patrol, and headed on to the barge.

It was about thirty minutes later that I spotted the barge. It was a squat and ugly thing, sitting out in the middle of the river. It looked like someone's homemade houseboat, and not very well kept, either. Some rusty pontoons, a flat deck, and some poles holding up a rusty sheet-metal roof was all there was to it. Instead of bulkheads enclosing the superstructure, there was a low wall of sandbags and a steel mesh screen, probably to keep grenades out. Rusty. Jesus, I'd never seen the Navy let anything get so rusty. I learned later it was deliberate: Rust was the perfect camouflage out in that muddy brown river.

We tied up to the port side and climbed out. Brewster tossed our seabags out to me. Some sailors came over to unload the supplies we'd brought back.

"Welcome to the Mekong Hilton," said Lieutenant Commander Gray.

"I hope you enjoy your visit with us," said one of the sailors in what was obviously his best doorman's voice.

"Right this way, ladies and gentlemen," said the Lieutenant Commander. He led us through a gap in some sandbags. There was a rectangular space there—I wouldn't call it a room—walled about three feet high on all sides with sandbags. Tarpaulins tied up near the roof could be let down to darken the area, but they had been left up to let in any vagrant breeze that might chance to come that way. The floor and the roof were both made of sheet metal, and the place was an oven. About twenty cots were crowded together, leaving space for a few more. There were a half-dozen off-duty sailors sacked out.

"Here you are—a lovely, spacious suite overlooking the scenic Mekong River, with a view of both banks. A gorgeous color scheme, don't you think? Olive drab and battleship gray. There is coffee in the lounge at all hours,

and open-air dining in the Galley. Sometimes after dinner
there is live entertainment, provided by roving native
bands, including fireworks displays. A delightful group
called Charley plays here with some regularity." The
Lieutenant Commander was obviously enjoying his little
joke. Well, hell, it was as good a way to get squared away
as any.

We picked out vacant cots and threw our shit down
beside them. The Chief flopped down on his and propped
his hands behind his head.

"I'd really prefer a king-sized bed," he said with a wry
grin. "And this mattress isn't firm enough!"

"Oh, we'll do our best to please, Chief," said the Lieutenant Commander, with a wink to one of the sailors. "I'll
have a sheet of three-quarter-inch plywood sent in at once."

He turned to go, hesitated, turned serious for a moment, and then broke out in that grin again. "River tours
begin promptly at oh-eight-hund...at eight o'clock, noon,
four P.M., and eight P.M.," he continued. The brief lapse
into Navy jargon was hardly noticed. "And they continue
around the clock. May I suggest that you take this opportunity for a brief nap? We have some special activities
planned for tonight, to sort of welcome you to our estab-
lishment: You'll be given the opportunity to participate
in a fabulous night safari into Indian country, where you
will be given the opportunity to experience first hand the
unusual stalking techniques practiced by the natives."

He turned and left.

Brewster looked at me, confused. I looked at the Chief.
He was lying on his back, looking at the underside of the
roof. His eyes were black and flinty.

"What'd he mean by that?" I asked.

"An ambush," the Chief said, sounding like a man who's
driven all night to get to the big game by kickoff time,
only to have a flat just outside of town. "It's like an
initiation...they put all the new guys out in the bush their

first night in-country, if they can, on a patrol or an ambush. Gets you over th' jitters. I don't need it...I ain't goin' if I can get some other duty. You guys are goin' to be bait for an ambush. Like stakin' out a goat to catch a tiger. It ain't always healthy for th' goat."

I wish they wouldn't do that—that is, tell you to get some sleep, and then tell you something that's bound to worry you half to death. I laid on the cot, and I sweated, and I thought about all kinds of things. I didn't sleep.

We'd done the same sort of thing during training: Two or three guys would set up a phony ambush and would sit there and talk and smoke like they didn't really give a shit. Meanwhile a sniper or two would cover them from off to one side. If an enemy team tried to slip up and attack the decoys, they would be picked off. It was sort of a game...you always knew what they were doing, but you tried to slip in and get the decoys without getting spotted. Sometimes you made it. Over here, it wasn't going to be a game, and if Charley got to us without being seen...

And there was something else that bothered me. I might have to kill someone tonight. I was raised to believe that killing was wrong, that taking another human life was about the most awful thing you could do. Now my government was telling me I had to go look for some Vietnamese people who I didn't even know and kill them. If I do that, I thought, I'll be a murderer. And if I don't, I'll be a traitor. I'm caught between a rock and a hard place. Killing is wrong...but my daddy always said that the government was right, the American government anyway, because whatever they say to do is the expression of the will of the people. And Americans are good, Christian people.

Can I really do it? I wondered. Could I really shoot a person down? Or could I stick a knife in his back or strangle him with my hands? Sure, I was trained to do it—I could do it without really thinking about it, just by instinct. But if I'd seen that sniper running earlier today, could I have machine gunned him?

Yes.

I know I would have. I might have hesitated.... My mind would say, No! you can't take a human life...but my fingers would have pulled the trigger, just like they've done hundreds of times in training.

But what about afterward? How would I have felt, seeing the blood and intestines splashed all around?

I shuddered, for that thought caused me to recall another death. A memory of blood splashed all over the room. Guilt rode on one shoulder still, and the specter of insanity on the other. Did insanity run in the family? The news media made a big thing about 'Nam vets who went bananas after they got home, and I knew there were a lot of returnees in mental hospitals. War is hard on the mind—even a stable mind—and I had reason to doubt the stability of mine.

CHAPTER 2

I woke up with a headache. Oh, yes, I finally went to sleep, despite all the worrying. I was exhausted from the trip over. But I shouldn't sleep in that kind of heat, not in the afternoon, anyway. There had been a nightmare of some sort that I couldn't remember, and I woke up soaked with sweat. The sweat could have been because of the heat, I guess, even though I was wearing nothing but my tiger shorts. The sandbag wall was just high enough to block out any breeze there might have been, and the sheet-metal roof radiated heat downward. Droplets of sweat trickled through the hair on my arms and legs and stomach, feeling like a swarm of flies running around. My scalp began to crawl—a sure sign of dehydration. The place was an oven, and I was baking like a turkey.

Brewster was still out of it. Nothing ever disturbed his sleep. He lay on his back in his tiger shorts, big beads of sweat on his stomach and forehead. He was snoring, the sound of it like a wood rasp on hardwood, but I was used to that sound from long months in the barracks. Something else had woken me up.

One of the off-duty riverboat sailors was threshing around in his bunk, making frightened, wordless sounds and shaking his head in a NO! NO! gesture so hard that his cot was about to topple over. From the sounds he made, I judged he was trying to shout a warning to someone, but his lips wouldn't form the words. Only formless sounds came out.

I wondered what he was dreaming about. I stood watching for a minute, wanting to get the hell outside but entranced by the thrashing figure on the cot. Could I do anything to help? Should I do anything? Just as I decided to wake him, he stiffened suddenly and muttered, "Ohmygod!" Then he seemed to collapse into himself, lying totally limp, his eyes open and staring, unseeing, at the roof.

I hurried out of the place. Outside the sun still beat down, but the faint breeze wasn't blocked off by anything, and I felt considerably better out there.

The mess was just some folding chairs and tables under the forward—upstream—part of that sheet-metal shed. There were no sandbag walls to block off the breeze. A big coffee urn sat on one end of one table, with some styrofoam cups scattered around it, but coffee was about the last thing I needed.

A man sat at the other end of the table from the coffee urn. I hardly noticed him. My attention was riveted on the can of Coca-Cola he was drinking from, and my throat constricted from craving. I walked over to him.

"Hot, ain't it?" I croaked.

He looked at me for a moment like he was going to say: Well of course it is, dumbshit—it's hot every day. Instead, he just said, "Yep."

"Where could a feller get one o'them cold dranks?"

"Saigon," he said without a blink.

My face fell so far it bounced on the deck. Seeing my desperate situation, he grinned and waved toward the sandbag bulkhead. "Or he could wander over beyond that bulkhead there and look in the cooler."

I didn't exactly wander. The cooler was well stocked with beer and Coke. I wasn't sure about the beer regulations, so I took a can of soda. I began to feel better as soon as I popped the top and let some of that luscious cold fluid trickle down over my tonsils.

I went back and pulled up a chair opposite the man.

"It affects everybody that way at first," he said. "You'll get acclimated." He waved his hand at an open box of little yellow tablets in the middle of the table. "Better have some of them," he added. "If you drank much on the plane coming over, you'll need 'em for sure."

I noticed there was an open box on every table. Salt tablets. Evidently the guys here consumed quite a few of them. I washed a handful down, then stuck out my bony paw to the man.

"I'm Tyler," I said. "J. E., but everybody just calls me Tyler."

His handshake was firm, but his gray eyes flickered my way only for a moment, then went back to the distant shoreline. His smile was sort of sad—resigned-looking, I thought.

"They call me Poppa," he said. "You're one of the new SEAL team that just came in."

He was an older man, certainly not your average baby-faced combat soldier, for his hair was beginning to gray a little at the temples, and his face was dark and coarsened by years of weather and wars. He wore jungle greens with no insignia. A crucifix on a chain hung from around his neck.

Poppa plus crucifix plus older man equals chaplain. I added two and two and got three and a half, as usual. This outfit was too small to have a chaplain assigned to it, but I supposed he might travel from unit to unit the way the itinerant preachers back home used to ride their mules from town to town—that was before my time, but I'd heard the old folks tell about it.

"Are you the chaplain?" I blurted.

I laughed with him, but I didn't know what was so funny.

When his laugher had died down, he told me, "I'm a Marine—a sniper. I guess you could say I've laid some people to rest in a manner of speaking, but that's about all I have in common with a chaplain!"

A sniper! I knew at once, by intuition, I guess, that this was the man who would have my life in his hands that night. My life would depend on how good he was. I desperately wanted to know, but I was afraid to just come right out and ask him—he might get pissed off at me and hesitate just a little too long at a critical moment. Maybe I could sort of coax it out of him.

"How long have you been in the Corps?" I asked him. It must have been quite a while, I knew.

"Twenty-seven years." He emphasized each word so that it sounded like an incredibly long time indeed. In fact he'd had more years in the Marine Corps than I had months in the Navy! Hell, he'd already had eight years' experience when I was born!

Somehow, his age created a sense of confidence. It implied that he was war-wise and thoroughly competent. He had to be doing something right to have survived all those years.

"Seen a lot of action, I guess?"

"Yep."

It was his eyes that were old. The touch of gray in his hair and the weathering of his face could have put his age anywhere between thirty and fifty. Hell, I'd seen twenty-five-year-old vets who looked older than this guy. But his eyes were cloud gray, as if they, instead of his hair, had turned color with the years. They were clear, though. Like the Chief, he seemed to be seeing the slightest details even over great distances. He would never look right at you. Always he looked past you, over your shoulder, or away from you.

"You must've been awful damned young when you signed up."

"I was sixteen. But there was a war on, and I was afraid I'd miss it." He smiled that faint, sad smile again. I knew he was smiling at himself as a young man.

"What'd your family think about that?"

"The orphanage was glad to get rid of me. I was a wild'un."

"I reckon you've been all around the world, bein' in the Corps that long?"

"All around the Pacific."

"Just the Pacific?"

"Hawaii. Guam. Japan. The Philippines. Australia. Korea. Vietnam. That's half the world right there."

He was right—it was half the world and his service span included three wars fought in that area. But he still hadn't told me anything about his experience or his ability. And it was obvious he wouldn't volunteer much information—you would have to ask him a direct question, and it would have to be the right question, or he'd cut you off.

"Where was the first campaign you were in?" I'd often heard the old-timers sitting and spitting on the courthouse square talk of the different "campaigns" they served in.

"New Guinea."

"Is that when you became a sniper?"

"Yeah. Hey, look, if you're scared or something . . . if there's something bothering you, spit it right out. Let's hear it."

"Well . . . well, hell . . . did you ever *miss*?" That's what I really wanted to ask, I guess.

He leaned back in his chair and took a pipe out of his pocket. He looked thoughtfully toward the river bank as he began to pack it.

I finished the can of Coke. It was warm and flat by now, but it and the salt pills had done their job. I felt better. Still hot, but better. I lit a cigarette and waited for his answer.

Poppa lit his pipe with great deliberation and puffed on it a few times, studying the shoreline intently. Then he removed his pipe from his mouth and folded his arms, exhaling with a long sigh.

"Yeah," he said. "Once."

God, the Coke nearly came right back up.

"Oh, my God...I have to draw you of all people! A sniper that misses!" I choked.

He looked at me briefly, coldly. It was an appraising glance, level, though his eyes didn't meet mine but for an instant before he glanced away. It was very disconcerting.

"Don't you ever look at anybody you're talkin' to?" I exploded.

He glanced at me briefly again and went back to studying the jungle shoreline.

"I don't like to look at friends too close," he said. "I look real close at the people I shoot."

I smoked the cigarette down to the butt and snuffed it out in the Coke can before I spoke again. So he'd missed once. He might miss again. Tonight.

"Was this in 'Nam?"

"Yeah. Up by Da Nang."

"Did you have a decoy?"

"Yeah."

So far, so bad.

"How did he die? The decoy, I mean. Was it quick?" I asked. I felt like I needed to know.

Poppa said, "He didn't die!" in an offended tone.

I said, "Hell, you just told me you missed your target,

and now you tell me your decoy didn't die? Charley was coming in to get your decoy, wasn't he?"

Poppa grinned. "I was aiming to hit him in the head, and I hit him in the throat. A clear miss!"

I laughed, in relief. "The hell it is!" I said. "You're talking about six inches difference on the target. Shit! How far away was he?"

"Oh, he was about three hundred meters out, I guess."

"Go-od damn! That's no miss! I'll take ye any day!"

It made me feel better to know that Poppa was really good, but it didn't completely stop me from worrying. I killed the rest of the afternoon pacing the deck and drinking coffee. I'd rather have had a cold beer, but I drank the coffee, because I didn't want to chance falling asleep on patrol.

I measured the barge a few times, pacing its length and width, studied the jungle through binoculars, and checked out a PBR just for the hell of it, but all the time my thoughts were racing through the many things that could happen on tonight's patrol. Would I have to kill someone? Sooner or later, I would. There was no way out of it. . . . The chance to run to Canada had come and gone.

My uncle used to tell us stories about combat in World War Two. He was in the Pacific, and he fought in the jungle. He said that a lot of the time, they'd just fire into the damned bush—at sounds or at the source of the enemy fire. He killed some men, he knew, but most of the time you never even saw the men you killed, or you'd find their bodies later. But in training they told us: Don't waste a shot; make each bullet count, if possible—that extra round might sometime save your life.

I tried to imagine what my first kill would be like. Would someone just point at the bush and say, "Now, you shoot at that tree," or "Shoot at that bush," and then would we go looking to see if I killed somebody? How would I feel, knowing I'd pulled the trigger and ended a life?

The Lieutenant Commander got us new guys together at about 1600 to brief us on what our jobs would be. We sat at a table and drank cold beers while he told us in his soft voice about himself and his family, just to get us familiar with him and to make us feel at ease. He said that he was forty and had a wife and three daughters at home, that he wanted a promotion very badly and had volunteered for a third tour in 'Nam to help him get it, and that he was not a disciplinarian but wanted us to maintain a little discipline and a military manner.

He stood with one hand on his hip and gazed out across the river when he talked. The other hand held a cigarette between the second and third fingers; he held the hand across his body with the knuckle out, and except for the cigarette, you could almost imagine it stuck in his shirt in a Napoleon-like pose. He wore a baseball cap pushed back on his head. . . . I never saw him in anything else except when there was some visiting brass.

He turned to look at us, and as he talked, he looked each one of us in the eye in turn.

"You'll be working primarily for Naval Intelligence. You'll pull a few daily river patrols with my men, especially at first, when you're just getting used to being here, and getting acclimated. But your job is reconnaissance. You're here to find out all you can about Charley: where he is, where his camps are, what he's doing out there, when he's moving. Sometimes, who he is. You'll be working with the Vietnamese a lot: interpreters, Provisional Recon Units—we call them 'prews'—and the people in the villages. Now get this straight: You're here to liberate them, not annihilate them. After a while, it will seem like they are all the enemy. That's because we operate primarily in territory controlled by the Viet Cong. . . . They don't need us anywhere else, you know.

"You'll get together with Poppa later and get organized for the ambush. Those of you that haven't yet met Poppa should get to know him—he's been out here a long time, and he can teach you some things that will help you stay alive."

Late in the afternoon, we ate a little bit and drank a lot of coffee. Poppa divided us into two teams. He and Brewster were to be one team, the sniper and a spotter. They would carry a Starlight scope in addition to the one on Poppa's sniping rifle. Ivy League and I were the other team, and we'd do double duty, both as decoys and spotters. We'd have a Starlight scope ourselves. We were to talk, smoke, and carry on in general like a couple of fools, to attract Charley's attention to us. Poppa had preselected the site for the ambush, a jungle clearing with a little high ground overlooking it from the edge of the bush. It was in an area with a lot of traffic from both sides. Charley had been very active in that area lately, and snipers had hit several of our patrols and caused some casualties. Tonight our own patrols would stay clear of the area. There was to be radio silence, except to call Poppa in case we spotted someone coming in.

"And one more thing," he added. "If you hit the god-damned button on the radio and tell me there's somebody coming in . . . there'd better by God BE somebody coming in, or I'll damn sure kick your asses all the way back to the river! I *don't* like to give my position away unnecessarily. Any questions?"

"There only going to be four of us?" Brewster asked.

"Yeah," Poppa replied. "I like to keep my groups small. You all know that a few people can travel through the bush a lot faster and quieter than a big patrol."

"You're gonna be carryin' your snipin' rifle, and only us three are gonna have assault weapons—what if we run into a big force of Viet Cong?" Brewster went on. "We ain't got much firepower."

"We'll hide and watch 'em go by," Poppa said. "Anyway, didn't they teach you guys that a SEAL is worth twenty or a dozen of those guys in a shootout?"

"Yeah," Ivy League put in. "They were full of a lot of other bullshit, too."

"That's not bullshit," Poppa corrected him. "If it was, you think I'd risk my ass in the bush with three green kids?"

There wasn't any arguing with that kind of logic, and it kind of made you feel better to know he thought that way. But I still had lingering doubts. The others probably did, too. None of us had yet come up against Charley, except Poppa and the Chief. I wished the Chief was going along with us. At least he'd captain the boat that would take us out and pick us up. I knew what the Chief would say if anybody asked him whether a SEAL was more effective than a dozen Viet Cong: *"Hell yeah!"* After all, he'd been a SEAL for twelve years, and you wouldn't stay with an outfit like this unless you believed in it.

I didn't ask any dumb questions this time. Ivy League did.

"How do we tell friendly Vietnamese from Viet Cong?"

Poppa studied him for a moment with hard gray eyes.

"Son, friendly Vietnamese won't be slipping around out there in the dark, trying to stick a knife into your back." His voice was kindly when he spoke, but it had an edge to it. "Out there . . . in the jungle . . . at night . . . there ain't any friendly Vietnamese. If it moves, it's VC."

We checked out our gear then: M-16s, banana clips, hand grenades, Starlight scopes, radios. We blackened our faces with camouflage paint. We went to the head. Then we got aboard the PBR and shoved off.

I wanted to say, wait, I'm not ready yet, but I didn't. I looked around and I thought, So this is what it's like, going into action the first, and maybe the last, time.

We went west, upriver toward Cambodia. The setting

sun was just touching the river and seemed to be melting and flowing into it, for both the sun and the river ahead were blood red. The jungle was a dark green wall along the banks of the river, like a high hedge along some broad avenue. Astern, the river was purple—white where it was disturbed by our wake—and out over the China Sea towered a great high cumulus cloud, its bottom purple and its top an angry-looking red.

Going into battle on a blood-red river, under a blood-red sky. A bad sign. A bad sign, indeed. But beautiful.

It got dark quickly. Ivy League and I sat facing the starboard shore. Poppa and Brewster were facing to port. They were not far away, for a PBR is not large, but soon, whenever I looked over my shoulder at them, I couldn't make out their features at all. The camouflage paint made them hard to recognize even in good light. In the dark all I could see was an occasional gleam of white as someone moved his eyes.

There was nothing I could see in the way of a landmark, but the Chief or the coxswain apparently could. All too soon, the boat turned abruptly and roared toward shore until I began to wonder if we were going to crash into the jungle at full throttle. Then the coxswain throttled back, and the PBR mushed down into the water and slowed quickly.

There was a long, agony-filled minute of waiting, a few seconds, really, as we drifted in, waiting to ground and jump out, waiting for the Viet Cong to open fire, waiting for mortar rounds or rockets to streak out of the dark. I felt awfully, awfully sick, and my breath came in short, shallow gasps. My knees and hands were trembling as I squatted there, ready to leap out. I was glad the darkness hid my trembling from the others and the throb of the engines covered the sound of my gasping breaths.

Then we grounded with a slight bump, and Poppa slipped over the port side and waded ashore. He checked

out the bush at the water's edge, then disappeared into
it. The Chief, who was standing near me, hit me on the
shoulder and hissed, "Go!" And I went.

The bottom was soft silt, and the water knee deep. The
footing wasn't the best, and I splashed and stumbled
ashore, making more noise than a stampeding water buffalo. At least it seemed that way to me. There was no
more than ten meters of open river to cross, and it was
dark as hell, but I felt so exposed that it seemed I would
never get ashore.

Then I thought about booby traps. The fuckin' bush
was *full* of booby traps. I could feel them...every step
might be taking me closer and closer to a trip wire or a
punji stick or some other devilish contraption....I hesitated for a second...but if I stopped where I was I'd be
a sitting duck for any VC sniper in the bush! My feet just
kept pumping away, on their own, and within seconds I
was crouching in the bush.

Brewster and Ivy League followed me ashore, and the
PBR reversed its engines and roared away.

For a while after the boat left, we crouched there. The
jungle was pitch black and silent at first, but slowly the
jungle noises began again—first the insects and then
the birds. Our eyes grew accustomed to the dim light, so
we could see one another and the bush. Poppa led off,
taking the point, and we headed for the ambush site. Poppa
carried an M-16. His sniper rifle was still in its case, and
he gave it to Brewster to carry.

We went about a mile through the jungle, and then
waded across a rice paddy. It was knee to waist deep,
and every step I took, I expected to hit a mine or step on
a punji stick. I was still that psyched up about booby
traps. The ambush site was a clearing beyond the paddy.
Ivy League and I slipped out to the middle of it and sat
down back-to-back. Brewster and Poppa took a position
where the paddy dike met some high ground just inside

the jungle edge. From there Poppa would have a clear shot to the jungle on all sides of the clearing and the rice paddy, and down both sides of the dike.

Obviously, there had been a lot of recent activity in the area. The sawgrass was full of trails, and the spot we sat down in was beaten down for about twenty meters across, as if a bunch of people had converged there.

We sat quietly for about ten minutes. It wasn't as hot as it had been in the midafternoon, but it was still intensely humid, and our little walk had soaked us with sweat. The night air was full of foul odors, not the least of which was our own body sweat. There was a muddy, swampy smell from the rice paddy, a lot of that smell still clinging to our clothes and boots, and the pungent air of growing green things and rotting vegetation from the nearby jungle. And there was another sharply pungent, faintly familiar smell that I pondered over for a while before I recognized it: manure. The essence of cow lot. Water buffalo, I decided. Water buffalo could account for the way the sawgrass was beaten down in wide trails.

"What time is it?" Ivy League asked in a low voice.

I looked at my watch and told him.

I wondered how many Viet Cong were out there in that jungle. Maybe some had been there when we showed up, and had watched us take up our stations. They might be out there right now drawing a bead on us...or on Poppa and Brewster. Or they might have gone back to their camp to bring back a patrol to wipe us all out.

I felt as big as a barn, and just about as hard to miss. Would they have rifles or crossbows? I'd heard stories of Viet Cong snipers hitting a patrol with crossbows, the bolts striking so silently that three or four men might be killed before anyone knew anything was up. I became very aware of Ivy League's back pressed against mine. Not only was he sweating, he was trembling. Or was he? Would I know if he was hit by a crossbow bolt? Sure, I told myself. I would feel him jerk from the impact. We sat back-to-back so that no lone VC could slip in with a knife or garrote, and kill one man silently without the other's knowing about it. Of course, it made us more vulnerable to other forms of attack, such as grenades or machine-gun fire . . . but Poppa was supposed to take care of that.

After a few minutes of silence, Ivy League said, "Goddamn, it's hot. Aren't you hot?"

"Shut up, for God's sake!" I blurted out. "Do you want Charley to hear you?"

"But we're supposed to be talking," he reminded me. "He's supposed to hear us."

"I know it! But who's gonna know if we don't?"

He was right. As much as I'd rather lay low and be quiet, as much as instinct cried out for me to do so, we had a job to do, and we might just as well do it. It was no worse to be shot by the Viet Cong than by Poppa for being a poor decoy. (Or so I rationalized.)

"What'll we talk about, then?" I asked. He was the college guy—let him think of something.

"What time is it?"

I'd already looked down at my watch when I realized that I'd told him the time only a few minutes earlier. I'd set decoy during training with guys that kept asking all night what time it was. They could drive you crazy. I had to put an end to it right quick.

"It's five minutes later than it was five minutes ago. Can't you think of nothin' else, for Chrissake?"

He didn't say anything for a while. He was thinking, I guess. Finally he asked, "Do you suppose that sniper's any good?"

"Yeah, I suppose so," I told him. "I talked to him a little while this afternoon, an' he's not supposed to've ever missed."

"There's a first time for everything, isn't there?"

"Shut up, God damn it! He ain't gonna miss!" I told him, but down deep in my mind, some mischievous devil kept whispering, "Well, *isn't* there a first time for everything?"

"I wonder if he cuts notches in his rifle stock," Ivy League said.

"He told me he used to cut off their ears," I told him.

"No shit! What'd he do with them?"

I was too scared to think of a suitable smart-assed answer, so I just told him the truth. "He saved 'em until the bag was full, an' he didn't have no other place to put 'em, then he threw 'em all in the river."

"I wonder how many he had," he mused. Then after a minute or two of silence, when I didn't answer, he said, "How damned barbaric can you get! Cutting off people's ears for goddamned trophies! Like some damned big-game hunter."

I felt obliged to defend Poppa. "He ain't barbaric. He's a damn nice guy. Anyway, he threw the damned things away, didn't he?"

He just grunted.

It was still hot. I got to thinking about home, and how it would start cooling off after dark, even in the summer. The mists would start rising on the night air, and you could smell the honeysuckle and hear the buzzing of the locusts and the calls of the doves and the whippoorwills. How different it was from this! Unidentifiable insects ratcheting and birds squawking, and rustlings in the bush that might be rats with either four legs or two.... Yet, with a stretch of my imagination, I could see myself at home, on a quiet summer night in the Ozark woods, in the darkness under the canopy of the trees. I wondered if there was anything in Ivy League's background that might have prepared him for the jungle nights.

I wanted a cigarette desperately, and they encouraged you to light up: The glow might attract the Viet Cong. But I wouldn't let myself give in and light one. The hell with the job, I intended to stay alive.

CHAPTER 3

The jungle sounds and bird calls had died out so slowly that we didn't notice at first, but now the silence was overpowering. We sat without speaking for several minutes, studying the bush within the arc of our vision, turning our heads ever so slowly to widen that arc...never looking directly at a spot, but always to one side, to get the advantage of the cone of night vision. Ivy League passed me the Starlight scope, and I scanned all of the jungle and the clearing visible from where I sat.

"Do you see anything?" Ivy League whispered.

"No," I whispered back. "Do you?" The night sounds had begun again.

"No, but I don't like it. I wonder if a patrol passed close by."

"Somethin' spooked them birds, all right," I said.

"Yeah, I guess so," he agreed. Then we sat in silence for a long time.

"What time is it?" Ivy League wanted to know again. I couldn't help glancing down, but it pissed me off, him asking so often.

"Didn't you wear your own fuckin' divin' watch?" I snapped at him.

"Yeah," he replied, "but I don't want to look at it. The Viet Cong might see the glow." Oh, great, what a good buddy—wants the VC to see my watch instead of his! Maybe Charley will blow me away and overlook him!

I wondered why the night sounds had stopped and then started up again. If a man sat very still, the animal and bird life in the jungle would forget about him, or decide he wasn't a threat, and the sounds and the cries would start up again. There might be a Viet Cong out there right now, drawing a bead on one of us...or waiting for an opportunity to slip through the sawgrass and cut a throat or garrote somebody. If you moved slowly, a step every two or three minutes, say, the jungle creatures might just ignore you, and the night sounds might continue. I tried to estimate how far it was to the nearest bush, and if a man moving a foot a minute could cover that distance before we would leave the ambush site. It was about one hundred and twenty feet to the nearest stand of trees, and it was now—I glanced at my watch—2230. We would be on the ambush site until at least 2400. He might make it.

I thought about Ivy League and wondered what had brought him to 'Nam. I was here because I'd tried to avoid getting drafted into the Army and sent over. But why the hell would Ivy League, with all his family's wealth, want to be over here? I knew that with all that money and influence he could have gotten a berth on the Atlantic Fleet, or permanent duty ashore in the States. It just didn't make any sense to me.... Why would anyone not use that influence? And why did he join a hard-assed outfit like the SEALs? I asked him straight out.

"My father," he said finally, in a voice so low I could

hardly hear him. I'd really expected some smart-ass remark on the validity of the war or the redeeming social value of sacrifice, or some shit. I didn't really expect him to bare his soul, but something about sitting out there in the dark, waiting for someone to slip in and kill you, made you want to communicate . . . even if the person you told might be dead soon.

"My father," he went on, a little louder, "he's the reason I'm here. He is president of Boston–Inland Bulk Carriers, you know, as was my grandfather before him—it's a family business. Father takes great pride in 'running a tight ship.' He always gets what he wants from his employees . . . and from his business associates . . . and from his family." He paused for a few minutes. I shifted my position a little bit to keep my legs from getting numb.

"He wanted you to be a SEAL?" I asked. "Hell, I've never talked to anyone outside the Navy that ever even heard of the damned SEALs."

"My father was a Navy officer," he pointed out. "And so was my grandfather, and his father before him. . . . It's a tradition in my family that all the men serve in the navy—as officers, of course—before going into the family business.

"Boston–Inland specializes in shipping wheat, coal, and ores," he continued. "Anyway, none of the family has seen action since the Civil War, despite their Navy service. The . . . well, the timing's been all wrong. Grandfather served between the World Wars, and during World War Two the Merchant Marine was so important to the war effort that the Navy refused to call him back, although he was in the Reserves. They insisted that he remain in charge of the firm, and that he keep the supplies moving. Father enlisted, but the war was over before he could see any action, and he had just resigned his commission to take over the business from Grandfather, who was ailing, when the Korean Conflict began. So since the Civil War, no Hartford has had the opportunity to 'distinguish himself in conflict,' as Father likes to put it. Except me."

"Well, there's been Tylers in almost every war this country's been in," I told him—I just had to get that dig in. "But here's one Tyler that would've been just as glad to let this war go by without him." That didn't surprise him, I guess.

"Yeah. You've made that clear. But you can see why I was in Navy ROTC in college," he went on. He said it "rot-see." "Father is also very big on sports. He wanted me to be an athlete. *HE* was a hockey player . . . has all kinds of trophies and junk. . . . He says a contact team sport, like hockey, develops the character, develops courage, initiative, and leadership, and all that crap. Well, I tried out for the hockey team, but I didn't make it. I couldn't skate well enough. But I tried out for the swimming team and found that I could do well there. Father wasn't happy, of course—swimming doesn't afford the same kind of opportunities for leadership—but he decided that swimming was better than no sport at all."

He paused for a while.

"All the practicing and training and meets took up a lot of time, and I'm not a quick study, like some people—I have to work hard to make my grades. So after a while, I found myself on scholastic probation. I called Father, to see if he'd let me quit the team. I thought he might. After all, it was only swimming and not hockey. But he told me that I'd never succeed in anything unless I learned to stick with what I'd begun, that I should continue swimming and keep my grades up, and that I could do both if I quit partying and running around. Of course, I'd given all that up already—I couldn't party and stay in training for the swimming team. Finally, I flunked out. I was committed to serve four years in the Navy because of the ROTC program," he went on. "But I didn't complete the program, so I couldn't make officer."

"But why'd you volunteer for the SEALs?" I asked. "Looks to me like just bein' a riverboat sailor would've been enough to satisfy your old man—it would've got you into the fightin'."

"It really wasn't that at all," he replied. "Father would have preferred that I become a fleet sailor and learn about handling large ships, but we had another big scene the night I told him that I'd flunked out, and that I'd be going into the Navy, but not as an officer. He cursed me a lot, said I was gutless, said I was a quitter—that wasn't true. He said I didn't have balls enough to make it in anything. I got mad and left."

I didn't make any comment. I was thinking about scenes like that, that I'd had with my dad, when I was in high school. Over the plowing or feeding the hogs, when he didn't think I'd done it just right. Or the way I drove the pickup—too fast and reckless, he said. Or when I stayed out all Saturday night and came in too drunk to get up and go to church on Sunday morning.

"About six weeks into boot camp, I got a letter from Father. He said he was going to fix things up for me. He was going to see that I was assigned to the Second Fleet, where I would get plenty of ship-handling experience. He also thought he could arrange for me to advance quickly, due to my education, perhaps even to warrant officer."

"Shit!" I interrupted. "Could he do that?" I wasn't surprised that he could, just that Ivy League would admit to it.

"If anyone could, he could. But I was pissed off at him, and I didn't want any of his favors.... I knew I'd be the loser in the long run. So, just to screw up his plans for me, I put in my chit for the SEALs as soon as I got through boot camp. I didn't say anything to him about it, until I heard that I'd been accepted. I had a short leave before BUDS, and I went home to tell him."

"Was he pissed?" I asked. Somehow I knew he had

been. I could just imagine a pompous, fat old fart in a Brooks Brothers suit, chewing a big cigar and snorting and blowing like an old worn-out steam engine.

"He was really pissed," Ivy League said. "But he just laughed sarcastically and said that inside a month I'd be out because I couldn't make the grade. He told me that I was just wasting my time, that whatever I would learn in the SEALs was useless and wouldn't benefit me at all when I took my place in the company. Of course, when I went home for my two weeks just before we shipped over, he was full of that 'chip off the old block' and 'I knew you could do it' bullshit, bragging to his friends and business associates about what an elite outfit the SEALs were. He couldn't believe it when I told him to stow the crap and quit being such a damned hypocrite. He blew his stack again, and I turned around and walked out. That was the last time I saw him."

"The last time I saw him." Those words had a chilling effect on me. Despite the heat of the night, the mists rising from the earth seemed suddenly cold; it was as though someone had opened a freezer door and the frigid air had crept down around me, turning the sweat that soaked the back of my shirt into frost. "The last time I saw him." The last time I saw Dad I saw his blood splattered on the floor. . . . There had been one of those stupid arguments— over nothing, really. He didn't like it that I'd left the spare tire on the pickup instead of putting the good tire back on after I'd fixed it, and I was tired and hot and had been drinking a lot of beer. The flat tire had delayed me. I wanted to go into town with some of my buddies, and I had a lot of chores to do yet. I just didn't want to change that tire right then. So a few words led to more, and soon we were snarling and spitting at each other like two tomcats with their tails tied together. My stomach churned as I recalled the scene. I'd really loved that old man . . . but how I'd hated him right then! How had I let it happen?

There could be only one explanation: He'd gone insane. Temporarily, perhaps. Hell, anybody would be a little bit crazy after a lifetime of nothing but raisin' hogs—he must have been getting worse and worse each day until it reached a peak on that hot July afternoon when he'd gone into the house after our fight. The county sheriff had decided it was an accident. But I stood there, sick, reeling from waves of nausea, shocked, and I looked at the blood stains and thought: You had a hand in this, J. E. It's your fault. If you hadn't been so hotheaded, if you'd let him have his way, he wouldn't have done it.

The things that you try hardest not to think about are the things that keep coming to mind. I kept trying to turn my thoughts in other directions, but they kept coming back to the same things: Dad's death and his insanity. Maybe all the Tylers are a little bit insane, I thought. If that's true, it'll be found out; a few more nights of this and I'll be nuts for sure. I'd heard of guys going over the edge on these ambushes, or on patrol. They jump up and start screaming and shooting in all directions....

It would almost be a relief if something did happen.

The minutes ticked by. We listened and watched and occasionally scanned the treeline and the paddy dike with the Starlight scope. We still saw nothing. I was still nervous, but much less so than at first. Sometimes there would be a rustling sound in the jungle, and my breathing would get shallow and quick, and my pulse would pound wildly for a few minutes, only to slowly subside when the Starlight scope revealed nothing.

When we sat there without talking, the tension seemed to get worse, because we had more time to think on all the bad things that could happen, I guess. Sometimes the tension got so unbearable I thought we'd have to keep talking or I'd start screaming and shooting. During one of those times I asked Ivy League if he had seen his girl on his two-week furlough just before we shipped over.

"Yeah," he said. "I went to see her a few times. She was in school, of course."

There was something in his voice that told me things hadn't gone well.

"Just a few times?" I asked. "I reckon I'd'a spent all the time I could with my girl."

"I spent some time with Father and my family," he replied. That was the first time he'd mentioned any family besides his father. There might have been just the two of them for all he talked about anyone else. "And she was busy at school. She's carrying a heavy load this quarter, and she has lots of homework. And on top of that, she's very involved in . . . ah, campus politics."

"Looks to me like she'd'a made time, with you coming over to 'Nam, and all. Or doesn't she know you might not be comin' back?"

"She knows," he said in a kind of strangled voice.

"What d'ya mean, she's in campus politics? She a-runnin' for school president or somethin'?" I persisted.

"You know damned good and well what I mean, Tyler!" he snapped, not loudly but with a lot of emotion. I thought he was going to cut me off right there and not say anything more, but he went on. "She's in on these damned antiwar protests. Marching and carrying signs and all that garbage. She claims she doesn't understand why I didn't run off to Canada when I flunked out, or why I didn't desert when I was home on leave before BUDS. This time she was very cool to me . . . kept calling me an assassin and a hired killer—she's found out what a SEAL is, you see. When I tried to explain to her how the Viet Cong is trying to force its brand of politics on these people through murder and terrorism, all she did was chant 'Ho . . . Ho . . . Ho Chi Minh!' so she couldn't hear me."

"Sounds like you had a rough trip, what with that and the fight with your dad," I sympathized.

"Well, hell, things had been going sour in both relationships for a long time," he pointed out. "I should have known better than to go back. I've changed a lot since I joined the SEALs."

I knew what he meant. I didn't seem to be able to get along with the people I once knew, at least not as well as I had before I joined the SEALs. A lot of it was the training: After you'd been through Hell Week and all that, you couldn't help but be different. It couldn't help but change your personality, even without seeing combat, and in ways that weren't understandable to people who hadn't been through it, or something like it. Especially to people who'd known you before, like family and friends.

"What did you do on your leave, Tyler?" Ivy League asked, probably to get his mind off his fiancée. I knew he didn't really give a shit.

"I went home for a week," I said. "To Arkansas, but I got kinda bored around there. I couldn't talk to those people anymore. After I found out how the crops were, an' how the pig market was, an' who was runnin' around with whose wife . . . there just wasn't anythang to talk about. So I went back to San Diego. Anyway, I was dyin' for a beer—my home county's dry, you can't buy no beer or liquor there. I laid around San Diego for a week, and drank a lot of beer, an' some hard liquor, an' worried, mostly."

"Did you worry a lot?" he wanted to know.

"Yeah," I told him, but I didn't tell him what I worried about. Some of it he already knew. He'd probably worried about it himself: losing an arm or a leg or both legs or both balls, being blinded or being disfigured or being captured and tortured. All of us had that kind of thing on our minds before we came over. I didn't tell him, of course, that I worried about going mad.

"I thought about going over the hill," I admitted. "An' the night just before we shipped over, I worried a lot more.

I couldn't sleep, I just laid there all night an' worried,
wonderin' if I was gonna come home in a baggy. I thought,
man, after all you've gone through, you're gonna wash
out tonight. I figgered I'd have a narvous breakdown. So
I got up about three in the mornin' an' went down to the
lounge to get my ass some coffee. I just about fell over
to see a bunch of the other guys in there. All of 'em with
faces so long they'd'a tripped over 'em if they tried to
walk. Brewster was in there, lookin' like a rich uncle had
just died an' left everythin' to the church! Hell, even the
Chief was in there. He was drinkin' his coffee with whiskey, an' after a while he quit drinkin' the coffee an' just
drank whiskey. I could tell that they'd been at it all night,
some of 'em, because the coffee was fresh-made, an' there
was a big pile of grounds an' starfoam cups in the trash-
can. It was a relief to see the other guys. I'd thought I
was the only one worried like that. I said to the Chief,
'You've been there before. Why are you so fuckin' worried?' An' he said, 'Tyler, I'm worried *because* I've been
there before!'"

I had paused for just a second or two and was just
about to start up again with my story when I felt Ivy
League tensing up.

"Did you hear that?" he whispered.

I hadn't heard anything other than the usual night
sounds, and told him so.

"It wasn't an animal sound," he insisted. "It was
more . . . substantial." He used those two-bit words every
once in a while. After a moment, he got even more tense,
if that was possible, and whispered, "There . . . did you
hear it?"

I had. It really was more substantial than the sounds
we had been hearing. It was made by a bigger body, for
sure.

One by one, the night birds quit calling and the frogs
quit piping. It was like someone was going around turning

off their switches. Then the locusts began to fall silent, too. I could feel Ivy League's back getting stiffer and stiffer, and the flexing of the muscles as he turned his head slowly, trying to hear or see something.

Through the silence, there was another stealthy rustle in the underbrush.

The sound came distinctly from behind me and to my left. I couldn't force myself to sit still, although I should have. I slowly turned my body to the left—not very far, and very, *very* slowly—just a quarter-turn. I could feel Ivy League shaking, and I was sweating like a stevedore in August. Sweat ran down my back and soaked my shirt in front, trickled through my hair like I'd just taken a shower, and got into the corners of my eyes, making them burn and sting until I could hardly see. My throat got suddenly dry, and it was hard to swallow. Or talk.

"Do you see him?" I finally managed to croak.

"No," Ivy League hissed, "but God damn it, I heard them talking. Listen!"

I thought I could hear it too: a voice, very faint, with a singsong inflection.

Ivy League searched the treeline with the Starlight scope. I could tell from his movements that he saw nothing.

"Call Poppa and tell him Charley's over there," he admonished.

"No, not until we see somebody for sure. You heard what he said about false alarms," I reminded him.

There was another rustle in the brush. Ivy League stopped sweeping the treeline with the scope and froze on a certain mass of bush.

"Call him, damn it! There's someone over there!" he insisted. He was breathing in short gasps.

I could hardly get a breath myself. The night air had suddenly become suffocating. I held my thumb on the button of the radio. Should I call? I didn't want to face

Poppa's ridicule if we did call and there was nothing out there but jungle animals.

"Call him!" Ivy League said again, in a loud, forceful whisper.

"Sh-h-h-h. . . . Don't shit in your pants," I told him. "Gimme the damn scope." He passed me the Starlight scope, and I scanned the treeline in the direction the sound seemed to come from, but there was nothing to see.

We heard the sound again . . . a muted rustle.

"They're out there!" Ivy League insisted, louder this time.

"Where, God damn it! I don't see anything," I insisted, keeping the scope aimed in the direction the sound seemed to be coming from.

"Over there! Over there!" He was pointing. "I can see him without the goddamned scope! Give me the fucking radio!" He reached for the radio. Luckily my body was in the way. I handed him the scope instead. Ivy League cursed me, but he put it to his eye and searched the treeline again. He didn't see anyone where he thought he'd seen them with his naked eye, so he fell silent.

The rustling came again. Could there be someone out there, concealed from us by a wrinkle in the land or by unusually thick underbrush? I wanted badly to call Poppa. . . . So what if he chewed us out; we'd know for sure if Charley was out there. But Poppa had made his point so strongly I just wasn't going to call unless I saw the image of a man in the scope—with my own eyes, not Ivy League's.

The stealthy sound came again. Why didn't Poppa shoot? Could Charley be hidden from Poppa by the same brush or fold of land that hid him from us? My heart was pounding so loudly it seemed like Charley should be able to take aim at me in the dark just from the noise it made. My thumb crept by itself to the little button on the radio, only to lack the strength to push it. I kept waiting for the

crack of a sniper rifle . . . or a burst from an AK-47. In my
imagination, I could feel the impact of the rounds knifing
into my left side, smashing ribs and puncturing lungs and
blasting flesh.

Ivy League had moved when the sounds began, moving
so as to face them more, just as I had—instinct, I guess.
We were sitting almost shoulder to shoulder. Now I suddenly had the thought that those sounds might just be a
ruse to draw our attention to that part of the treeline,
while someone sneaked in from the other side to knife
us. I turned quickly to look over my shoulder, and Ivy
League jumped a foot in the air.

"What is it?" he whispered in a near panic.

"Just checkin' behind us," I told him. "You don't want
a knife in the back while you're a-worryin' about a bullet
in your chest, do you?"

"Don't move so goddamned fast. . . . I thought you were
shot!" he said.

Either he had a powerful case of body odor, or he'd
pissed in his pants.

Poppa didn't shoot.

Instead the radio buzzed. That was the signal to move
out to the rendezvous point and meet up with Poppa and
Brewster. I scanned the treeline one more time with the
Starlight scope and passed it on to Ivy League, who
scanned his sector. I could feel the tension draining away,
second by second.

"All clear," he whispered.

I hit the button on the radio—at last—and told Poppa
it was all clear and that we were moving out. Then we
moved, alternately, in short, leap-frogging bounds, each
one covering the other's movements. It was a long way
back to the treeline and the rendezvous point—at least
two hundred meters. I began to wonder if Poppa really
could have seen someone in the treeline on the opposite
side of the clearing. I knew he'd scouted it out in the

daytime. He wouldn't have picked the spot if he couldn't cover the decoys from any part of the treeline. I think.

We made it back to the rendezvous with the PBR without incident. As the boat cut its throttles and mushed down into the water, we raced out to meet it, one at a time. Poppa stayed until last, covering the rest of us as we withdrew. As soon as we had tumbled aboard, the engines roared, and the PBR began to back away from the shore. Seconds later, it spun around and raced toward the middle of the channel. Despite the nonexistent protection provided by the fiberglass hull, I relaxed for the first time all night. I was back in my element.

I leaned over to Poppa and shouted in his ear—I had to shout to be heard over the roar of the engines. I asked if we'd done well.

"Nope," was his terse reply.

I was really let down. I thought we'd done a good job of chattering out there. So I had to ask why not.

He grinned—I could see his teeth gleam in the dark.

"We didn't get one, did we?"

CHAPTER 4

Despite the late hour when we got in from the ambush, there was to be no sleeping in the next morning. We were rousted out early, me and Brewster and Ivy League, and made the rounds with the Chief. He briefed us—lectured is a better word for it—on the necessity of inspecting the boats and the barge every day. We checked the guns and made sure they were well oiled. They could rust overnight if they weren't properly dried off after a patrol, and they might jam if the rust was in a critical place. After looking things over topside, we stripped down to our shorts and dived into the river to check the underside of the boats and the barge, to make sure the VC hadn't attached a mine to them during the night. Only when we were finished did we get any coffee or breakfast.

The rest of the day we sat around. We were off-duty until evening, when we were to go out on patrol. I slept awhile, as best I could in the heat, then bullshitted with some of the sailors and cleaned my rifle. Finally the Chief came around and called us together for a briefing on the patrol.

To my surprise, there was a Vietnamese there. He was a chunky, solidly built man, about thirty-five or so, as best I could judge, and he wore no insignia of rank. Only his tiger suit marked him as an ARVN Ranger, and he seemed a little bit old for an enlisted man in the Rangers, at least to me.

"Who's the gook?" Brewster asked the Chief.

"Ah, he's supposed to be a kind of a guide and interpreter," the Chief said. "He just come in this afternoon. Somethin' to do with we don't take enough prisoners. He's supposed to talk 'em into surrenderin' or somethin'. Everybody calls him Hercules—his gook name ain't pronounceable."

We took our seats for the briefing. I got myself a cup of coffee and sat down between Brewster and the Chief. Everybody was smoking, but I smelled no marijuana. There were other smells in the air, though, the odors of men who'd been several days without a bath. I made a mental resolution to check the boats every morning. At least that way I'd get a bath of sorts.

Besides Brewster, the Chief, and myself, Ivy League and Poppa were there, and a half-dozen sailors. Lieutenant Commander Gray sat at the head of the table with Poppa on his right and Hercules on his left. It looked like a meeting of the board of directors.

"Fellows, this is Hercules," the Lieutenant Commander said, nodding toward the Vietnamese. "He is attached to our unit temporarily from an ARVN Ranger battalion. He is to act as a guide or interpreter, as needed. He's from Kien Phong Province, just up the river a ways, and he's very familiar with the people of the Delta and with this area in particular. He will be accompanying you on many of your patrols, in an attempt to entice some of the enemy into surrendering, not only so that we can interrogate them, but also so that we can attempt to sway them to our side. Every Viet Cong defector who comes to us in a propaganda victory, and will help to win this war in the end."

"If they don't help us *get* it in the end!" one of the sailors joked.

"This program has been *quite* successful in First Corps areas," Poppa interjected, scowling, "because the Vietnamese who join up are usually the ones who were forced to join the VC in the first place, either by kidnapping or by having their families held as hostages. Many of them later saw their families starve, because there was no one to work in the rice fields, or saw them murdered, as 'examples,' by the Viet Cong. Many people who would've been neutral or even pro-VC were made their enemies by atrocities committed against their families or friends. Weaker souls may be converted to VC, or at least neutralized, by terrorism, but many rebel instead. Hercules is one of those. I've worked with him before. You can have confidence in him."

"What keeps hard-core Communists from joining up with us as a scout and leading people into traps?" Ivy League wanted to know.

"Nothing," Poppa replied. "Except the Vietnamese intelligence boys who screen the volunteers are pretty good at their business."

"We're sort of getting away from the subject of the briefing," the Lieutenant Commander said. Then he outlined the plan for the night's patrol. "The VC have been slipping men and supplies into the Delta area in sampans, coming downriver at night from Cambodia. Aerial infrared recon has picked up concentrations of sampans nightly in this area." He pointed to a place on a chart he'd laid out on the table. It was upriver quite a way from our barge, but well within patrol range of a PBR. "We're going to go up there tonight and try to intercept some of those sampans. Remember, there may be legitimate river traffic on the river. Don't open fire until you have signaled the sampan to heave to and it has refused to do so. There will be boats from several other units up there, too, so don't open fire until you've definitely identified your target. I don't want you guys getting spooked or overeager and blowing away some of our own guys. Poppa and the SEALs will go along to give each boat some added firepower and manpower. Take as many live prisoners as you can carry. We'll turn 'em over to intelligence to find out the details of how they get their supplies and reinforcements into the Delta. Maybe we can be instrumental in stopping the flow."

I checked my gear again, stowed it in one of the boats, then checked out the boat thoroughly before we pulled away. When the Chief came aboard, he repeated the check of the fifty caliber that I had just completed. I didn't resent it at all. He took a position manning the fifty, and I knelt beside the starboard gunwale just aft of the coxswain den. The rest of the crew took their places, and Brewster knelt just on the port side opposite me. We cast off and roared up the river.

I felt differently about going out tonight than I had last night. Then, we'd gone out to make a target of ourselves in hopes of attracting Charley's attention. Tonight, we were looking for Charley. And two PBRs with six men apiece made a formidable force, for each boat was armed with fifty-caliber machine guns, an automatic twenty-millimeter cannon, and a forty-millimeter grenade launcher, not to mention the personal weapons of the men on board.

As we sped up the river, the sky darkened to deep blue, and the green jungle became a black wall broken here and there by rice paddies. The evening star had just become visible low down on the horizon when I noticed a winking light in a clump of bushes between two rice

paddies. I was just about to call someone's attention to
it when something went zip! past my ear like a bumblebee
in a power dive. I ducked, and just then the PBR heeled
over as it went into a ninety-degree turn at flank speed.
The turn sent me sprawling sideways. By the time I had
regained my balance, the Chief was checking his fifty
caliber by firing off a couple of rounds, and I heard the
other machine gunner on the other boat doing the same.
I checked my rifle to make sure there was a round in the
chamber and that it was off safety.

The P.A. system boomed out: "Hold your fire. Let's
try to take him prisoner!" It was Poppa.

The light continued to wink, in quick pulses at odd
intervals, as the gunner squeezed off bursts. He either
had a machine gun or an AK-47. The rounds passed with
a zipping or popping sound, some of them hitting the water
and ricocheting away. The Chief fired a burst from his
fifty into the rice paddy near the bushes, kicking up geysers of water and mud, to force the VC to get his head
down. It didn't work: The snapping and popping of near-
misses grew more intense. It was enough to make me
want to duck down behind the flimsy fiberglass of the
gunwale. . . . It must have been twice as bad up front, but
at least the Chief had partial protection from the guntub.
He walked the next burst into the brush, and the winking
light stopped.

By this time the two boats had virtually reached the
shoreline. I could tell where the shoreline was by the
scattered bushes that stuck up through the water there—
the river at this high stage just continued right on out into
the paddies, but the water was a lot shallower there. We
roared toward it at an insane rate. I braced myself for the
crash as we grounded, but it never came. We swept on
into the paddy without the slightest hesitation.

As we roared into the paddy, a single figure broke out
of the clump of brush and dashed madly for a nearby line

of trees. I say madly because he had no chance of making it, but there was no other path of retreat. I thought we would probably run him down with the boats, but instead we slowed to a halt, and the P.A. system on the other boat boomed loudly, this time with Hercules's voice. He spoke in Vietnamese, but I knew that he was telling the runner to stop and surrender. He repeated his words several times in an urgent voice, but the man didn't stop running. Finally, Hercules said in English, "Stop him."

Brewster and I already had our M-16s pointed toward the fleeing man. He was about fifty meters away when we were told to open fire. I lined up the sights and began to swing the rifle gently to overtake the runner from the rear. As the barrel swung toward the man, I thought, Tyler, if you pull that trigger you'll be a killer. All your drinking and fighting and whoring around will be forgiven, but you know that killing's one sin that the Lord will never forgive. Then the sights lined up on him, and as the barrel swung slightly ahead of him, my finger squeezed the trigger on its own, as it had been trained to do, and condemned me to an eternity in hell. There was no doubt in my mind that I had hit him. As the rifle popped, he lurched slightly, but he didn't fall, or even slow down that I could see. So I squeezed the trigger again and again. At least six of us were firing, and I think Brewster was firing semiautomatic fire like I was, but some of the sailors had their M-16s on full automatic. We kept hitting him and knocking him forward, but he wouldn't go down. He just kept stumbling across that rice paddy, with geysers of water spurting up around him and chunks of flesh flying off his arms and legs and chest. . . .

The Chief finally let off a burst from his fifty caliber, walking the shots into him, and knocked the guy down. He didn't get up. The Chief had probably held off for a while, hoping that we'd knock the VC down and we could

take him alive. But the fifty caliber left little chance of
that.

We dismounted from the boats and went over to check
our kill. I paced off the distance as best I could across a
rice paddy. It was about fifty meters to the spot where
we'd first opened fire on him, just like I'd estimated. It
was another forty meters, more or less, before we got to
the body. He was lying face down, and the back of his
head was blown off. I think it was the fifty caliber that
killed him, because when we turned him over, he was full
of little holes about the size of a pencil where the twenty-
two caliber bullets had come out. There was one big hole
in his chest, and the Chief said that was caused by the
fifty. His legs were damn near cut off, by several hits
from the fifty.

"Shit," I said. "If that little fucker'd been runnin' toward us, he damn near woulda made it! If he'd had a hand
grenade, an' run toward us...."

"Christ," said Brewster. "I know I hit the sumbitch at
least six times."

"He must have been on dope," said Ivy League. "He
had to have been on that shit."

The Chief said, "That ain't the first time that ever
happened. That's about all them little popguns are good
for. And sometimes they do run toward you. I've seen
gooks overrun a position because somebody with an M-
16 didn't hit a vital spot, an' that little twenty-two bullet
don't have the clout to knock a man down, if you don't."

"I thought they were supposed to tumble, and generate
hydraulic shock," Ivy League said.

"Sometimes they do, sometimes they don't," the Chief
said. "If they do, they'll tear a man to pieces. You might
hit him in the arm, an' the bullet come out the top of his
head. That hole in the gook's head, that's from an M-16.
I've seen 'em hit a man just right, an' make a hole in him
like he was hit by a howitzer shell. But more often than

not, I've seen 'em punch little holes like these, an' not stop a man at all. An' the least little twig will deflect 'em. You can't fire through brush like you can with an M-14."

I thought about that. I thought about it long and hard while we spread out and went to check on the clump of brush he'd run out of. We halted at the edge of the rice paddy while Hercules called out in Vietnamese. To my surprise, there was a reply.

"He says he is wounded and will surrender," Hercules told us. "Go in cautiously, and do not kill him if he keeps his hands behind his head." Then he shouted something else in Vietnamese and received a reply.

The Chief went in with Poppa and Hercules, to get the VC. In a few moments they came out with him. He was pretty shot up, and the Chief was carrying him. He dumped the little guy in one of the boats, and we huddled for a while to decide what to do.

"He's *bo doi*—plenty dumb. He's not worth taking prisoner—he will know nothing." Hercules said. "Let him die here. We can go on to find the sampans."

"He's plenty dumb, all right," said the Chief, "or he wouldn't have shot at us. They had no way to retreat from that clump of brush."

Just then the coxswain of one of the boats came over and put an end to the talk.

"We gotta get moving, you guys. We're taking on water. We've got bullet holes in one of the boats. Anyway, the strainers will clog up if we set dead in the water in these rice paddies much longer."

Poppa quickly decided that one boat would go on with the patrol, and the one that had been holed—the one I was in, as it turned out—would return to the barge with the wounded prisoner.

Before I got back on the boat, I walked over to that clump of trees, took the clip out of my M-16, and ejected the round in the magazine . . . and then took the damned thing by the barrel and smashed that plastic stock against a damned tree. A bamboo tree, or something like that. Then I walked over to the boat and tossed the pieces in. The Chief looked at me kind of funny, and then grinned and winked.

"Got a little excited in the heat of action, eh, Tyler?" he asked.

"Yeah," I told him. "I fell agin a tree."

He just laughed.

Brewster, Ivy League, and I went on the boat that went back. Poppa, the Chief, and Hercules went on the other boat. We bandaged up the wounded VC and put tourniquets on his worst wounds. It felt kind of strange, taking care of one of the enemy that way, but he was just a kid, and more frightened than hostile. He just lay there, expressionless despite the pain he must have been feeling, and watched us with wide eyes.

When the barge was in sight, we radioed ahead and told them we were bringing in a VC prisoner, and for them to call a Medivac chopper in for him. They gave us back a roger, and the all-clear to come in. As we approached, a couple of sailors on the deck kept us covered with an M-60 set up in some sandbags. That was just in case the boat had been captured by VC. Of course, we kept them covered with our fifty caliber, just in case the barge had been taken over while we were gone. It was standard operating procedure.

While we were unloading the prisoner, Brewster reached out a hand to help and dropped his M-16 in the water. Then he just looked at me and shrugged.

I later reported that the stock of my M-16 had been hit by a VC round and shattered. Brewster said his dropped overboard, which was the truth. He said it was an accident, which wasn't. I requested, and got, an M-14. I felt more confident with the heavier, thirty-caliber weapon. I knew it would knock a man down if you hit him squarely, and I knew I could hit with it. Brewster was issued a twelve-gauge shotgun and steel buckshot loads for it.

It was a good chance to get some sleep, since we got in at about 2100. But all I could see when I closed my eyes was that man running across the rice paddy. I was a killer now. My fate was sealed. I was still awake when the other boat got back about 0200. They'd seen nothing. Either it was a wild goose chase or the enemy had been warned.

The next morning was a repeat of the one before, except that the Lieutenant Commander sent the Chief into Saigon in a PBR "to get some fresh meat." I couldn't see anything wrong with the stuff they had in the 'fridge— there were some damned good hams in there. Three or four sailors threw their seabags into the boats when they got aboard, and their friends stood around and wished them luck and told them to take it easy, if they could get it that way, and others told them to "get some"—any way they could, I suppose. I thought maybe they were being transferred to another outfit where there was more fighting or something, from the long faces of their friends, but I finally caught on that they were being rotated home. Then I realized the other sailors had such long faces because they were wishing they were on their own way home. They were scared they would never make it themselves. And I think that down deep they knew the guys going home were facing an even tougher fight than the one they were leaving: trying to fit in back in the world again.

The Chief came in late in the afternoon with about twelve sailors and a new boat, to replace one that had been shot up before we came. The new sailors were the "fresh meat" he'd been sent to get. The new boat meant we would have three boats operating, and we could patrol the river a little better and carry bigger forces when we needed to hit a camp or something. The Chief had stopped at a couple of bars, and he was a little bit loop-legged. He kept sucking oxygen out of a Mark VI SCUBA tank to clear his head.

One of the sailors he brought in was a colored man, a coxswain. The Chief was down on him from the start because he was black—not an attitude I expected from an Indian. The coxswain was to go on a patrol that night. They were putting him right out into action, like we went out as decoys on our first night. After all, you're supposed to be thoroughly trained by the time you get over there. The coxswain was worried about it, too, just like I'd been. He cornered me while I was oiling my rifle. We'd already been briefed, so he knew what he was going to do: He was going to stay in a PBR and hold it just offshore so that when we came back we'd have a boat waiting for us and our prisoners and wouldn't have to wait for a pickup. We'd probably come back at a run, with the Viet Cong right behind us.

He sat down on a cot next to mine and watched me field strip my M-14 and check it out. I noticed he was a little agitated. He took out a package of cigarettes and broke one in two trying to get it out. When he finally did get one out, he dropped it, and then stepped on it while he was looking for it. I gave him one of mine, and I'll be damned if he didn't light the filter end. I watched him while he drew a long taste of it and choked, and then I cut the filter end off for him with my diving knife and relit the cigarette.

"What's wrong? You gettin' a little wearied an' narvous?" I asked him. He wasn't too tall, about normal height, I guess, but stocky. He had great long arms that hung down almost to his knees. He was dish-faced, with a protruding lower jaw and thick, fleshy lips over a great big mouth full of yellow teeth. He had big eyes that showed a lot of white around the colored part. His hair was short and kinky and reminded me of a piece of black carpet stretched over his head. His ears stuck out like handles on a jug, as they used to say back home. Altogether, he was about the ugliest man I'd ever seen.

"Oh, shit, yeah, man. I'm flat-ass scared!" he replied.

"Well...what're you a-scared of?" I asked him, thinking how I'd damned sure rather stay out there on the river in that boat than go ashore to bring back some Viet Cong.

"Man, I don't want to die," he said.

So I said, "Well, hell, do you think anybody in this outfit *does*?"

"No...but you guys are all Special Forces, an' you know what you're doin' out there. Hell, I'm just a little ole riverboat sailor, an' all I know about is boats."

"Well, shit—that don't make no difference. We're all ass-deep in it anyway. You know about boats, an' the rest of us have to go out there in the bush and find the little fuckers." Meaning the Viet Cong. "What's really botherin' you?"

He said, "Man..." and then he thought for a minute. His voice had been high-pitched and kind of quivery and nasal, but when he spoke again, it was lower and more controlled. "Is it really true, whenever you're shot at, you can hear them bullets go 'pop' like that?" He snapped his fingers. "Do they really go 'pop'?"

"Yeah," I said. "An' if you hear one go 'pop,' you duck! If you hear one pop over here"—I snapped my fingers, too, beside my ear—"you move away from it...an' if you hear one pop over *here*, you move the other way, because they're a-gettin' close."

That night we went out, all in one boat. There were Poppa, Hercules, four SEALs, and two sailors, besides the coxswain. Before we shoved off, the Chief took the coxswain aside. I overheard him talking.

"Whatever you do, God damn it, don't you let this

boat get on that beach!" the Chief told him. "Keep it away from the goddamned beach, and don't let it get hung up. If you start getting shot at, if Charley starts snipin' at you, you just wrap around that fifty—we'll hear it. If you shoot, we'll hear it an' we'll come runnin'! Your main concern is that PBR.... It's our only way out of there."

The tide was going out when we went in. It had been a surprise to me to find out that there were tides that far up the river, but we weren't that far above sea level— only three or four feet, I guess. Even in that time of year, when the river was at its highest level, the tide made it rise and fall enough to strand a boat, if you let it stay too long too near the shore when the tide was going out.

We had about twenty feet of open, muddy ground to cross and a slippery little bank we had to scramble up before we got into the bush. Then we formed up and moved off with the Chief taking the point. I had second thoughts about the Chief being out front this time, re-membering how drunk he was when he came back with the boats. He had to keep taking shots of oxygen on the trip out, too. I wasn't sure the oxygen had done him all that much good. But he got us there all right, and Poppa and Hercules went in to look the village over for a while. When they came back Poppa filled us in on the plans.

There were fifteen or eighteen people in the village, not counting the kids running around. Most of them were assembled in the clearing beside the huts, where one man was harassing them about something. Hercules said it was a political speech. There were two sentries out, one on the near side of the village and one on the far side. Poppa would take one of them out. Hercules wanted the other one, but Poppa insisted he was too important to risk, because no one else could talk to the villagers. He told Ivy League to get the other sentry. I was glad he hadn't picked me. Shooting a man at a range of forty yards or so is one thing, but cutting his throat is another thing entirely. It's much more...intimate.

After they got the sentries, we were to surround the village and set our claymore mines....Each of us was carrying two. Poppa would fire a few shots into the clearing, to get their heads down. Then Hercules would call out for the Viet Cong to surrender. If they started shooting, we'd pick off a few, then try again. If they kept on, or if anything went wrong, we'd set off the mines.

"Any questions?" Poppa asked when he was finished.

"Yeah...what about the kids?" I asked. "We s'posed to kill them, too?"

"Tyler, this is a Viet Cong camp. Those kids hate your guts just as much as their mothers and daddies do, and they'd kill your ass if they had the chance. If they get in your line of fire, blow 'em away. This is no place for bleeding hearts." I thought that was a real poor choice of words. "The claymores won't leave much anyway, if we have to use 'em." I couldn't believe my ears: Those words were coming from Poppa—who told me just three days before how much he liked Southeast Asia, and the Vietnamese in particular. I looked over at Hercules, and to my surprise he was agreeing.

We moved in close to the village to surround it, and Poppa took one of the sentries out. His garrote was a piece of piano wire with a couple of little steel bars connected to the ends for him to grip. He kept it well oiled and coiled around his neck, underneath his collar. He took it out and held it in one hand, keeping his M-16 in the other while he crept up on the sentry. I stayed behind and covered him. He slipped up right behind the man, who never even looked his way but kept staring off the same direction into the jungle. Poppa carefully laid his M-16 where he could crouch down and grab it if anything went wrong, then took the garrote in both hands. He moved and had that garrote looped around the guard's neck so fast that the man never knew it was there. I saw Poppa's arms straighten out and down, and the gook's head just popped off his shoulders. Blood spurted everywhere. The thick, slaughterhouse smell of it rolled me in a wave, and I was sure the people in the clearing must have been able to smell it, too. I just crouched there and stared at the body for a minute. I could see its heels through the underbrush; they twitched rhythmically. I could picture the blood spurting out the other end in gushes, like when Mom used to pop the head off a fryer for Sunday dinner. Poppa saw me staring and motioned for me to move on.

I moved on around the village to set my claymores on the other side. Ivy League was on the other side. I got around there just after he'd taken out his sentry. He was squatting by the trunk of a tree, steadying himself with one hand. The gook's blood had sprayed over him. I had to step over the sentry's body. Ivy League had used his knife, and it was a messy job.... He'd ripped him open all the way up his spine to the back of his neck. If you can get to the sentries without being heard and get your knife into the vertebra and go on past it, into the heart, usually they won't have much reflex and won't make much noise. Especially if they don't have their fingers on the trigger. If you catch a sentry with his gun up on his shoulder or down at his side, or if he just has his hand on the stock—and if you're fast enough—then you can get him: Put your arm around his neck and your knee in his back and ram that knife in at the same time and rip him.... Usually you can take him out before he can get his finger on the trigger or shout. If you can get his neck stretched all the way back, and his chin up in the air, he can't holler. But if you aren't fast enough and he yells, or if he is carrying his rifle right, with his finger on the trigger and a round in the chamber, the safety off...he's going to warn them.

I had just got my last claymore set and aimed when the Viet Cong started shooting. I don't know what tipped them off. Maybe the sentries were supposed to report in or something. Maybe it was the sound of Ivy League puking. Anyway, bullets began to sing and pop through the bush, and we started shooting back. The commissar, or whatever he was, herded a bunch of the people into one of the huts, and we put a lot of lead into it. Somebody had their claymores set and discharged them, and that cleared out one end of the village. The huts went down like they were made out of cards and toothpicks. We moved out into the edge of the clearing around the hut where the villagers had taken shelter. I poked into a couple of the huts that were still standing, but there was nothing in them except some straw mats and some jars and bags of rice. I moved up and crouched beside Hercules, facing the hut where the villagers had holed up. A few scattered shots came out of it, wild, answered by short bursts of automatic fire. I didn't shoot.

Hercules was yelling something in Vietnamese. There was no answer. He yelled some more, and then someone stepped out of the hut.

It was a girl. She was about twelve or fourteen, I judged—the Vietnamese don't show their age like Caucasians do—and she'd been hit. She held her side and walked bent over and wobbly. Her face was contorted with pain. She wasn't a pretty girl. Her face was a hard face, thin and bony, with sunken cheeks—undernourished-looking. There were a lot of faces like it back home, with harsh lines etched there by pain and poverty. In fact, she'd have looked right at home in a hogpen with a big bucket of slops in each hand. I felt at once a sort of kinship with her, as if she and I had something in common: hard lives and hard times.

I stood up to go and help her. Hercules quickly grabbed my sleeve and pulled me back down. He yelled something in Vietnamese and turned loose of my sleeve only long enough to gesture with both hands.

"I'm telling her to lie down. If she lies down, we will come to her and help her," he told me between shouts and gestures.

She just kept walking toward us, holding her side.

Hercules began to back up slowly, keeping about twenty meters between us and the girl, and I backed up because he tugged at my sleeve. He kept telling her to lie down, but she kept coming, her thin little face grimacing in what I could see now might be hatred as much as pain. Her jaw muscles worked as she clenched her teeth. Blood oozed from the wound in her side.

We backed up again.

Hercules looked toward me for a second and then back toward the girl. I don't know what he read in my face, but he said, "I am going to tell her one more time to lie down. If she doesn't, kill her. Do you understand?"

I nodded, only vaguely aware of what he'd said or that he wasn't looking at me anymore. My full attention was on the girl: her pock-marked face, her skinny body, her wound. Why didn't she stop?

Hercules yelled again in Vietnamese.

The girl kept coming.

"Kill her," Hercules said.

I wanted to say, well, god damn, she's just a kid, and she's hurt. Maybe she's in shock and doesn't understand.

Her black eyes glinted with pain, or hatred. Her gaze bored into mine.

"Kill her!" Hercules repeated.

I balked. I couldn't shoot. I didn't even aim at her. I had my M-14 pointed in her direction, from waist height. Hercules turned to look at me, and said very clearly but slowly and through clenched teeth: "Take...her... head...off...*now*!"

When he said it that way, I stopped backing up, and

threw the rifle up to my shoulder and shot. I guess I was
nervous and scared, because I didn't aim. Or maybe I
really didn't want to kill her. The bullet hit her just below
the breastbone.... I saw a little red spot appear there just
a split second before the bullet's impact knocked her
backward and around. When she hit the ground she blew
up. She just...blew up.

We all ducked down when the blast went off. When I
looked again, she wasn't there anymore.

Little pieces of meat were splattered all over me. I
could feel little wet, sticky spots on my face and on my
upper lip, and I picked one off and looked at it for a
second, without really realizing then just what it was. I
looked at Hercules. I was kind of dazed, I guess.

"Now go puke," he said.

I did. I ran back to the edge of the bush, away from
the huts, and bent over, feeling hot and nauseated, but I
had the dry heaves. I heaved and sweated and heaved,
but nothing came up. I was still in that position, head
down and ass up, several minutes later when I saw two
men coming out of a hole in the ground. It was the commissar, or whatever he was, who had been giving the little
political talk, and a younger man with a scarred face. They
looked around before they came out, like a couple of rats
testing the air for the cat before they head for the grain
bins, but they kept looking back toward the hut and never
toward me.

Should I shoot? Should I yell for Hercules? I knew we
needed prisoners. That was the whole point of the raid.
But I forgot suddenly how to tell them in Vietnamese to
surrender. If I yelled for Hercules, they'd either get away
or I'd have to kill them. I made my decision in a lot less
time than it takes to tell it. I had to move fast and get
close before they saw me. I had to take control of the
situation and keep them off balance. I had to attract the
attention of the others in my patrol. And I had only a

second or two to do all those things. That's where training takes over and thinking is left behind. As soon as I had sized up the situation—and that didn't take but half a second—I lunged toward them, my M-14 held about shoulder height and thrust out in front of me, ready to fire. After about ten steps, when I was already so close they couldn't react before I was on top of them, I yelled the most maniacal Rebel yell I could come up with. It was to shock them, to scare the piss out of them, to let them know they'd been spotted just when they thought they were getting away...to let them anticipate for just a split second the impact of the bullets in their backs. It was a little bit of pyschological warfare, softening them up to be captured if they got a chance to surrender.

My Rebel yell started from the tail end of a dry heave, and it came out sounding more like a loud *urp*, but it had the effect I wanted, anyway. The two men jumped and looked my way in midstride. Both of them tried to turn and raise their AKs to fire, but I was on their offside, so they had to turn completely around my way, and as we were all running and just a few steps apart, they didn't have the time. I fired one shot that went between the two of them, and I was so close that the skin on the commissar's face was burned by the muzzle blast. Then I got the barrel of my M-14 tangled up with the barrels of their AKs and neatly disarmed both of the bastards. Actually, I was trying to poke Scar Face in the guts, but the Chief said later it was a really slick move, and would I teach it to him. As their rifles went flying, I bashed Scar Face in the head with the butt of my M-14 and kicked the commissar in the nuts. Both of them went down, and there wasn't any fight in them after that.

So we had ourselves two prisoners.

There weren't any others. Someone flattened the hut where the people had been holed up with a claymore mine. There were no survivors. Not even the kids.

Later, I remembered seeing Brewster standing by a burning hooch, staring down at something that looked like a little bundle of rags. He had the strangest goddamned expression on his face that I ever saw him get. At the time, I didn't think much about it, because I was so shook up over the girl and so high over getting the prisoners. When I remembered later, it seemed like those streaks of sweat down his cheeks might have been tears. I never asked.

Everybody was wrung out. We mopped up quickly, grenading the bolt-hole shut, checking the bodies, and destroying the weapons. Then we kicked our prisoners in the ass and started them toward the boat.

I avoided going past the place where the girl had blown up.

On the way back to the boat, though, I thought about her. She'd obviously been sacrificed, sent out to create a diversion so the commissar and Scar Face could escape. I wondered which one had the idea and which one had strapped the bomb to her. Scar Face looked mean enough—he looked like he could tie one onto his own sister. But the other man, the commissar, had given the orders, I was certain. I remembered that it was the commissar who herded all those people into the hut. I began to hope Hercules would be the one to interrogate him and would let me work him over, maybe cut on him a little, to make him talk. He was still limping a little from my kick, and Brewster kept jabbing him hard in the back with the barrel of his M-14, to hurry him along. I didn't feel sorry for him at all.

We had a couple of miles to go to the river, but we were moving pretty fast, just in case some VC patrol had heard the shooting and came to investigate. We were still a quarter-mile from the boat when we heard that damned fifty caliber on the PBR go off.

CHAPTER 5

Right ahead of us we heard some short bursts of automatic fire. The fifty rapped briefly again and then quit. There was more rifle fire, a few short bursts, and finally, silence.

We came together in a loose group, keeping a close watch around us. "Okay," the Chief told us. "Here it is: They've got that little nigger. They've killed him. But it's likely the boat is still there. There wasn't any explosion, and there's no glow from a fire. We've got to get the boat before they do, or we can't get out. We're going to split up in groups of two, and we're going to move fast for about three hundred yards. Then take it a little slower. Look for snipers. Spread out about fifty yards between groups. That'll give us a hundred-and-fifty-yard front, and we're sure to find the Viet Cong. If it's a big patrol, use your own judgment. If there's just a few, hit 'em. If you get in a hot firefight, we'll be there to help out, but our

71

first objective has to be to get to that boat before the Viet Cong do. Any questions?"

Brewster spoke up. "Yeah. What do we do with these here little fellers?" He pointed to the prisoners. "They ain't movin' fast enough to suit me."

"The prisoners have to come second," the Chief said. "We have to get to that boat." Poppa nodded. The Chief started to say something else, but before he could, Brewster had slit Scar Face's throat and thrown him aside. He was moving to get the commissar when Hercules stopped him by poking him in the ribs with the barrel of his M-16. I thought Brewster was going to turn on him for a second.

"We keep that one," Hercules said.

"Git yer goddamn gun barrel outta my ribs, you gook shit, or there's gonna be three dead gooks here," Brewster growled.

Poppa put a hand on Brewster's shoulder.

"None of that shit, now. Save it for the VC." he said. "Let's keep at least one prisoner to make the trip worth it. I think you just put the fear of God into 'im. He'll move faster now."

We split up and moved out. Poppa and Hercules took the commissar with them. Brewster and I went off together at something just less than a run. We moved out on the far right flank.

Brewster cursed Hercules under his breath as he went. He kept threatening to cut "that smart-ass gook's" throat, and I didn't doubt that Hercules would cut his if he got the chance.

About twenty meters from the river, Brewster motioned me to hold it, so I crouched down and looked around. Sure enough, there was a gook, moving carefully and quietly through the bush, looking back. He was coming from the direction the boat should've been in. He'd obviously seen or heard one of the other pairs and was slipping away from them. He kept looking back too long. Brewster raised up in front of him and gave him just a second to realize what was happening before he cut the man from bellybutton to gizzard. The guerilla just walked right up onto him.

Brewster slung the sniper's AK-47 over his shoulder, and we went on down to the water's edge.

There sat the PBR, about twenty meters away, up by the beach. Its bow wasn't up out of the water, though, like it would have been if it had grounded before the tide turned. It looked like it could be pushed off.

"What do we do now, Tyler?" Brewster whispered.

"We go get it," I told him. There was about twenty meters of open water to cross before we could get to the PBR.

"Do you suppose the gooks are on it?" he asked.

"Nah. They would've blown it up or burned it or scuttled it. They might have a patrol on the shore, though, waitin' to ambush whoever goes to it."

We patrolled down the shoreline to our right about fifty meters, then swung back. There had been no sign of anyone. Poppa and Hercules were at about the place we'd started from, looking out at the PBR. We decided to wait until the others came in to try to go out to the boat.

Just then a firefight erupted to our left. There were several bursts of fire, some of them from AKs and some from M-16s. Brewster and I moved out that way while Poppa and Hercules watched the prisoner and the PBR. Someone ran out into the river, leaving a white trail of splashes against the dark water. Another trail of splashes appeared in the river, near him, but they were smaller and there were many of them.... This trail moved quickly, closer to the runner, and there was one big splash as he fell. There was no more firing.

Brewster and I went about thirty meters to the left, and then held up. Several men were coming through the brush toward us. We could hear them before we could see them. I was straining to see anything moving in the shadows when I heard a whippoorwill call. That was no jungle bird! It was the Chief! I whistled back, and they came on in to us.

"We hit a little gook patrol," he said when he came up to us. "Three of 'em. One of 'em almost got away."

"Brewster got a fourth one," I told him. "The boat's still out there, but there's no sound or movement out of it. I guess the nigger's dead."

"Any gooks on it?"

"Not that I can tell," I told him. "Guess we'd better go on out there and get it."

"Well..." Brewster said. He studied the PBR for a minute. "Let's go, then. *Are you ready?*"

"Let's do it!"

And we were off in a mad rush through the mud and ankle-deep water. That seemed like the damned longest stretch of open water I'd ever crossed, but it was probably only a couple of seconds before we were throwing our weapons in and tumbling over the gunwale after them. I laid there for half a second, expecting a burst of machine-gun fire, or a mortar round, or for some gook to jump me with a knife, but none of those things happened, so I got up and looked around. The coxswain wasn't anywhere to be seen.

"I guess he fell overboard," I told Brewster. Brewster jumped down into the coxswain den.

"I'm gonna crank it up," he said.

I went aft and threw a round into the twenty millimeter. Somehow I didn't want to see what might be in the forward guntub.

Two figures came splashing through the water from a spot just a little upstream of where we'd come from. I swung the twenty around to cover the shoreline. It was

Ivy League and one of the sailors. They tumbled on board, knelt behind the gunwale, and watched the shoreline.

The others came in a rush, five of them, with Hercules pushing the prisoner ahead of him. When they got to the boat the Chief scooped the man up like he was a sack of hog feed and tossed him on board. His hands were tied.

"You could've broken his damned neck," I heard Poppa growl.

We got the engine started and backed off without any trouble, and got out of there without taking any fire.

The Chief climbed on board and went forward to the guntub with the fifty caliber. When he looked down into it, he hollered back to the rest of us.

"Here he is! He's in here!" He reached down, first with one hand, then with both, and gave a heave. Then he started cussing. He shined a flashlight in. That wasn't like the Chief at all, to break blackout discipline like that, so I knew something was up. I could see him saying something to whatever or whoever was in the guntub—it had to be the coxswain, of course. I figured he was wounded. But then the Chief started yelling, and he got up on the edge of that guntub and put one big foot in it and started stomping.

"Th' goddamn nigger is *hidin'* in here! He ain't hurt. He ain't hurt at all, th' cock-suckin' yellow bastard!"

After he'd stomped a few times, he reached down with both hands again and picked the coxswain up. The black was pretty heavy, but the Chief was awfully damned strong, and he was *mad*. He dragged the unfortunate man over the edge of the guntub and threw him back toward the coxswain's den. The coxswain hit the deck, with both hands holding his steel pot on his head, and he never moved.

"My God!" howled the Chief, "he's shit all over hisself! It's all over th' fuckin' guntub!" He looked around at the coxswain, who was sort of hunched over on the deck with

his arms over his head, and took a couple of quick steps toward him and kicked him in the ass with such force it moved him a foot or more along the deck. "Get up on your feet, you lily-livered, yellow-bellied, kinky-haired, chicken-stealin' cockroach! God damn you from hell to breakfast, you worthless, shit-eatin' dog!" He stepped to one side and planted his boot in the coxswain's ribs hard enough, it looked like, to break a rib. Then he grabbed him by one arm and jerked him over and threw him against the gunwale so hard the coxswain had to let go of his helmet and grab for a handhold to keep from going over into the river. His eyes were big and white in his dark face, and his mouth was open, so his teeth flashed white as well. He blubbered something to the Chief, his words mostly just gasps and sobs.

"Shooting at you!" The Chief was screaming in his rage. "The slopes were shootin' at you, were they? You think they were just playin' tag with us? God damn, they weren't anywhere close to you! There ain't no holes in this boat! You fuckoff! You dipshit! You're gonna wish they'd'a killed you before I get through, you . . . you stinking, slimy . . . worm!" The Chief was running out of things to call him, so he punched on him some while he tried to think of something else. The coxswain covered his head with his arms and bent 'way over to cover up, so the Chief drove him down to his knees with kidney punches and rabbit punches, and then kicked his ass again and again. Finally he grabbed the coxswain's steel pot and tried to rip it off, but the coxswain was holding on to it too tight. The Chief grabbed him under the armpits and dragged him over to the gunwale and threw him half across it, so he had to grab on again or go overboard. When he turned loose of the helmet, the Chief grabbed it and sent it sailing out over the water. Then he grabbed the coxswain by the hair and pushed his face down toward the water.

"We're gonna let you go for a little swim, you little

black lump of dog puke! We're gonna troll for alligators, and you're gonna be th' bait!" he yelled. He started trying to push the coxswain over, but the man managed to hold on.

Poppa had been picking his teeth and watching all this impassively from the den. Now he walked over and casually offered the Chief a cigarette. The Chief looked at him open-mouthed for a second, still trying to jerk one of the coxswain's hands off the gunwale. Finally he got the point and let go. He glared at the coxswain's back for a second, then took the cigarette and lit up and went over to sit with Poppa.

The prisoner, bound hand and foot and lying in the bottom of the boat, had tried once to look up at the ruckus, but Hercules put his head down again with a whack from the barrel of his M-16.

Brewster cut the engines 'way back, until they were just idling. The PBR mushed down into the water and started slowing down.

"Let's take him back!" Brewster said, with a toss of his head toward the coxswain. "Let's put him ashore where you hit that patrol. Give 'im to th' slopes."

The Chief grinned from ear to ear.

The coxswain cringed and hunkered down over the gunwale. "No...oh...oh!" he sobbed. "Don't take me back there! Do-on't!"

"Shit, yeah!" said the Chief with enthusiasm, like a kid planning a trip to the candy store. "We could take off his boots...hell, all his goddamned clothes...leave him nekkid, with no gun or nothin'. If the gooks didn't get 'im, th' snakes an' bugs would!"

The coxswain's shoulders shook with sobs.

Poppa pointed ahead. "Let's get this prisoner back to the barge," he told Brewster.

So Brewster opened the throttle up, and we went on back.

A few miles from the barge, the coxswain puked, over and over, until finally he slid down to his knees, resting his head on the gunwale, and stayed that way the rest of the trip.

When we got back to the barge, Poppa and Hercules took the prisoner up to the bow and manacled him to a post. Brewster and I took care of the routine things like offloading weapons and drying off the ones mounted on the PBR. The Chief helped the coxswain off the boat and onto the barge. He took him gently by the arm, coaxed him to his feet, then led him to the other side, where we were tied on. I couldn't believe it.

He gently pushed the coxswain over toward the center of the deck and stopped just behind him, his legs spread a little apart and his hands on his hips. I noticed then that his jaw muscles were bulging as he clenched his teeth. The coxswain took a few hesitant steps aft.

"NOW HEAR THIS!" the Chief roared. Everyone stopped what they were doing and looked up. "YOU ARE LOOKING AT A COWARD! A DIRTY, DICK-SUCKIN', SHIT-EATIN' COWARD! A SNIVELING, YELLOW, USELESS, SPINELESS NIGGER CRY-BABY! HE PUT ALL OUR LIVES ON THE LINE TO-NIGHT, 'CAUSE HE WAS AFRAID! HE HID IN THE GUNTUB INSTEAD OF MINDING THE BOAT. I WANT YOU ALL TO KNOW THAT SO YOU'LL UN-DERSTAND WHY I'M ABOUT TO BUST HIS ASS!" He lost his temper again with his last sentence and hit the coxswain in the back with all his strength. The coxswain's head snapped back, and he went down to his knees. Before he could pitch forward, the Chief backhanded him across the ear and sent him sprawling. He then sent a half-dozen well-aimed kicks into his ribs and kidneys. He started in cussing again while he kicked, some real gems he'd picked up from all his years in the Navy. The crew just stopped work and watched. Some of the black sailors looked kind of unhappy, but nobody made a move to stop him. They figured he had good reason, and anyway, he was acting crazy enough to kill anybody that tried to stop him.

All the ruckus attracted the Lieutenant Commander, who came forward with Poppa and Hercules. He watched the Chief drag the coxswain to his feet and knock him down again. He took the pipe out of his mouth (he smoked a pipe to make him look older, I think), tapped the ashes out of it against a bulkhead, and took out a knife and began to clean the bowl. Meanwhile, the Chief had picked the coxswain up and pinned him against a bulkhead so he couldn't fall down again, and now was slapping his face back and forth—just slapping it. All this time, he hadn't hit the guy in the right place to even knock him out. One punch would've finished the coxswain off, but the Chief wanted to punish him. Now he worked himself into anger again and started pounding the coxswain's ribs with short, hard punches, holding him against the bulkhead with his left hand. The coxswain tried to cover up, but the Chief got his punches through, and the coxswain began to grunt every time he was hit.

"That's enough, Chief," the Lieutenant Commander said mildly. The Chief kept throwing punches. He probably hadn't heard.

"That's enough, Chief!" the Lieutenant Commander said more crisply. The body punches continued. A black sailor stepped forward, thought better of it, then took another step. *"Belay that!"* The Lieutenant Commander's voice cracked like a rifle shot. I jumped. I'd never heard him bark like that before. *"Mackintosh!"*

The Chief's head snapped around, and he quickly stepped back, letting the coxswain slide to the deck. The Chief went to attention. I hadn't seen that position assumed by anyone since I'd been on the barge.

The Lieutenant Commander looked sternly at the Chief,

then casually filled his pipe, lit it, and, leaving the Chief at attention, puffed on it awhile. Finally he blew a little stream of smoke and said softly, "Do you want to tell me what this is all about, Chief?"

"This man is a coward, sir—"

"I already heard that much, Chief," the Lieutenant Commander interrupted. "They probably heard you all the way to Cam Ranh Bay. Tell me the details, please."

"We left him in the boat to keep it close in case we had to get away fast. A VC patrol came along and sniped at him a little bit, and he hid in the bottom of the guntub. We were coming back with two prisoners when we heard the shooting. We drove the slopes off and boarded the boat and found him hiding. I was just . . . correcting his attitude, sir," the Chief explained.

"Two prisoners? Where's the other one?" the Lieutenant Commander asked Poppa.

Poppa took full responsibility, something I've always admired him for. He could've blamed the other prisoner's death on Brewster.

"We weren't sure how many Viet Cong there were in the boat, and whether we could guard two prisoners during the firefight. So we eliminated one of them," he said.

"How many VC were there?" asked the Lieutenant Commander.

"Three," said the Chief. "In the patrol we hit, there were three."

"Four," I said quickly. "Brewster got one down by the boat."

The Lieutenant Commander, puffing on his pipe, looked at the coxswain for a while. He nodded at the black sailor who had started forward to help, and the man helped the coxswain to his feet. The coxswain was still crying. His face was puffy and streaked with tears, and he smelled awfully bad. Fear-sweat stinks worse than work-sweat, I think, and he had been sweating and puking, and he'd urinated down his legs from all the kidney punches, not to mention messing his pants when the shooting started. He was a sorry sight, all right. It was enough to make you ashamed for him.

"Now tell me your side of it," the Lieutenant Commander said.

The coxswain was slobbering and bawling until you could hardly understand him. "Man, them dudes got to shootin' at me! There was bullets on this side goin' like this"—and he snapped his fingers beside his left ear about five times—"an' so I dodged that way"—he ducked his head to the right—"an' then there was bullets on that side"—this time he snapped his fingers beside his right ear and ducked to the left—"an' so I ducked this way. But pretty soon there was bullets on *this* side goin' like that, an' bullets on *that* side goin' like that"—this time he snapped his fingers on both sides of his head—"an' I didn't know what to do excep' get the hell down and stay there! I was afraid to dodge—I'd've dodged right into a bullet!"

I nearly doubled over with laughter, and so did everybody else, except the Chief . . . even the black sailors. The Chief was cursing and wanted to kick him around some more, but we held him back. The Lieutenant Commander, between chuckles, told the coxswain to go bathe and wash his gear and to report to him in the morning.

All this business with the coxswain had taken my mind off the girl. After I'd cleaned up, I went in to lie down, and there was Brewster, snoring away, all covered with mud and blood and shit, and I thought about those little pieces of meat that stuck to my uniform and my face, and I felt sick. After a few minutes of dry heaves, I went and got some beer. There were no more patrols out, and the barge was quiet. Everybody was in the sack except for me and the sentries, so I sat there in the still, hot night and drank beer and thought about the girl.

I was damned glad Hercules had been there. If he had not been, I would have run up there to help that girl, and little pieces of me would be sticking to Brewster's uniform, mixed in with pieces of the girl. And Brewster would be lying there snoring, not giving a shit. Lieutenant Commander Gray would be writing a letter to my mom, and someone would be packing up my gear to send back. Poppa had told me that even the kids hated us and would kill us if they got the chance. Well, I'd just found out he was right, and I damned near found it out the hard way.

Having to shoot her like that hit me hard. I could justify killing soldiers, but it was hard to justify killing children and girls. The society that I grew up in put women and children in a special category. They were to be cared for, protected, and looked out for. They were definitely noncombatants. There was just not supposed to be any reason to kill women and children in a war, and women and children weren't supposed to try to kill you in a war, either. I knew my family would never understand why I had to shoot that girl. They still thought of war in a romantic sort of way, at least those that had never been in one did. War was, to them, still a field of honor.

I knew better now.

I told myself, I don't care if they're six years old or a hundred and six years old, if we go in to hit a camp and they're in there, I'm going to blow them away. If it's a free-fire zone and I meet 'em on a trail, I'm going to shoot their asses. I don't care if they're kids or grandparents. If they're friendlies, they aren't supposed to be there, and it's their tough luck. I'm going to survive. I'm not going to stick my neck out to help any damned kids or old women that might stick a knife in my guts or a live grenade in my drawers. They booby trap their own kids and their own women and their own houses. . . . I'm not going to take any chances.

All during training they kept hammering at us to be

hard. "Hard hearts win battles." Mine had just been hardened.

I was still sitting there, drinking beer, when the cooks got up and started breakfast.

CHAPTER 6

When I woke up just after dawn, blue gray shadows of morning mist still hung over the river, but in the east the sky was tinted with the gold of early morning sunshine. Another beautiful morning in Vietnam.

I swung my legs over the edge of my cot and sat there for a minute in my undershorts. It was already hot. I felt in my shirt pocket for a pack of cigarettes, took it out, and lit one. My hands were trembling.

A nightmare had awakened me, the same one I'd been having for the past several weeks. Almost every night I dreamed about that Vietnamese girl, about killing her. Sometimes she got mixed up with the flamethrowers or the man that tried to run away across the paddy. But this night had been worse. This night I'd dreamed that I was back in Arkansas, going to visit some relatives, and as we stepped up on their front porch, a cousin came out to greet us. It was that same girl, and I shot her. In that last second of the dream, as she fell and blew up, my family all turned to face me with accusation on their faces. I knew they would never understand why I had to do it.

My God, I thought, if the nightmares are this bad now, what's it going to be like by the time my tour is up? How bad will it be when I get back home?

My rifle was leaning against the sandbag wall within easy reach of the cot. I looked it over: It hadn't been moved, or so it seemed.

Even though there were sentries watching the barge, there was no guarantee Charley couldn't slip someone aboard and booby trap your weapons. There were no wires attached to the rifle. The butt rested on the spot where I always placed it—a file mark on one of the ribs of the steel grid deck. It was off safety. I picked it up. There was a round in the chamber. I knew it hadn't been tampered with.

I left a round in the chamber in case I needed it in a hurry during the night. If Charley could slip a man aboard, say around 0300, when almost everyone was asleep, he might knife the sentries, slip a whole force aboard, and be on you in a second. Maybe I was a little bit eccentric about it, but I intended to go home alive.

I removed the clip and worked the action, ejecting the unused cartridge. The bolt was clean and worked smoothly. The spring in the clip was free, and the cartridge-retaining lips weren't bent. I replaced the live round and snapped the clip back in the weapon.

I took the rifle with me when I stepped out onto the afterdeck. I stood there for a moment while I smoked my cigarette and watched the sun break through the morning mist.

There was many a day I thanked the Lord I'd been raised in Arkansas, because it's hot and humid there in the summer. I worked hard in the summers, haying and slopping hogs, and all the other things you have to do around a farm, and I got used to working in heat and humidity. Vietnam was worse, and I did have to get acclimated. But it was a lot easier for me than for Ivy League and a lot of other people. Ivy League came near to sunstroke a couple of times, but finally he learned to control his sweating with salt tablets. At first he'd drink beer and water and pop until he was all swelled up, and then he'd get sick and throw up. But he finally adjusted. Only Brewster seemed to have no problem. He said Vietnam wasn't any worse than working in a coal mine.

We hadn't gone on any raids in a while. We did patrol around, checking on the villages and looking for Viet Cong camps. We found a few booby traps and destroyed them. Sometimes we'd set a few claymores around them so that when Charley came to check on them, he'd trip a wire and blow himself away.

Once, Poppa stopped me just before I stepped down on a booby trap. It was a thirty-caliber cartridge held tight in a piece of bamboo, with a nail in the bottom for a firing pin. The whole thing was buried except for the point of the bullet. When you stepped on it, the cartridge would be driven down onto the nail, and it would fire upwards into your foot. If you stepped on it with your heel, it would probably shatter the bones of your ankle and leg and cripple you for life. If you hit it with your toe, it would go through your boot and into whatever was above that: your knee, your thigh, your chest.

As I thought, by God, ol' Poppa has got his shit together, and I'm going to stick close and love him like a father, Poppa said, "Well, asshole, when are you going to start paying attention? I don't want to have to lug your fat carcass all the way back to the boat. Keep your goddamned eyes open!" My daddy used to talk to me the same way.

Mostly, we were just showing Charley that we were there, and that we controlled the ground. We were harassing him, interfering with his supplies, making him go hungry or sleepless once in a while. Sometimes we patrolled the riverbank near the barge to keep the Viet Cong from coming in with mortars and shelling us. We also ran river patrols.

It was all part of my everyday life. I got up every morning and went to war, just like I used to get up every morning and go to work. Like the farm, it was always there—you had to work nights a lot, and around the clock sometimes, and you could never let down. Sometimes on the farm you put in twelve or sixteen hours haying, and then you had to get up after two or three hours' sleep to help a sow give birth or shoot a polecat in the chicken shed, or maybe there was lightning off in the southwest and you'd have to get up and finish bringing in the hay before it rained. Sometimes in Vietnam we'd spend most of the night watching a village and have to roll out after an hour or two of sleep to go check sampans on the river or go patrol the riverbank, because a sentry saw something, or respond to a call for assistance by a PBR on patrol. It was the same sort of twenty-four-hour demand.

I finished my cigarette. Then, rifle in hand, I went to the head.

The afterdeck was already hot from the morning sun, and I was barefooted, so I ditty-bopped right on back there. Luckily, there wasn't anybody on the head. It was just a little metal box, hanging out over the river from the "stern" of the barge.

Next I went over and got a cup of coffee and wandered over to the boat I was going out in that day. The Nigger was already aboard checking the oil in the engines. "Nigger" was what the Chief called the colored coxswain, and the name just sort of came into general use. It made him madder'n hell when we called him that, and when he got mad, he was the best goddamned coxswain in the Mekong Delta, if not in the whole damned Navy. He could make that PBR sit up and beg biscuits off the table. It was like the boat was part of him. But that was only when he was pissed off and forgot to be scared.

Since I just had on my shorts anyway, I set my rifle and the cup of coffee down on the deck and slipped into the water. Catching a quick breath, I ducked under and swam down along the underside of the boat, checking for mines or any other monkey business. I cleaned out a few blades of grass that were caught in the strainer, and then I climbed on the barge deck again and went over and picked up my rifle and coffee.

I went on board the boat and checked out the fifty-caliber machine gun mounted up front. Actually, it was a twin fifty—it had two barrels—set in a steel guntub that you sat in for more cover. Between the barrels it had a gunshield of sorts, just a little rectangular metal plate. Mounted on the starboard side and aligned with the barrels was a spotlight. When it was on, you aimed it at what you wanted to shoot at, and the gun fired right at the spot.

The fifty was working fine, so I went aft and checked out the twenty millimeter. I guess you'd have to call it a machine cannon: It shot pretty fast, like the fifty, but it shot explosive shells. The fifty would shoot about as fast as a jackhammer hits, and, like running a jackhammer, it'd shake the shit out of you. The "twenty Mike Mike" shook pretty hard, too, but it only shot about half as fast. The twenty was mounted on a pivot, so you could fire it in all directions. It had a gunshield on it, too.

Next I went up behind the coxswain den and checked out the forty-millimeter grenade launcher. It was belt-fed and fired special grenades about 1,800 meters. It was mounted on a pivot mount right behind the coxswain's den, so it could fire only off to the sides. You had to stand up to shoot it, so it had a gunshield, too. It shot a big shell that had eight or ten times the explosive power of those the twenty put out.

It was time for breakfast. I took my rifle and went over to get something to eat. The Chief and Ivy League and Brewster and the others were already over there. Brewster was first in line, of course.

"Powdered eggs *agin*?" he said to the cook. It was kind of a ritual complaint. He was the most likely of all of us to go back for seconds.

"If you don't like 'em, you don't have to eat 'em," the cook said. His hands still had grease in the little wrinkles of his knuckles, from working all night on one of the engines of a PBR. There was a little smear of black on his face, too. Nobody on the barge had just one duty, except the sentries. Everybody else did two or three jobs. "If you guys would run into Saigon and pick up some supplies, we could have fresh eggs for a change."

"How 'bout biscuits 'n gravy fer a change?" Brewster wanted to know.

"Or fried ham an' red-eye gravy?" I added. "I know you've got hams in the cooler."

"Why don'tcha just ask for steak? Or eggs Benedict? Or a Denver omelette? You're gonna have t'get you a full-time cook if you want that shit, or get in here and cook it yourselves." He slapped a big blob of eggs onto his own plate.

"That sounds like a good idea to me," I told Brewster. "Why don't we cook breakfast tomorrow?"

"Anything Brewster cooked, he'd have to eat himself," one big-eared sailor wisecracked. "Nobody else could stand it!"

Ivy League sat down in the last seat at our table. He tried not to look across the table at Brewster, who was stirring ketchup into his powdered eggs. "What's this about Brewster eating himself?" he asked. "I've seen him chewing his toenails, but I didn't know he was limber enough to eat himself! What's the matter, Brewster, won't anybody let you give 'em a blow job?"

The big-eared sailor laughed.

Brewster spread strawberry jam half an inch deep on a piece of toast and tore a bite out of it with his canines, leaving a smear of red jam around his mouth like gore.

"Shut your goddamn smart mouth, turd head, or I'll let you do a blow job on my shotgun," he growled.

"Better your shotgun than your prick," Ivy League shot back. "Aren't you afraid you'll get gonorrhea of the mouth from eatin' yourself?"

Again, a laugh from the other table.

Bob tried to grab Ivy League by the collar with his left hand. Ivy League deflected the grab. They both stood and glared at each other.

"Listen, dipshit! One more wise-ass crack outta you an' they're gonna send you home in a baggie!" Bob growled.

I put a hand on his shoulder. "Take it easy, Bob!" I pleaded. "I don't *like* blood on my eggs!"

Ivy League said, "Take your best shot, Brewster. Any time."

The big-eared sailor hoo-hawed.

Brewster pushed Ivy League back into his chair and turned on the sailor.

"What're you braying about, jackass? How'd you like them goddamned big ears cut off?"

"Stow that shit, Bob," growled the Lieutenant Commander, who was passing by with a tray. To the big-eared sailor, he said, "When the SEALs are having a . . . uh, disagreement, you'd be well advised to keep your damned mouth shut. Certain parts of your anatomy might end up as somebody's trophies—and I don't mean just your ears."

The sailor got very busy eating his breakfast.

"Who's going out with me today?" the Chief asked, by way of changing the subject. He knew damn good and well who was going.

"Me an' the Nigger," I told him. "An' Ivy."

"Oh, God damn," he growled. "Not that fuckin' Nigger!" He said it loud enough that a deaf man on the riverbank, four hundred meters away, could've heard him.

Nigger was checking out the twenty millimeter. (That didn't bother me at all.... The more they were checked over, the less likely something would be overlooked.) He glanced over at the Chief, then nonchalantly swung the twenty around and fired a burst toward the shore, drowning out whatever else the Chief had to say. But the Chief was determined to have the last word.

"Listen to 'im over there, wastin' goddamned amminition! Don't he know that shit's expensive?" He turned and shouted over his shoulder, "Goddamned taxpayers payin' through the nose for that!"

We loaded up and pushed off shortly after that. The sun was shining brightly when we ran down the river. The mist had burned off the main channel, and the only clouds in the sky were off on the horizon toward the China Sea. The first few days we'd been in-country, it happened to rain about noon and clear up in the afternoon, just in time for us to go out on our raids. It didn't make any difference that it wasn't raining those nights, because the bush was still dripping wet, and you got soaked anyway. After that, it started clearing up during the day, and the sun would beat down and the humidity would rise up like steam out of the saturated ground, making the heat stifling. On those days, it was better to have a river patrol, with the air hitting you to cool you off a little, than to sit around and bake on the damned barge. Patrols along the shore were worse yet.

In the afternoons, it would cloud up again, and the rain would pour down until evening, or maybe all night long. Sometimes it would rain all day long, too. At least the monsoon season was nearly over, and the rains were slowly tapering off.

The river was at its highest stage. Water flooded large

parts of the low ground near the banks and made the river seem wider than it really was. In places, tidal waters ran right up to villages a half-mile from the main channel. Some villages were built on stilts, because the water actually went beyond them at high stage.

When I say the river, I mean the main channel of the Mekong. There are several rivers in that Delta, some of them branches of the Mekong and some of them having no current, and maybe no water, during the dry season. The different channels all separate and come back together, with bayous and canals connecting them, twisting and worming their way through that jungle like a sackful of snakes.

We cruised along at about half-throttle, near the starboard bank. Ivy League, the Chief, and I all watched that bank. Nigger watched ahead. I was in the bow, on the fifty, and Ivy League manned the twenty back on the fantail. The Chief, being the boat captain, was in the coxswain den.

This was just a routine patrol: We were assigned to patrol a certain sector that had been relatively quiet for the past two weeks. There was another boat in this sector, in case we needed some assistance, some "backup," but we weren't traveling together. The Lieutenant Commander, Brewster, and two sailors manned that boat.

We had no schedule, and we tried to vary our patrol pattern as much as possible. When we left depended on who was on the crew and how soon they were ready. Sometimes, if Intelligence thought Charley might be moving by water early in the morning in a certain sector, we'd try to be there just about dawn, or a little before. Sometimes we'd patrol at night. There might be a certain area they'd send us to, or we might patrol the same stretch of river at the same time of day for two or three or four days and then switch up and patrol it a couple of hours earlier, trying to catch Charley moving between patrols. Or we'd "drag" a patrol boat along an hour or so behind another one, to catch Charley coming out when he thought the coast was clear.

We watched the banks for any sign that Charley was building up his forces or moving regularly through an area. We watched for snipers. If you patrol a certain area long enough, you get used to the look of it, and you can tell from looking if Charley's been there or if he's there now. Sometimes the bush will be so thick that he has to cut down a tree or cut a path, and you'll see a little patch of clearing you didn't see before. The undergrowth will look different. Then you have to go in and check it out.

Sometimes there would be signs that Charley was using a certain place as a river crossing, or some informer would tip off the Intelligence people that Charley was moving in a certain area, and we'd go in and set an ambush. If he was using boats at all, we'd pull a PBR up close to the bank somewhere up or downriver, camouflage it, and pursue the boats when we sprang the ambush.

We turned up a smaller channel. There was still some mist. The jungle towered up on either side, and some of the larger trees almost met above us. The banks were relatively clear of underbrush, because the canopy of leaves blocked off direct sunlight. We ran through a clearing, actually a wide, shallow lake overgrown with reeds and tall grasses, for about half a mile, then passed back into the jungle. It was like walking into a dark bar in the middle of a bright summer day, with your sunglasses on.

The channel made an S-shaped bend just before it joined up with another, larger channel, and the mist lay in a dense bank there.

I saw a python in some tree limbs.

We broke out of the mist, and there was a sampan. It was a narrow little wooden boat about forty feet long that could hardly have had a foot of freeboard above the water. In the middle, some woven straw mats thrown over bamboo poles made a sort of enclosure. There was an oarsman standing at a sweep oar in the stern, and three or four men sitting 'midships. They could have been fishermen for all we knew.

Except that the oarsman suddenly swung them in toward shore and started humping like hell to get them into a little narrow creek. If they'd made it, they'd have been out of sight in seconds, for the little creek ran right through some dense underbrush.

We turned to head them off, and Nigger hit the throttle. Still, it looked as if they would make the mouth of the little creek before we could stop them. I wouldn't have shot at them, for sure. But when they started firing at us, I raked them with the fifty. The oarsman, I think, dived into the water. Ivy League was manning the twenty, but he couldn't bring it to bear, because we were heading right for the sampan.

"There's another one!" the Chief yelled. Another sampan was making for the shore, about four or five hundred meters beyond the first.

I was already concentrating on the second boat as we shot past the first, but the Chief and Ivy League got their chance to fire as we went by. The twenty and the forty took that little boat apart. Pieces went everywhere, and there were pieces of boxes and crates, too. Something exploded with a blast that sent water a hundred feet into the air. There was no doubt now that it had been carrying supplies for the Viet Cong.

The next one didn't show any fight. The oarsman stopped working his oar, and they lay to until we came up on them.

I heard the Chief radioing our backup boat.

"Delta Six . . . Delta Five. Delta Six . . . Delta Five. Do you read me? Over."

"Five, this is Six. Go ahead." The Lieutenant Com-

mander's voice. As an afterthought, he added, "Over."
He always did that.

"Six, we're closing on a Victor Charley sampan. Can
you back us up? Over."

"A-roger, Five. Say your position." Pause. "Over."

The Chief looked at his map. I looked at the sampan.
Nobody in it was moving.

"Six... Five. Position: Mapsheet G three, Sector Mike-
one-niner, grid coordinates thirty-two-fifteen. Over."

"Negative, Five. You are not in the China Sea. Say
again.... Over."

The Chief cursed. Without looking back I could imagine him frantically unfolding the map to double check the
coordinates. This time he read them right.

"Roger, Five. Our ETA fifteen minutes." By taking the
shortcut, we'd put them into a position where they would
have to swing 'way upriver to come to our support. "Has
the Victor Charley shown any hostile action... Over."

"Six... Five. Not yet. We just encountered one hostile
and destroyed same. The other is making like a Friendly.
Over."

"Five... Six. Hold your position till we get there.
... Over."

It was too late.

We heaved-to alongside the sampan. I covered it
with the fifty, and Ivy League covered it with the twenty.
The Chief had his M-14 pointed at them. There was apparently just the oarsman and an old papasan and a mamasan who sat quietly in the bow. None of them moved
or spoke. I think they saw what happened to the other
boat, and they were too scared to even blink. In the bottom of the boat was a woven straw mat. It might cover
rice, it might cover weapons, it might even cover Viet
Cong. We watched the mat and the people with equal
suspicion.

"You Viet Cong?" the Chief asked.

Nobody answered.

"Papasan! You Viet Cong?" the Chief snapped.

It was the old mamasan that reacted. She understood the words "Viet Cong" and let out a wail: "No veecee! No veecee!" She half stood up, her arms extended toward the Chief in supplication.

"Papasan Viet Cong!" The Chief was insistent now. He pointed his M-14 at the papasan, raising it to his shoulder as if to take aim and fire.

The old woman screamed again. "No veecee! No Viet Cong!" she insisted.

The Chief swung the barrel of his M-14 around to cover the oarsman, who stood absolutely still. I don't think he even took a breath.

"Viet Cong?" he said.

"No Viet Cong! No Viet Cong!" the old woman insisted.

The Chief looked them all over very slowly, as if he was thinking all this over. Then he quickly swung his rifle toward the old woman and fired a burst of about three rounds into the river between us and the sampan. The old woman screamed and crouched down in the boat. The papasan half stood up and then sat down abruptly as the Chief swung the muzzle of the M-14 back toward him. The oarsman barely twitched a muscle and remained frozen at the oar.

"Mamasan Viet Cong!" said the Chief, as if he had it all figured out now and was very proud of himself.

"No veecee! No Viet Cong!" the old woman wailed, shaking her head. She hugged her bony knees, rocked back and forth, and really sobbed now.

The Chief was insistent. He took careful aim at the papasan, who grasped the gunwales of the sampan with both hands and started chanting a Buddhist prayer. He thought he was going to die right then, I'm sure.

"No veecee! No Viet Cong! No Viet Minh!"

"Mamasan Viet Cong!" the Chief persisted. "Mamasan boom-boom Ho Chi Minh!" Mamasan slept with Ho Chi Minh.

"No veecee! No Viet Cong, no Viet Minh. *Dien cai dau! Khong biet Ho Chi Minh!* Numba ten, Ho Chi Minh!" the old woman insisted.

You are a crazy man, she was saying. I don't know Ho Chi Minh. Ho Chi Minh is bad. Ho was dead, of course. He'd died the year before.

Now the Chief took a different tack. He lowered his rifle and used it to signal to the old woman to stand up.

"*Lai dai, didi. Do chieu day!*" he told her. Come here, quickly, and lift the mat carefully! With his rifle barrel, he signed for her to throw back the mat in the bottom of the boat.

She hesitated, looking at papasan.

"*Kiem chieu mau len!*" snapped the Chief.

Papasan started to stand up. The Chief sat him down again with another short burst into the river. Mamasan shrunk away, throwing up her arms as if she could ward off bullets with them. When she realized she was still alive, she turned back toward the mat and hesitantly flipped it back.

The Chief whistled.

"Well, God damn . . . would you look at that," said Nigger.

Under the mat were a dozen or more bales of marijuana, twenty or thirty pounds to the bale, all bound for Saigon, no doubt, to sell to the pushers, who would retail it to the servicemen there.

The Chief had exhausted his Vietnamese vocabulary. Now he resorted to yelling "*Didi song*" and gesturing with his rifle. The Vietnamese got the idea finally and slipped over the side into the river. They clung to the side while the Chief went aboard. He kicked around at the bales of marijuana while keeping his rifle pointed in their general direction. There seemed to be nothing hidden under the bales. Satisfied, the Chief stooped and picked up a bale with his left hand and tossed it back into the PBR. Then he jumped quickly aboard.

The Nigger had picked up the bale and was smelling a leaf he'd pulled from it. The Chief pushed him back toward the coxswain den.

"Get back to the goddamn controls," he said. "Let's go back up the river and check out that other boat—if we can find any of it now."

The Vietnamese were crawling back up into the sampan as Nigger revved up the engines and we started moving away.

I hollered back to the Chief: "You want me to shoot, Chief? Are they Viet Cong?"

The Chief laughed and waved the bale of marijuana. "Shit, no. Don't shoot, Tyler. Of course they're not Viet Cong. They'd know Ho Chi Minh is dead if they were! They don't like us, for sure, but they paid their toll. Let 'em go on to town.... We don't want to cut off our own supply of grass, do we?" As we looped around the sampan and headed back upriver, the Chief laughed uproariously and yelled at the Vietnamese, "Mamasan veecee! Mamasan boom-boom Ho Chi Minh!"

We went back up the river, to sift through the debris from the first sampan, to look for bodies, and to pick up anything we could find that might be of some value to Intelligence. That's where we were when the other PBR came up and the Lieutenant Commander hailed us.

"Christ, did you blow them both up?"

"Naw. We let the other one go. It was just an old couple with some marijuana," admitted the Chief.

The Lieutenant Commander made us divvy it up.

We completed our patrol and ran back up the main channel to the barge. We killed the afternoon there writing our report and drinking beer and playing fantan with Hercules. He cleaned us all out of ready cash, so Ivy League offered to put up his G.I. life insurance. Hercules didn't understand G.I. life insurance. The ARVNs didn't have such a thing, I guess.

"Just as well," growled Brewster. "If'n he won, he's jus' as likely as not t'slip in an' cutcher throat t'git it." He said throat "thote."

The cook made fried chicken.

"Well, lick mah fangers," said Ivy League, and then he and Bob were into it again.

"God damn," the Chief said to me, "those two are goin' t'give me ulcers. They fuss like my damn kids."

About dark, we chose up sides and went out again. To my surprise, the Chief chose Nigger to be coxswain again. But he did take him aside and tell him, "Okay, asshole, if we stop another sampan: *This time stay at the wheel.* We'll take care of the sampan. We may have to get out of there in a hell of a hurry."

The sun wasn't long down when we pulled away from the barge, but it had clouded up and was drizzling rain, so it was pretty dark already. We ran downriver, without lights. The Lieutenant Commander wanted us to go down toward Sector Q14. That was between the barge and Saigon, on a rather narrow connecting channel where the boats going from our part of the Delta to Saigon and back passed through. Lately, Charley had been setting up in there and sniping at the boats as they went by. It wasn't much, just a little harassment, but we didn't want it to get any worse. We were going to sweep through the area that night. We might draw some fire and knock out one or two of the VC, or at least pick up some more information about Charley's whereabouts. If he was moving in by water, we might surprise him on the move and damage his forces.

I jumped on board and grabbed the fifty before anybody else could get it. Brewster was right behind me. He got the twenty. Ivy League brought an M-60 machine gun on board and sat aft of the coxswain den. The Chief would use his M-14, or the forty, or whatever was appropriate. There were a couple of M-79 grenade launchers back there in the coxswain den. "Blookers" or "thump guns," some people called them. We were a pretty heavily armed outfit.

I hunkered down in the guntub as we ran down the river, and let my eyes adjust to the darkness. The drizzle continued, steady, even, not heavy—Charley's weather. In the jungle, the gentle rustle caused by the raindrops and the tap-tap-tap of water dripping from the treetops onto the leaves of the undergrowth camouflaged any sounds of movement. On the river, the rain reduced visibility.

Shit, I'm tired, I thought. Nights without sleeping because of those damn nightmares were getting me down. We got precious little time to sleep anyway, and I couldn't afford to be missing any of it. I had to do something about it. I wished I was like Brewster. That son of a bitch never missed a minute's sleep. His conscience didn't bother him at all, no matter what.

Then I thought, I wonder if that marijuana is as good to relax you as everybody claims it is. Might be worth a try.

I'd never smoked any of it, you see.

When the Chief divvied up the stuff, he had given me my share, which I then gave to Brewster. Where I came from—at that time, anyway—you didn't smoke pot, at least not openly. Hell, even the moonshiners and bootleggers wouldn't sink that low. It was a long-hair habit, and rednecks weren't having any of it back then.

But maybe it was worth trying. It seemed to help some of these guys relax. Beer and liquor seemed to make things worse. Of course, I'd have to wait until we got back to the barge to try it. We didn't use the stuff on patrol.

I got to wanting a cigarette, but the pack in my shirt pocket was empty. I knew there'd been a couple in it right after we ate. They must've fallen out. I felt around in the guntub, but they weren't there. That just made me want one worse.

I endured for a while. Then I glanced back and saw the Chief lighting up, and I couldn't stand it anymore. I climbed out of the guntub and went aft—something I normally wouldn't do—but we were still in well-patrolled waters, and the crew was large enough that one of them could sub for me and watch forward.

"God damn, I need a cigarette," I told the Chief. "An' I'm fresh out."

He handed me one. It felt different between my fingers, and I realized it was a roll-your-own variety. From the smell of the smoke, I knew he'd lit up one of his funny cigarettes.

"Naw," I said. "I don't smoke this shit. Not on patrol, anyway. Give me one of your rag'ler ones."

"This is all I've got," he lied.

"I'll get one from Brewster," I said, giving the roach back to him.

Brewster said, "What's the matter with Chief's cigarettes? I saw him give ye one, an' ye give it rat back."

"It was marijuana," I said. "That's all he's got."

Brewster dug in his pocket and came up with a bent Camel. There were all sorts of unidentifiable stains on it.

"Ye better have one uh these," Brewster insisted. He stuck a roach out at me, and when I pushed it back at him, muttering something about "not on patrol," he laughed, and said, "Shit, what better time? Ye may not get another! Better take one. . . . They smooth out the bumps."

I went on back up to the guntub and smoked the stained and bent Camel. It tasted like it was made out of camel dung. All of them back there lit up joints.

Every once in a while, one of them would holler at me: "Hey, Tyler! How about a *good* cigarette?" Then they'd laugh. "Aw, come on, Tyler! It ain't gonna hurt ye!"

They kept it up while we cruised on down into Indian territory, and I started getting uptight having a bunch of potheads to depend on. Finally I gave in. I don't know if I just got so uptight I wasn't thinking clearly anymore, but I thought: Maybe it'll relax me, an' I can get some decent sleep tonight—without nightmares.

"All right, all right," I said. "Gimme one of your goddamned funny cigarettes. I'll smoke it! Anything to shut you damned people up!"

Ivy League brought me up one of his, and I lit the thing and puffed on it awhile. It tasted a little different, but it didn't seem to have any more effect than an ordinary cigarette. So I puffed a while longer. I still didn't feel any different. I decided that old weed didn't do anything for me, and I told them so.

"Just keep a-smokin'," they yelled.

So while we cruised on down the river, I hunched down in the guntub and smoked, with the cigarette cupped in my hands so the glow wouldn't be visible from shore.

After a while, I yelled back at them again.

"Hey, what do you guys see in this shit, anyway? It's just like smokin' a rag'ler cigarette, only it don't taste as good. It don't have no effect on me at all. Am I a-doin' it right?"

They just laughed at their little private joke and said, "Hell, there ain't no trick to it! You smoke it, that's all."

Sector Q14 was an area of exceptionally thick bush and high jungle. The trees were so thick that helicopters couldn't land, and Huey gunships—or even a big, fixed-wing Puff with a cannon—couldn't do much good. The channel was a good hundred meters wide at the narrowest point, but the trees were at least forty or fifty meters high, and they made it awfully dark and spooky. The banks were covered with a tangle of bamboo and rattan, and the vines, lianas, were so thick it looked like fishnets had been thrown up in the trees. I could feel thousands of tiny eyes watching us, and I would have bet a month's pay they didn't all belong to four-legged furry things.

They didn't.

We were cruising along in midchannel, at about half-throttle. That was a mistake in itself and just showed how marijuana had robbed Nigger of his good sense. The channel was wide enough that we should have been pushing right on through at no less than three-quarters throttle. At slower speeds, we were just asking for it.

Of course, they started shooting at us.

I was scrunched down in the guntub with my knees sticking up about level with my ears—I'm pretty long-legged, you see—and I was pretty relaxed, and feeling like the king of the mountain, when the shooting started. I could hear those damned bullets coming. They didn't "pop!" like they usually do—instead, they buzzed past like some damned big old June bugs. Not only could I hear them coming, but I could hear them going past and going away.

I hopped up and grabbed that fifty and cocked it back.... It seemed like my arms were moving through molasses, they moved so slow. I was excited. And scared. It was like being in a slow-motion movie.

I thought I could see rifle flashes in a treetop off to the starboard, so I swung the fifty around and squeezed off a short burst. The button stuck, or something. That short burst just went on and on... but the gun was going BOOM...BOOM...BOOM only two or three times a second, like the forty, instead of ripping out the rounds, like it should have been. Something was screwed up, but I'd never had anything like that go wrong before. Then I realized there was something else wrong: Every fifth round that came out of that machine gun was a tracer so that we could see where you were shooting, and when I hit that button, those tracers would come out of there and go about fifty feet, and *then they'd just about stop*! You could count the tracer bullets just slowly creeping over toward the trees. I wondered how they could stay in the air, they were going so slow. Of course, going that slow, they wouldn't do any damage to Charley if they did happen to hit him. They'd just bounce off. I might as well have been chunking rocks.

"There's something wrong with this fuckin' gun!" I yelled to the Chief. "Look at them damn tracers, what they're a-doin'! They're just stoppin' out there! God damn, how do they do that?"

But the Chief didn't hear. He was back there aft of the coxswain den, with an M-14 on his hip, squeezing off single shots and war-whooping at the top of his lungs. Christ, I thought, why doesn't he at least fire it automatic? Brewster was back on the fantail, hollering "Whooooyaaa!" at the sniper and shooting the twenty. There was something wrong with it, too: It only fired about one shot each second, and each round boomed out like a broadside from a battleship. It sounded like it was going to explode any second.

Ivy League was sitting back in the coxswain den, leaning up against the gunwale like he was watching TV in his living room, and grinning from ear to ear.

"Get up an' shoot, you crazy bastard!" I yelled at him. He had the M-60—if it was working right, it could make a hell of a difference. But he just sat there.

Those strange slow bullets were buzzing a little louder, and each one that went by was a little closer. I could almost reach out and grab one.

I tried another short burst into the trees, to make the sniper get his head down, and the fifty kept on with that slow-firing shit.

The PBR was only making about five knots. I hadn't

noticed us slowing down so. Nigger must have done it
gradually. If we didn't speed up and get the hell on out
of there, Charley was going to find the range. But we just
kept plowing along.

"Go-od damn! Let's go! Let's get outta here!" I yelled
at him. "These damned guns ain't workin' right! Let's
go!" I glanced back at him.

Nigger looked like he was frozen at the controls. I
couldn't really see his face, only his silhouette faintly
outlined by the brightness of the muzzle flashes from the
twenty—most of which was shielded from our eyes by
flash suppressors. I could see his hand moving slowly
toward the throttle, and I could see the whites of his eyes
against the black of his silhouette. They were as wide as
saucers. Nigger was scared. Somebody was shooting at
him again. I watched, half expecting to see him duck
down. Instead, his hand moved slowly to the throttle and
began to inch it forward.

I was impatient, I want you to know. I wanted to break
off this little engagement. We had made contact, and that
was enough. No one but Nigger and me seemed to be the
least bit worried, though. The Chief and Brewster just
kept on "whooyaa"-ing and war-whooping and shooting.

Then I saw another white flash on the coxswain's silhouette, this one too low to be his eyes. It was his teeth!
Nigger was grinning from ear to ear! Was I the only one
that was scared? Was I the only one that knew what was
going on? Were the others all high on that damned dope
and just not realizing that we were in bad trouble?

I began to wonder if Nigger had fucked up the damned
guns, just to get back at the Chief. Then I decided no, he
couldn't have. Nigger didn't know enough about the guns
to make them do what they were doing. He could jam
them, but how the hell could anyone make them slow
down like this?

He turned the wheel, and we began to lean 'way over

and turn—slowly, like a battleship instead of a river patrol boat.

It all added up for me, in a flash—the slow-firing guns, the slow acceleration and turning of the boat, the slow bullets buzzing by. . . . The problem wasn't with the guns or the ammunition or the boat; it was with time. Time was all screwy. I just tilted that fifty's barrel down toward the water and hunkered down in that guntub with my head in my hands—to keep it from rolling off, I guess. And I hollered to the Chief, "Get me the hell outta here!"

It seemed like it took an hour, but we turned around in midchannel and headed back the way we came. The engine was roaring louder, but our speed through the water seemed to be just as slow as ever. The June bug sounds of the bullets stopped, but I kept hearing shooting. I raised my head and looked around and saw the Chief still blazing away to starboard. The sniper would've been off our stern and to port, but the Chief didn't even know where in hell he was, much less where the sniper was. Brewster was back on the fantail yelling, "Did we get 'em? Did we get 'em?"

Ivy League, grinning, hadn't moved.

It didn't take more than forty minutes to get back to the barge, but it seemed like forty hours. That was the slowest time that ever passed for me in my whole life. I sat there in the guntub and tried to look for Viet Cong, but I think we could've run over a sampan and I wouldn't have seen it. I'd be flying high for a while, feeling great, thinking about Lord only knows what, and then I'd snap back for a while, to the cool air in my face and the spray and the roar of the engine and the dark of the night. . . . The Chief kept wandering around in a daze and damn near fell off the boat once, when Nigger swerved to miss something. "An alligator," he yelled. "Shoot the fuckin' alligator!" So Brewster obliged, blasting into the water astern with the twenty Mike Mike and kicking up big geysers of spray. Then he raked the shoreline just to make sure no others swam out toward us. I hadn't seen any goddamned alligators and when Nigger yelled and pointed ahead and told me to shoot the alligators over there, I just sat in the guntub and held my head on. It was so light I was afraid it would float off and blow away like a kid's balloon.

When we got to the barge, Nigger went straight at it until the last possible second, and then turned the PBR hard a-starboard and chopped the throttle, so we slid sideways into the barge like a runner sliding into home base. The M-60 machine gun crew that always covered incoming craft thought we were coming aboard boat and all, and they scattered. We belayed a line to the barge and climbed out, and I felt like letting everybody know we were back, so I yelled "Whooooyaaaa!" at the top of my lungs. Brewster and the Chief joined me, and we "whooyaa"'d all over the place. That got the attention of our little Lieutenant Commander, who came out to see what all the ruckus was about.

"Belay that, Tyler. You want to wake up Ho Chi Minh?"

I told him, "Man, I'm just glad to get back in one piece!"

He wanted to know what the shit had happened.

"God damn, it was weird," I told him. "We started gettin' some sniper fire, an' when I opened up with the fifty, the fuckin' thang wasn't workin' right! That gun has *got* to be fixed. There's somethin' wrong with it. They got them tracers in there ass-backwards or somethin'. They just go out, and they kind of explode and hang there!"

The Lieutenant Commander looked at me hard for a minute.

"Tyler, are you on something?" he asked. "Like pot? Or speed?"

"Hell, no, I don't use that shit!"

The Chief reminded me I'd smoked a marijuana cigarette.

"Well, that one don't make no difference," I said. "That
stuff don't affect me none."

The Lieutenant Commander just grinned.

"Better scrub this patrol," said he, "and get some rest.
We'll talk tomorrow."

So I went off to my cot, but the damned barge was
pitching in a heavy swell, and I had to make several tries
to get aft. The sailors kept making smart remarks about
the strange way the gun was fucked up. I tried to explain
to them, but they just kept asking questions and giggled
about my answers until I got plain pissed off and told
them to shove off. I couldn't see what was so damned
funny.

When I got up the next morning, my mouth tasting like
the Russian Army had marched through it barefooted, I
had only one thought: What was wrong with that fifty
caliber? So I broke my usual routine and went first thing
to find out.

Well, I field-stripped that damned machine gun and put
it back together, and I couldn't find a fucking thing wrong
with it. I even shot a couple of bursts through it to check
it out, and it worked just fine.

Maybe, I thought, it was the ammunition. Maybe the
ammunition was screwy.

The twenty millimeter had been firing slowly, too. So
I went back to check it out. Before I field-stripped it, I
jacked a round into the chamber and fired a burst. It
worked just fine.

There was a crew of sailors patching holes in the boat
and doing maintenance work on the engines. I looked at
them suspiciously and asked them if they'd fixed the guns.
They just grinned at one another and said no.

There wasn't any more I could do there, so I went and
got some breakfast. I sat with the Lieutenant Commander

and Poppa and the Chief. When I sat down, Poppa and the Lieutenant Commander looked at me funny, but the Chief didn't look at me at all. He got real busy eating his eggs, as if they tasted about halfway good. Poppa looked at me like I was a roach that just crawled up on the table— one of those Vietnamese cockroaches about as long as your hand, with a shiny black shell. The Lieutenant Commander's eyes were kind of twinkling. He spoke before I did.

"Did you find anything wrong with that fifty, Tyler?"

I narrowed my eyes down and looked at him real hard.

"Why—did you have somebody fix it last night?" I asked.

He grinned.

I took a long sip of coffee and tried to read his face. He looked like he was enjoying a good joke at my expense. Poppa was still looking at me like I was a cockroach. I expected him to wallop me with a gun butt at any minute. The Chief must've found pearls in those eggs, the way he was digging into them.

Very slowly, making every word clear, I said, "What was wrong with the goddamned fifty?"

Poppa spoke up. "There wasn't anything wrong with the fifty, Tyler."

And I said, "The hell there wasn't! I shot the goddamned thing—I know! Them tracers were in there wrong or something! That gun was fucked up."

"The gunner was fucked up," Poppa replied.

"What the hell d'you mean? I didn't do anything to that gun!"

"Tyler," the Lieutenant Commander asked, "did the Chief give you a marijuana cigarette?"

"No . . . yeah . . . hell, yeah—Ivy League give me one. It was from that sampan we stopped yesterday. . . . You took some of that stuff yourself. It don't make no difference anyway. That stuff don't have no effect on me!"

The Chief finished all his eggs and picked his plate up in both hands like he was going to go for seconds or something. Nobody but Brewster ever ate seconds of that crap. I guess he had second thoughts about getting seconds, because he didn't leave, but he sure looked like he wanted to be somewhere else.

"When you came back aboard last night, you were walking around like a damned goose: two steps forward and one backwards. We damn near had to lead you to your cot so you wouldn't go overboard," the Lieutenant Commander said.

There wasn't any reply I could make. I remembered the time I had working my way back to my cot across that pitching deck . . . and I knew damned good and well there hadn't been any heavy sea to cause it.

Then Poppa spoke up. "I've been tryin' to teach you somethin' since you've been here, Tyler. I thought you had some common sense. Now . . . I don't know. It's your life. If you want to fuck up, if you want to die . . . that's up to you. I don't give a damn. Just don't you ever put my ass in a bind while you're doin' it." Then he raised his voice so everyone on the barge would hear him. "NOW HEAR THIS, ALL YOU SWABBIES! IF YOU COME OUT ON PATROL WITH ME AND YOU'RE SMOKIN' GRASS OR YOU'RE DRUNK OR YOU'RE ON SOME OTHER KIND OF DOPE, AND YOU FUCK UP AND GET HURT . . . YOU'LL LAY THERE, BY GOD, UNTIL THE VIET CONG FIND YOU. I'M NOT BUSTIN' MY TAIL TO GET YOU BACK. *AND* . . ." He emphasized the "and" even more. "AND IF YOU FUCK UP AND BRING THE SHIT DOWN ON ME, I'LL KNEECAP YOUR ASS AND LEAVE YOU FOR 'EM!"

Fair enough, I thought.

We were all quiet for a while. I ate my eggs and thought about it. If we'd hit a big force of Viet Cong, instead of a solitary sniper, none of us might have survived. It'd

been extra-cautious in other ways, but last night I blew
it all. I was just damned lucky to be here this morning.

Poppa lit up a cigarette and leaned back in his chair.

"Tyler," he said, "I don't know why I bother....I
guess I thought you had more on the ball than Brewster
over there. You and Hartford." He meant Ivy League.
"It wasn't but about three or four months ago that I took
a platoon in to provide security for a Graves Detail....It
had been an Army outfit, a heavy weapons platoon in a
temporary firebase. They were dug in all right, with bunkers and wire and mines and the whole bit. Heavy machine
guns covering all approaches. But they got overrun. Wiped
out to the man...fifty or more of them. We didn't find
a single Viet Cong body, not even a blood trail. And it
wasn't hard to figure out why: They hadn't fired a shot—
not a blessed shot—to defend themselves. Every fuckin'
one of them was either asleep or stoned out of his mind.
There was dope all over the place: marijuana cigarettes,
pills, syringes. The little second lieutenant in command—
he hadn't been cut on or anything, no mutilation. They
just shot him full of heroin and left him to O.D. From the
needle scars on his arms, he was pretty far gone before
they ever got to him. But there hadn't been a damned
shot fired. They must've walked in like they owned the
place. Most of the soldiers were bayoneted or had their
heads bashed in with rifle butts. If any Viet Cong was
hurt, he scratched himself on the wire...or wrenched his
back carryin' off all the shit they made off with: mortars,
mortar rounds, fifty calibers, and belts of ammo....We'll
be getting it shot back at us for months."

"If all the guns were gone, how'd you know they hadn't
been fired?" a sailor wanted to know.

"There weren't any cartridge cases on the ground or
anywhere in the bunkers," Poppa told him. "Even if they'd
policed the place, they couldn't have done that good a
job."

That's when I realized you couldn't depend on anybody but yourself. Not and survive. You had to have a mind of your own.... You had to think for yourself.

I looked over to where Brewster sat—alone, of course. He was finishing up his second helping of eggs and looked like nothing out of the usual had happened at all. I can't even count on him, I thought. Not even Brewster, even after all the bar fights we've been in, all the times I pulled fleet sailors off his ass.

He saw me looking at him, and shot me a finger.

CHAPTER 7

It must have been December—getting close to Christmas—when Billy showed up. I didn't know him then, of course. I think it was a Sunday when Poppa and the Lieutenant Commander came back from a trip into Saigon with four new men, all SEALs. They'd gone in, partly for a day in Saigon, I think, and partly on business. Poppa knew some little three-striper in Intelligence that he went to talk to every once in a while. Anyway, it was one of those days when we took a break and didn't run any patrols and just sat around on the barge and relaxed a bit. Ivy League and I were playing reverse strip poker with Nigger and another sailor.... That's where you start in your undershorts and the loser has to put on his clothes. Nigger was losing—we even had him wearing his slicker—when the boat pulled in.

The Lieutenant Commander turned the new men over to an enlisted man to show them where to stow their gear,

113

and handed the mail to another and told him to start mail call. Then he and Poppa went back to his quarters with a couple of bottles of hard stuff. The sailor we were playing poker with had to go help unload supplies, and Nigger and Ivy League both got letters from home, so I started a little game of Solitaire.

Nigger got a letter in a little pink envelope all stinking with perfume, and he didn't even take off the slicker before he tore it open and read it. He sat there sweating and grinning like apeshit, and once in a while he'd say, "Whoooooee!" or "Hey, momma! All right!"

Ivy League got two letters. He laid them down on the table and looked at them awhile while he drank his beer, like he didn't know which one to open first. He'd pick up one envelope, look at it, and put it down, then pick up the other and do the same thing. Finally he slit one open with his diving knife. As he took the letter out, a newspaper clipping fell out also and blew across the table. I grabbed it before it blew away and handed it to him. He took it without really looking at it. I didn't read it, but I saw the headline: STUDENTS ARRESTED IN CAPITOL SIT-IN. His face remained expressionless as he read first the letter and then the clipping. After a moment, he carefully folded the letter and clipping and put them back in the envelope. Then he looked at the sandbagged bulkhead for a long time.

For a while there, I'd been kinda let down that I hadn't gotten a letter. Now I decided maybe I was better off.

I went and got another beer. It was the last cold one, so I put half a case of warm ones in the cooler to chill.

Brewster got a letter from a guy we went through SEAL training with who used to go with us on tours of the bars around San Diego. He looked at the return address and threw it over the side without opening it.

"I never liked that asshole anyway," he said.

"Where is he?" I asked. I thought the guy might be in Viet Nam.

"Hell, I didn't notice," Brewster said. "Some ship."

I went inside. One of the new guys was taking gear out of his seabag and laying it on my cot. I dumped it off on the floor and laid myself down.

"Hey, God damn, I'd've moved it," he said.

"'S okay," I told him. "I did."

"Well, shit!" he said, real sharp, like he was going to do something about it. But when I raised up on one elbow and looked at him real hard, he got busy with his gear and didn't say any more. I laid back and then rolled over and found myself looking into a pair of green eyes.

"Hi!" said Green Eyes brightly. Green Eyes was a sandy-haired All-American-Boy type, a good-looking kid. Even I had to admit that. He had the cheerful attitude of a Boy Scout who's just done his good deed for the day. His cot was pulled in between me and the bulkhead.

"I'm Billy," he said, offering his hand to shake, like a puppy offering his paw.

"I don't give a shit," I told him, ignoring the paw. "I don't allow nobody to bunk there. It blocks th' breeze off'n me, if there is one. Not t'mention my view."

"Well, I can appreciate that," he said. "But there wasn't any other place to put my cot. I'll trade with you, if you want."

It was getting a little bit crowded in there, with all the new men coming in. But the guy didn't have to be so goddamned accommodating. I wasn't used to it. I rolled over and looked at Brewster's bunk, with a wad of mud-caked clothes and a pair of mud-caked boots stuck underneath. The canvas of the cot was as black and shiny as leather from sweat, grease, and grime. Brewster wouldn't have been accommodating.

"Do you want to trade places? I'll trade," the kid insisted.

Why wouldn't he quit wagging his fucking tail and let me be depressed in peace?

"Shit no," I growled at him. There was no use fighting it. "Keep yer bunk there. If Charley comes over th' side, he'll cut yer throat first."

I heard him shake the steel screen that was there to keep out RPGs and mortar shells.

"How could he get through that without waking us?" he asked.

I ignored him. I didn't want any conversation right then. I wanted to sulk.

"Maybe they'd hacksaw through," said the rat-faced guy that was still taking stuff out of his seabag.

"Hell, no—a hacksaw would make too much noise," said a new voice. I opened my eyes to see someone sitting on Brewster's bunk. Brown skin, black straight hair, lots of white teeth...and almond-shaped eyes. Chinese, or something like it.

"God, I'm surrounded," I muttered.

The Chinese was looking speculatively at the screen.

"They'd just stick a rifle barrel through it and blaze away," he pointed out. "They wouldn't have to come inside."

"They are inside," I said.

"What?" one of them said.

"Charley...he's on the barge right now," I told them.

"Shit...what are you talkin' about?"

"How could they get on the barge, in broad daylight?"

"Charley's got his ways."

"Shit, I didn't see anything on this tub but blacks and honkies, man," said the Chinese. "Maybe a chicano or two. How could Charley be on the barge? There's no Vietnamese on it."

"Maybe he's a-settin' on a buddy's bunk a-lookin' at me right now," I said. I let it sink in for a minute before I said anything else.

He was looking at me very seriously. He didn't quite know how to take me. Good.

Finally one of them said, "Vic's not Viet Cong. . . . He's Chinese-American. I went through SEAL training with him."

"But how do you *know*?" I pointed out. "How do you know he's not an English-speaking Vietnamese? A Chink that infiltrated us? Viet Cong could make it through SEAL training—a picked one. They're tough sonsabitches, some of 'em."

I gave them a second to think about that, and then went on: "On the other hand, how do ye know Charley isn't layin' on this bunk right here, a-talkin' to ye?"

"But . . . you're not even Oriental," said Rat Face.

"But how do you *know* Charley hasn't got to me? Maybe I got a little girl friend I'm a-screwin' in some village around here, an' she's Viet Cong, an' she finds out all this shit from me? Or maybe she's been workin' on my mind, an' one of these nights I'll ketch ye all in here asleep at th' same time, an' frag the whole lot! It's happened before! *How do you know?*"

They didn't have anything to say to that.

I rolled over and sat up, and stuck out my hand to the Chinese. "I'm Tyler. An' I ain't no VC."

"I'm Vic Lee, an' I'm not VC either. We'll just have to trust each other, I guess," he said, shaking my hand.

"I don't trust nobody!" I told him. "That asshole that bunks where yer a-settin'? If I trust anybody, I trust him. He takes no chances. Kill me if he thought I was goin' t'get him killed. We been in lots of bar fights together. . . . I've pulled a lot of fleet sailors off his back . . . covered his ass lots of times in San Diego. Waste him in a minute, if he fucks up. You go out with me, *don't you fuck up*."

The other new guy had joined us now. It was a good time to point out something to them.

"You see that rifle there?" I pointed to my M-14, leaning against a support post at the side of my cot. They all nodded. "That's *my* rifle. It's got a special place, a mark on the floor that I know about. It sets a certain way—I turn it that way ever time I put it there. If it's ever moved, I'll know it. It's got a round in the chamber, an' it's off safety. Nobody touches it but me—ye all understand?"

They nodded. Yes they understood.

"Y'can borrow my money, y'can read my mail, y'can drink outta my bottle, y'can wear my underwear...but don't you *ever* touch my rifle. I want t'make that clear right now."

Then I pointed to Brewster's bunk again. "That's Brewster's bunk. He is a crude motherfucker. Another one of us ignernt hillbillies. He is a *mean*, crude motherfucker, an' a dirty one besides. Don't ever set on Brewster's bed, an' don't ever handle his stuff. He gets pissed off, an' violent. Ye want a beer?"

I showed them where the cooler was and got me another beer and went and sat down in the mess. Brewster, Ivy League, Poppa, and the Chief, all the old hands, were sitting around drinking, so I joined them. The new guys sat down, too. Somebody had a news magazine they'd picked up in Saigon, and it was full of news about protests and riots back in the States. They were talking about it.

"Don't that just burn you up?" I said. "I mean, them kids marchin' around over there protestin' an' everthang? What've they got to protest about? They're a-goin' to college, they got nice air-conditioned rooms to sleep in an' women to sleep with, an' they don't have powdered eggs for breakfast ever blessed day."

"They're protesting because they don't want to give all that up to come over here," Ivy League pointed out. "They don't want to be drafted."

"A bunch of fuckin' cowards," said Brewster.

"Ah, I think a lot of 'em are just a-raisin' hell," I told

Ivy League. "Kids always raise a lot of hell. You did it, an' I did it. . . . Protestin' th' war is just the way they're doin' it."

As a reply, Ivy League took the newspaper clipping out of his pocket and gave it to me to read.

"You never done that fer me," Brewster said. "You never let me read your mail. Nobody ever lets me read their mail!"

"You can't read, anyway," Ivy League shot back.

"I read good enough t'know thet little gal o'yours sure do like t'fuck," Brewster told him.

I thought another fight was brewing, but Ivy League didn't bother to reply. The newspaper story just said a girl from a certain area of Boston—the name didn't mean anything to me, of course—had been arrested with a group of war protestors who had been marching with North Vietnamese and Communist flags and had invaded the Capitol Building in Washington. She was quoted as telling the reporter: "We support the People's Army of Vietnam against imperialist aggression by the United States. The American fascist pig Army is murdering women and children. The people of the United States do not want this immoral war; they will join us in bringing an end to it. End the atrocities! End the murders! The Freedom Fighters of Vietnam will be victorious. Impeach the warmonger Nixon!" The reporter asked if she was a Communist. "We are all loyal and patriotic Americans," the girl was quoted as saying. The "loyal and patriotic Americans" then drowned out any further conversation by chanting "Ho, Ho, Ho Chi Minh" and scuffling with the police who came to remove them from the building.

I handed the clipping back.

"What does she say to you?" I asked him.

"About the same old shit," he said. "I've spent hours talking to her, talking long distance a lot of times, but it's like talking to that sandbag over there. I write her letters, tell her what goes on over here, how the Viet Cong really treat the people . . . how they liberate them of everything they have, even the rice they have to live on, how they steal the young girls to make whores out of them. About the murder and torture. She just writes back that I've been brainwashed by the government, and that what I think I see isn't really what I see."

"Rape's rape, stealin's stealin', murder's murder," I said. "How can you make a mistake about that?"

"She says that the people it happens to deserve it . . . that they are traitors to the Vietnamese people, because they support the puppet government or black-market profiteers or local thugs."

"Sounds like Communist Party drivel," Poppa said.

"It is," Ivy League told him. "In her last letter, she finally admitted she had joined the Communist Party. Can you believe that shit? I'm over here fighting . . . hell, we used to plan to get married after I got out of school . . . before all this Vietnam shit."

"Ye still a-plannin' to marry her when you get back?" Brewster wanted to know.

"No," said Ivy League flatly. I looked at him to see what he might be thinking, his voice sounded so strange. He was deadpan, his face revealing no emotion at all, but his eyes showed more whites than usual—they were open real wide, and he was staring toward the sandbag wall. His teeth were clenched. I guessed what else was in the letter: She'd probably told him she hated his guts, that she'd been screwing one of the Commies, that she hoped the Viet Cong cut his nuts off. Women are like that: When they turn on you, they turn on you all the way.

Poppa shook his head. "I just don't understand America," he said. "I guess I've been overseas too goddamned long. Why do they spend millions of dollars fighting Communism over here and let them roam around the streets over there? There's really only a few Communists at the core of the whole mess. If they'd just lock 'em up, shut 'em up...all these protests would die out. They're all planned by the Communists.... Look at the timing. Look at the way it's done: Somebody organizes these things, somebody puts them together.... They're too complex to 'just happen.' Somebody keeps a careful watch on the government, on the Congress, and they schedule these things in advance, when Congress is debatin' the war. And then they're not there when trouble starts. They bug out and leave the damned dumb students holding the bag.... It's always some 'innocent bystander' that gets hurt, did you ever notice that? Nobody that gets caught or hurt was ever part of the demonstration—they were just there watchin'!" He paused for a drink of beer.

"Those kids," he went on, "they don't know what the diddlyshit they're protesting about. None of them has ever been over here. But I've been here—a hell of a long time. I was here right after the Japs were kicked out in World War Two. Ho Chi Minh was a hero then: He helped us kick the Japs out! But we liberated the French from the Germans, and the Vietnamese from the Japanese, and then turned our backs while the Frogs took over Vietnam again. If we'd stayed right after the war and helped the Vietnamese set up a government, things might have been different.

"The North Vietnamese and the South Vietnamese, now they're two different breeds of people. Really. The northerners, on the whole, they're more industrious and more honest. We could've worked with the northerners.... Maybe the government that was set up wouldn't have been an exact little copy of our own, but what the hell? Italy and France have Communist parties, and they're NATO allies. Now...it's hopeless. We're trying to prop up an incompetent government, a corrupt bureaucracy. And there's the Catholic-Buddhist problem. It's a can of worms, and it's too late to sort it out.

"The protestors, they keep saying the division of the country into South and North is artificial, and the Viet Cong are fighting to unify it again. Well, they're right, but they're full of bullshit at the same time. The *unification* of the country was the doing of the French. . . . This whole peninsula—Thailand, Laos, Cambodia—it's been like the Balkan states: shifting borders, changing names, constant wars and fighting. There's a dozen different tribes and ethnic groups, and all of 'em hate each other. The only time they get their act together is when they're fighting some outsider, like the French or the Chinese. Anybody that says we're trying to preserve an artificial division of the country while the Communists are trying to unify it is full of shit. They're just following the Party line."

"You sounded pretty sympathetic to the Viet Cong," one of the new guys said, "until you said that last part."

"I'm sympathetic to the Vietnamese," Poppa told him. "I'm sympathetic to the rice farmer out in the paddy and the merchant in the marketplace that want to get rid of the French and the Americans and the North Vietnamese and the Chinese and everybody else, and just get on with the business of growing rice and selling chickens. I believe in stopping Communism now—right here—but I don't believe we went about it right to start with, and we're not doing any better now. We've beaten them militarily. We're pulling troops out now. The newspapers and reporters will try to sell the line that we're beaten, that we've lost, that we'd better just pull out. Partly that's because those damned people, the correspondents and broadcasters, are still fighting World War Two, or think they are, and don't understand guerilla war, and partly it's because the newspaper reporters and editors are left-wingers. Have been for years."

Poppa didn't usually talk that much. All the bitterness in him seemed to be coming out.

"It ain't just the newspapers. It's the fuckin' Army an'

Air Force an' Marines...an' Navy," the Chief said. "They're all fucked up. Don't you see how much crap is wasted? How much effort is wasted? They figger only one out of every ten or twelve Americans in Vietnam is a combat soldier. The rest are all support units. Where does all the crap go? Do you think the soldier with his ass out there in the grass ever sees any of it? Visit a firebase one of these days.... Those guys are always short of everything. We live like we were in th' goddamn Hilton Hotel on this barge, compared to those guys, and all I hear around here is bitchin' about powdered eggs and dehydrated meals.

"I'll tell you where all the shit goes: It all goes to feed and clothe and equip all those gold-brickin' support personnel, all the fuckin' clerks an' paper pushers. Anything left over is sold on the black market.

"How much ground have we gained in this war? Huh? None, that's how much! We take it over, we kick the Viet Cong out of it, an' then we walk off an' let 'em have it again. Guerilla war or not, you win by controllin' ground, an' the only ground you control is what you got two feet on. You gotta patrol an' patrol an' patrol. An' you gotta have garrisons. You can't just hide in th' cities, or in firebases. Then there's this Neutral Zone crap.... You can't fight a war by givin' th' enemy a place to hide, an' rebuild his forces. D'you think the Viet Cong will pay any attention to those Neutral Zones? When he's ready to hit something in th' Neutral Zones, he'll hit it."

He shook his head sadly from side to side. "Waste... waste..." he said.

"Do you think the air strikes in North Vietnam will bring the North Vietnamese to their senses now that Ho Chi Minh is dead?" Ivy League asked of Poppa and the Chief and, I guess, all of us in general.

"Air strikes! Air strikes! You can't win a war with air strikes.... You gotta occupy that ground!" the Chief said.

"We won the Second World War with air strikes," Ivy League argued.

"No, we didn't," Poppa told him. "That's flyboy propaganda! Germany didn't quit until ninety percent of it was occupied." When Ivy League protested that Japan did, he went on to say: "No, you're wrong again—Japan quit after we kicked them off of New Guinea and th' Philippines an' Okinawa, an' they knew Japan was next . . . they couldn't stop us. The bombing, the atomic bombs, they just showed the people at home what it was like to die in a war and convinced 'em they didn't really want to. If they'd had to wait to find out, to wait until they experienced it personal, we would've had to invade Japan. Tarawa and Iwo were bad—just think about invadin' Japan."

"You don't think bombing does any good?"

"Sure it does, if it kills troops and interferes with moving supplies. But it's a waste," the Chief went on. "There was a bridge. . . . It was close to Tchepone, in Laos, on the Trail, th' Ho Chi Minh Trail. The flyboys, they bombed it and bombed it and bombed it. . . . They never could knock it out. The VC put up antiaircraft guns around there, and missiles . . . and they shot down plane after plane and helicopter after helicopter brought in there to knock out that one bridge. Talk about waste."

It was time for another round of beer. By the time we sat down again we were back to bad-mouthing the protestors. We all agreed it was like striking against the country, and that it was bad for our morale.

"Poor folks don't have time for all that shit," Brewster said. "They're too busy earnin' a livin'. If th' guv'mint didn't support them damn kids with welfare an' all that stuff, they wouldn't have time t'protest. Let 'em work."

"I'll bet as many of them are from wealthy homes as from poor ones," Ivy League told him.

"They work," I said. "They peddle that damn marijuana and heroin and stuff. They don't pay no taxes on what they make, either. But they git welfare and food stamps, 'cause they got no legal income!"

"I know one," Poppa said, "that isn't living on welfare: Jane Fonda."

"Go-od damn that bitch," said the Chief. "D'you know she went up to Hanoi an' told 'em what a great job they were doin'. They oughta *hang* her ass! She's a traitor! That's givin' aid an' comfort to th' enemy! She deserves publicity, all right—the kind you get when they stand you up in front of the wall and shoot you!"

"Hell, they won't do nothin' to her," Brewster said. "If she was poor, they'd throw her tail in jail an' throw away the key. But she can hire enough fuckin' lawyers t'get her off."

"Any lawyer that would defend her—" the Chief started, but Brewster cut him off.

"A lawyer'll do *anything* for money," he said. "Anything. Screw his own mother for money."

"It just isn't right," I insisted, "her pullin' some shit like that and gettin' away with it. Makin' money, not just some money, but thousands of dollars, millions maybe, runnin' around bein' a traitor to her country, while we wade around in th' stinking mud and get our butts blowed off for a few dollars a month."

"I don't understand," said Rat Face. "You complain about what the war is doing to you, what it's doing to your mind even if you don't get wounded or killed, but you object to what people are doing to try to stop the war. The protestors want to stop the war, Jane Fonda wants to stop the war, the Vietnam Veterans Committee is trying to stop the war...."

"In th' first place, " I told him, "Jane Fonda don't give a shit about th' war, except as far as it helps her career. In the second place, no committee's gonna stop a war and no protests are gonna stop a war. Wars got a life of their own: They start when they're ready and they stop when they're ready, and if you're there when they start, why, you fight in 'em, that's all. Wars are like floods an' earthquakes. You can plan for 'em, but you can't stop 'em from hap'nin'."

"What a morbid outlook," Rat Face said.

"I agree with Tyler," Ivy League said. "It's the balance of nature: Predators keep the size of the herds under control. So do disease and floods and droughts."

"There is one way to control wars," Poppa said. "Make 'em less profitable. If we had a law that required industry to supply war materials to the government *at cost*, with no profits, and if we drafted people to work in war industries at lower wages...they wouldn't be so eager to get us involved."

Brewster was talking to Rat Face, but his words filled a gap in our conversation: "Well, they can gripe all they will," he was saying, "but this war ain't so bad. It sure as hell beats mining coal. Th' hours are long, but th' work ain't hard to take. I like killin' gooks."

Billy, looking at Brewster, had his upper lip all snockered up, like a little girl that's just been offered a handful of nightcrawlers. I leaned back in my chair and grinned and crumpled up my beer can to throw it over the side.

"Yessir," I agreed. "You just might call us th' predators."

CHAPTER 8

The next night, Poppa took the new guys out on their break-in patrol. Billy and Rat Face (his name was Yancey) went out as spotters; Vic—Chinese Lee, we called him—and the other new guy (his name was Bacon, so Brewster immediately started calling him Fat Back) sat decoy. Before they went out, I took them aside and told them: "Look, you're gonna be scared shitless out there tonight. I was. Brewster was. Ivy...Ivy League was." I decided not to tell them Ivy League pissed in his pants. "Don't let it get to you. Don't let your imagination do it to you. You got three people out there lookin' out for you, an' you got your own eyes. Chances are you won't see anything. If Charley comes along, Poppa will take care of ye. If there's one or two gooks, Poppa'll get 'em. If there's ten or twelve, he'll get you outta there.... He'll cover your tail while you withdraw. I know you don't feel like it right now, but the five of

127

ye can handle ten or twenty of them little bastards, no sweat, *if* ye keep your heads."

They came back in at dawn, looking kind of shook. "Well," I said as they got off the boat, "did ye have any luck?"

Nobody spoke. They just walked on by and went and got themselves a beer. Poppa was still on board. He nodded slightly and winked.

I went over and got myself a beer and sat there a long time waiting for somebody to break the silence. Finally I said, "You know, th' first time I sat decoy, I saw all kinds of Viet Congs sneakin' around out there in the bush, an' Poppa never did shoot. All of 'em turned out to be either shadows an' fog or little jungle animals—rats an' such. I never did find out how good a shot Poppa was."

"Oh, he's a good shot," Vic said.

"How d'ye know?" I asked, innocently.

"He got one," Vic said, sort of strained, like he was choking back tears or something.

At that Billy jumped up, ran to the side of the barge, and puked.

"Why, what's th' matter with you? Was th' gook a friend of yours or somethin'? You oughta be a-celebratin'."

Rat Face Yancey was the only one that didn't seem to be a little bit sick.

"Took his head right off," Yancey said. "Shot him in the neck and took his head right off...."

December was the beginning of the dry season. At least that's when I noticed it wasn't raining so much. The undergrowth along the banks of the streams and canals was as thick as ever, but there was less of it back away from the water. Of course, it was still hot—the rain didn't seem to affect the temperature any. And it was steamy, down there in the Delta. The waterline of the Mekong was going down drastically. Villages that a month ago were right by the river were now a hefty walk back from the bank. Some of the tributary streams began to show sandbars at their mouths.

And, of course, December was also the month of the Christmas holidays . . . and the Christmas cease-fire.

The troop withdrawals were going ahead as planned. Fifty or sixty thousand U.S. troops had been pulled out in 1969, at least according to the news. "Vietnamization" of the war was in full swing. In February, before I came, the Navy had started turning over PBRs and other shallow-draft boats to the ARVNs, who had taken over most of the riverine warfare down in the Delta. By December, ARVN patrol boats were venturing as far upriver as our barge, but not much further. Things got too hot for them upstream.

On shore, the pacification program was making tremendous strides, according to Armed Forces Radio, Saigon. Couldn't have proved it by me. Oh, there were villages where you knew the people were friendly—you could feel it in the air. There were lots of others where you could feel the unfriendliness. It seemed like things got a little better when the regular forces pulled out and stopped running Search and Destroy missions through the villages. Maybe because they had usually searched little but had destroyed a lot. But generally, American faces just weren't welcome. We were outsiders, invaders. The funny thing was that ARVN was about as unwelcome as we were.

As the regular troops pulled out, the SEAL teams got larger. SEAL Team One and Team Two both had platoons operating in the Delta; a lot of the SEALs were involved in training and advisory roles with Vietnamese outfits. There were always odd jobs to do: blasting out obstacles in channels so bigger ships could get upriver, checking fouled screws, recovering bodies or downed aircraft. The war went on. The regular troops were still blundering around in the boonies, trying to come to grips with the enemy, but units like ours were seeking out the enemy in his "safe" bases, on his own ground—and hurting him.

One day, the Lieutenant Commander stopped us from going out on the morning river patrol—Ivy League, Brewster, and me. He got us to sit around a table in the mess and drink coffee while he told us what he had in mind.

"Boys, I've got a little surprise for you," he said, and I thought, uh-oh—that means trouble. He only talks that way when it's going to be nasty.

"Christmas is next Thursday, and there's going to be a Christmas cease-fire."

"Oh, goody," said Brewster, "we gonna put up a Christmas tree?"

"No."

"We gonna get leave t'go chase whores in Saigon?" Brewster again.

"Nope. The thing about Christmas cease-fires is that Charley is Buddhist, and he doesn't believe in Christmas. So, it's always been the case in the past that we stop shooting, and Charley doesn't."

"I got a feelin' that ain't gonna be the case this year," I told Ivy League.

"I have a hunch you're right," he replied.

"The word is we want to keep the Viet Cong off balance and unable to attack, while most of the regular troops get to observe the cease-fire. That means that from now through New Year's Day, we're going to be running a twenty-four-hour river patrol out of this barge. Crews'll come in just long enough to chow down and fuel up and make any repairs they may need, and then out they'll go again. I'll be taking my turn on patrol with everybody else—everybody but the regular sentries—the cooks, the mechanics, everybody. We have to patrol more often, and we also have to widen the area patrolled. We'll be going farther up into the Plain of Reeds, and we'll cover the canals down south toward Rach Gia."

I started getting a feeling like heartburn. The further you went into the Plain of Reeds, the better your chances of getting hit. The place crawled with Viet Cong. And it wasn't much better down south, on the Ca Mau Peninsula.

Then he dropped the bomb.

"Of course, that won't affect you guys that much. . . . You won't be here."

What now? I thought. Where are they sending us now? Quang Tri? Rung Sat? Laos? I thought of just about every possible alternative except the right one.

"You're going on a recon patrol in the Seven Mountains area, the Nui Kto Highlands, between Ba Chuc, Phum Tampo, and Cau Sac." He passed a little xeroxed map sheet over to us, with the area circled on it, and our barge marked off. "That's Viet Cong country. Hardcore. I guess they've been giving ARVN hell up there, and the Special Forces, too. Nothing big, just an ambush here and there and hitting a bush camp every once in a while. But the Intelligence boys think Charley's building up, up in the high country bush there, to attack somewhere during Christmas. So we're sending patrols up there to scout around and see what they can find. Special Forces will have recon patrols out, but they wanted more people in the area, and My Tho agreed to send some of ours up." That's the Naval Support Facility at My Tho.

"I can only spare you three. Poppa and Chief Mackintosh are needed here—we can't put these new guys up in the Plain of Reeds or down on the Ca Mau without an experienced man along. So you'll be going out with Hercules and two SEALs from My Tho. I know that Hercules is the only one you've worked with, and you'll be a little bit unhappy about going out into the bush with strangers. At least they're SEALs, not Army types. You get together with the other SEALs and decide who's going to be squad leader. If I were picking one, I'd pick you, Hartford. But I don't know who they're sending up from My Tho besides Hercules—one of them may be an officer or an old hand.

"Anyway, the six of you will be in the bush for a week or ten days. You may or may not be able to resupply— you'll have a radio, and there's a Green Beret outpost you can get in touch with to call a helicopter. But who knows what you'll run into. A helicopter might not be able to get in. So take enough to get by on for four or five days without resupply. I don't have to tell you what you need.

"The guys from My Tho will pick you up in a PBR this afternoon and run you up to the airstrip at Cao Lanh. You'll helicopter in from there. Here's a map—one of you take charge of it.... Hartford, you take it. Pick-up arrangements will be made with the pilot after you leave the ground—that way, Charley won't get wind of the coordinates and be there waiting for you. The same pilot will pick you up. That's all I've got to say.... Get your shit together."

All of us had a queasy feeling, I guess. This was our first time for this kind of operation. Yet it would have been a lot worse if it had been dropped in our laps four or six weeks earlier, before we had time to get used to the country and get our confidence built back up. I knew that the grunts, given a choice, would pick chasing Viet Cong in the high country over wading after them in the swamps and marshes, any day. I was packing C-rats when Brewster voiced his opinion on the matter.

"Reckon them slopes up there in th' hills are hillbillies? Reckon they're more back'ards than the ones down here?"

"It would be hard to be more backwards than these

here in the lowlands," Ivy League said, folding up the map and putting it in a plastic bag.

"Fold that thang where you can read it through th' bag," I told him. "Not with th' map side in."

"Well...it cain't be too bad," Brewster said. "Any places with names like Nooky Toe an' P'foom Tampon...whut'er them others? Oh, yeah, Botchup an' Cow Sack...gotta be sump'n like Bug Tussle an' Possum Trot—jist ragler ole country folks."

"Yeah, well, down home, them ragler ole country folks'll blow yer ass away if they don't know ye...'specially if yer out messin' around their stills," I told him.

"Let's try to avoid their stills," Ivy League suggested.

We had time to get our gear packed up and our weapons cleaned and loaded, and get nervous and pace around before lunch. After lunch I said the hell with this and lay down on my cot and tried to take a little nap, nervous or not. Ivy League drank coffee and paced and got more nervous. Nerveless Brewster sacked out, of course. Once, I got up and checked the stuff I was taking and added some concussion grenades and a couple of clips of M-14 ammo. Finally I did doze off, just about the time the PBR came in to pick us up. Hercules came aboard and talked to the Lieutenant Commander for a minute while we got our gear together, and then we all climbed aboard. The PBR was fully manned, so there wasn't anything to do except drop our packs and sit down. I looked around at the crew. It wasn't hard to tell which were the SEALs.

They were a couple of bushwise-looking bastards. Both of them had scraggly beards, four or five days' growth, anyway, and both had smeared their faces with camo paint. One wore cut-off jeans and tennis shoes, and an old olive-drab sleeveless T-shirt well camouflaged by what looked like dried coffee and ketchup stains, with some motor oil and sweat thrown in. He wore a dirty, ventilated baseball-type cap of the kind that usually says "Caterpillar," turned with the bill backwards. The other SEAL wore jungle green pants and G.I. boots, but no shirt. He'd covered his torso and arms completely with black camo paint. His slightly long hair was pulled into a ponytail in the back, and held by a couple of rubber bands. He wore one of the soft-brim jungle slouch hats.

Definitely not your rear-area commandos.

I relaxed a little when I saw them—I'd been a little worried that they'd be a couple of greenhorns, or maybe spit-and-polish officer types. After all, as scruffy-looking as those two characters were, we looked almost as bad. After a few weeks of crawling around in the swamps and jungles, our uniforms were getting a little raggedy-ass. My shirt had the sleeves ripped off, and I never buttoned it up, so it always hung open—it was cooler that way. My headgear was a sweatband. Ivy League wore an olive-drab T-shirt. I'd have worn my tennis shoes and cut-offs, except I didn't know what I was getting into, up in the high country. Brewster wore his jungle greens, but they were so ragged and ripped up he looked like a scarecrow, and so mud and sweat-stained they were almost black.

They looked us up and down while we looked them up and down, and then Ponytail spit in the river—he was chewing tobacco—and the coxswain opened up the throttle, and we roared off up the river.

At Cao Lanh, the harbormaster got us a jeep and a driver, and the six of us threw our gear in the back and climbed on, and off we went. Hercules climbed in by the driver. Ivy League, Ponytail, and I sat in the back, on the little metal seats that are like the wheel wells in a pickup bed. Baseball Cap climbed onto the middle of the hood and sat there cross-legged, and when the driver tried to get him to move, he gave the poor fellow such a hard look that nothing more was said. Brewster hooked one leg inside and clung to the spare tire and a handrail, his other leg dangling outside.

Cao Lanh seemed to be about the same size as my hometown, but it had at least twice as many people, all scurrying around like ants in a nest that's just been uncovered. People were carrying loads on their backs, pushing them in handcarts and carrying them on the ends of bamboo poles. There were no sidewalks. Pedestrians, bicycles, motorcycles, and Army deuce-and-a-half trucks filled the streets from shopfront to shopfront. There were scruffy kids in rags and naked kids and scruffy men and women in pajamalike clothing, all of them with that haggard look that poor people have just about everywhere. And there were fat Chinese in white suits and pretty girls in long, brightly colored dresses called *ao dais*, with parasols to shade them. Our driver used his horn about as often as his brake, and much more often than the gas pedal.

It was slow going in the busiest streets, creeping along in low gear with the horn going almost constantly. It looked like a good place for an ambush, with us going so slow and all the people around to hide in... so I made sure my rifle was ready, Neutral Zone or not. A girl in an orange *ao dai* caught Brewster's attention. She was walking the same direction that we were going, and she alternately overtook and passed us, and was left behind as we found an opening in the traffic. Brewster began leering at her. She managed to keep her parasol between them most of the time, and ignored him until he started talking to her in what he thought was an enticing fashion, in a mix of English and the few Vietnamese words he knew. At that, she ducked into a shop.

"Damn bitch.... Is that any way t'act when somebody's bein' friendly?" he said.

The street was blocked up ahead, so the driver took a hard right down a street so narrow it wasn't much more than an alley. Halfway down was a lumbering bullock cart, and to maneuver around it he had to wheel the jeep over almost to the wall of a shop. Just then, the girl in the orange *ao dai* popped out of the back door of the shop, almost into Brewster's arms. She stopped, startled, when she saw his leering face so close, and he took the opportunity to pinch her on the left tit. Then the driver got clear of the cart and we raced on down the street, with Brewster shouting, "Whooooya! Mer-ry Christmas!"

When we walked into the office at the air base, the little noncom behind the desk looked at us like he couldn't believe his eyes. But when Ponytail showed him our orders, he checked a board on the wall and told us where to go out on the flightline to find the helicopter. Then he told us where we could get some coffee. We had about an hour to kill.

We drank a lot of their coffee and had some fresh-baked pie before we went out to the helicopter.

"Fuckin' flyboys," Brewster said. "Live like civilians. Eat like civilians. Fly around over all th' mud an' shit, up above all th' shootin' an' go home an' brag they been fightin' a war. Closest them fuckers ever get to a war is hagglin' with a whore on Tu Do Street."

I agreed with him, until we took off in that helicopter. Then I started wishing I was back down on the ground, in the jungle, where Charley had some trouble seeing me, instead of sitting up there in midair, where I was an easy target. One man down there with a surface-to-air missile, and all my caution would be for nothing.

There was a metal-framed canvas seat that went almost all the way across the width of the helicopter body, and I sat on the right side, on the open hatch. There were no doors. There were seat belts, but no one belted in. A gunner sat cross-legged on an ammo box by the portside door, with a swivel-mounted M-60 machine gun. Ponytail sat facing me. When we crossed the barbed-wire perimeter around the base, about a hundred feet up, he grinned at me and spit tobacco juice out the door.

A couple of armed Loaches—Light Observation Helicopters—took off right after we did and took up a position on either side of us. They were faster than the Huey, and they would zoom off to investigate something, and then come zooming back to their positions. They flitted around like dragonflies.

Outside the base and the town, rice paddies stretched out as far as you could see. Here and there a canal ran through them, straight as an arrow, for miles. Along the bank of the canal there were usually some trees and brush and maybe some houses—huts, really—for fifty or a hundred meters. A road ran along beside a lot of them. Beyond the line of trees would be the rice paddies, thousands of them, each one a different size and shape. After we crossed the Mekong and the Bassac, the paddies continued for a few kilometers, but you started to see patches of unreclaimed marsh between them, and some islands covered with jungle. Gradually the jungle and the marsh took over from the paddies.

I kept waiting for a line of tracers to come arching up out of the trees into the door where I sat, or the streak of fire as a SAM hurtled toward us, but when I did see tracers, they were 'way off to the right and behind us. They couldn't possibly have hit us. Charley just wanted us to know he was watching.

One of the Loaches went zipping off that way and squirted the trees with his machine guns where he thought the fire came from. Then he made a return pass and headed back toward us. . . . As he zoomed away, a yellow stream of tracers rose after him, like a lone finger raised in salute. Fuck you, Round Eyes.

The LZ was a clearing near the foot of some hills. We came in low and fast, so as not to give Charley any warning. The Huey rolled back from its forward-tilt and slowed, dropping quickly until it was just above the tall grass, then settling hesitantly, as though testing the ground. I had my M-14 ready when I went out the door, but there was no firing. I went about thirty meters out from the Huey, bent 'way over to avoid the rotor blades, and expecting at any step to hit a punji stick or trip a booby trap. I'd hardly got away from the chopper when the beat of its rotors changed tempo and the sound of its engine changed tone as it pulled away. It headed away to the south, leaving me crouched in a grassy clearing God knows where in Vietnam. The Loaches had circled to their right and came back past the clearing heading south as the Huey lifted off, attempting to mask the sound of its landing and takeoff with their own noise, which was like a pulsating buzz.

I didn't think the trick would fool me, and I was sure it wouldn't fool Charley. It was time to get the hell out of there.

I glanced around. There was no one else in sight. For a moment I thought the others had seen something and gotten back on, and I was alone here. Then I saw a ripple in the grass that wasn't the wind, and beyond that, toward the opposite side of the clearing, a figure darted quickly toward the jungle.

I did likewise.

We formed up just inside the treeline, and after studying the map of the area we were supposed to recon, started up toward the hills. The patrol area extended up to and along the crest of a low ridge for several kilometers. Other recon patrols would cover the sectors on either side of us and on the other side of the ridge. We decided to work our way up the ridge in a shallow Z, looking for trails or other signs that VC had passed that way. We decided to move some distance away from the clearing we'd landed in, and laager until daylight—we'd see signs better by daylight than at night.

As I moved at a crouch through the bush, turning first this way and then the other, listening, looking, lurking in the shadows and avoiding the clearings, I thought to myself: This is the real thing. The breaking-in period is over. And then: Oh, boy . . . Hell Week all over again!

CHAPTER 9

We moved up out of the lowlands into a tree-covered area on the side of a low hill. There we found a stand of trees with very little undergrowth around their bases, the result of the leaves being so thick overhead that little light could get through to the forest floor. The trees were quite tall—you couldn't tell just how tall in the dark, but there were no branches in sight. I'd seen very few stands like this in the lowlands. It was pitch dark in there. Little light could get to the ground even during the daylight hours, so it was a perfect place to hole up for the rest of the night.

We split up into pairs, each "watching" a different direction. Brewster and I sat where we could reach out and touch each other, because it was too dark to see hand signals. We decided to take two-hour watches and try to grab some sleep. It might be the last chance we would

have for a long time. I took the first watch, and Brewster
was asleep, I think, in less than a minute.

When you're watching like that, in the dark, you haven't
got a lot to do except think. Of course, the first thing I thought
about was Charley. Did he hear the helicopters? Did he see
them? Did he know they dropped us off, or think they were
just patrolling around? I was sure if Charley heard those
helicopters, he knew that one of them had landed, and if he
saw them, he knew where and was there by now. Whether
or not he would find our trail and follow it would depend
on how good Charley was. Viet Cong were just people like
everybody else: Some of them were really sharp, and some
of them were really dumb.

Like me.

I mean, how else could you really look at it? I was
being used. . . . I was a sucker for being here in the first
place. Back over in the States, unemployment was low,
because the war industries were booming. Wages were
high. The banks and the munitions industries were raking
in the money. Good times were being had by all, except
the poor fuckers stuck over here in the boonies. I thought
about what Poppa had said, and I knew it was the truth.
We were fighting over here to stimulate the economy, so
the war industries could make fat profits, and so the pol-
iticians could enjoy themselves in public office a few more
years, taking bribes and payoffs and playing swat-the-
baloney with their secretaries.

And when you got back, what then? Was there any
gratitude? Shit no! I knew enough veterans to know they
had trouble fitting in, trouble getting jobs. That's why a
lot of guys came back on second and third tours—the
South Vietnamese showed more gratitude than the American public.

It made me mad. Mad enough to shoot a Congressman,
if one ever came over on a tour again.

I was beginning to see the world as consisting of the

screwers and the screwees. The screwers always screw the screwees, seldom each other...and if that sounds a little bit like Karl Marx, well, that's just the way it is. The only difference in my viewpoint was that I could see that Ho Chi Minh and General Giap were screwers, too, no matter how they tried to pretend otherwise. Charley, now, was a different matter: He was a screwee, just like me...only he didn't know it. He believed all the shit the Communists put out. He screwed the villagers, and his political bosses screwed him. The villagers were the lowest screwees on the totem pole. They got screwed by everybody—by the Viet Cong, by ARVN, by us. Now, Jane Fonda, on the other hand, was a screwer. Nixon was also a screwer, and so was Johnson, Westmoreland, and the whole fucking lot. I was born a screwee, and I'd been getting it all my life—from the bankers, the draft board, the Navy, the college students....No wonder I sometimes felt closer to the peasants out in the rice paddies than those fat and sassy bastards back in the States.

I knew if I kept thinking along those lines, I'd go over the hill. So I tried thinking about my family. About my brother. What was he thinking, knowing I was over here because only one of us could be deferred? Did he realize I'd saved his ass? He'd have gone into the infantry for sure, and the damned infantry were sitting ducks for Charley. They hadn't been trained enough, or in the right way, and worst of all, neither had their officers. I wondered if he'd be grateful, if he'd show any gratitude when I got back, for the years he'd had at home because I gave up some of my life....

What about Mom? What was she thinking? I knew very well how she felt about things like killing. She'd hated my drinking and whoring around when I was at home, but those were sins that could be forgiven....Those were human sins. Killing another person was the most ungodly thing a man could do; there wasn't any forgiveness for

that in her book. Deep inside, I felt the same way. She'd
made sure that I went to church every Sunday when I
was younger, and she'd preached to us herself, to make
sure we grew up with the proper Christian attitude. Some
of it soaked in, like believing that killing's a mortal sin,
even in war, but some didn't take, I guess. As a kid I'd
drink until I was sick if I got the chance. And I'd still
throw a few drunks every now and then. The last week
or so, I'd been drinking pretty heavily, enough that I had
to have a shot or two of oxygen to clear my head in the
mornings before going out on patrol. And if I could get
to Saigon, or even My Tho, I firmly intended to find me
a whore. I could sort of sympathize with Charley when
it came to raping some of the village girls, too—when you
face death every day, or almost every day, the urge to
gratify that need gets awfully strong, sometimes strong
enough to overcome any personal reluctance to use force.
The shrinks called it the urge to "seek immortality through
reproduction." I couldn't sympathize with what Charley
did to the girls afterward: the torture and mutilation. They
did a lot of it, to keep the villagers frightened and in line,
and it seemed like they got to enjoying it and thriving on
it and doing it when there was no point. Would I start to
enjoy killing? I didn't think so. But I didn't feel sorry that
I'd killed most of those people I'd killed. Only the death
of the girl bothered me at all. Would I start torturing
people to make them talk? Could I cut on them, burn
them, skin them? No, not me.... Hell, when I was back
on the farm, it was all I could do to castrate a calf or a
pig.... I sure as shit couldn't do it with people, even
gooks.

Is this what it will be like when I get home? I wondered.
Will I sit awake in the dark and try to justify it in my own
mind? Will I have nightmares, like I do here? Will my
family be afraid of me? Will I care about them and the
things that happen to them, like I used to? Maybe I'll be

so used to killing, get so much of a thrill out of it, that I'll have to kill someone every now and then, just for kicks. They won't put up with that over there. Even though They are responsible, even though They send you kicking and screaming into a war where you stay alive by killing the other guy, you're not supposed to bring that home with you. You're not supposed to be any threat to Them.

When dawn came, with only a faint increase in light underneath the canopy of leaves that roofed our hideaway, we got our battle packs on and moved out. Baseball Cap—his name was Harlow—took the point. Very slowly, he moved out about thirty meters or so, and called us up by thumbing the talk button on his radio. We moved individually, each of us at a low crouch, stopping, moving ahead, looking around intently, then moving again, a different distance. We'd keep it up all day.

Harlow led us out of the thick copse into an area where the tree cover was broken. It was considerably lighter there, but the undergrowth was thicker. By now the temperature was in the eighties, and climbing.

We came to a running stream, and that helped us locate ourselves on the map. We then took a compass bearing and started the first leg of our patrol. Our route took us first uphill, then down, then back up again. All day long.

It got hotter as the day wore on. My shirt had been soaked with dew earlier in the day, but as that evaporated I began to sweat, and my clothes never dried out. After almost three months in the country, I was used to it. One of the jokes going around was that you could tell an old hand in the Special Forces—Green Berets, SEALs, and so on—because they were the ones that didn't have to put on camouflage paint before they went into the bush. They were so overgrown with mildew and fungus you couldn't tell they were human anyway!

In the more broken parts of the jungle, our travel was

faster, even though there was more undergrowth. You had to move pretty slowly in the tall-tree stands, because you couldn't see that well in the darkness. We tried to avoid those stands just like we tried to avoid the open ground and the grassy clearings. Our route wasn't straight at all.

There didn't seem to be much human life up here. Of course, there were lots of monkeys and birds, and snakes and insects. At times, the monkeys and other critters made so much noise it sounded like a bunch of kids playing on a schoolground. And at times it was so still you could hear sweat dripping on the leaves. . . .

We hit the first trail late in the afternoon. It was wide and nearly straight and had footprints all over it—human footprints. Sandaled feet and bare feet, no boots. We watched it awhile but saw no one moving on it. We scouted along the sides of it and saw no sign that it was booby-trapped.

"Do we follow it, or keep on the patrol path we laid out?" was the question Mike—Ponytail—asked. It was a rhetorical question. We'd selected him squad leader, and he would make the final decision. He was a W-2, a warrant officer, so he outranked everybody present.

"Follow it—we're here to look for Viet Cong, not just cover ground." We all agreed. So we followed it to a village. We didn't walk on the trail itself, of course. We worked our way through the bush beside it and got to the village after dark.

It was a poor village, just a dozen or so raggedy-ass hooches—"huts" is too substantial-sounding for those ramshackle things—perched on the banks of a little creek. About two-thirds of them were on one side, and on the other side the rest were built along some little narrow rice paddies. Right back of the paddies the jungle started and the hill sloped. We lay in the brush of the hillside and watched.

We watched all night. There didn't seem to be any sentries—we circled the village a couple of times looking for them—and they didn't seem to be mounting any patrols, but we waited until well after dawn to make sure. The only evidence of a weapon we saw was when one old man left the camp early in the morning to go up in the hills. The rifle he carried was incredibly long—Hercules said it was an old French rifle or else a Japanese Arisaka left over from the war. The hill people used them a lot for hunting, he said, and he was sure that's where the old man was going.

The women came out and cooked, and the men came out of the huts to eat their morning meal, and then they all went to work in the paddies. There did seem to be an unusual number of older men and women, and plenty of younger children, but few young men or young women. To me, that looked bad.

About 0900, after the hunter had come back in with a dead monkey on a pole, we decided to go in and talk to them. We knew which hooch had the gun in it—we could keep an eye on it.

We left Harlow and Ivy League in the bush to watch over the village, and Brewster and I slipped up to the back of a couple of the hooches. Some dogs smelled us and started barking. I was afraid the villagers would get suspicious, but just then a couple of pigs that had been rooting in a vegetable garden got scared off by our approach and ran away, squealing. They probably had been chased out before. Anyway, the dogs took off after them, and our approach was covered by the yapping of dogs, the squealing of the pigs, and laughter and shouts on the part of the villagers. Just at that moment Hercules walked out of the woods.

He walked into the village along the trail, his rifle slung barrel-downward over his shoulder. He looked very relaxed, as if he was just out for a Sunday morning stroll in Saigon. He called out to the nearest villager, an old woman in one of those wide-brimmed coolie hats, in such a cheerful manner that I could almost understand that he was bidding her good morning.

She stopped her work and stood looking at him suspiciously. She moved not a muscle except to turn her head as he walked closer to her. All over the paddies, heads lifted in unison, and expressionless faces turned toward Hercules.

Hercules stopped and talked to the old woman for a minute, obviously asking her questions. Her answers were short and curt and suspicious-sounding, even to me. After a minute or two, Hercules squatted down on his haunches, into that so typical Oriental posture, and seemed to launch into some sort of a story. He went on for some moments, his voice rising and falling in pitch and changing tone almost as if he was singing, gesturing frequently with both hands. Something seemed to put the old woman at ease; her answers got longer, and she made a few peremptory passes with her hoe at the paddy muck. Then she turned and called one of the children to her and in singsong phrases sent it scurrying toward a hooch. None of the other villagers had so much as moved a step. Hercules stood up and called back toward the jungle—in Vietnamese—and waved for someone to come on in. Mike walked in. There was a stir among the villagers when they saw he was an American. They began to chatter to one another.

The kid ran across the bridge to one of the hooches across the creek and disappeared inside. Within seconds he reappeared, leading a rather startled-looking old man by the arm. The old man planted his feet a few steps outside the hooch and would go no further until the boy pointed to Hercules, standing on the trail. Then when he saw the stranger, he began to hurry in that direction, with short, quick steps. He wore ragged, white, pajamalike

clothes, and he had a white goatee and a white fringe of
hair around his scalp. He hurriedly slipped on his coolie
hat so his bald head wouldn't get sunburned. He wore
sandals made of old rubber tires. They made a peculiar
slapping sound on the trail as he half shuffled, half trotted,
toward Hercules. He was across the bridge and several
meters down the trail before he noticed Mike coming out
of the jungle. He stopped abruptly, putting his hand to
his brow as if to shade his eyes, although they were well
shaded by the coolie hat. Perhaps he was near-sighted.
He chattered something to the boy in a plaintive voice,
and the kid responded with what sounded like sass. The
old man teetered uncertainly, then apparently decided to
wait for the intruders to come to him.

At this time, I wasn't more than thirty feet from him.

Everyone's attention was riveted on Hercules and Mike,
so I waved Brewster across the bridge. He moved quickly
and quietly for all his size. Not one head turned as he
slipped across the old rickety wooden bridge and into the
nearest hooch. Meanwhile, I kept my rifle pointed toward
the paddies just in case. Sometimes Charley kept a rifle
hidden in the mud, and he could pull it out of the muck
and dust your ass off before you knew anything was going
on. But none of the villagers had moved from where they'd
been standing. Brewster began to work his way from hooch
to hooch, quickly checking out the interiors while the
villagers' attention was rooted elsewhere. Finally he
waved—all clear. It was my turn now.

Mike was up even with Hercules, and both of them
were walking down the trail toward the village elder, the
old man. I only had a few seconds to check out the hooches
on my side of the creek. The elder stood not fifteen feet
in front of one of them. I'd get it last, I decided, and
quickly slipped around the side of the hooch nearest to
me, keeping it between me and the old man, and went
inside.

It was black as pitch except for a few narrow beams of light slipping through cracks in the thatch. There was no one there, so after a hurried look around, and glancing out to make sure no one was watching, I slipped over to the next hooch. It seemed an incredibly long distance, but it probably wasn't over fifty feet. I was sure someone would hear my footsteps, but when I glanced back, all the peasants were still looking at Hercules and Mike.

This was the one with the rifle. There was also an old woman, on a reed mat on the side farthest from the door. I didn't see her at first—I took her for just a bundle of rags. I was looking for the rifle, and found it. It was either Japanese or Chinese, from the inscriptions on the metal. It definitely was not a modern weapon. It took only a second to strip out the bolt and slip it into my pants pocket, and then I was ready to go back outside.

Then the old woman moaned. I was startled, and I turned quickly toward the sound, ready to shoot. Then I saw her. After a moment of hesitation, I went over to her. Either she was very sick, or senile, or both. She looked right at me and didn't blink an eye. I expected her to be frightened and begin to scream, but she only moaned some more and touched her lips with one leathery old hand. I was going to leave, but with her other hand she had a hold on my trouser leg and tugged insistently at it. She kept touching her lips with her fingers. Finally, I got the idea: She wanted a drink. She probably was so blind or so senile, she thought I was just one of the villagers. I thought, shit, why should I give water to an old gook? Her kids may be shooting at me in ten minutes. But I found myself pouring some water out of a pot into a bowl and holding the bowl to her lips. She drank a little, maybe four or five drops, and then lay back. I set the bowl down and backed away.

When I stepped outside, Hercules and Mike were standing in front of the other hooch with the old man, and Hercules was talking to him in a low-pitched voice. One or two of the villagers saw me then. I watched them closely. Had one of them bent down, as if to pick something up, he would have been dead before he could have straightened up.

Hercules said something to him, and he called out to the people in the paddies, waving with his arm for them to come in. It was a peculiar gesture, not the bent-arm wave of an American but a pushing away. I could imagine what he was saying, although I could understand none of it. He was probably saying to come here, these young men wish to ask us questions.

Brewster came quietly across the bridge, and this caused another stir among the villagers. The boy saw us and tugged insistently at the sleeve of the old man's pajamas. The old man brushed him off a couple of times but finally said something sharply to him. The boy replied and pointed, and the old man turned slowly. His face registered surprise, confusion, and fear for a moment, before he got control. Brewster and I were by that time thirty feet behind him.

"See anything?" I asked Brewster.

"Jist a bunch of bowls and crap," he said. "Pigs an' dogs. Shacks, like th' pore folks in th' hills back home. You see anything?"

"I found th' rifle," I told him, "an' took this." I showed him the bolt. "There was an old woman in there . . . sick or dyin', I reckon. She saw me, but she never knew but what I was one of them."

"She's prolly Viet Cong," he replied sarcastically, "playin' possum. Ye should've drug her outside, where we could watch her."

"None of these people has gone to check on her," I pointed out. "Bet they don't give a damn if she lives or dies."

"Prolly wish she'd die," he pointed out. "One less mouth to feed."

"Yer a cheerful bastard, ain't ye?"

"Jist reelistic."

When Hercules finished talking to the villagers, he waved to us to come on, and we walked out. We walked off down the trail until we got out of the villagers' sight around a bend. Then we slipped off into the brush and watched to see if anybody left the village or tried to follow us. They stood around in a group talking to one another for a half an hour or so, then the old man went back to his hut, and the others went back to the fields. If one slipped away, we damned sure missed it.

We worked our way across the creek and up the hillside in back of the village and met up with Ivy League and Harlow.

Hercules briefed us on what he'd learned. He'd translated for Mike as they'd talked to the villagers, so now he directed his words to the rest of us.

"They know the Viet Cong here," he said, "but they say they do not like the Viet Cong; they are not Viet Cong themselves. When the Viet Cong first came here, there were not many, and they ate little rice. They were men from the lowlands. They were nice men—they paid for their rice, or worked in the paddies to earn it. Now there are many Viet Cong. They come from the north, and they are not always nice men. Sometimes they pay for their rice, sometimes they take rice and pigs without paying and say it is a tax. They have taken the young men from the village to make soldiers of them. They have taken the young girls for prostitutes in their camps and have not paid for them. This makes hardship for the parents, for there are not enough hands to work the fields or to cut trees in the mountains. They have also told the young men that they must be brave and not run away—if they run away, the Viet Cong will come and kill their parents.

Last week, the Viet Cong came and killed the parents of
Quoc Kim, who ran away in a fight. Now the grandmother
is very ill, and her care is a burden on her remaining
family, and indeed on all the village. This much I believe.

"They also say they will not tell the Viet Cong we came
if the Viet Cong come into their village again, nor will
any one of them go and tell the Viet Cong. This I do not
believe.

"I told them we would watch their village for three
days, in case the Viet Cong come, and if they come, we
will kill them.

"They say they do not know where the Viet Cong camp
is, but they told me with their eyes that the Viet Cong
come down the stream from above the village."

"I think we ought to go upstream and look for this
camp," Mike said. "But let's hear from the rest of you."

"That's what we're here for, ain't it?" I said.

"Let's go get 'em," said Brewster.

Harlow didn't say anything. He just grunted and spit
tobacco juice at an ant.

Ivy League nodded in agreement, and added, "I think
we ought to prepare a surprise for Charley, if he comes
up here looking for us."

"What?" said Brewster.

"A booby trap?" asked Mike, nodding his head thoughtfully.

"Sure," Ivy League said. "Something like Charley
would leave for us. A calling card, so to speak."

We didn't really want to leave many of our claymores
behind, so we got busy and came up with something like
what Charley would've thought up. Brewster and I slipped
back down the hillside and across the creek, and I watched
while he set a claymore to cover the main trail right where
we'd left it to come into the bush. He set the trip wire so
that if anybody came just a little ways off the trail, along
the way we'd come, it would get him and anybody stand-

ing on the trail, too. When we got back to the creek, Hercules and Mike were there. Hercules put a trip wire across the log we used to cross the creek—obvious enough that Charley would see it, but concealed enough to make it look like he'd tried to cover it up. Then he cut dozens of punji sticks and stuck them in the mud of the creek bottom on either side of the log, and at reasonable-looking crossing sites up and down the stream for ten or fifteen meters. The trip wire wasn't connected to anything, of course.

Back at the spot where Ivy League and Harlow had watched the village, Harlow had rigged up a broken sapling so that if you put any weight on it when you stepped over it to get to the scuffed-up area where they'd sat and watched, it pulled a white phosphorus grenade off a limb overhead. The grenade would fall far enough to yank the pin, which was partly out already, but a little piece of wire kept it from falling very far. It would go off about eight feet in the air, and scatter that shit all over. . . . Diving for cover wouldn't help any, either. He was a sly devil, that Harlow.

We moved off the hillside toward the creek and came to it about half a click above the village. Sure enough, we cut a trail along the creek bank. It obviously didn't see a lot of traffic, but there had been some. And there were different kinds of tracks on it, too—boot tracks, like those made by the boots the NVA wore. We didn't follow the trail but worked our way through the bush slightly up the slope from it, moving down just often enough to check and make sure that we were still moving along beside it, that it hadn't turned away from us somewhere along the way.

We kept moving until it turned quite dark, then held up for a while, to let our eyes get adjusted. After a short conference, we decided to press on. We would keep moving up the creek under the assumption that the Viet Cong camp was up this way.

Then we came to a fork in the stream. Of course, we couldn't see that that's what it was, in the dark, but we could see in the moonlight, where the trees were thin enough, that the main valley went on in the direction we'd been traveling, but the slope of the ground had changed as we pushed on that way, and we soon came to the stream. Which way to turn? Up the tributary, or follow the main stream? We didn't think we'd crossed the trail, but we might have missed it in the dark.

We were split about whether to go on or wait until daylight. So Mike made the decision. We'd wait until it got lighter. We pulled back up the hill and found a spot of very dense undergrowth to conceal us and settled down to wait through the darker hours of the night.

I swallowed a salt tablet with some water, and then cleaned off my M-14 with my shirt tail. I broke out some C-rats and ate enough to keep me going and went to sleep. Brewster had first watch.

We got going again before it was fully light. We worked back across the valley and couldn't find the trail. So we backtracked and tried to find where we'd lost it in the dark. We came upon the patrol about 1100.

There were seven of them, and they were moving very carelessly. Several of them even had their rifles slung, and they sort of slouched along. We followed them and found the camp.

CHAPTER 10

The camp was tucked away in a patch of extra-thick bamboo and ferns on a side tributary of the main stream. It was built at the base of a horseshoe-shaped ledge that hung over a spring. The trees were pretty tall here, and the VC had cleared out a little patch of underbrush to put their hooches on. You'd have to fly right over the spring in a helicopter to see the camp, and they'd cleared the underbrush back from the ledge, too, so no one could slip in and spy on them from that direction without being seen.

Hercules and Mike slipped on in closer to get a better look. After an hour, they came back and said there was a better spot on the south side of the clearing, so we moved over that way.

We had to cross the trail leading in, and we were hardly ten meters beyond it—I was bringing up the rear this time—when the VC sent a patrol out. It wasn't hard to avoid them. They were chattering like a bunch of school kids. There were ten of them—an awful lot for a perimeter patrol. Hercules listened to their monkey chatter and said they were a foraging party going to get rice, probably from the village down the creek.

It was only a matter of time, then, until they found out about us.

We moved on around to the spot they'd picked, and this time I slipped in with Hercules and Mike to look at the place. There was a sentry close by, and we had to be really quiet, but we sneaked in close enough to get a good view. We needed to count the people and to see how often the sentries were changed. If there was an ammo dump or something in the camp, we wanted to know about that, too. Hercules would try to listen in as they talked, to pick up anything important they might be saying.

There seemed to be three or four sentries around the camp, at first observation. Two or three other fellows standing around with slung rifles were probably sentries, too, guarding something inside the camp. They were lax, and we were pretty sure this camp hadn't been hit in the past.

We kept watching all the rest of the day. They changed the sentries every two hours, and we finally figured out that, counting the patrol that went out, there were forty-five or fifty men, plus a few women and children.

About 1800, a runner came up the trail the patrol had gone out on, and there was immediate excitement. While he was catching his breath, Hercules slipped in as close as he dared, to hear what the runner had to say. There was a lot of arm-waving and chattering, and then someone who was obviously in charge sent out eight men. They went out with their weapons unslung, and two of them carried what looked like rolls of canvas over their shoulders.

Hercules worked his way slowly back to where Mike and I were crouched, waiting. Now there was an unusual amount of activity in the camp. A Viet Cong, a noncom, I'd say, went around to all the sentries and harassed them a little. An empty spot on the odd watch was quickly filled. They put together a six-man patrol that went out into the bush a hundred or two hundred meters to prowl around—a security patrol.

"That patrol we saw going out earlier went to the village," Hercules told us when he got back to where we waited. "The villagers told them we'd been there, as we thought they would. When they heard there were but four of us, they made the village chief show them where we'd gone. The claymore killed four of them, including the village chief, and there are some injured. They have gone out to bring the injured back. A search patrol will be organized from the rest to look for us. There will also be patrols close around the camp for security."

It was too bad about the old man. That's the bad thing about booby traps—they're not selective. Of course, he was half blind and pretty old. He didn't have too many years left, anyway.

We worked our way past the sentry and back to the others to tell them the news. The question for now was, did we have enough information, or should we stay around and try to learn some more?

We were strongly outnumbered here, by at least six to one, and the VC were now aware that we were in the area. The helicopter was due in tomorrow to resupply us, or to pull us out if need be. We could pull out now, and no one would blame us: We'd done our job. We could stay in the area and harass Charley, keep him off balance, until a stronger force was assembled and brought in. Or we could hit the camp ourselves. I knew what the Chief would say: "Six or eight of them to one SEAL? Hell, that gives 'em a fightin' chance!" But I knew I didn't want them to have a fighting chance. Not at all.

"I'd sure as hell like to know what's in that one hooch," Mike said. "It might be an ammo dump."

"But how are we going to find out?" Ivy League asked.

"I will go in," said Hercules. "I would like to know also. I will walk in as one of them."

"Shit, no, man—that's too risky," Mike told him.

We tried to talk him out of it, but he was subborn, and in the end, we worked out a plan. Two stayed behind, watching the camp. Four of us, including Hercules, went out along the trail, keeping a careful eye out for security patrols, and waited for the patrol to return from the village with the wounded. When they came up the trail, they walked only a few inches from my face, and none of them ever saw me in the dark. They were following the trail, which of course wasn't a good idea with Special Forces around, but then I guess it would have been awfully tough to haul those litters through the underbrush at night. There were two litter cases, and one walking wounded. Counting the three who were supposed to be dead, that was five down. They must have bunched up.

There wasn't any chattering as they went by. The point man—they had one out about twenty-five meters ahead of them on the trail—was looking around really carefully, or so he thought. He didn't see any of us, of course. He stopped so close to me I could've reached out and tied his shoelaces together, if he had any. A couple of soldiers followed him, also crouching and alert, and then the litter-bearers. They were huffing and blowing, and cursing under their breaths. After the litter-bearers was the fellow who was walking wounded. I couldn't see how bad he was hurt, but he was getting along without help. Slowly. Two more brought up the rear. They would move and stop and look around and move again.

The last one stopped and looked around a little too long, and his companion moved out of sight. When he turned to go on, I put my hand over his mouth and pulled his head back and cut his throat. He stiffened and tried to fight when I got my hand over his mouth. If he'd pulled the trigger, he would've warned the others, but his only thoughts were for survival. He dropped the rifle and tried to grab my wrist and pull my arm away. Of course, he was too late. His hands had just touched my wrist when I put the knife against his neck and pulled it across. It went smoothly—my knife was sharp. His head nearly came off in my hand. His blood spurted out all over me. I pulled his body over into the brush while his legs were still jerking. Hercules stepped in, stripped the rice bag off the man's shoulder and slung it over his own, picked up his rifle, and took his place in line in a matter of seconds.

I dragged the body off into the brush and hid it. Tomorrow, they might find it by following the blood trail. Not tonight.

The remaining three of us went back to our vantage point by the camp, so we could help cover Hercules's escape if he was detected. On the way, the gook security patrol almost stumbled over us. We had to hold up while they went past, but they were not sharp. After that night, they would be more alert. The delay was enough that the litter detail got back to the village before we could get into position to watch. I almost expected firing to break out before we got there, when they discovered Hercules, but the only sounds were the commonplace jungle sounds.

"It was *so cool*," Brewster whispered. "He just walked rat in there like he was one of 'em! The first ones to get there was all tellin' their stories, an' there was lots of 'em gawking' at th' wounded ones on th' stretchers, an' he jist walks rat in, an' nobody ever blinked a eye or looked at 'im twice. He jist went rat on about his business, like he done that everyday."

"Which one is he?" I asked. In the light from the fires, they all looked just alike to me.

"Don't know," he whispered back. "He jist kind of blended in with 'em. Sort of disappeared."

It sure seemed like a long time before he came out, the same way he went in: He just attached himself to a relief security patrol and got lost from them. Of course, we couldn't tell it was him from where we were, and we goddamned near cut his throat when he came up through the bush from one side. We'd been expecting him to slip out from behind the hooches. I noticed a blood smear on his knife sheath.

He'd found out that the guarded hooch held a radio. He hadn't been able to get into the hooch, but he had heard the receiver, and saw an aerial strung from the roof to a tree. There was also an ammo dump of sorts, in another of the hooches, but it was nothing really big.

There had been some talk, though: They were expecting some large rockets in a matter of a few days, and then they expected to strike a camp somewhere.

Everyone agreed we had what we had come for. So we picked up our claymores—we'd set them out in case we had to give Hercules covering fire if he was discovered—and slipped away from the camp, back down toward the village.

We traveled pretty fast once we got away from that camp, even though the jungle was quite dark and thick. I was glad to get away—there were just too damned many of them in there, and they were so spread out it would have been hard to get even half of them with our five remaining claymores. As we approached the village, though, I began to feel a little bit tense again. There was a patrol looking for us that we knew might be anywhere in these hills.

We decided to circle the village on the near side. We climbed up a hundred meters or so, and then started moving very cautiously across the hillside. Where the jungle opened up a little, you could see across the creek. Ivy

League squatted down and studied the village with a Starlight scope. There was nothing moving in the village, along the creek, or up on the hillside, so we crossed the creek down below the rice paddies, where the jungle covered both banks.

Half a click out from the LZ clearing, there was some evidence of patrol activity: tracks, broken twigs, and such. We had to check first to make sure that it was the right clearing, and second to make sure that Charley hadn't set up an ambush there. We'd sprayed patches of paint that fluoresced under blacklight on several of those broad-leaved bushes that look like big rubber plants, along the path we took away from the clearing, so it was easy to identify. Then we began to patrol around it to make sure there wasn't an ambush or booby traps waiting for us.

We spread out about forty meters into the jungle, in a sort of zigzag line, and moved clockwise around it. We each tried to keep at least one other person in sight as we moved, so as it got darker and darker, the line drew together. I carried a Starlight scope, and Mike, on my left, and Harlow, on my right, both had blacklights. Mike had gotten a little bit ahead of me when we found a sign that Charley had been there. It was a booby trap, and it was Mike that found it.

I heard him grunt—a sort of "Hunh!"—and then I heard a *whish* and a meaty *thunk*, followed by a low groan. My first thought was that he'd been hit with something. In a low crouch, looking all around, I moved toward him. So did Harlow and Brewster. Hercules came in from the other side.

"Oh, shit!" Brewster said.

I was glad it was pretty dark when I saw Mike, or the others would've seen how green I turned. He was about six feet off the ground, hanging by one foot from a snare. It was a sling-snare, like you might set to catch game with. It had been attached to a bent-over sapling, and when the sapling was released, it had yanked him off the ground and over into a bed of sharpened bamboo spikes—punji sticks—imbedded in a tree. He was dead. One of the spikes protruded from his chest, and another through his throat.

"He never said a fuckin' word," Brewster said. "Never screamed . . . nothin'."

Mike's rifle lay near him. He'd held on to it until he hit. A gouge in the dirt showed where he'd tried to dig it in and stop himself.

"Not a fuckin' word," Brewster said again. There was admiration in his voice.

The patrol all gathered around us. Fortunately, the Viet Cong didn't hit us while all our attention was focused on getting Mike's body down.

Harlow was pretty shook. He kept trying to find signs of life, even though we kept telling him there was no fucking chance. When he finally accepted that the guy was dead, he started weeping. Not crying—that's what kids and women do. He sat there and swallowed hard, and didn't make any noise except for a low moan sometimes, or grinding his teeth, but tears made tracks down both his cheeks.

"God damn, Mike," he kept saying. "God damn . . . God damn."

We sat there a few minutes, all of us feeling sick, all of us glad we weren't the one that stepped in that hellish contraption, and all of us wondering whether or not if we had, could we have kept from screaming out when we realized what was happening. Then Hercules began to get agitated about the Viet Cong finding us and wanted to move on. We helped Harlow get Mike's body over his shoulder, and moved out. We had to finish the patrol. I hunted around the area of the snare until I found the blacklight. We didn't want Charley to get his hands on that.

You'd better bet we moved a lot slower, and looked around pretty sharp. Harlow, carrying Mike's body, slowed us down—he got tired, part way around, but wouldn't let anyone else carry it. And, of course, no one wanted to repeat Mike's final experience. When we finished our patrol, it was already time for the helicopter to get there.

We still wanted to check inside the clearing, so Brewster and Hercules worked their way toward its center in a zigzag pattern, moving, stopping, looking around. They weren't halfway when I first heard the whop-whop of helicopter rotors.

I called Hercules and Brewster on the walkie-talkie.

"How does it look out there?"

"Clear, so far as we kin tell," Brewster called back. "Tell 'im to come on in."

So I called the helicopter on the pack radio.

"Whiskey One-Niner, Badger Four. Are ye a-listenin'? Over."

"I read you, Badger Four. Go ahead. Over."

"It looks clear. Ye can come on in. Over."

"Roger, Badger Four. ETA about two minutes. Can you be waitin' at th' station? Over."

"Mighty fine, Badger Four. Out."

The sound of the rotors was getting much louder. It was obvious they would be here in a matter of seconds, so we shouldered our loads and started out. Harlow picked up Mike's body, with some help from Ivy League and me, I took the pack radio, Ivy League took Mike's M-16, and we started humping out toward the middle of the clearing. With a sudden fluttering roar, two Huey gunships swept low over the clearing and on toward the hills. The Huey slick was close behind. He slowed over the clearing, tilting back like a horse rearing up, and then settled into the grass about twenty meters from Brewster and Hercules. We started running, but not too fast, Ivy

League and I both keeping an eye on Harlow, who had the biggest load. He breathed noisily, in loud rasping gasps, and he sort of stumbled and crashed through the grass under his load. He carried the body in a fireman's carry, and the one free arm dangling down kept hitting his heel. For a moment it was like watching a scene in a movie: In a shell of darkness, I saw two legs pumping in short quick steps, and a dangling hand that kept flopping against one heel and getting kicked up and back. . . . I was acutely aware of the sounds, as if it was the movie soundtrack: Harlow's hoarse "unhh-hunh!" as he gasped for breath, the thump of our feet hitting the ground, the crackling of the grass as we crashed through, the muted beat of the helicopter rotors, the backfires of its engine . . . backfires?

"What the hell?" said Ivy League just about that time.

I jerked my attention away from Mike's hand.

We were taking fire from the treeline to our left. It was semiautomatic, small-arms fire, making sharp, firecrackerlike snapping sounds. AK-47s. Hercules and Brewster were answering it—Hercules's M-16 sounding like a popcorn popper at high heat, and Brewster's shotgun puncturing the night with authoritative booms. The VC fire seemed to be directed at the helicopter. At least it wasn't hitting around us.

For a moment I thought how crazy it was to be running right into enemy fire like this. Just then, Harlow went down, sending Mike's body rolling over and over through the grass. I thought he'd been shot.

"Oh, *shit*! Oh, God *damn*!" he shouted.

Both Ivy League and I hesitated for just a second. Then I tossed the pack radio to him and went back to get Harlow.

"Put it in th' chopper!" I yelled to Ivy League. "I'll help Harlow!"

He was struggling to get to his feet when I got to him. His right foot seemed to be anchored to the ground.

"Unh...unh...unh," he was groaning as he hopped in an arc on his left foot. What the shit? I thought. He can't be shot and be acting that way! I got to him and slipped his arm over my shoulder just as his foot came loose. "Aaargh!" he cried, not so much a scream as an angry snarl. "Punji stick! Aaaah, God Almighty damn it to hell, motherfuck! It's still in there—it's still in my foot!" He'd wrenched the stick loose from the ground. His arm over my shoulder, we started toward the helicopter, him hopping along on one foot and cursing to beat the devil.

The helicopter had come in with its nose toward us so we wouldn't have to approach past the tail rotor. That meant its M-60 machine gun was on the wrong side to fire at the treeline, but it was detachable, and the gunner was already in the right-side doorway, cradling the weapon in his arms and pouring a stream of tracers into the treeline. Brewster, having tossed his useless shotgun in, grabbed Mike's M-16 and started emptying the magazine in the appropriate direction.

When we passed Mike's body, Harlow began yelling. "Don't leave him! Don't leave him!"

"I'll get 'im. I'll come back," I lied. I had no intention of getting him. I just wanted to get my ass on the helicopter and out of that clearing before the VC started working it over with mortars.

Ivy League ran back to help me with Harlow. Harlow pushed him away.

"Get Mike...get Mike!" he kept yelling. He tried to break free and go back. I thought I was going to have to deck him before we could get him on the bird. In less time than it takes to tell it, though, he stepped down on that injured foot and passed out with a short yelp of pain. Ivy League helped me carry him.

"Get in! Get in! Let's get the fuck outta here!" the helicopter pilot was yelling—he was yelling in my ear, or I wouldn't have heard him over the sound of the machine gun firing. I turned to look at Brewster and Hercules, who were backing toward us and firing as they came. Harlow had come around, and as he lay there on the floor of the chopper, he was hollering at me, too. I couldn't hear him, but I could tell what he was saying.

"Don't leave Mike! Don't leave him!"

The pilot grabbed my arm and gave a pull.

"Come on, God damn it, get in!" he yelled in my ear. He was tanned but had turned pale, giving his face a yellow hue. He was sweating, and his eyes were big and wild.

I guess it was the pilot's fright that changed my mind. I had had every intention of leaving that body out there and saving my own ass. But I sort of resented the flyboys, and this one was so scared he was about to shit in his pants. . . . I didn't want him to think I was, too, I suppose.

"There's one more," I shouted at him.

"Is it th' KIA?" I nodded. "Leave 'im. They can't hurt 'im now! Let's go." Harlow was shaking his head angrily from side to side. I liked Harlow.

"I ain't leavin' him out there fer them little bastards to cut on!" I told the pilot. I broke away and went back. Brewster and Hercules were by this time about ready to jump onto the chopper; Ivy League was firing from inside the door. Brewster shot me a wondering, wide-eyed look as I darted past him.

A rocket grenade exploded in the clearing about forty meters beyond the helicopter. There still weren't any tracers coming from the treeline, but I could see an occasional muzzle flash as I ran. Some of them came from the grass this side of the treeline. The helicopter engine began to rev up.

I had a devil of a time getting the body onto my back. He was still limber, and just absolutely dead weight—no pun intended. First I tried the fireman's carry. I could sit him up and get his arm over my shoulder, but I couldn't get his butt off the ground. I kept thinking about how we'd had to help Harlow pick him up and how I was going to feel like a goddamned fool if I had to leave him after all. I wished that someone would come help me, and I hoped they wouldn't hit the helicopter with a rocket grenade before I could get back.

Somebody else was worrying about those rocket grenades, too: the pilot. The roar of that engine kept getting louder and louder, the whop-whop! of the rotor blades sharper and sharper, and I knew he intended to take off without me. I took a quick look over that way to make sure he wasn't lifting off already, and I saw the gunships make their first run on the woods. They'd circled around over the hills, and it took them a little while to get back. Now they hosed down the edge of the woods with rockets and miniguns. It was like the Fourth of July. In the flare from the explosions and from the glow of the almost solid stream of tracers from the miniguns, I thought I could see several figures running, falling, cartwheeling through the air . . . but of course, they may have been just limbs from the trees. From out of that hell rose a single yellow trail of flame—a rocket grenade, probably fired just as the firer was hit and went down, shooting straight up then falling back harmlessly.

I got Mike's body sitting upright again, then got down on my knees astride his legs, stuck my shoulder in his belly, and grabbed the seat of his pants. I was able to pull him forward until his weight was on my back and raise myself on my hands and knees. I stood up, thinking it was a good way to get a hernia.

I got the body back to the helicopter all right. The gunships had taken care of the Viet Cong, and there were no more shots from the jungle. I found Brewster squatting behind the pilot, cradling his shotgun and grinning like a possum in a henhouse.

"This lettle feller thought he was a-goin' to leave ye," he said, "until I convinced 'im he wasn't."

"Horseshit," I told him. "I know ye better'n that. You was a-tellin' him to get yer ass outta there! In a hurry!"

CHAPTER 11

After we got back to Cao Lanh and Harlow was taken to the hospital, we reported to some Army Intelligence people—a Green Beret major was in charge. We told him where the camp was, how many VC there were, and that they were getting built up to hit one of our camps somewhere. We told him about the radio and about the rockets they were supposed to get. We told him how many we'd killed and how we'd been hit when we started to get on the helicopter. We told about the village and how many people were in it. Hercules did most of the talking. He knew the major personally. They seemed to be old friends.

"Can we get ye to call BSU-One and have 'em swing by to pick us up, sir?" I asked. I wasn't used to having to say "sir" to an officer anymore. Lieutenant Commander Gray didn't insist on it.

"Well, you'd better stick around," the major said. "We

aren't through with you yet. We'll have to hit that Viet Cong camp, and we'll need you fellows to beef up our patrol and guide it in."

"We gotta go back there *again*?" Brewster asked. He was a little agitated. The little Green Beret major blinked four or five times right fast, twirled his little pointy moustache, and grinned like he wasn't playing with a full deck.

"You fellows should know that place like your own backyards by now," he said.

"I ain't seen my backyard in goddamn near four months," I told him, "but I seen *that* fuckin' place yesterday."

"We want you to go back and keep an eye on them, that's all. Let us know if they're building up to attack somewhere, or if our patrols in the last several days have caused them to cancel their plans."

"They'll be waitin' fer us," Brewster told him. The Lieutenant nodded his head; he agreed. But the major shook his.

"No . . . we won't send you in the same way. This time we'll send you in by boat. See this river?" He pointed to the map. A narrow and sinuous river ran almost parallel to the Bassac for several miles, then swung up toward the Seven Mountains. It wasn't big, but when you looked at the water depths, it was deep enough to run a PBR on. "We can get a boat up to this point. There's a cut-off here, and where it leaves the main channel it forms a kind of lake about four hundred meters across—plenty of room to turn around, plenty of room to drop somebody off. A patrol could go ashore here. There's been a patrol boat running up this far every third day or so, so there wouldn't be anything to tip Charley off. And from here, it's not such a long walk up to that camp, either. You ought to be able to make it in two hours, maybe three. The boats don't usually go any farther upstream because of a sandbar across the mouth of the main channel here. They tell me there's a tidal effect—though I find that hard to believe—and it's enough that the bar is awash sometimes. They might get in and not be able to get back out. So you'll have a little walking to do.

"When you get to the camp, lay low. You're just there to report on activity. When, or if, it looks like they've built up their forces and are just about ready to hit somewhere, contact us, and we'll send in a strike force."

"Why don't ye just send the strike force in now, instead of us?" Brewster asked.

"We want to wait until the buildup has peaked...so the attack will cause the greatest possible damage."

"Damage to *who*?" Brewster inquired insolently. "Them or us?"

The little major ignored him. He pointed to the map with a long chrome pointer.

"This is the Special Forces camp we call Fort Ticonderoga—it's only about five clicks from the camp you'll be watching. The area in between is intensively patrolled by the Viet Cong, but if you need to get the hell out fast, you could probably get there without too much trouble. Your radio won't reach us from down in that valley—you'll have to move up onto a hill or onto the ridge to get in contact, and then I suspect you'll only be able to reach Fort Ticonderoga. Your code name will be Mohawk Sierra Four. Fort Ticonderoga will answer to 'Fort Ti' or to Choctaw Charlie One—use Choctaw Charlie One, because we think the VC may know where and what Fort Ti is.

"The same group that made the last patrol will go again tonight. I'll beef it up some, but there's really not many men available. Any questions?"

The major kept his promise to beef up the patrol. Just before time to load up and go out, a helicopter came in with a single SEAL aboard. It was Billy, his greens as neat and clean as if he was just climbing off the plane into Saigon for the first time.

"Jeezus Christ! The kid's still wet behind the ears!" Brewster growled.

"Hell, look on the bright side," I said. "At least he's a SEAL." And to the kid, I said, "Just stick with the rest of us. Do what we do. Keep yer eyes open—you'll be okay."

At least I hoped he would be. But there were lots of ways to die out there.

I thought about Mike, caught in that damned sling, knowing he was going to die but not making a sound louder than a grunt and a groan, so that he wouldn't give us away to the Viet Cong. Of course, he hadn't had a long time to think about it, just a second or so.

All the way back to Cao Lanh, with that damned punji stick sticking out of his foot, Harlow had gritted his teeth and had cursed the pain, but mostly he had cried about his buddy Mike.

In addition to Billy, the Special Forces major got us a lieutenant and three enlisted men from the 101st Airborne and one of his own Green Berets. The problem was, nine men were too many to move quickly or escape observation for long without a large helping of luck.

A PBR took us upriver about sunset. We skirted around floating snags and skimmed over sandbars as we got further up the river, and the jungle along the banks got thicker and taller. By the time we got to the oxbow where we were to drop off, it was pitch dark, and you couldn't see the hills, just big black shadows blotting out the stars.

I took the point.

Being point man is a lonely sort of a job. You're mostly out there by yourself leading off in the general direction the patrol is to go. But you don't follow a straight line. You go over here and over there, and if there's a thick clump of brush that might be hiding a Charley you check it out. If you come to a trail where there might be an ambush, you check it out. If you think there might be mines or booby traps somewhere, you check it out. It's your job to find the ambushes, the mines, and the snipers before the rest of the patrol gets there. You have a radio—the little walkie-talkie kind. If it's all clear, you call up the patrol.

There may be somebody else in command of the patrol, a lieutenant or a sergeant or a chief petty officer, but the point man is really in charge, regardless of rank. It's his responsibility to see that a patrol gets where it's supposed to go without being ambushed or spotted.

The little radios had a button you pushed to talk, and you could signal with it. We usually set up a series of signals in advance: one buzz—come on up, it's clear; two buzzes—come on up, but be cautious, there's a Charley up here; three buzzes—hold where you are. Something like that. If you could talk without being overheard, it was better to give instructions: "Come on up, but watch to the right, there's a Victor Charley patrol over there." Or: "I've found a booby trap . . . I've disarmed it, but there might be others. Hold there while I check it out." The point man was usually the first one killed in a firefight; he was the one that stepped on the mines and set off the booby traps; he was usually the one that got sniped. Not always.

When the patrol moved, the men would come up one or two at a time. They'd zigzag from bush to bush and look around, all directions, and come on again. That's just how the point man moved, too. You had to look in ALL directions: front, back, sides, up, down. And it was dark most of the time, because we patrolled at night by preference. But you didn't just look for Charley, you listened for him, too. He made noises moving through the brush, just like you did. He talked . . . not always in a low voice, either. A lot of them used dope—heroin, that kind of stuff—and they'd chatter away like they were walking down a goddamned street while they were out there on patrol, and you could hear them fifty or a hundred meters away. And you smelled him out.... You used your nose. Charley smoked, and sometimes he smoked pot; you could smell it twenty or thirty meters away. Campfires, of course, you could smell a lot further. And he loved a damn stinking fish sauce called *nuoc-mam*. If he was close you could smell it on his breath. Sometimes you could just sense that somebody was looking at you, watching you. On a really dark night, or in those places where the trees were so thick overhead, that's all you had to go by: hearing, smell, and what they call "sixth sense."

If that sounds slow . . . well, it wasn't. An Army patrol, or somebody not familiar with the jungle, might take an hour or two to move one click. We would move three in two hours.

This night, we passed through a fringe of jungle down by the river, then we had to cross rice paddies. Fortunately it was quite dark by that time. We stayed away from the paddy dikes. That's where the Army liked to walk, and the ARVNs, so that's where Charley put his mines and booby traps. We waded through that stinking sludge in the paddies, black fine mud, rotting plants, and manure—human and otherwise. I'd go maybe forty or fifty yards ahead, hold, and call the patrol up. On the other side of the paddies was broken, open jungle and scrub brush, so we made good time there. Just a little over an hour passed before we found a landmark and knew we were within half a click of the camp. Time to take it easy and look for perimeter patrols.

Shortly after that, we heard them.

I called the Lieutenant up. "Hear that?"

He listened for a few seconds.

"What th' hell?" He scratched his head and his chin and thought about it.

The rest of the patrol moved up one by one, listened, shrugged, and said they didn't know.

Ivy League ventured to answer. "Sounds like they're having a pep rally."

"You may not be far from right," the Lieutenant said.

We went in closer, moving very cautiously, on the lookout for security patrols around the camp. We didn't see any. The sounds grew louder and louder as we got closer, and you could start to pick out individual voices. Some of them were just hollering; others were chanting. The sound came in waves, louder for a while and then receding.

When I got near the edge of the clearing, I got down on my hands and knees and slipped in a little closer. They had a bonfire going that lit everything up. All the people in the clearing were armed, and a lot of them had packs on their shoulders. Some had their weapons slung, and others carried them in their hands. Most had on the typical Viet Cong black pajama outfit, though a number of them wore green uniforms: NVA. A bunch were just milling around, shooting up dope, and drinking beer or wine—something in bottles, anyway. A bunch more were standing around listening to another fellow chant. He'd say some things in a singsong voice, his voice rising and falling, and he'd end on a high, loud note, holding it for a second or two. When he did that, all the group standing around watching him would roar back at him. Not only did it sound like a pep rally, it looked like one, too.

I called the Lieutenant up.

"Come on up here, Lieutenant," I said to the radio. "But fer God's sake, keep down. They got a fire goin' that lights up half the goddamned valley. You'd better come on up here an' look at this."

He came up, and he studied the situation for a long time. At least it seemed like a long time to me. Then he slipped back out, and signaled me to come with him.

Back in the jungle, we got together for a council of war.

"They're gettin' ready for an attack," the Lieutenant said. "What they're going to attack can't be too far away. They're getting all boozed up and doped up, and there must be seventy, maybe a hundred, of them in there. They're going to overrun something. Probably Fort Ti . . . it's the closest camp anywhere around. To make it worse, they're just about ready to move out. We haven't got much time to act. The question is—what do we do now? Do we hit them before they move out, or do we head over to Fort Ti and try to warn them? Or do we climb up on the ridge and call in an air strike?"

Nobody said anything for a little while. We were all thinking over the odds, I guess. Then one of the 101st paratroopers spoke up.

"If they're about ready to move out, an air strike wouldn't get here in time."

"You're right," the Lieutenant said.

"I reckon we got to do both them other things," I said finally. We were wasting time squatting there in a circle and spitting on the ground. "We better get word to that Fort Ti place, an' we got to hold 'em up here so our runners have time to get through. Them Viet Congs'll move pretty fast when they move out."

Just about everybody agreed, though nobody wanted to be the one to say it.

The Lieutenant picked one of the 101st Airborne troopers and the Green Beret. He gave our radio to the trooper.

"You get up on that ridge," he said, "and get them on this radio, and warn them an overrun attack is coming. If you don't raise them in five minutes, get the hell out and try to make it on foot." He turned to the Green Beret. "You know where Fort Ti is. . . . Go straight there on foot, in case the radio doesn't make contact. We can give you a fifteen-minute head start. No more. You have any explosives? Any claymores? Leave them here. Just take your rifles. Good luck, and get moving!"

We pooled our resources then. We had four claymore mines; five pounds, more or less, of C-4 explosive; Brewster's shotgun, a grenade launcher, and five rifles. Not much to stop a hundred doped-up men. But we had something else: surprise.

We split up the claymore mines and the explosives among the seven of us. We decided to creep in as far as we could and set the mines and the charges, timing them so that some went off right away, and others at odd intervals. Three claymores would be fired right off, to do the most damage. Then the C-4 charge and the last claymore would be set with trip wires, to cover our withdrawal.

"We have to move fast, to hit them before they start to move out," the Lieutenant said, "so you'll have exactly five minutes to spread into position and set your charges. No more than that, so don't try to go too far. At the five-minute mark, we'll trigger the first claymores, and then we'll start shooting. Conserve your ammunition. . . . Just snipe at them. Don't spray the whole goddamned area. We can hold them ten minutes or so. . . . There's so damned many of them, they'll swamp us after that. We'll rendezvous right here in fifteen minutes exactly. Anybody that's late will get left. Got that? Fifteen minutes exactly. All right . . . check your watches . . . now! Let's move out, and remember: fifteen minutes. See you here."

He started moving out. I looked over at Brewster. He was scratching his butt. He'd been complaining about worms lately. He slipped off toward the camp. I didn't expect ever to see him again.

Ivy League shot me a funny look as he moved out, like he wasn't expecting to come back either. The two troopers moved off toward the same flank. I turned around and went back in to the spot where I'd been observing the camp.

I crawled in even further to set up the claymore. The Viet Cong were obviously about to move out. They were all bunched up into three or four different groups, and a bunch of fellows I took to be noncoms were running around chewing them out, making sure they had everything they were supposed to have, making sure they had enough ammunition, just like they do in any other army. I aimed my claymore at the nearest group and crawled back about fifteen meters to the edge of the taller brush. I checked my watch: one minute to go.

I didn't have time enough to catch a cigarette, but there was enough for the Viet Cong to mill around a little bit and shift the center of their group some so that when I triggered the claymore only a few got hit.

It was a hell of a shock when the claymores went off. Those VC that weren't cut down by the seven hundred little steel balls that thing spews out just stood there stunned. I got my rifle up and fired and hit at least two before they started diving for cover, and running into each other, and yelling. Then they started shooting back. The return fire was ragged at first, with just one or two of them shooting. Then it grew, crackling as if somebody had turned up the volume on a radio. But they were shooting high, cutting leaves and twigs off the trees over my head, so it didn't bother me that much. I shot at anybody that moved, and I know I hit several of them. The trooper with the grenade launcher was flattening the huts one by one. An NVA regular with a rocket grenade launcher raised up to a kneeling position to get a shot. He should have stayed down. I hit him, and at least one other shot hit him at almost the same time. His head split open like a watermelon falling off a pickup truck.

Over to my left, some of the VC were beginning to move up toward the treeline, some of them crawling and firing, others running up in short dashes. When the first C-4 explosion went off, they held up for a while, not wanting to advance into a booby trap. Then they got bold and started forward again. I shot at a few of them, but mostly I was worried about those in front of me.

Second C-4 blast. Brewster's shotgun plainly heard— probably ineffective at the range he had to use it. Grenade hits radio shack. Viet Cong fire getting closer. Shots snap past my ears, and I move to one side. I've been standing in one spot too long. VC rocket grenade hits in treeline to my right. I think, I hope you burned your butt, shooting it from a prone position like that. In front of me, a Viet Cong leaps from behind a bush, throws a grenade, and runs forward firing a submachine gun. He dives into the grass and disappears. The grenade is wide of the mark. Another moves up on his right, firing his AK-47 from the hip. I move away from the submachine gun fire and drop the AK gunner with a short burst. Then I concentrate on keeping the submachine gunner down. Out of the corner of my eye, I see two or three VC jump up, run forward, fall. Another raises up for a shot, jumps like a dog pissing on an electric fence. And falls back.

Third C-4 blast... the signal to get the hell out and back to the rendezvous. Already the fire from the treeline has diminished. Either someone was hit or we have some clock watchers in this outfit. Clip empty. VC moving like ants through the grass and bushes... shooting and crawling. Time to move: bullets snapping past my ears again. I chuck a grenade at the last place I saw the submachine gunner and put in a fresh clip. Spray the area one last time.

Run like a scalded dog.

From far to the left: Brewster's shotgun blasts, then there is a long, drawn-out "Whooooya!"

Turn and spray the area behind with automatic fire. Run some more.

The rendezvous point. Two men waiting. Two more run up as I do. Where's the kid? Here he comes. Brewster is last, five seconds later.

"Okay, let's get the hell outta Dodge!"

Run through the goddamned dark brush, eyes dazzled by fire and explosions, expecting to step on a punji stick or trip a goddamned mine. Expecting a bullet in the back. Much yelling behind us. Explosions: The last C-4 and claymore have been tripped.

Trip over roots. Step on a rotten log and almost twist an ankle. Vines snag the barrel of my rifle, seem to reach out and twist around my neck, my arm, my foot. "Now I know what they mean by a 'clinging vine,'" somebody says. Gasp for breath and get a mouth full of cobwebs. Choke but keep going.

The shouts behind us are fainter. Gradually we slow down. Everyone breathing hard, not talking, looking around. Especially looking back.

"Up the ridge." The Lieutenant, talking in short sentences. Tired. "Try to make it...to Fort Ti."

Brewster chuckling. "Blowed them cocksuckers away. Yessir! Got me a dozen, at least."

"So cut notches on your shotgun," Ivy League, looking wide-eyed and sort of shaky.

I'm feeling high. We hit 'em and got away with it! Actually got away with it! Unbelievable. Seven men attacked a hundred and got away with it!

So far.

High ridge to climb. Rough going. Thick undergrowth, muddy steep banks. Always looking back. Can't stop—they've surely got patrols out by now. There may be patrols on the ridge—the Greenie Beanie major said the ridge was heavily patrolled. What's that over there? Shadows, some kind of an animal maybe. Check it out. Probably imagination. Take two steps uphill and slide back.

Trail along the ridge top. Booby traps. Check it out,

move slowly. Mines. Ours or theirs? Leave 'em. Let's go, down the other side.

Form up. More like a patrol now. Point man out: Brewster. He has the only radio, but it has a tiny signal light. Hit the button, light flashes. Have to look sharp. He can't get too far ahead.

Cooler up here in the hills, probably sixty, sixty-five degrees, but the exertion keeps you sweating, stinging in the corners of your eyes, while tears blur your vision. Sweat in your hair, clothes are wet like you've been swimming. Sweat runs down the crack of your ass fast enough to turn a millwheel.

"Hold up. Let's try to raise Fort Ti."

"What the hell was that call sign? Comanche?"

"Choctaw. Choctaw Charlie One."

"Choctaw Charlie One, Mohawk Sierra Four. Over." Pause. "Choctaw Charlie One, Mohawk Sierra Four. Over." Over and over.

"Let's move on."

Moon is out now. Easier to see. Come to a creek but the ford looks too well used. Might be booby-trapped. We move downstream to a steep bank. Cross there. Cut a bamboo pole, poke the mud in front of me. Brewster stops short of the far bank. Hand signals: palm in, fingers up, arm moved up and down. Punji sticks. Moves on. Red flash from bushes on the bank. Come ahead. Water up to the armpits. The creek is too wide. We're too good a target. Step carefully. Look out for punji sticks. Into the brush, spread out, cover the next man's crossing.

Form up and move out. Country flatter, slopes less steep. The jungle is more open.

Voices.

Two flashes. Hold up there. Load and lock. Weapon ready, level, pointing toward the sound. Sit tight while the voices slowly die away. One flash. Move up.

"Viet Cong patrol. Six men. Want to take 'em?"

No. Move on.

At last: "Mohawk Sierra Four, Choctaw Charlie. We read you, weakly. What is your position? Over."

Read the map by the glow of a taped-over flashlight. Read off the coordinates. Do they have any of our men?

"Roger, Mohawk. Two men in the compound. Dirty and scratched up, but okay. Said they heard a hell of a firefight. Any casualties? Over."

"Ah, negative, Choctaw Charlie. No KIAs, no WIAs this side. Boocoo other side. Can we come in?"

"Mohawk, Choctaw Charlie Actual. . . . Hold up five. We have a patrol out. . . . We'll tell them to look for you. You're about one click out, if you have the coords right. There are minefields inside the cleared perimeter. . . . Hold up at the clearing and we'll guide you in. Any Victor Charley activity out there? Over."

"Roger, Actual. A six-man patrol about half a click back, moving away. We'll hold here five minutes, then come in. Not too long—there may be boocoo Victor Charleys hot on our asses."

"Mohawk, Actual. . . . Come again? There are boocoo Victor Charleys?"

"Thicker'n flies on a dog's butt, Actual. Last seen coming out of camp like a swarm of hornets."

Hold up five minutes, looking behind anxiously, then move out. Hold up again on the edge of the clearing while a guide comes out. No sign of patrol.

Handshaking, slaps on the back, congratulations. Give me a cup of coffee and some chow, and stow that congratulations and thank-you shit. Let me sit down. I sit in a sandbagged dugout, ass on the dirt floor. Lean against sandbag. Coffee's good, pork 'n' beans better, peaches best.

CHAPTER 12

I woke up the next morning and experienced a minute of panic, because I didn't know where I was or how I'd come to be there. I was damned near as sore as after my first day of BUDS. I was covered with mud and cut up and scratched up. . . . My greens looked like something off a scarecrow. I was propped up against a sandbag wall with my legs sticking straight out in front of me, and some of my gear was gouging holes in my back. The taste in my mouth would have done justice to a Vietnamese sewer, if there ever was such a thing. My head pounded. I felt like something the dog dragged in after the cat was through with it.

I needed to take a piss very badly.

I stood up, with many sighs and grunts, and made my way outside. I was on a slight mound in a clearing in the jungle. Holes dotted the mound, all more or less half full of water. Whether they were shellholes, or stumpholes

where trees had been bulldozed up, I wasn't sure. Three
slightly raised watchtowers guarded a number of small
hooches. There were a half-dozen small bunkers, just
roofed-over slit trenches, and there were bigger bunkers
like the one I'd just come out of, roofed over with sandbags supported by log beams. The dirt was piled up around
them almost to the roofs, to protect the occupants from
anything but a direct hit by big rockets or mortars. Two
or three sandbagged gunpits filled in the gap between the
three guard towers. Outside all of it was a more or less
ring-shaped barricade of sharpened stakes, driven into the
ground to point outward, about six inches apart, with
barbed wire interlaced around them, and—I learned this
later—punji sticks underneath, and claymore mines and
daisycutters with trip wires woven into all that mess.

This camp was home for eight Green Berets and almost
two dozen ARVN Rangers. There also seemed to be a
number of refugees, or else the ARVN forces included a
full complement of camp followers. The ARVN and the
Green Berets operated out of this camp just about like
we operated off the barge. They'd patrol around, make
their presence known, let Charley know they controlled
the ground. The civilians, it turned out, were the families
of some of the ARVNs and some people from a nearby
village that were allowed in to work. The ARVNs' families
stayed in the compound to keep them out of the VC's
hands. The villagers left before dark.

I found a secluded spot behind a bunker and got all
set to piss in a hole when somebody yelled at me.

"Don't piss in that hole! You might have to hide in it
tonight!"

I looked around, and there was a big Green Beret sergeant standing and looking at me with his hands on his
hips and kind of a sneer on his face.

"Use the piss tube. Don't they teach you fuckin' swabbies nothing? Go use the latrine; don't bleed your lizard

here in public. If we let everybody piss just anywhere they wanted to, the goddamned place would be a sewer inside of a week."

"War sure is hell, ain't it?" I said. "Last night you fuckin' people loved us so much ye wouldn't hardly let us get no rest, tellin' us what a great job we did savin' yer tails, an' this mornin' we ain't good 'nough to piss in yer mudholes. Where is this damned latrine, Sergeant?"

"This week it's over there." He yanked his big thumb toward a sort of screen standing out by itself. He watched me with a belligerent interest while I walked over to the place he'd pointed out. He didn't just watch until I got started the right way.... He watched me until I stepped around the screen out of his sight.

Sergeants and chief petty officers can be a hell of a bother, if they like to throw their weight around.

That started the day off wrong, and then the cook tried to tell me and Brewster that we were too late for chow. We convinced him otherwise, but the shit wasn't fit to eat. When we got together with the Lieutenant in the command bunker, we found out that the Green Beret major would be flying in about noon to be briefed on the previous night's action . . . so we had time to kill. We went out and prowled around inside the compound.

There were Vietnamese kids all over the place, playing in the mudholes and fighting and squealing and all the other things that kids do. I don't mind telling you all that monkey chatter made me nervous as hell. The women were out there, too, making bread and washing clothes and scolding the kids.... Every one of them looked like a Viet Cong spy to me. Some of them would look at Brewster and me and giggle, like they'd never seen such a couple of tramps. Most of them just ignored us, and we tried to ignore them.

But four of them were washing a python.

Now, I won't say Bob Brewster is scared of snakes—

I don't think he's scared of anything much—but he does have a healthy respect for snakes, and the bigger they are, the more he respects them. So when he called my attention to the python, it was more than just a casual observation.

"Jeeesuz fuckin' H. Christ on a bamboo raft! Lookit that snake! Sumbitch must be twenty feet long!"

The four of them had stretched that damned snake out as much as they could and were washing him off. He must have weighed almost two hundred pounds and was almost all they could handle. When we stopped to look, they sort of giggled and jabbered, like they were tickled pink to show him off. I walked over for a closer look, but Brewster stayed a respectful distance away.

"Look out, Tyler, that sumbitch might be hungry! He ain't in no goddamn cage, ye know!"

I went up to look at his head. It was really sort of small for the size of the body. I judged him to be about twelve or fifteen feet long. The gal holding his head held it out toward me, so I could get a better look, or pet it, or something. It looked at me through half-closed eyelids, a lazy sort of look, like it was saying, "Wouldn't *you* like to stretch out in the sun and get bathed by four women?" I tentatively scratched it between the eyes.

"Numba one? You like snake? Numba one?" asked the gal holding the head.

"Number one," I agreed. It was the biggest goddamned snake I'd ever seen, for sure.

"Number *ten!*" Brewster insisted when they offered the snake for him to pet. "Number fuckin' ten, damn it! Don't get close to me with that sumbitch! I don't wanta pet it!" I scratched its head some more. "Ugly fuckin' thang," Bob grumbled. "Where do they keep it? If I'd knowed it was here last night . . . I'druther sleep out there with th' goddamned Viet Cong than a python!"

"I see you've met Brucie," somebody said.

I turned around to see who it was. A couple of Army corpsmen stood there grinning.

"Brucie?" said Bob with a tone of absolute disgust.

"Sure. Did you ever see a fag that was more limp-wristed?" the taller corpsman asked, pointing to the long loops of snake that hung down between each of the women.

"Where'd ye git 'im?" I asked.

"Where d'ye *keep* 'im?" asked Bob quickly.

The corpsman grinned. "Bought him off a native. You'd think you guys would've seen a lot of 'em just like him out in the bush."

"I seen lots of 'em out in the bush," Brewster told him. "An' I left 'em out there, too!"

It turned out they kept him in a cage between two bunkers. They took him and wrapped him around their bodies ... just draped him around their necks like he was a scarf or something. The gooseflesh rose up on Bob's arms at that. Finally they gave him back to the women and told them to go put him back in his cage.

"Come around this evening and watch us feed him," they told us.

We wandered over behind the women and watched them put the snake in his cage. He lay there, stretched out in the sun, and seemed to be dozing.

"Numba one? You like?" asked the one who'd held the head. I had to look away from the snake to answer, and when I did I really saw the gal for the first time. She was young ... maybe seventeen, maybe twenty ... and not bad-looking at all. No raving beauty, but there wasn't anything wrong with the way she looked either. There were definite bulges in her peasant blouse from high, youthful breasts—unlike most of the other Vietnamese women around, whose teats sagged down like deflated balloons—and she flashed bright, even teeth when she smiled.

"Number one," I agreed.

When she walked away, I couldn't help but notice a well-rounded butt under those shapeless trousers.

The major showed up right at noon, before we had lunch, twirling his stupid mustache. We missed lunch, because we spent the next hour and a half with him going over the events of the night before. Then he and the Lieutenant got into the helicopter with the Green Beret camp commander, and they flew up into the hills to take a look at the Viet Cong camp.

"Maybe they'll get shot down," Brewster muttered hopefully.

"Why?" I asked. It was the first time he'd indicated any dislike for the little major. My only source of irritation with the man was his ridiculous moustache and the vain way he stroked and petted the damned thing. And his idiot grin.

"'Cause if they get shot down, we won't have to go back to that damned place again," Bob said.

"Yes, we will," I said. "We'll have to go up there an' get 'em out."

"Fuck 'em. . . . I might not be able to find the place again."

"I wonder . . . if they captured the major, would they cut off his moustache?"

I missed the dip in the river I was used to getting every day when I checked out the PBRs. Anyway, I wanted to clean out some of the scratches on my legs and arms, so I went and took a shower and put disinfectant on the worst scratches. Then I just lay out in the sun in my tiger shorts to dry off.

I lay down on some sandbags that were piled up around a bunker. Even if it was hot, the sun still felt good. I lay there and thought about the firefight and shook my head to myself. I didn't see how any of us got out alive. The odds were just too long. Don't you ever get yourself into that kind of a bind again, I told myself. Next time you won't make it back. You just won't be that lucky twice.

I must have dozed off for a few minutes. I woke up to the sound of giggling. Looking around, I saw Number One You Like and one of her friends. They were looking me over from stem to stern and chattering to each other and giggling about something. Had I forgotten my shorts? I had a feeling like I was lying there naked or something.... The knowing look on Number One's face made me think she knew to the inch just how long my pecker was and somehow it just didn't measure up. That's the way it looked to me. When she noticed that my eyes were open and that I was looking at her, she stopped giggling and chattering long enough to flash me a big bright smile, and then they hurried off, covering their mouths and giggling some more.

I wondered if we were going out on patrol come nighttime.... Most likely we were, but if we didn't, things might get interesting.

It was starting to cloud up and looking like it would start to rain any minute, and the flies were getting bad, so I gave up on the sunbathing. I sat up and got dressed and looked over to where Number One and her girl friend were, and thought, shit, why not? Why wait? I found Bob Brewster asleep in one of the bunkers, his big mouth open and the flies walking around on his face. An empty bottle lay on the floor beside him. I had no idea where he'd gotten it. Maybe he bought it from a Greenie Beanie, but more likely he saw it and just took it. I shook him, and he woke up right in the middle of a snore.

"What the hell, Tyler?"

"You want a piece of ass?"

"Are ye pimpin' now?"

"Do ye or don't ye?"

He rubbed his face for a minute and sniffed and snorted. When he had woken up a little bit, he said, "What's th' matter? Couldn't ye handle it yer own self? Need me to hold yer hand?"

"No . . . I can handle it myself. It's just that she has a girl friend. I thought ye might like a piece yerself . . . but if yer not interested, I'll jist have to take 'em both on."

"Hold up a minute, god damn it! Let me get my boots on. . . ."

We looked around for them once we were outside, but we didn't see them anywhere. It was such a small place it didn't seem like you could overlook them, though. We walked around the compound looking into the hooches, and Bob started to gripe.

"Hell, Tyler . . . I thought ye had this *arranged*! I didn't know we was goin' to have to bird-dog the damn women all over hell an' creation! Why didn't ye jist let me sleep till ye had it all set up?"

I finally spotted them going down the road toward the village. Any other peasant woman just looked like a Vietnamese peasant woman, from that distance, but there was no mistaking that shapely little ass.

"There they are!" I pointed. "Let's go git 'em!"

"Shit, Tyler, it's about to rain! Lookit them clouds! It'd be a-rainin' before we could get their pants down! Do ye wanta fuck in the mud?"

"You think they'd walk to the village if it was goin' to rain? They know th' weather around here better'n we do. It hasn't rained over three or four days this month, anyway. It ain't goin' to rain. . . . It's jist gonna look like it. . . . Come on."

We hurried down the road after them, but before we could get out the gate and past the sentry there, I heard the beat of a helicopter rotor behind us. It had to be the major coming back from his reconnaissance of the Viet Cong camp. He'd probably want to assemble all of us to go over his plans for the night's patrol. I stopped and thought about going back.

"What're ye a-waitin' for? Ye turn chicken?" Bob asked.

"Ye know what that means," I said, indicating with my head the helicopter that was circling the compound before coming down on the pad.

"Fuck 'im. If he was five minutes later, or ye was five minutes faster, we'd a-been in th' village. Won't be no difference if we jist keep goin' now."

I looked at the helicopter, and then I looked back at that swaying ass disappearing down the road, and then back at the helicopter.... I knew what I ought to do. I should go back and hear what the major had to say. Then I thought about that firefight, and how we all ought to be dead now, and I was sure we'd go back again tonight. I might be dead tomorrow.

So I said to Bob, "Well...hell! Duty calls, I guess," and I started walking down the road. Then, as he stood looking at me with his mouth in a little round O and a confused wrinkle between his eyes, I yelled, "Don't stand there like ye growed roots! Them women will be plumb to the village if ye don't move yer ass!"

We didn't catch up to them before they reached the village, though. In fact, they'd done their business and started back out when we met them just at the outskirts. Each of them was carrying two ducks.

"Hi," I said.

Number One smiled real big and looked at me blankly. Her girl friend looked at Bob and me suspiciously.

"Ducks?" asked Bob. "You eat *ducks*?"

"Dugs?" said Number One blankly.

"Them thangs," Bob said, pointing to one of the ducks under Girl Friend's arm. She half turned, as if to keep him from grabbing it. "Quack, quack. Ducks."

"Ah...docks!" said Number One brightly, and then started rattling on in Vietnamese and pointing back toward the compound.

"What the hell, Tyler. . . . They gonna cook us a duck dinner?"

"I don't know," I told him. The girls started walking down the road, moving sort of quickly, and Bob and I had to follow along at a fast walk just to talk to them.

Bob tried talking Vietnamese: "You boom-boom me, mamasan?"

Mamasan just walked faster.

"Hey, come on, lady—let's get it on, whaddyasay?"

She said something in Vietnamese.

"How much did ye say?" Bob insisted.

I caught up with Number One and took her arm. She obligingly handed me one of the ducks. I put the duck under my arm and took her arm again, trying to lead her toward the bushes beside the road. She shot me a funny look and pulled back and said something in Vietnamese, the same thing Girl Friend had said. I smiled at her real wickedly, or tried to anyway, and said, "You boom-boom me, Number One?"

At that she brightened up. I brightened up, too. She understood something anyway.

"Ah . . . number one . . . you like?" she said, smiling and showing even white teeth. My old pecker was trying to push its way out of my pants, and I thought she glanced down at it.

"Number One, I like. I like boom-boom Number One!"

At that, she chortled, and hid her laugh behind her hand. She pointed to the duck under my arm and to the compound, and said, "Numba one, you like!" Then she chattered something in Vietnamese and pointed to the clouds.

I began to understand. "Number one you like" was the only English she understood . . . and she used that for just about anything. She figured it was going to rain, and she was telling me she had to get the duck to the compound before it drowned. Or some bullshit like that. She was playing hard to get.

Bob wasn't having any more success than I was. He had the other broad by the arm and was pulling her into the bushes. She kept pulling back and chattering something.

Bob kept saying, "Oh, come on, damn it.... I want to fuck!" and she kept shoving the duck at him and chattering in Vietnamese.

"I think she's telling you to fuck th' duck, Bob!"

He shot me a dirty look and made a grab for her trousers.... He yanked them down far enough that the black curly hair of her crotch showed... and then it started to rain. We froze at the sudden shock of it. Not Number One and Girl Friend—they broke loose from us and started running down the road with those short, quick little steps that women use. Number One held her coolie hat on with one hand as she ran, but Girl Friend still had both ducks, and her hat fell off, hanging down her back by a chin string, and bobbing as she ran. Her pants were still at half-mast. I just stood there and looked at Brewster, and he stood there and looked back at me, and the rain plastered our hair down to our heads and ran down our necks and soaked our clothes.

"'Nah... it ain't goin' to rain,'" he mocked. "'They wouldn't walk to the village if it was goin' to rain!' God damn, Tyler, I told ye it'd be a-rainin' before we could get their pants down! 'Oh, no,' ye said, 'it ain't rained but three or four days this month. It ain't goin' to rain'!"

"Why don't ye shut yer fuckin' mouth," I told him, "before ye drown?"

It didn't mess around any, that rain. It hit us like somebody had turned on a fire hydrant—almost a solid wall of water moving across the rice paddies—but I could look out and see where it wasn't falling, because there the paddy water was still as glass. In fact, the sun was shining not a hundred yards away, while I walked down the road already soaked to the skin.

We trudged up the damned wet road like a couple of mongrel dogs, wet clear through, and me still carrying that damned duck. Ivy League saw us come in the gate. He was standing in the door of a bunker, dry as you please.

"Nothing like a cold shower to dampen the old ardor, eh, boys?" he shouted.

"Oh, shitcan it," Brewster hollered back. To me he muttered, "What th' fuck is he talkin' about arders for? We ain't carryin' no arders!"

Of course, by the time we got to the compound, the rain had stopped. Brewster headed for a bunker to find somebody with a bottle, and I found Number One and gave her the damned duck. After I had wrung out my clothes, I went looking for Bob. Sure enough, he had a bottle.

It turned out we didn't go out on patrol. When the major hadn't been able to find the Viet Cong camp from the air, he decided we'd hit them hard enough that they wouldn't be attacking anywhere for several days. Anyway, he figured we needed a rest, and he thought the patrol ought to be beefed up before we went up there again. I wasn't going to argue about that.

Late in the afternoon, the Army corpsmen came by and wanted to know if we wanted to watch them feed Brucie. We were both pretty well lathered up by then. I won't say we were drunk, but we were in a good humor. So we went over to the cage to watch the show. It was raining lightly, but we were already wet anyway. There were twelve or fifteen people out there, including Billy and Ivy League.

Number One was there with one of the damned ducks, saying "Number one, you like" to the snake and looking at me and giggling.

Suddenly it all got a lot clearer.

"Number One" was what she called the snake. No damned wonder she'd laughed when I said I'd like to boom-boom Number One. She probably thought I was some kind of pervert.

She put the duck in the cage with the snake, and we all stood back and watched. The duck flapped and quacked and beat against the bars, trying to get away from the snake. The snake just lay there for a few minutes, watching until the duck forgot why it was afraid and quit beating against the cage and started walking around looking for a way out. Then it saw a bug and chased it over close to the snake before it caught and ate it. It quacked contentedly and shit a big white turd. The snake raised its head and turned to look at the duck with both eyes. The duck looked back with one eye, and its quacking sort of died out like a car running out of gas.

"Stupid fucking duck," Brewster said.

"Quack?" said the duck.

The snake's little black tongue flicked in and out. The duck started backing up. The snake started moving, slowly, swaying from side to side. Its little black tongue kept flicking in and out, in and out. The duck backed up some more. Its head was cocked to one side, and its tail twitched nervously.

"Quack?"

The snake kept moving back and forth, silently. The duck sat down. It wasn't backed into a corner or anything. . . . It just sat down to watch the damn snake. Every once in a while, its tail feathers quickly switched back and forth a half-dozen times and then quit.

The snake slowly moved closer, its head swaying ever so slightly. It never blinked. It never hissed. Its little tongue went in and out, in and out.

Then it struck.

It looped its body around the duck once, and in a flash it had the duck's head in its mouth. Then it was just a matter of time. The duck struggled. The snake held it firm. When the duck relaxed, exhausted by its flapping and kicking, the snake swallowed a little more. Soon only the duck's tail and feet were sticking out. The tail switched violently for a little while, and then it was still. Soon nothing could be seen but a big lump behind Brucie's head, moving slowly toward his midsection.

"There's got to be a moral in that," one Green Beret said.

"Stupid fuckin' duck," said Brewster.

After the snake had eaten, it just lay there and digested its dinner. Since it was still raining, things broke up and everybody went back to whatever they had been doing. I thought I'd make one more try with Number One (the girl, not the snake)... but then I saw her walking off toward a hooch with the big loud-mouthed Green Beret sergeant I'd had the run-in with. She said something to him in Vietnamese, and they both looked back at me... her laughing and him glaring.

Brewster and I slept in an empty bunker that night. It was only a few yards from the snake's cage, but nothing in the compound was very far from anything else, and it was fairly comfortable, so Brewster didn't complain too much about being close to the snake. Billy and Ivy League bunked with us. The damned place actually had wooden shelves for beds—no sleeping on the dirt floor! We borrowed some blankets from the corpsmen. After shooting the shit and smoking a cigarette or two, we turned in.

Along about 0100, something woke me up.

I lay there for a few seconds, listening. What had I heard? Had someone slipped into the bunker? Was I woken up by a rat running around? I noticed that Brewster wasn't snoring—he'd been woken up, too.

Then: CRASH! a mortar round hit outside, followed almost immediately by a faint *pop*! as a second round was fired. That's what had woken me, I was sure—the pop when the mortar fired the first round.

The second explosion was closer than the first, and it was obvious the Viet Cong thought they had the range. They immediately began to fire as quickly as they could load. They had several mortars out there. The firing sounds sometimes overlapped, making a noise like *popopop*! and the sounds of the explosions came as close together as a man can clap his hands.

I didn't lie there but a few seconds, looking up at the flimsy little canvas roof over our heads and wondering what they had zeroed in on. We were safe from just about everything but a direct hit...but those damned mortar rounds come almost straight down, and if we were hit, it would come right through the roof.

I said to the others, "You think they got this hut zeroed in?"

Ivy League said, "Maybe they think it's the ammo dump!"

I said, "Yeah!" and we grabbed our rifles and scooted out. Billy and Ivy League went out the front, and Brewster and I went out the back way.

I sort of had it in mind to run to one of the log-roofed bunkers, but about the time we ran out, the mortars hit the generators, or somebody killed the lights, and everything went black except for the flash of explosions. The damned rounds seemed to be coming down about as thick as hail in an Ozark hailstorm. Bob and I made a one-eighty and headed for the nearest hole. It was half full of water, but right then even that was inviting. We ran right into Brucie's cage.

Just as we were backing off and going around the damned thing, the Viet Cong fired a flare to light up the compound. The door of the cage was open, and Brucie was gone.

"That damned ugly snake is out here somewheres!" Brucie shouted.

Just then a round hit close by, and shrapnel went rattling around in the cage. The ground shook, and we got shook and headed on the double for the shellhole. The hell with Brucie.

The flare didn't last long, and things got dark again.

When we got to that hole, it was just a black pit. It wasn't lit at all by the flash of the mortar shells. We both stopped right on the edge. We were both thinking the same thing.

"That damned snake's in there!" Brewster said.

"Well, what's it goin' to be? Brucie or the mortars?"

"Shit, I don't know!"

Just then a mortar round hit nearby. We went on down in the hole, snake or no snake. The water was waist deep. I hunkered down so my head was below the edge of the hole and felt around in the water with my free hand. I couldn't feel anything but slime. Then another flare lit up, and I could see Brewster. He had the barrel of his rifle down in the water, just a-pokin'.

"Oh, God . . . I jist *know* that ole ugly thang is down in here."

I just couldn't resist it: "I wonder if he likes a midnight snack?" I asked.

The shelling lasted about forty-five minutes, and then cut off as abruptly as it began. There were only a few casualties, and not as much damage as you might have expected. The ARVNs got together a patrol to sweep the perimeter, and someone found Brucie curled up in a bunker. Bob and I went back to sleep.

The patrol came back about dawn with no contact and no casualties. They'd found where the mortars had been set up, but of course there weren't any more Viet Cong around. The little 101st Airborne lieutenant and the camp commander were on the radio to the major, though. They

thought we ought to get together an attack and get rid of
that Viet Cong camp once and for all. The major was
strapped for people to do the job, because of the Christmas "ceasefire," but the camp commander wanted the job
done "*Tonight*!" He was afraid the VC would come back
in force and overrun the place. The major said he would
call around and try to scrape up somebody to do the job,
but it would probably be tomorrow.... Couldn't the
ARVNs do the job? The camp commander said he couldn't
strip the garrison to form up an attack force, and if he
sent half his men with all the patrol—us—that would only
be twenty-two men...and ten of them were ARVNs.

"Shit. Leave them gooks at home," muttered Brewster.
"We can do better without 'em—jist have to keep one
eye on them an' one on the Viet Congs."

A patrol went up the ridge at about 1000, and Brewster
and Ivy League and I went with it. There were only two
Green Berets and six ARVNs, so we figured it needed
beefing up a little. Three SEALs ought to just about double the firepower. Anyway, we didn't want to spend another day lying around that stinking compound. Billy was
trying to learn Vietnamese from one of the ARVNs. I
urged him to come along—it would have been good experience for him—but he wanted to take his language
lesson, so he stayed back.

We left the compound through the gate and walked
down the road away from the ridge, until we came to
some little white plastic flags stuck in the mud beside the
road. That marked a path along the paddy dike that had
been cleared of booby traps and mines that very morning
by ARVN sappers. Moving parallel to the ridge, we followed the paddy dike out across the paddies toward the
jungle beyond.

"I feel like a big ol' bull'seye on a target range," I told
Bob. I didn't like walking out across the rice paddies that
way.

"Ye look more like a big ol' pile of bullshit on a cow pasture," he said. Bob always comes back with something, but I knew he felt the same way I did. He was antsy as hell to get off that paddy dike.

It was a relief when we got into the bush, but I noticed the ARVNs, who'd been pretty relaxed out on the dike, were now alert. They spread out and moved in a crouch, their weapons ready. They didn't look anything at all like the slipshod ARVN outfits I was used to seeing.

We went out into the bush two hundred meters or more before we turned back toward the ridge. We crossed a little creek, and beyond it the terrain rose gradually toward the ridge. It started getting hot. The jungle was very open here, and there were great patches of sunshine to dazzle your eyes and make it hard to see what was lurking in the shadows. The air was so hot and sticky that before long even the ARVNs were soaked with sweat. Gnats swarmed around our eyes and noses. Where the ground started climbing toward the ridge, it was an even, rounded slope like the valley below, but the higher it got, the rougher it got, and soon it was quite steep, rocky, and treacherous. Not that it was any more open up on the ridge. Really, the jungle grew considerably thicker, and you constantly had to climb around stumps and large roots and moss-covered rocks.

After an hour or two the patrol stopped for a break at a little stream, hardly a foot wide, that ran over some flat rocks in a series of little cascades. The splashing muffled any sounds from the jungle, so we wet our faces, and the ARVNs filled their canteens, and we moved twenty meters or so off into the bush to squat down in the shade.

Ivy League was wearing a floppy old bush hat. He took it off and mopped the sweat off his forehead with a handkerchief.

"These are a different sort of ARVNs, aren't they?"

he observed. "I mean, they've got more on the ball than ARVNs usually do."

"Yeah," I said. "I was jist noticin' that, myself. I don't feel too bad about goin' out with these little fellers. . . . They seem to know what they're a-doin'. I guess they're about th' best the South has, though."

"Jist more fuckin' gooks," Bob said.

When we moved out, one of the Vietnamese and one of the Green Berets took the point. Brewster, Ivy League, and I trailed along behind, not letting the gap get too great, but not following in there tight either. That's when I came upon one of the ARVNs lying down.

He was lying on his back, with one leg twisted up behind him. There was no doubt he was dead. On his chest was a big, wet, spreading bloodstain. But I hadn't heard a shot, and everybody else was going on as usual. If I hadn't been bringing up the rear, I'd have missed him.

I called Ivy League over with a hoarse whisper as I crouched near the guy and looked around into the bush.

"What the shit?" he said when he saw the body. He crouched down on the other side of the ARVN, and we both scanned the trees and bushes for a while. We saw nothing. Satisfied that Charley wasn't drawing a bead on me, I decided to take a closer look at the dead man. I kept my M-14 ready to fire one-handed. There wasn't anything unusual-looking about this body. The eyes were open; the face had a shocked and surprised look. . . . It didn't look any different from dozens of others I'd seen. But when I reached down and tried to roll it over, it seemed stuck to the ground.

"Gimme a hand here," I told Ivy League.

Together, we were able to sort of lift it up and roll it to one side. When we did, it was easy to see why I hadn't been able to turn it right over: A steel shaft was sticking about four inches out of its back and had buried itself in the ground.

Ivy League whistled. long and low. "Crossbow," he said, almost in a whisper. "That's why we didn't hear a shot."

"Went all the way through," I said, suddenly feeling a sharp pain between my shoulder blades. "Pinned the little fucker right down."

"Look at the angle to his body. . . . It had to come from a tree," Ivy League said.

I agreed—it was sticking out of the poor fellow's back at about a forty-five degree angle and would have had to come from above, even if he was crouching when it hit.

"It must have come from that direction," he continued, pointing. "Unless he turned as he fell. Do you think he might have turned as he fell?"

"Nah . . . he fell like a goddamn pole. That thang pinned 'im rat to the ground."

"Then it must have come from over there," he said, pointing to a tree.

"Yeah . . . but do ye see anything?"

"No. . . . Let's hose it down anyway. Let's not take any chances."

"Hold it! The patrol's up that way," I told him.

So we split up. He went off to the left, and I circled around to the right, so we were approaching the tree at right angles to each other and at about forty-five-degree angles to the patrol's route. It took us a full ten minutes to move in to meet at the base of the tree, but neither one of us saw a damned thing. Ivy League wanted to back off and spray the tree with our assault rifles, but I couldn't see that it would do much good, and it might attract a VC patrol. Obviously the ARVNs hadn't missed us or their buddy yet. They hadn't come back to look for us and there was no use taking a chance that the VC would get to us before they could. Anyway, that was a damn big tree. A fellow could use up all the ammo he was carrying, spraying it in hopes of hitting something he couldn't see.

"Do you suppose he might have turned a little bit as he was falling?" Ivy League asked. "Maybe it was another tree."

"Maybe he was a-bendin' over," I pointed out, "an' the shot came from a bush somewhere."

"And we've been walking around out there concentrating on that one tree while he reloaded," he said, gazing thoughtfully toward the bush.

I began to look nervously around.

"It do make yer asshole pucker, don't it?"

"It sure does," he agreed. His knuckles were white where he held the pistol grip on his M-16, and his eyes were showing a lot of white around the irises. I expected him to start blazing away at any second.

Well, we searched that clearing for half an hour before the patrol came back to see what had happened. They came very cautiously, expecting an ambush. When we told them what had happened, they spread out and joined the search. We hunted around there for another two hours before we packed it in, and the whole time every one of us felt like he was about to get a crossbow bolt between the eyes or in the chest, like the poor ARVN did. I guess you always expect to see the other guy first if he's right in front of you. But we never did, despite the fact that there were ten men out there looking in a confined area. Either the sniper was hidden awfully damned good or he'd left the country. It ended the patrol, though. The ARVNs made a litter out of bamboo poles and carried their dead comrade back to the compound. The Green Berets ran point. Bob and me and Ivy League held back like before.

We didn't talk until we got back. Not being able to find the sniper sort of shook us up.

"I wonder why he didn't shoot somebody else," Brewster said at last. "We wouldn't a-knowed he shot till they fell down."

"I'll bet the crossbow was so powerful it had to be

cocked with a level or a ratchet, and he couldn't do it without making so much noise he'd have given himself away," Ivy League said.

"Yeah... whatever," Brewster muttered.

A Vietnamese woman was screaming and carrying on over the victim on the litter. Brewster shot her a bitter look as he walked past.

"Shit... feed 'em ta th' goddamned snake," he growled.

CHAPTER 13

Sometime in the afternoon, the Green Beret major succeeded in finding a Marine company that was on standby for the holidays, and arranged to have them hit the VC camp up in the hills. The Airborne lieutenant came by to tell us to expect to go out on patrol that evening. We'd be split up into two groups. One would go up to the camp to keep it under surveillance while the other group would provide LZ security for the Marines and guide them in to the camp. We were to decide how to split up our people, but we would have the services of two Green Berets and six or eight ARVN Rangers from Fort Ti.

How to make the split was the problem. Obviously the Green Berets and the ARVNs should go as a unit, not only because they worked best together as a team but because none of the rest of us could speak Vietnamese well enough to communicate with the ARVNs. On the other hand, they didn't know the way in to the VC camp.

In the end, we split them up. The Lieutenant, Brewster, Billy, me, two Green Berets, and three ARVNs that spoke some English would go up to the camp and keep it under surveillance. Ivy League, three of the paratroopers, a Green Beret, and three ARVNs would provide LZ security for the Marines. The Lieutenant at first planned to go with the security force...then I think he realized that whoever was commanding the Marines would outrank him, and he changed his mind. He put Ivy League in charge of the patrol and made one of his own men second guide.

The next order of business was to chow down. Everyone that was to go ate early. It was decent food—one of the Green Berets cooked it himself, instead of the Vietnamese cook they usually had in there.

"Tyler," Billy asked around a mouthful of chicken, "where are you from, anyway?"

"Arkansas...why?"

"He wonders why yer so fuckin' dumb," Brewster said.

"Dumb? Me? Now...why would anybody thank that?"

"You volunteered, didn't you?" somebody asked. I think it was Ivy League.

Billy ignored the wisecracks and kept on with his questions.

"I heard you say something about a farm," he said. "About raising hogs. I grew up on a farm, too."

"Yeah? Gee-whiz." I don't know why I wanted to be so sarcastic, except I just didn't want to know anything about the kid. I didn't want to get to liking him. In three months, he'd be a raggedy-ass, crude, mean motherfucker—a killer like all the rest of us—or he'd be dead. Either way, the baby-faced, cheerful, All-American Boy Scout would be gone.

"My family has a farm up near Maumee, Ohio," he went on. "We raise corn, mostly. Hogs, too, though—"

"Make any corn liquor?" Brewster interrupted.

"It's flatland . . . rich bottomland. Trees here and there, and miles and miles of cornfields. A lot like Arkansas," Billy persisted.

"You ever been to Arkansas, you wouldn't say that," I told him.

"I was down to Little Rock just two years ago," he said in a hurt voice.

"Little Rock!" I snorted. "No wonder ye thought Arkansas was flatland! We got lots of flatland up in the Ozarks, all right—only it's all a-standin' on edge! Yer fat ole Ohio hawgs would get to rollin' down one of our hills an' roll all the way to the bottom—why d'ye thank we raise razorbacks? So when they fall down, they get wedged in th' cracks in th' rocks, and won't get killed a-rollin' downhill!"

Brewster snorted.

The Green Beret sergeant said, "Shit!"

Billy just grinned. "That sounds like a tall tale to me."

"It may be a mite tall," I told him, "but it ain't so goddamn far from th' truth."

"Of course, it's home. . . . You'd go back there in a minute," he insisted.

"Hell, no. I'm a-gonna live in California. Somewhere there's a beach, an' lots of pretty girls in bikinis, jist a-waitin' fer somebody to take their bikinis off an' screw 'em! Ain't you?"

"I'm married," was all he said, as if that explained it all.

"I thought those hillbilly girls ran around in short little skirts with no underpants and were ready to screw anytime," said the Green Beret sergeant. "Like Daisy Mae, or—what's her name?—that other gal, the one with th' pigs." He haw-hawed.

"That's what ye get for thankin'," Brewster said, and he spit a small chicken bone on the floor. "Most of 'em

look like their daddies crossbred with a horse. An' they
go to church six times a week and twicet on Sunday."

"Are you from Arkansas, too?" Billy wanted to know.

"Naw. Kentucky."

"Ain't Kentucky the Bluegrass State? You know, thor-
oughbred horses, the Kentucky Derby, big rich farms..."
the sergeant said. Was he being friendly or sarcastic?

"There ye go a-thankin' agin," Bob replied, and he said
no more.

It was time to go. I smoked a last cigarette and drank
another cup of coffee and made a pit stop at the latrine.
Then we formed up and shoved off. A helicopter came
to pick up the security force just as we walked out of the
compound.

So we went up over that ridge again and back to the
camp, to watch them and, if necessary, to snipe at them
and hold them until the Marines got there. Bob and I
synchronized our watches.

"Time flies when yer havin' fun, don't it?"

Those people were in the camp in force again, and they
were whooping it up just like before. We heard them some
time before we got there, and we slipped in to see what
was going on. They had machine guns and RPG-7 rocket
launchers, like before, but this time they also had a few
mortars, broken down for carrying, and some of those big
rockets they launch from a hog trough. There were NVA
soldiers in green uniforms and peasants in black outfits.
If I looked real hard at some of the faces, they looked
familiar, like I might have seen them in some village or
another... or around the compound at Fort Ticonderoga.
One thing sure was different: They had a lot more sentries
out.

The Lieutenant was all for hitting them again. I think
he could smell awards and decorations in the wind. All I
could smell was trouble. Bob was reluctant, too.

"We caught 'em with their pants down before," he

pointed out. "That ain't likely to happen agin. We was jist damned lucky to get out that time without gettin' stomped on."

The Green Beret sergeant wanted to hit them, though, before they could get off to attack the compound. Maybe he was thinking about his girl friend back there—hell, maybe he really gave a shit about the little slant-eyed cunt. Or maybe he just felt we were hogging the glory. Anyway, he convinced the other Green Beret we should give it a try, so Bob and I told the Lieutenant we'd go along.

We arranged a rendezvous time, and then crawled in as close as we dared to set claymore mines. We backed away, laying the trip wires as we went, and waited for the time to detonate them.

This time, when the mines went off we mowed down quite a few Vietnamese. Then we started throwing fire in and cut down a few more. For a few seconds, it seemed like a rerun of the last time. Viet Cong and North Vietnamese soldiers were dropping like flies. There was a tall, skinny asshole in a brown uniform with a little brown fatigue cap tilted down over his eyes—it had a red star on the front—who looked like he was yelling orders. I think he might have been Chinese. I aimed right at the little star and smoked him. Hit him right in the middle of the forehead. Then I dropped a little fellow in black pajamas with a rocket launcher on his shoulder. But then the volume of return fire started to grow, and it didn't just gradually swell, like it did before. . . . It started out with a few scattered shots and suddenly crashed like a breaker on the beach. The shit really started flying. Leaves and limbs off the trees beside me came down till it seemed like I'd be covered up pretty soon. The rounds were popping past my ears like firecrackers on Chinese New Year.

I didn't tarry any. I couldn't see any use hanging around. The shooting wasn't all coming from the front, either. . . . Some of it was coming from behind me and off to the left. There had to be a gook patrol over that way—one we'd missed.

It all came apart on us.

I mean, I got the fuck out of there.

I turned around and headed for Saigon just as fast as I could run.

There were little men in black pajamas running everywhere and shooting at everything that moved—bushes, birds, and boa constrictors—even each other, I think. I was shooting at everything, too. I mean, I was shooting over to the left, I was shooting over to the right, I was shooting from the hip, and with one hand. I was even shooting back over my shoulder like the trick shots do on television. It sounded like I'd got into a nest of rattlesnakes and bees, there were so many AKs firing and bullets buzzing around. I ran through some neck-grabber vines and bear-trap bushes and jumped over a little waterfall and slipped on a moss-covered rock. AK-47 rounds were blasting the moss off the rocks beside me. I'd emptied the clip in my weapon, so I grabbed a couple of rocks and chunked *them*.

The Lieutenant was just off to the right, running just as hard as I was. He suddenly went down. I started over that way, but three Viet Congs were already there, having a shoving match to see who got to kick him first. I went on back into the jungle, toward the rendezvous point.

Bob was there already, breathing like a plowhorse that just ran in the Derby.

"You motherfucker," I told him when I got my breath. "You beat me here, and ye was way over there to th' left! How'd ye get here so quick?"

"I had about a thousand little monkey faces to help me."

"Th' Lieutenant got hit."

"Yeah . . . I saw 'em pickin' him up. He ain't hurt bad."

"I saw him go down... but I couldn't help him.... They was all over 'im."

The others started trickling in, one at a time, slow and quiet. We kept a sharp eye out, in case Charley had spotted and followed them, but finally we had all come together again, except the Lieutenant. We could hear the Charleys crashing through the brush and jabbering and laughing... hell, yeah, laughing! They must have had a dozen ten- and twelve-man patrols out beating the bushes for us. It wasn't those patrols that worried me; it was the ones you couldn't hear—the real pros.

"Where's that damned Lieutenant?" asked the Green Beret sergeant after he counted noses and saw we weren't all there.

"Gooks got 'im," Bob said.

"Is he dead?"

"No."

"We gotta get the fuck outta here."

"They'll make him talk."

"Yeah. We gotta get the fuck outta here."

Bob sighed, like he was real tired.

"He talks, he'll tell 'em where th' Marines are landing. They'll ambush 'em. Anyway, that's our only way out. Charley'll be all over the ridge.... He knows that's where we went last time, and it ain't too hard to figure we'd go that way agin. We gotta go to the LZ."

"But Bob..." That was Billy talking. "If they make the Lieutenant talk and he tells them where the LZ is, they might get there before the boats could get us out. Wouldn't it be better to take our chances going over the ridge?"

"Somebody's got to warn them Marines they ain't walkin' into a cinch deal," I pointed out.

"But it won't help if the Lieutenant talks.... Charley'll be all over us anyway."

"We got to make sure he don't talk," Bob told them.

"We've got to get him out. . . . " I put in my two-bits' worth.

". . . Or shoot him," Bob finished up for me.

Billy's eyes were big and round and glowed like foxfire in the darkness.

"Jesus!" he whispered. "Are you going to kill him?"

"Not if we can get him out," I told him. "But if we cain't, we'll kill him to shut his mouth."

"I don't think I can be part of that," Billy said.

"I don't thank you'd want to be part of leavin' him in their hands, neither," I told him. "First they'll gouge out his eyes, to make sure he can't git away . . . then they'll cut off his nuts while he's still whole enough to care . . . then they'll really start to work on 'im."

"But you can't just . . . kill him."

"Th' hell we can't. We'd be doin' him a favor. I'd want ye to do it to me, if they ever take me alive."

"Holy shit," somebody said. I think it was Billy. He didn't much curse or use four-letter words, so I figured I was getting to him.

"Somebody's got to get to th' Marines an' warn them," I said. "Somebody's got to get to th' LZ an' tell 'em what happened up here, tell 'em Charley's alert and mad as a nest of hornets that's jist been stirred with a stick. I'll go back an' get th' Lieutenant, but you others've got to go tell 'em."

"You can't do it alone," someone else said.

"He ain't gonna be alone," Brewster said. "I'm goin' with 'im."

But the Green Beret sergeant was stubborn and insisted on going back over the ridge at once. He told the other Green Beret and the ARVN Rangers to come with him. The ARVNs started getting ready to move out, but the other Green Beret told him to fuck off.

"I've got friends with the Marines," he said in a nasal

Eastern accent. And he went off with Billy to the LZ to warn the landing party.

Before they left, we got their hand grenades, and we made the ARVNs fork over some of theirs, too. I'd been carrying three, but I had none left. I'd had the pins hooked to the buttons of my shirt, and they must've pulled out as I ran, because I couldn't remember throwing any. I hoped they blew some of the people chasing me to kingdom come.

Bob and I watched the others go. I was wishing like hell the Chief and Ivy League were there. They would've stayed to help us.

We checked our weapons for the fourth time, and then Brewster looked at me, and I looked at him.

"Well... what're we a-waitin' for?"

"Let's do it!"

The Viet Cong still had patrols out everywhere, looking for us. It wasn't as bad as it might have been, though, because they were working their way away from the camp, looking for somebody that might be wounded or hiding or trying to escape. They'd just sent us scampering, and they were all excited about their victory. They were laughing and chattering, and shouting back and forth. They weren't looking for anybody fool enough to be heading *back* toward the camp. Still, we had some close calls. We had to lay up for half an hour while a bunch kicked through the bushes nearby.

Finally, they moved on, and we slipped in toward the camp.

Once, Bob whispered, "I wonder if they've got his eyes out yet?" I knew what he was thinking. If they had, we'd have no choice but to shoot him. We couldn't be stumbling through the brush leading somebody that couldn't see where he was going. Not with patrols out looking for us.

We were almost back to the camp when I started feeling like we were being followed. I didn't see anything, but . . .

Brewster stopped and looked at me with his little pig eyes squinted up real tight. "You gettin' narvous about this?" he asked.

I just nodded my head and kept looking around. He looked at me hard for a while longer, then crouched down and started on toward the camp. When I followed, he gave a quick hand signal for me to come up. When I got there, he whispered directions. "Circle around to th' left. I'll go right. Meet ye here in five minutes. . . . I'm gettin' narvous, too."

We circled in opposite directions and came back to the place where we'd separated. I didn't feel nervous anymore, and neither did Bob. His left arm was covered with fresh blood up to the elbow. I didn't need to ask him what had happened.

I had been worried we might have to slip into the camp and look in every hooch for the Lieutenant, but he wasn't hard to spot. The gooks had tied him up to a post, like cannibals do to missionaries in the cartoons. The light from the burning hooches showed everything up real well . . . just like it would anybody that tried to slip in there.

There were four people standing around him. Two were just yelling at him. I figured them for officers. The other two were probably enlisted men, since they seemed to act when the others told them to. They were hitting him in the face and the belly and kicking him in the nuts and in the knees. They'd beat him up pretty well, but they hadn't started cutting on him yet. It was obvious he wasn't telling them anything, either. Yet.

We both studied the clearing without saying much. It looked mighty grim, from the rescue standpoint. But I knew I couldn't pull the trigger on him, not without at least trying to get him out first. I wasn't so sure about Bob.

There were about fifteen other people visible, mostly wounded wandering dazedly around. Some seemed to be medics—at least, they were patching the others up. There was one hell of a shitpot pull of bodies lying around, too. If they weren't all dead, they were so badly wounded they were going to be out of it for a long time to come. And there were pieces of flesh and tatters of clothing everywhere.

"Well...who's it goin' to be? Who's goin' in after him?"

We drew straws.

Brewster won. Or lost, however you look at it.

He slipped in from bush to bush. It took him a while to get in close enough. In the meantime, one of the Viet Congs had taken out a knife and had ripped open the Lieutenant's shirt. He started peeling the skin off his chest.

Bob got into position and gave me a nod. I shot the gook with the knife, right through the ear. It blew the far side of his head off. Then I put a couple of rounds into the chest of the other enlisted man. His chest cavity kind of foamed up, like a strawberry pop that's been shaken. I wanted to zap the two officers, too, but it was time to move around and pretend to be a dozen cowboys. I threw some more rounds from the new spot, then threw a grenade off to one side, so it wouldn't hurt the Lieutenant. Then a few more shots. Then moved and threw another grenade.

I had Charley's attention now. Shots were coming my way. Bob ran in to cut the Lieutenant loose. I shot another gook, emptied my clip, and had to reload. Bob had to kill a gook that stood up right in front of him. I shot a few more times and then threw a grenade way over to the right. It must have hit a gasoline dump or something, because when it went off, the usual blast was followed at once by a loud whoosh and a fireball that would've seared the balls off a welder. Several Viet Cong ran away burning. Others just ran away. Bob cut the Lieutenant down, slung him head downward over his shoulder, and ran. I shot some idiot that tried to run up and stop him. Bob thundered by like a runaway draft horse. Then, shooting and throwing grenades, I started to withdraw. Now fire was coming from over on the right, as the search patrols moved quickly toward the sound of our shots and the explosions.

We got the hell out of there, first withdrawing to the southeast, then cutting back toward the north and the LZ. Bob carried the Lieutenant for a while, with me covering the rear. Then, when Bob got tired, I took over. Finally we set the son of a bitch down and let him make his own way. He wasn't hurt that bad. He was moaning and limping a little bit—the bullet had hit him in the thigh—but the wound wasn't deep enough to keep him from making it. I guess his balls hurt with every step he took, too. But he kept going. He was scared, and he didn't want to be taken again.

When we thought we'd put enough distance between us and the other guys, we stopped and bandaged him up. We didn't want to leave a blood trail. He moaned and held his balls while I wrapped his thigh wound and Brewster bound some bandages to his chest.

"Ye'll be all rat," Bob growled at him. "Jist don't plan on breast-feedin' yer kids yerself!"

I started getting this funny feeling along my backbone, like somebody was watching. I sat and listened for a while, but didn't hear anything. Bob finished binding the Lieutenant's leg and stood up.

"Hold up a minute, Bob. . . . I gotta go take a piss," I told him.

He looked at me funny. "So piss," he said. "Since when ye gotta ask my permission?"

"I mean, I don't want ye to leave while I'm gone."

"Leave? Gone?" Now he really looked at me hard. What I was saying wasn't making sense to him, and that was just what I intended. I *knew* someone was watching... and I knew by now that a lot of Vietnamese could speak better English than they let on. I didn't want to tell Bob what I had in mind and tip off an English-speaking Viet Cong. But I wanted him to know something was up. I rolled my eyes wildly at the trees around us, but he didn't react. Not that I could tell, anyway.

I stood up, and though it was like twisting a knife in a wound to do it, I thrust my M-14 into the Lieutenant's hands.

"Here, hang on to this," I told him. He had been un-armed. Now I seemed to be, but I still had my .38. I made a show of walking off into the bush and stopping and standing straddle-legged. Then I looked around at the clearing and moved a little deeper into the underbrush, as though the first spot wasn't private enough. Bob stood up slowly and paced a step or two away from the Lieutenant, as if he were patiently waiting for a rather eccentric companion.

Of course, once I got deeper into the bush, I dropped to a low crouch and took out my .38. I looked quickly around, but I just didn't *feel* like any Viet Cong were close and watching. My instincts were focused on an area partway around the clearing. I didn't have long to act before the VC got suspicious—if there was one there—and slipped away. On the other hand, I couldn't get careless and move too fast, for if there was a VC there, he was good. One of your run-of-the-mill soldiers couldn't slip up on us that easily.

I began moving, crouched very low, almost at a fast duckwalk around the spot where Brewster and the Lieutenant were waiting. I stopped every few feet to look and listen. As I got closer to the place I thought him to be, my heart began to pound and it got hard to breathe but I can't honestly say I was *scared*—not of the Viet Cong, at least. I was more afraid that I would see him, shoot him, and Brewster would react to the noise and blow me away.

I got near the place, but I couldn't see anything. I crouched behind a bush, and listened and watched. Brewster and the Lieutenant were talking in low voices. The Lieutenant's voice began to sound a little higher pitched, slightly hysterical. I had to spot the VC soon, but I could see absolutely nothing. I began to doubt there was anyone out there.

Fifteen seconds more, I thought, and I'll give it up. There's nobody out here. I'm hallucinating. I'll start shooting at shadows next.

After fifteen seconds, though, the feeling was just as strong, so I waited fifteen seconds more. Bob's voice again, this time positive and forceful. I could make out the words: "I'm goin' to go check on him."

Then a shadow moved.

That's all I saw, just a shadow shifting slightly. The VC, probably as nervous as Bob because I hadn't come back, started moving when Bob moved. Of course, Bob didn't just walk into the bush calling for me. . . . He assumed the worst. He and the Lieutenant were concealed, and Bob took care to remain concealed when he moved. It was enough for the VC. I caught only a second's glimpse of a figure in black moving between two bushes, and I cranked down on it with the .38 held in both hands for a steady shot, but I never saw it again. I worked my way over. There was no one there.

"Tyler?" A low hiss. Bob.

"Here."

"See somebody?"

"Yeah."

"Get 'im?"

"He's gone."

"Ye sure?"

"Yeah."

We didn't say any more. We just went back to the Lieutenant. I took my M-14 and gave him the .38, and we slipped away.

We met the Marines going in as we came out. Billy and the Green Beret had already warned them, and they had several men out as flankers on the point. We spotted the flankers first, and they radioed the main body that we were coming in. They called a Medivac for us, and it took Brewster, Billy, and me back to the barge on its way into Saigon with the Lieutenant.

As we were getting off the chopper, the Lieutenant grabbed my arm.

"I want to thank you guys for coming back to get me out," he said. "Thanks a hell of a lot."

"Shit," Bob said. "We didn't do it for you. . . . We did it to save our own asses."

I looked at my watch.

"Merry Christmas," I told him.

The barge heaved a little as the helicopter took off. It felt a little unfamiliar to feet that had been on dry ground so long.

It felt *good*.

CHAPTER 14

Ivy League told us later about hitting the camp with the Marines. They went on in and surrounded dozens of VC patrols that had got back in and were swarming around the camp, cleaning up the mess we'd made, laying out the dead, taking care of the wounded, and putting out fires. The VC were still shook up and didn't have the sentries out that they should have had, so the Marines were able to get into position and call in an air strike. When the helicopters came in and the Cong started running for cover, they ran right into the Marines' guns. After the choppers were through, the Marines went in and mopped up. Ivy League figured they got eighty or ninety percent of the gooks who were in the place. The Marines used explosives and flamethrowers on some tunnels they found, probably killing a bunch more. Then they moved in and decided to stay awhile. They started building themselves a compound.

After the Christmas and New Year "holidays," things settled down, and the Lieutenant Commander started rotating the boat crews that went into Saigon for supplies. Somehow he found he needed a lot more supplies from Saigon than from My Tho. Eventually it got to be our turn—the Chief and Bob and I—to crew a boat that went in. You didn't get a whole hell of a long time in Saigon...no weekend pass or anything...but it was a break from the routine. Sometimes, if there was a delay in getting the supplies, you might have an hour or two to kill, and you could go into a bar and have a drink. If you could get into a bar.

Some sailors who had been in Saigon a few days before said the bars were so packed all hours of the day that you couldn't push into one with a shoehorn. And even if you got in, it took an hour or more to get a drink. So we talked about it and hatched this idea of taking the boat in through Sector Q14. There was a canal through the swamps and rice paddies there that was a short cut over to Saigon, but Charley was almost always in there. He was pretty regular about sniping at single boats that went through, so most of the supply boats took the long way around.

We said, "Shit, if we get shot up a little bit, we'll get a whole afternoon, maybe an evening, in Saigon while they patch the boat up. Time enough to get in a bar. And if we don't get shot up, well, we'll get there an hour sooner, and we can take the extra time to go have a drink anyway."

The little canal that ran through Sector Q14 was surprisingly straight, almost as if it had been dug by machines, but I guess it was partly natural and partly hand-dug. In places, there were thick clumps of trees right along the banks, and rice paddies or jungle farther back. In other places there was only swamp. Little strung-out villages, one house wide, had been built on the levee, on the dirt that had been dug out to make the canal.

Anyway, we had to slow down a little. There were always little one- or two-man sampans being poled around, and sometimes the villagers got right out in the canals to fish with toss nets. We tried to give them time to hear us coming and to move over toward the bank. Sometimes they wouldn't. Of course, we made quite a wave when we went by, and more than one fish basket, floating on a little raft made out of bamboo, got turned over. The fishermen would wave and yell, and it wasn't hard to guess what they were yelling about. Fishermen on the lakes back home used to yell at us kids the same way when we went roaring by towing water skiers.

Of course, this time we got the shit shot out of us.

They'd set up two machine guns, on opposite sides of the canal, right where it made about a thirty-degree bend. The banks here were not tree-covered but grown over with a lot heavy brush, which hid our view of the channel around the bend as we approached the curve. We didn't see the little sampan out in the middle until we came around the point. They were probably fishermen. . . . I don't think they were part of the ambush. Anyway, when they saw us coming, they dived overboard and swam for shore. The coxswain throttled back and managed to miss the little boat. Just then two machine guns opened up. There wasn't any room to maneuver, so we just threw some fifty-caliber rounds into the bushes and got the hell out of there. A little later, the Chief inspected the damage. He said we took a little more than we'd counted on.

When we pulled in to the dock for repairs, there were a couple of other PBRs in there, and we were told it would take most of the afternoon to get ours ready to go.

The supply dock was right close to Saigon. From the repair dock, though, it was a bit of a walk. No one would let us take a jeep.

"Are you kidding?" they said. "You take a jeep into Saigon you got to mount a guard over it. Even the Shore Patrol, hell, if they leave one of their jeeps unguarded, the slopes'll cart that motherfucker off in little pieces."

So we started walking up the road toward the bars.

"Better take our shit with us," the Chief said, slinging his M-14 over his shoulder. "Or it won't be here when we get back."

"You guys can't carry them things into town," one of the sailors on the dock said. "This here's a Neutral Zone. . . . No weapons allowed."

Brewster snarled something at him, and the sailor shut up.

It really wasn't far into town, but the sun was beating down and the road was dry and dusty, so by the time we met the first little knot of soldiers, we were pretty thirsty. They were sitting in the shade of the only tree for two hundred yards in any direction, panting and passing a bottle. We stopped and bummed a swig out of their bottle.

"You guys look like shit," they said. "You just come out of the boonies?"

"Yeah . . . we got a few holes shot in our boat an' th' damned thang wanted to sink on us, so we brought it in to get it patched up. While we was waitin' we thought we'd go into town an' find us a bar."

"Good fuckin' luck!"

We went on down the road a piece and stopped another couple of soldiers to bum a drink off them. They were drunk out of their minds.

"If it's so goddamn hard to get a drank, how come they're all so damn drunk?" Bob wanted to know.

"Well," I said, "maybe they had to wait so long to get it, they was drankin' on an empty stomach."

At the first bar we came to, we couldn't even poke our heads in to see how crowded it was, for the line at the goddamned door, so we went down the road a little farther. The next bar was the same story. When finally we came to one without a bunch of soldiers standing around outside we tried again. They weren't outside because they were all packed inside, watching some little slope broad doing a bump-and-grind in a G-string. There wasn't even room to wedge ourselves in. We stood around outside and looked up and down the street and tried to decide just what to do.

"I gotta have a goddamn drink," the Chief said.

"I gotta have another look at that broad's tits," Brewster said.

"I seen bigger tits on a boar hawg," I said, and I meant it. "But I gotta have a drank, too."

"What're we gonna do? Roll a grenade in there?"

Just about then this soldier came up with a guard dog. It was a Doberman, and it growled at us.

The Chief looked down at the dog. Then he looked over at the sentry and asked, "Is that damned dog workin'?"

The guy said, "No."

"Then you better tell that sumbitch to quit growlin' at me, or I'll blow his damned head off."

The guy just laughed. "Ah, shit . . . he just does that. It's the only noise he knows how to make. You can tell real easy from the tone if it's a mad growl or not. You can reach down and pet 'im. . . . He's friendly as a puppy to Americans. Hates gooks, though. We taught him that."

"Ye can jist reach down an' pet 'im, huh?" Bob asked, and the guy nodded. So Bob did.

I looked down at the son of a bitch, and I got back away from it. It was a hungry-looking, black motherfucker, with just a touch of brown around the eyes and mouth, and there were scars across its muzzle. It had that old spiked collar on it, the kind they like to put on guard dogs so you can't grab it by the neck or collar and control it or choke it. Or cut its throat. The damned spikes are sharp as razorblades, and they paint them black so they can't be seen at night. But Bob petted the damned brute on the head and tickled it under the chin, and it growled and slobbered on his hand and beat a damned hole in the ground wagging its tail.

The guy looked at us and said, "You guys look like hell warmed over. You just get into town?"

We looked back at him silently. We knew we stunk a little bit. Well... Brewster stunk a lot, but it was honest human sweat. The guy himself smelled absolutely *doggy*.

He waited a minute for us to reply, and then said, "I mean, I can see you haven't run into any MPs or Shore Patrols yet. Or the Vietnamese police. They kind of frown on armed gangs walking around the streets of town, you know. Unless they've been paid off, anyway. That artillery you're carryin' is kinda hard to overlook. And don't be surprised if somebody hassles you about bein' out of uniform."

We weren't out of uniform. We didn't exactly have on dress whites, but we were wearin' what the well-dressed riverboat sailor wore on patrol just about every day: I had on my cleanest G.I. bush greens cut off just below the pockets, a sleeveless G.I. T-shirt, my tennies, and my little black beret. And my K-bar and a .38 and an M-14, with two banana clips of ammunition, and a half-dozen hand grenades. I admit I hadn't shaved in a week, and it *had* been two months since I last let the Chief cut my hair.

"If we could just get in a goddamn bar, outta sight, we'd be happy as hell," the Chief told him. "We been tryin' to get in one of these bars to get a drink, and hell, there's a line outside of just about every one of 'em, waitin' to get in. We saw this one didn't have a line, but it's jammed full, too, inside. Every fuckin' bar we've tried to get into has been packed with every kind of rear-echelon asshole there ever was." A long speech for the Chief.

The dog handler laughed again. He wasn't any rear-echelon asshole. They took those guard dogs out in the bush to track down Viet Cong, and they patrolled nights around fire-support bases and other kinds of installations, and brother, that was just as "up front" in Vietnam as the A Shau Valley or any of those other places you heard so much about on the news.

"We thought about rollin' a grenade in," Brewster said, "but we didn't feel like havin' to serve our own liquor."

The sentry grinned. "God . . . I've been tryin' to get a beer at every bar along this street, an' I been thinkin' about clearin' one out, myself."

"You ain't carryin' no weapon," said Brewster suspiciously.

"Yes I am," the sentry said, and reached down and patted that damned Doberman. "You know I could . . . he could clear that bar out damned quick. We could get in there . . . but we'd get our butts in trouble."

So the Chief said, "Well, we'll just go in an' ask 'em right polite to let us have a place. An' if they won't do it, we'll go back in with th' dog an' our weapons, an' we'll clear us out a little corner an' have our drinks."

We all agreed to it.

The Chief and I went in, Brewster not being so diplomatic as we were, and we spotted a table of airmen, over in a corner, who'd had at least three drinks, because there were three empty glasses in front of each one of them.

"Boys," the Chief said, "we just got in from the bush, an' we need a drink an' a rest in th' worst way. Now, we haven't got long in town to wait for a table, so would you mind if we had your chairs for a while . . . maybe twenty minutes?"

They looked at the Chief like they were amazed that anybody would ask anything so stupid. Then they looked us over like the Ladies Literary Society would look at a garbageman.

"Jesus, who let you bums in?"

"You better go back to th' boonies. They got laws against vagrancy here."

"This is our table. You can fuckin' well wait like all the other swamp rats."

"God, let a stupid grunt into town, an' he thinks he *owns* the fucking place. Shove off, sailor."

The Chief got pissed off, but instead of jumping the lot of them, like Brewster would have, he just turned around and went over to a table full of soldiers and tried again. That was why we picked him as the spokesman, instead of Bob. Of course, at this table, the reception wasn't any better.

"Okay, thanks anyway," he said. Then he went back to the door and got the guy with the Doberman. I stayed there between the two tables.

The airmen thought it was all a big joke. They had a goddamned good laugh at our expense. I'm glad they enjoyed it, because in a minute they quit laughing. The Chief came back with Brewster and the sentry and the dog.

"Okay, put that sumbitch to work!" the Chief said.

"Which table you want?" the dog handler asked. The Chief pointed at the airmen. "Okay, fellow. Go to work." The soldier said it very quietly and gently, but the dog's whole character changed right then. The handler pointed at the table. The dog started for it.

The airmen were laughing to beat hell until one of them noticed the dog. He sobered up right fast. The others turned and also saw the dog, who by then was almost to the table. There was a scrape and crash as their chairs were pushed back and fell over. and they started yelling. Then other people saw the dog and *they* started yelling. A barmaid screamed, threw a tray of drinks right over her head, and jumped up on the bar, scattering glasses and booze everywhere. A big ugly Chinese came out of nowhere—I think he may have been a bouncer—but when he saw the dog, he disappeared back to wherever he'd come from.

The bartender, a Vietnamese, was yelling at the top of his lungs in Vietnamese and English.

"Whattafuck you t'ink you do? You no can do that! Get hell out my place! I call MP! I call Shore Patrol! I call police!"

"You forgot the mayor an' th' dog catcher," the Chief told him.

"Hit," said the handler, and the dog went up on the bar in one jump, and right toward that bartender. The bartender's eyes got big and round and bulged out.... They looked like hen's eggs. He started backing away. Of course, the handler stopped the dog before he got too far, but the bartender felt the hot breath of death on his cheek.

There was lots of room now. At least half the bar was empty. The people were all crowded into the other half, watching us watching the dog. We must have looked like a bunch of pirates, standing there with those weapons. Anyway, we sat down at the table, and the handler put the dog on guard. The dog sat down on the floor between us and the nearest table.

"Get somebody over here. We want to order drinks," I told the bartender. He shoved a reluctant bargirl our way. She edged along the bar until she got to the wall and then tried to slip past the dog. He stood up and looked at her. I thought she was going to pass right out.

But the handler spoke, and the dog sat back down, and she sidled on up to the table. She watched that animal the whole time we ordered our drinks. We had to remind her to take the empty glasses.

I felt kind of sorry for her.

"What say we order four or five dranks, so she won't have to come back but once?" I suggested. So we ordered two pitchers of beer, and the Chief ordered two whiskeys.

We leaned our weapons up against the wall behind us

and made ourselves at ease. The braver souls in the crowd—there weren't too many of them—started drifting back and sitting down. But if any of them got too close, the dog would stand up and walk around a little and sit back down. That was all he had to do. Nobody sat at the tables next to us until some Marines elbowed their way through the crowd. They looked around at the airmen and soldiers, all standing over in half the bar, and at us, over in the empty half, and at the dog, too. They grinned real big.

The Chief waved at one of the tables.

"Have a seat, boys," he said. They waved thanks, and sat down, laughing at the soldiers and the flyboys.

By the time we started on the second pitcher, we were all getting a little drunk. The dog handler—his name was Mac-Something-or-another—had gone over to play the jukebox.

Some son of a bitch had called the Shore Patrol.

A couple of MPs and a Shore Patrol came in and pushed through the crowd. They only hesitated a second to see what was going on. Nobody needed to point us out.

The Chief just looked at them. Brewster was sitting there with his hands in his lap, watching the bubbles in his beer. I had my feet propped up on the Chief's chair, and the dog was behind me. Mac's empty chair was between him and the MPs, so they didn't see the dog. I heard him growl when the MPs started our way, but they didn't. The dog sat there, as he'd been told to, but he kept edging further and further out between the MPs and the table, sort of scooting along on his hindquarters. Finally, he couldn't stand it any longer, and he crouched down to spring, and growled again—a warning growl.

The MPs noticed him then, and they stopped dead in their tracks. They started to reach for their sidearms, but froze when the dog tensed like he was just about to spring.

Brewster started whistling to the dog and snapping his fingers.

"C'mere, boy! C'mere, little feller!"

The Chief told the MPs, "You'd better not move, boys—that sumbitch'll take your throats. It's just a question of which one he wants first. We don't have no control over him. . . . That's somethin' for you to think about before you go for your pistols."

About that time Mac turned around and headed back toward the table. "Oh, my God!" he said when he saw what was going on, and he ordered the dog to heel.

The MPs came over then, the SP with them, and demanded to see some identification.

"I don't have to show you no goddamn ID," the Chief said, but the rest of us shook our dogtags.

"What're you boys doin' in town?" one of them asked.

"We're here on business," the Chief said, "an' our business is Naval Intelligence, an' it ain't none of yours."

"We jist got our boat shot up an' put in for repairs," I told them, wondering why we'd ever thought the Chief was diplomatic. But the Chief was a long-time Navy man, and he'd had more dealings with MPs and SPs than we had.

"Well . . . what the hell you mean, coming into a place of business and creating trouble?" the SP asked. They had to keep up that public-relations B.S. The bartender had come over and was raising five kinds of hell with them. Every time they tried to ask us a question, he started yelling, and they finally told him to shut up.

"Who are you and what did you have to do with this?" they asked the dog handler.

He told them his name, and that he was guard dog handler in the something-or-other security outfit.

I interrupted. "He was jist doin' what we told him to do," I said.

The Chief took over from there. "We came up to this

bar.... It was the only one we could find that we could even get to the door... and we were tired, and we wanted to sit down for five or ten minutes, so we asked some guys to lend us their table for a few minutes, and they wouldn't. Then this nice sentry man here come up, and we borrowed him for a few minutes... him an' his dog. He was very cooperative, 'cause if he hadn't been, we would've shot him!"

"We intend to have a few drinks while they're a-fixin' our boat," I told them. "Then we're gonna get the hell outta here... 'Cause we got a job to do for th' spooks."

They doubted us, I could see that, but they were kind of sympathetic, too, with us wanting a drink and finding the bar full of flyboys and rear-echelon commandos. There was quite a disturbance outside: A bunch of guys we'd run out were standing around in the street hollering and cursing, and the racket attracted more people, who came to see what it was all about. The SP went outside and told them to quiet down and either come in or move on. So about half as many more people crowded in as we had run out.

To the bartender the MPs said, "You got more damned customers now than you've had in a week. Just shut the fuck up and serve them some drinks, before we have a riot here." To the crowd, they said, "You just leave these guys alone... give them space.... They'll leave after a while. Just go back to your drinkin' and give 'em a little room over here."

They were getting ready to leave when the damned Vietnamese police came in. They figured the MPs had the trouble taken care of by then, so it was safe to come in and hassle the survivors.

They didn't give a second thought to the disturbance, or anything the MPs told them. They just saw our weapons, and they got all huffy.

"Saigon Neutral Zone. You don't need weapons here," the head policeman said.

We just looked them over for a minute.

"Did you hear what we say?"

"Yeah. I heard you," the Chief told him. "What about it?"

"This is Neutral Zone. You are not allowed to carry weapons here."

The Chief pointed to one of the MPs. "This feller here told you about our boat. We couldn't leave the weapons there. . . . They might be stolen . . . regulations, you know. We're suppose to have them on our persons at all times. Navy Intelligence."

That didn't seem to make any impression on them.

"Are they loaded?"

"Well, hell, yes, they're loaded! They're no use unloaded!"

"We will have to take them," the head policeman said.

Brewster was suddenly on his feet, his face about two inches from the second policeman's, who he towered over. I flinched a little. I didn't want any fucking gook taking my weapon either, but I didn't want Bob in the brig for killing him. But he took a completely unexpected approach.

"Ain't I seen ye somewhere before, asshole?" he hissed.

"No!" the man said, startled, and stepped back.

"Yes, I have! I seen ye before!" He stepped toward the man again, thrusting his head forward and down until he was glaring eyeball to eyeball with the little Vietnamese, who was leaning a little backwards. Bob half turned toward the Chief then, and said loudly, "It's him! It's that fuckin' VC! It's him, I'm sure!"

The gook was shaking his head no, looking from one of us to the other.

"You goddamn Viet Cong sumbitch! You turncoat dog vomit!" Bob was hollering at the policeman, pretending to pull toward him while I restrained him with a hand on his arm.

"I not VC! I not VC!" The man was shaking his head desperately.

I picked up my rifle while the Chief shook his dogtags in the other policeman's face, and growled, "Naval Intelligence. Your partner is a suspected Viet Cong. We'll have to take him in for questioning."

"He not Viet Cong. He my wife's brother," the other man said in confusion, as if that explained everything.

"This man's probably one, too," I told the Chief. "We ought to take him along, too. Anyway, ye get more out of 'em if ye let one watch t'other bein' questioned for a while." I winked at one of the MPs, who was standing there watching all this with an absolutely blank look. "Ye know what I mean, don't ye?"

"I not VC! You make mistake!" protested the policeman.

"You wanta castrate 'im first, or skin 'im?" Brewster asked the Chief.

The MPs stirred to life. "Now, wait a minute, boys. Are you sure? I mean, they check these guys out pretty well."

"Oh, shit, yeah, I'm sure," Brewster said. "I'll never forget that fuckin' face! It's him, all right!"

The MPs steered the Vietnamese policemen back into the crowd. They weren't too sure themselves that we weren't serious. The policemen were convinced. The MPs held a couple of seconds' serious conversation with them, and then the Vietnamese left. Hurriedly. The MPs followed them out.

We settled back down and started on the second pitcher of beer.

When things had quieted down a little, we noticed a couple of U.S.O. girls—they were real noticeable, because they were the only white girls in the place. One was a tall, kind of bony-looking blonde, and the other was a brunette. They each had quite a set of knockers, or else they were padded to beat hell. We watched them making a tour of all the tables. We noticed something funny in the pattern: They spent more time talking to the ARVNs than they did the airmen and soldiers.

"I thought they were supposed to be U.S.O. girls," the Chief said.

I called to the bargirl and told her to bring us another pitcher of beer. When she brought it over—edging around the wall, even though the dog was wagging his tail while Brewster petted him—I asked her about the girls.

"Oh, they just whores. They hustle soldiers just come out of boondocks—they pay more. ARVNs pay *beaucoup* more for round-eye woman than round-eye man pay, unless American soldiers in Vietnam *beaucoup longtemps*."

"D'*you* put it out?" I asked her. I already knew the answer, of course. She just shrugged. It was part of the job.

"You horny? Just wait...they hit on you soon," she said. "Anyway, you guys on job for CIA...remember? No time for focking."

"Navy Intelligence," I corrected her. "Anyway, them gals might know somethin'. We jist might have to question 'em."

"They hustle *gooks*?" It had just now sunk into Brewster what the girl had said. We were watching them make their rounds, and they were at a table with some ARVNs right then, but the ARVNs were shaking their heads.

"Word gets around," the bargirl said. "Some ARVNs not buy, now."

"Word of what?" I asked.

"Some ARVNs complain they get rolled. Get ver' drunk, no get focked. Girls take all their piasters. You go out with them, be careful. Take dog."

"Not a bad idea," I said, and laughed.

Brewster squinted at the girls. He always squinted at things when he was drunk.

"They fuck *dawgs*, too?" he said. "Gooks 'n' dawgs," he muttered. He thought about that for a minute, and then, giggling, leaned over to the dog and patted its head. "What d'ye thank, ole feller? Ye like the looks of them bitches? We owe ye a favor, y'know." He giggled some more. "Bitches," he muttered. Then he started whistling like he was calling a dog, and crooked his finger toward the girls. "C'mere, girls. C'mere. C'mon, now. I got a frien' I want ye ta meet."

The Marines were laughing and pointing our way, and the girls came over.

"Hi, guys. Would you like a little company?"

"Sure. . . . Pull up a chair. Join us in a drink," the Chief said.

The bargirl brought them a couple of drinks just as soon as they sat down. The bartender already had them ready. They were drinking whiskey and water. Mostly water.

"You guys really know how to liven up an afternoon," one of them said.

"Yeah, well, I'll bet you girls really know how to liven up an evening," the Chief replied.

"Who are you guys, anyway? We don't see many like you in here."

"They don't make many like us."

"Are you Green Berets?"

Brewster choked on his beer. I pulled off my beret and looked at it. "No," I said, "mine's still black."

"I can see that," the blonde said. "I mean, are you Special Forces?" Her face was bony and angular, and her eyes were narrow, with little crows' feet in the corners. She looked pretty hard and tough.

"We're kinda special, all right," I told her.

"We're SEALs," the Chief told her.

That didn't mean a damned thing to her. "Seals?" she repeated. "Like the little animals that live in the water?"

"UDTs. Frogmen, with some counter-guerilla training thrown in," I tried to explain.

She said, "Oh . . ." but I could tell that she either wasn't convinced or didn't know what the hell we were talking about.

"What are you doing over here?" the brunette asked. She had a round little face with a turned-up nose and freckles, and big round brown eyes with long, thick lashes. She probably would have looked like somebody's kid sister if it hadn't been for too much scarlet lipstick and green eyeshadow, and the top two buttons of her blouse unbuttoned.

"We do a little recon ever' now an' then," I told her. That covered a whole multitude of sins. "An' in between times we run up an' down th' rivers in our little boat an' shoot up thangs."

"What outfit are you with?"

"Boat Support Unit One."

"Oh . . . you're riverboat sailors."

"Yeah, kinda."

Brewster leaned over toward the blonde. "I want ye to meet a frien' a mine," he said, "but I don't know yer names."

"I'm Judy, and this is Pat," the blonde replied.

"Well, hi, Judy 'n' Missus Pat. I'm Bob, an' this here's th' Chief—he's 'n Indian, ye know—an' this thang over here is Tyler."

The girls said, "Hi, Chief. Hi, Tyler."

"An' *this* . . . this is my special frien'," Bob went on, leaning 'way over and petting the dog on the head. "This is Dawg. Dawg, say hello to the broads over here. This here's Julie an' Miss Spot." He raised up and leaned back in his chair, right proud of his good manners. "Dawg is responsible for us gettin' this table," he explained. "We owe Dawg a favor..." Fortunately, he tipped back too far in his chair, and stopped in midsentence while he recovered his balance, and the Chief was able to shut him up.

They talked about where we were from, and about our families, and all that personal shit until we got several drinks into them, or they got several drinks out of us, or something. Mac joined us again, and they chattered at him for a while.

Finally, the Chief got tired of horsing around and just asked them outright what they charged.

"We understand you girls put it out. How much d'you get for a piece?"

They got all huffy about it and acted insulted, but they finally named a price.

"Jesus Christ," Mac said to them. "I hope that's a package deal for both of you, and all three of them."

"What about you?" we asked.

"I got to go back on duty," he said. "Don't you guys get took by these two. Gook girls are just as good and they do it for a tenth of the price."

"Go on back to work, you cheapskate son of a bitch," Judy told him. "Go on back to your slope girls. Maybe you'll hook up with Saigon Suzie, and she'll cut your balls off."

We told him good-bye and thanked him for getting us the table.

He said, "Hell, I enjoyed it. You ever come back to Saigon, look me up.... I'm at the ammo depot right down the road here.... We'll do it again!"

After he left, we told the girls what we'd give 'em. They said no thanks, that the ARVNs payed double that, and they'd just go look for business somewhere else.

"How about a boat ride, then?" I asked.

"A boat ride?" They were interested right away.

"Shit, yeah. . . . We'll go waterskiing on the Saigon River!"

"Hey, no shit. . . . Will you guys take us for a boat ride?"

"Hell, yes, we'll take ye. Will you go?"

We checked our watches and decided to have a few more drinks first. I slipped the bartender five bucks to quit watering their whiskeys, so by the time we left we were all pretty drunk, none of us having eaten since morning. We took the girls down to the repair docks and smuggled them on board. As we cast off, one of the sailors on duty said, "Hey, I thought there were three of you guys!"

"We're just takin' it over to the supply dock to load up," we lied, and went off down the river.

"Where are the waterskis?" the girls wanted to know, so we lied some more and said we had to go get them. We went on down the river.

"Where are we going?" they asked.

"Jist enjoy th' ride," I told them. "We gotta go check out the place where we waterski."

We were planing along at max rpms, leaving a big roostertail of spray and weaving back and forth across the river to give the girls a thrill.

We turned off into Sector Q14 and cut up some more. I guess they started getting sober, or bored, or sick, or something, because they started wanting to go back to Saigon.

"Jist a few more minutes," I said.

Just then, Charley started shooting at us. Machine guns with tracers. . . . It was beautiful, just what the doctor ordered. Lots of fireworks and not much effect.

I grabbed the twenty millimeter and started shooting back, and Brewster jumped into the guntub and swung the fifty calibers around, and we started making a hell of a racket. The engine was roaring and the twenty was going and the fifties were ripping off two- and three-second bursts. . . . Brewster and I were "whooyah"-ing at the top of our lungs. . . . Empty cartridge cases were flying everywhere, and those tracers were zipping past. They would kick up spray if they hit the water, and you could feel them hit the boat. It was like the Fourth of July.

Those damned women started screaming and praying and wanted to know what to do. The brunette started promising God she'd never hook again if He'd just get her out of this. She jumped down in the coxswain den and peed all over herself. The blonde jumped in the guntub with Brewster and peed all over *him*. She started scratching at him and crying, and hollering, "Get us out of here! Get us out of here!" The brunette jumped on the Chief and started trying to grab the wheel. I was laughing so hard I could hardly hold on to the twenty.

The Chief took us back out of Q14 onto the Saigon River, and we throttled down to cruising speed. Brewster and the Chief and I were hollering and laughing, and the girls were begging us to take them back to Saigon.

"We can't take you back like this," we told them. "You've pissed all over yourselves. You got to clean up."

They wanted to know where they could do that.

"Why, right here," we told them. "There's lots of water right here. Just take off your clothes and jump in. We'll stop the boat."

They didn't want to do that.

"Hell, you've messed up your clothes, and you've messed up our boat, and you smell like a toilet. We don't want to be around you unless you clean up. Now, get in the water and wash off or we'll put you ashore right here," we told them. "What's the matter, can't you swim?" They both said they could.

"Where are we?" they wanted to know.

"Down below Nha Be," the Chief told them, "in Bien Hoa Province. It's a long walk back to Saigon. Chances are you won't make it without being picked up by Charley. Do you know what he would do to an American woman?"

"You'd get your fill of fucking gooks," Brewster told them.

"You wouldn't do that," the blonde insisted. She was right, but she didn't know that—she was just trying to convince herself and the brunette.

"You sure you can swim?" the Chief asked the blonde.

"Why?"

"'Cause you're goin' to swim to shore from here!" the Chief told her, and Brewster grabbed her and threw her over. She screamed and thrashed around for a while, and slowly drifted away from the boat. The Chief had us heading upstream at an idle. I could see she was treading water and doing all right, so I didn't go in after her.

"Now it's your turn," we told the brunette.

"No . . . please," she said.

"Then strip off, God damn it, and wash up!" She did as she was told. She stripped down to her panties and bra, and started to get in the water, but we stopped her and made her take them off, too. She washed her clothes, and we laid them out on the foredeck to dry. Meanwhile, the Chief reversed the engine and we backed down to the blonde. She gave up and took off her clothes while she was still in the water. While she washed, we played odd man out to see who was first, and I lost. Then we played to see who was second, and I lost again.

"God damn it to hell! You sumbitches have two-headed coins!" I protested, and made them show their coins. They wouldn't give up their turns. I had to cox the boat while they got their pussy and switched off to the other girl. "Well, fuck it. I get first feel, then."

So as I pulled the girls out of the water, I felt of their tits and their asses. The blonde had almost no cunt hair, and that really turned me on. I grabbed her in between her legs and started to throw her down on the afterdeck, but the Chief hollered, God damn it he was first. He and Brewster already had their clothes off, and it was two to one anyway, so I got down in the coxswain den and cursed and watched them screw. I found a bottle we'd brought with us and got to work on that and tried to decide which one I was going to screw first.

The blonde had a better figure, but she was kind of washed-out-looking with her clothes off. Like a dead fish. The brunette had saggy breasts with big brown prominent nipples, and a big mass of matted black hair between her legs, but she had a round little ass and she probably sun-bathed a lot, because she was brown all over. I decided she would be first.

I didn't notice at first that the boat wasn't handling right. I was still pretty drunk. First I noticed a dampness down around my ankles, and that my tennis shoes were wet. I leaned over and looked down into the hull. Sure enough, we were filling up.

"God damn!" I hollered, and threw the bottle of booze so it shattered against the guntub, and booze splashed all over the Chief and the brunette. "God damn it to hell!"

"What's th' matter, Tyler? You still pissed off?"

"Naw . . . we're just takin' on water, that's all. I'm goin' to have to open up the throttle, an' get th' hull up, or we'll sink."

"Sink?" the brunette hollered, and started to get up. The Chief just pushed her back down and went on about his business.

"Not if he gets us goin'," he said.

So I opened up the throttle, and we went on up the river toward Saigon.

"Hurry up, you bastards, or we'll be in Saigon before you get done!" They just laughed and went on enjoying themselves. "Ye'll jist have to jack off!" Brewster yelled.

The Chief got done first.

"Circle the harbor a couple of times," I yelled to him as I took off my pants. But I knew he couldn't for long.

It was too bad, too. The brunette and I really hit it off.

We let them off at the supply wharf. They were going to report us, they said.

"For not paying?" we asked. "You go right ahead. You know you're not supposed to be hookin'. You go right ahead, we don't give a shit."

And we didn't.

CHAPTER 15

Of course, late the next morning when we finally got the supplies back to the barge, we got chewed out for going through Q14 and getting the PBR all shot up. The Lieutenant Commander sure was pissed.

We didn't care, though. We'd let off a little steam.

The Lieutenant Commander made Brewster and me put on our monkey suits—our dress uniforms—and get into a helicopter and go over to Cam Ranh Bay because we were going to get a Silver Star for getting that little 101st Airborne Lieutenant out of a jam. It was one of these hurry-up-and-wait things. We got there in the afternoon, and the decoration ceremony was scheduled for the next morning on the carrier U.S.S. *Ticonderoga*. So we had a night to kill in Cam Ranh.

We went in and looked up the UDTs and SEALs there, to see if there was anyone we knew, and sure enough, there was one guy there, a diver we'd gone through BUDS

with. We asked him if he could go out drinking with us
that night.

"I'd like to," he said, "but I've got all these ships to
check out."

We said, "What the hell do you mean, check out?"

And he said, "When ships come in to the harbor, from
Da Nang or Saigon or Phnom Penh, we check 'em out,
to make sure there's no bombs planted on 'em below the
waterline. Some of these babies are tankers carrying avi-
ation fuel, and some of 'em carry ammunition. If the VC
managed to blow one of 'em up in the harbor here, it
could do all kinds of damage. It's not bad duty. The ships
usually treat us to steaks, and that kind of thing. But
there's so many going in and out, and so few of us to do
the job..."

We said, "D'ye have any extry gear? We'll help ye
out!"

So we gave him a hand, and that night we all ate steaks
and went out boozing.

We asked him if he ever found a bomb.

"No," he said, "but one day I did find this old geezer
all wrapped up in a cable. They sent me down to Can
Gio, at the main entrance to the Saigon River, where this
tanker had a fouled screw. I went down to check it out
and found all this damned cable. Then I found this old
son of a bitch all wrapped up in it. Or most of him—the
fish had been at him. We had to cut the cable off with a
torch. We figured he'd been out in a sampan looping the
cable over the screw when they started it up, and he got
tangled up in it. Makes you wonder, though... he could
have set a bomb just as easy. They probably wanted to
disable the ship and let it drift downriver, then sink it
somewhere and block the channel."

The award ceremony was a real circus. They had it on
the flight deck of the *Ticonderoga* so there would be room
for all the recipients to line up! Brewster and I were to-

gether down near the end—I don't know if we were lined up in order of the date of the award or if it was alphabetical order, and SEAL was last. Anyway, there were several of us down there.

By the time he got to us, we had been standing there damned near an hour. The sun was up pretty high, and I was starting to sweat, and so was the Admiral. The officer that read the commendation stumbled over the words, and the Admiral fumbled with the pin of the medal.

"What are you grinning about, sailor?" he growled under his breath.

"I'm proud to be *singled out* for this award, sir," I muttered back.

He stepped back and saluted, and I saluted him, all very proper. He waited while the next commendation was read, then stepped forward to pin it on, and growled at me again, out of the corner of his mouth.

"If you think this is so damned funny you ought to try pinning these damned things on three hundred chests!"

When it was all over, a little lieutenant (j.g.) stepped up to me and told me to report to the Admiral's office at 1100.

I thought, oh, shit, I'm in for it now.

But all the Admiral had to say was, "You didn't think much of our little award ceremony, did you, son?"

"No, sir, I didn't."

"Can you tell me why not?"

"Because there were too goddamned many sailors out there getting medals, sir. That sort of makes them worthless."

"There are all kinds of commendations, sailor. Some were receiving unit citations for their outfits. You got a Silver Star for rescuing a 101st Airborne lieutenant from enemy hands. Do you think that was a meaningless act?"

"I wasn't doing anything more than what I was trained to do. I was just doing my job."

He sighed and sat down behind his desk, and picked up a pencil. He started to write something down, and then stopped.

"Sailor, that's what we give awards and decorations *for*," he said. "Keeping your head and doing your job when the enemy is shooting at you and everything's going to hell in a hand-basket. Not many are able to do that. Dismissed!"

We went on back to the barge that afternoon and went back to work.

There were a couple of the guys missing.

They had been going in to extract the Chief and the "new" SEALs from a patrol, and saw a flare. They thought it was the signal to come in and get the SEAL team. It was Viet Cong. They shot their way out of it, but two of them were killed.

It doesn't pay to have friends in a situation like we were in. A friend is a handicap. You get to liking a guy, and you'll take chances for him that you wouldn't take for a stranger. And if he gets wasted, you really get down.

Brewster and the Chief I drank a lot with and raised hell with, but they weren't really friends. They weren't the kind of guys you'd look up when you got back to civilian life, and go visit on vacations or anything. They were members of the team, and they did their jobs. If they made it, fine; if they got blown away, well, they just fucked up, that's all. I could count on them to do their jobs, but not to look after my ass. I had to be responsible for that myself.

Billy *was* getting to be a friend, no matter how much I tried to avoid it. He was always so damned cheerful about everything, always had a positive outlook, never seemed to get his feelings hurt if you ignored him. And he did his job, too.

The other new SEALs...they were just a functional

part of the team. I didn't like them or dislike them. I used them, just like I used my M-14.

Ivy League had also made a friend in one of the sailors. I don't know what they had in common, but I think it had something to do with Ivy League's girl friend and the "Dear John" letter he'd gotten before Christmas. The friendship had just developed over the last few weeks. Then the guy was gone. They wrapped him up in a plastic bag and flew the body out on a helicopter, and Ivy League sat around and got drunk. He was plastered for two solid days before the Lieutenant Commander went in and had a talk with him and sobered him up. Right after that, he went out on patrol again, but he never seemed like the same old Ivy League.

He had always been a little bit high-strung. It was one of those things that didn't show up in training. But when he went into the bush, he saw gooks in every shadow and jumped at every little jungle noise. Many times, I would get close to him while we were on patrol, and he would be shivering—and it wasn't from being cold, either. We never put him in charge or let him be point man.

Now, after this sailor's death, he started wanting to be the point man.

We found that out when we went on an extended patrol to take some spooks up into the Parrot's Beak area, on the Cambodian border near Moc Hoa and Cai Cai. They had some electronic gear they wanted to set out on that part of the Ho Chi Minh Trail. When we got up there, there were more of Ho Chi Minh's trails than Carter has Little Pills.

The spooks milled around in confusion for a couple of days before they finally selected the sites they wanted to bug, and when they got busy, they got only about half their shit set out. We'd already been out too long. It seemed as if there was a gook behind every bush lately. So we told the spooks we'd have to get the hell out. They still wanted to set up the rest of their shit, but we told them, "Our orders are not to let you or your equipment fall into enemy hands." Then we took their stuff apart, smashed the bigger pieces with our gun butts, and buried it all in twelve different holes, which we then covered over with moss and dirt. We made the spooks carry extra dirt in their packs so their tracks wouldn't show them to be carrying less weight.

"You either move your butts or we'll bury *you* in twelve different holes . . . each," we told them.

We had to move back across the border before we could get a helicopter in to pick us up, so we would travel all night and day. As soon as it got dark, Ivy League said he wanted to take over as point man. I was tired, the Chief was tired, and Brewster was tired—we'd all had our shifts as point. It was time for Ivy League to carry some of the load—or so I rationalized, anyway. So Ivy League went out as point man—about his first time in the whole tour.

We were following a course to our pickup LZ, and after a while it led through some pretty thick woods. Ivy League led us out into this bamboo thicket, and then called us up. There were some bobby traps up here, and some punji sticks.

There didn't seem to be any real reason for them being there. Maybe they had been put out to harass the cane cutters or something. We sent him off in a slightly different direction.

He went off, and we followed him through the bush for maybe five or ten minutes. He was going a little too far before he called us up each time, and getting a little bit out of touch, but it didn't seem like anything significant to me at the time. This was my sixth night without sleeping, and we had been moving almost twenty hours without stopping. I wasn't thinking too clearly.

Then he got 'way out ahead and he didn't call us up.

We held up for a few seconds longer than usual, and it didn't bother me. But after a full minute, I suddenly got worried that he'd walked into a bunch of Viet Cong and they'd taken him out. I went up to where Yancey had the radio. The Chief and Brewster were on their way over, too.

There were shots fired from an M-16, at least a clip, on full automatic. We immediately faced outward in a defensive circle. There were no answering shots. I got Ivy League on the radio.

"What the hell . . . ?"

"I thought I saw something," he said.

"Ye *thought* ye saw something? Did ye or didn't ye?"

"Yeah," he said, and didn't transmit any more.

"Hold right where ye are. I'm coming up," I told him. To the others, I said, "Everybody stay rat here. Something's screwy up there."

I got up to where he should have been, and he wasn't there. But when I started forward again, he started shooting at me. There was no doubt it was him: It was an M-16 on full auto, spraying half a clip at a time.

"Hey, you sumbitch! You're shooting at *me!*" I hollered. He shot again, and the bullets came awfully damned close. I moved off to one side, and hollered again: "Hey, Ivy League, it's me. . . . It's Tyler!"

The son of a bitch shot at me again.

I thought, I'd better get the hell away from here. He's gone off his gourd. But every time I moved, he opened up.

I thought about throwing a concussion grenade . . . but I didn't have any.

I thought I'd try the old cowboy trick, and throw a rock only there weren't any rocks. So I threw a stick. He shot maybe five times, and while he was shooting I moved away from the place I'd thrown the stick, and toward him. Then I couldn't find any more sticks, so I pulled up a clump of grass and threw it, roots and all. While he was blazing away at that I moved in on him again.

This time, when he quit shooting, I could hear him whispering. "Tyler? Tyler? Where are you, Tyler?"

I thought I'd chance it.

"I'm over here, you sumbitch!" I said it in a low voice.

I could hear the rustle of bushes as he turned, but he didn't shoot.

"Tyler, they're out there! Be careful!"

"I'm goin' to stand up now. D'ye hear me? I'm goin' to stand up. Don't shoot at me, damn ye!" Slowly, I stood up. He didn't see me at first. He was looking over to my right, and had his finger on the trigger and his rifle pointed that way. I took a couple of steps toward him.

He turned his head and looked right at me, and I saw the black shadow that was his body start to turn. I was already starting to drop when I heard him say, "Oh, shit!" and start fumbling with the clip. I moved fast then.

As soon as I stepped close to him, I said, "It's me! It's Tyler!"

He said, "Oh, Tyler!" in a relieved tone as his clip clicked home, but I saw his body start to turn again, and that M-16 barrel start to bear in my direction. I stepped up close and blocked it, grabbing the barrel in my hand.

"Am I glad to see you!" he said.

I turned and pulled on his rifle barrel with my left hand, and whirled around and gave him a back elbow smash up beside the head with my right. I was aiming for his neck, but... it was dark, you know. Anyway, I got him separated from his rifle and threw it away into the bush. I had to hit the son of a bitch with my fist to get him down. He got up wanting to fight, but I clipped him on the chin with my boot, and he stayed down and groggy until I got the others up there.

We ended up giving him his weapon back, and he was okay as long as he was with the bunch.

We managed to get him to our pickup spot, and we called in a chopper.

The Lieutenant Commander just sort of sighed and said, "Okay," when we told him that none of us would ever go out on patrol with Ivy League again. When he heard the story, he sent out some message to Squadron headquarters. Then he went and told Ivy League.

Ivy League didn't take it very well. I thought he'd be happy as hell to be told he was going home, but he cursed us all and threw his stuff around the crews' quarters. Then he jammed it into his seabag, went and drank beer, and wouldn't talk to anybody.

Later in the day, a helicopter came and took him away. I never saw him again, or heard anything about him.

CHAPTER 16

The old man walked down the dirt road, driving his hogs with a switch. I waited in the bushes until he came even with me, and then raised up and pointed the M-14 at him. He stopped and looked at me, unafraid, as if he saw me every day of his life. I switched the M-14 to full automatic and blew his chest to a bloody froth. The hogs ran squealing down the road.

The old man's body lay in the road, an incredibly small heap of torn flesh and bloody cloth. I went over and looked down.

It was my father.

I hated that dream the worst.

The dreams came when we got back to the barge, or to whatever camp we happened to be staying in. Any place that was reasonably secure so that I slept. The cat-napping I did in the bush never caused me to dream, though sometimes, on patrol, a particular scene or circumstance might bring to mind a particularly vivid memory. But those memories never drowned out reality. At least not in the bush. But on the barge one evening, a sailor got hurt in an accident with some machinery. There was quite a bit of blood, and it made me remember Mike impaled on the punji sticks by that sling. I could picture in my mind his teeth clenched in his determination not to cry out as he was dragged across the ground toward the stakes, digging his rifle butt into the dirt to hold himself back. Then the final instant as it lifted him clear of the ground and swung him into the tree. That was ridiculous: I wasn't a witness to that scene, but my mind conjured up the picture to haunt me.

Some people were pissed off. They said I just sat there and stared when they needed me to help, and didn't even answer back when they spoke to me. Of course, I knew what was going on all the time—I was just remembering the other situation.

Of course.

The dreams were something else. They were sometimes about things that had really happened, like shooting the girl that had the bomb strapped on her, and sometimes about things that had never happened. And there were dreams where the two were woven together, so the dream began as a memory and became a nightmare. Sometimes the real things and the nightmare things from Vietnam got all mixed together with the real things and the nightmare things from home. Those were the worst. Like the one about the old man driving the hogs.

After that one, I got up and went outside and puked.

It was April, the dry season, but out in the Delta the air was humid and the nights were sultry. The night pressed down on me like a physical presence. I felt as if I couldn't breathe.

I walked around the barge for a while, but it didn't

help. I sat down on the deck and dangled my bare feet in the water. That was better, but the damned deck was uncomfortably warm.

The next thing I knew, I was in the water.

I thought, what the hell am I going to do, commit suicide? I'd always heard about people walking into the ocean and swimming out to sea to drown. I figured UDTs put that option out of my reach—they made me too good a swimmer, and drownproofed me until I could go through the drill without even being conscious of it. But splashing around in the water at night was a good way to get a bullet in the head from one of the sentries. Maybe that's what I had in mind.

However, the sentry was watching, and saw me go over.

"Hey, Tyler . . . you all right?"

"Yeah, I'm just going for a swim."

"Hey, guys: Watch out for Tyler—he's swimming around the barge."

I didn't swim around the barge; I swam away from it, out into the black river, with a slow Australian crawl, until it had shrunk to the size of a little matchbox behind me. I had thoughts of just keeping on and on; I felt as if I could swim all the way back to the United States. It was damned tempting just to try it. But the sane part of me kept saying, you'd never make it—you'll have to crawl out on the shore somewhere, and the 'Cong will get you . . . or worse, the Navy will get you and bring you back.

After a while, I dived under and swam underwater for as long as I could, in absolute blackness, not caring that I couldn't see. The war was up there, and I was out of it. It felt *good*, almost as good as being back in the States. I had no worries. I wasn't hurting anyone, and no one was trying to hurt me. I thought, is this what it will be like to go home? I turned cartwheels until I got disoriented and had to let myself float to the surface. The barge really was the size of a matchbox now, a penny box. Reluctantly I started back toward it, breaststroking for a while, then rolling over to backstroke. I was going against the current, but the current here wasn't anything compared to the riptides around San Clemente, and I was soon pulling myself dripping onto the deck.

"Jesus, Tyler, I thought you was goin' AWOL," one of the sentries said.

"I started to," I told him, and laughed. "I was a-headin' for home."

For the rest of that night, I slept better than I had for two months.

There were now fourteen SEALs operating off the barge, three times that many riverboat sailors, and eight boats. Some of the sailors were Vietnamese. We were training them to conduct riverine warfare. Poppa came back, and Hercules. As you can imagine, with all those boats going, we were busier than a one-armed paper hanger.

Being busy meant you didn't get a lot of sleep time, and having those nightmares meant I didn't sleep much when I did get it. It reached the point where I had to make a choice every day: Do I want to write a letter home? or do I want to go to sleep on patrol tomorrow? Do I want to get my hair cut, or doze off on ambush tonight? Do I want to play cards and bullshit with the guys, or do some other little thing that will make me feel more like a human being, or do I want to risk being a little too tired and a little too slow tomorrow and come out second best in a firefight?

Some guys just had to be human beings. I decided to save that for when I got back home. I was over there to kill, so I was going to be a damned efficient killing machine. It could make all the difference in whether I walked onto that big jet that was taking me back or was loaded on in a box.

I hardly went out with Brewster or the Chief anymore. There were a lot of recon patrols and attack patrols to take out, and only a few old hands to do the job. Poppa would take out a few, but mostly he was a loner, and we would take him out, insert him in the bush, and escort him back in a few days. Hercules didn't lead patrols. He was sharp as a tack and always knew what ought to be done in almost any situation, but he didn't want to lead, and most of the Americans there wouldn't have followed him anyway. So us "old-timers" led the patrols, and the less-experienced SEALs and sailors were the manpower. The Nigger was a boat captain now, and even the Chief didn't call him Nigger anymore. He said he still got scared . . . but when you're the only one on the boat who knows what the hell to do, and not doing it can get your ass killed, it's a lot easier to overcome your fear and do the things you have to do.

With more people, we were able to expand the range of our patrol action. The PBRs were really restricting Charley's ability to move by water, and we had an ambush out on some trail almost every night. We were hurting him, and we knew it. Then we started getting more aggressive, and going out of our immediate area, which he was starting to avoid, and seeking him out.

One place Charley kept giving us trouble was the goddamned Sector Q14. There were others: The Ca Mau Peninsula had a hard-core contingent in the interior, and the crossings of the Mekong just over on the Cambodian side were always "hot." But that damned Parrot's Beak area and the Plain of Reeds right next to it were a major source of infiltration. And they pointed like an arrow right down to Sector Q14.

So, in late April, I took a recon patrol down into Q14 to see what the hell was going on.

Recon patrols were almost all six- or eight-day affairs now, so you took along the very best people available. The problem was that few of the very best were available, since they were leading their own patrols. So on this one I took Billy, Yancey, Chinese Lee, and two other guys whose names I have since forgotten. We had Nigger drop us off along the Ky Huong Canal, and we walked in.

Things went bad from the start. Charley was all over that area, patrolling, setting up ambushes, collecting taxes and rice from the farmers. And it wasn't just your ordinary stumble-through-the-brush Charleys either; it was *Mr.* Charles. Mr. Charles was a lot more sophisticated than the local recruits. He was trained, and trained well, for what he was doing. On the whole, in the jungle, he was probably equal to the 101st Airborne, maybe the Green Berets, but definitely superior to the average Army or Marine unit. The sappers that infiltrated the wire and electronic defenses around U.S. bases and blew up helicopters and shit were trained by, and recruited from, Mr. Charles.

In a mechanized war, a World War II–type slug-it-out tank-to-tank brawl, we'd have beaten them, hands down. But this was the jungle, and we were fighting their war, and we just didn't have the units to match them.

They carefully dispersed their people and hid them until it was time to bring them together to hit something, and afterwards they scattered back into the jungles and rice paddies. While they were dispersed, they slipped around and killed one or two people here and there and burned or blew up a few things—no more, really, than a mosquito bite. But we kept slapping at the mosquito bites with big battalions, with the Air Cav and B-52s, instead of beating them at their own game.

Except, of course, for outfits like ours.

We had a tough time getting in, but we worked our way in as far as we could go, and spied on several camps.

We didn't want to call in air strikes or anything, because that would have tipped Charley off that we were in there, and in that heavy brush they wouldn't have been very effective. We got all the information we could, and located the camps as best we could on a map, and then slipped back out.

It had been a tough patrol, and I started having trouble keeping my mind on what I was doing. As I led the patrol out of the bush, there would be blank intervals when I couldn't remember what had happened five minutes before. I would come upon a particular scene, a certain situation, and suddenly I would be thinking about some other place, some other scene, something that had happened months ago. At first, it wasn't too bad, but then I realized that these memories were starting to blank out the real situation for the scene in my mind. I got worried that I would see a VC patrol, then blank out and forget it and lead my patrol right into them.

I called the guys up.

"Look," I said, "I'm jist too tired. I can't keep my mind on what I'm a-doin'. I'm goin' to lead us into an ambush. We've got to hold up here until I get over this."

"You won't get over it here," Billy said. "You won't sleep until we get back, and sleep's what you need."

"Let's keep moving," somebody else said. "I'll take over the point. Let's get out of this damned hornet's nest!"

"Hell, the sun's gettin' low. It'll be dark soon. Let's hold up here till dark. We can move easier then."

"We might miss our pickup and have to wait until tomorrow night. Let's get on out of here."

They kept on until they convinced me. Then they odd-manned to see who would be point man, and one of the new guys won. I didn't like it, but they overruled my objections.

"You weren't doing too hot a job, and anyway, he

needs the experience," they said. "This war'll go on after you're gone, Tyler.... Give some of us a chance!"

"Hey, it'll be all right," Billy said. "We'll make it okay." He always said that.

I thought, what the hell, they're right. Let 'im go ahead and take it.

The new kid did a good job on point. At least he started out doing a good job. He'd go out fifteen or twenty yards, look around, and call us up. We'd move up, and he'd leap-frog out in front of us again. We kept that up for quite a way, and I started to relax a little—as much as I could. Those damned blank-out periods kept coming back on me.

Then he just took off. He went up and stopped, where we had him in sight still, and then he moved on. It couldn't have been very far, because after just a few seconds he hit the transmit button on his little radio and told us to hold up where we were. We did. We waited, and we waited... and we never heard from him.

"We'd better go and see what's up," I told the guy nearest me, who happened to be Chinese Lee.

We went up to where we'd seen him last, and then went on, maybe five or ten yards more. There was no sign of him, or of a struggle. There was no blood, no broken branches... nothing.

"Where th' fuck is he?" Lee asked.

"They got 'im," I said. "Took him prisoner. Let's get back and warn th' others."

They waited until we got back, and then, when the VC had us all together, all hell broke loose. Luckily, it was mostly small-arms fire. They threw a few grenades, but we were all belly-down by then, and all they did was stun us a little. If they'd thrown the grenades first, they probably would've gotten us all.

I low-crawled over to where I could talk in Billy's ear. He was the nearest one to me.

"I'm gonna radio out fer help," I told him. "But they won't be able to find us unless somebody leads 'em in here. I want ye to delay five minutes an' then pull out. . . . Go back to th' LZ an' lead 'em in here to git us out." I had another reason for sending Billy, I guess. I wanted to get him the hell out of here, in case help couldn't get there in time. The situation looked pretty hopeless: They were shooting into us from three sides, and I knew they would close off the fourth side soon, if we didn't start to counter their ambush.

I called out on the radio and got hold of Nigger, who had his PBR camouflaged in an ambush site on a river close by, waiting to come in and get us out. I told him we were surrounded, and in a bad way, and we were going to try to hold out until we got some help. I told him we'd send Billy out to guide the relief team back in. Nigger relayed the message on to the barge, and then called back and said they were getting a team ready right then and would be in as soon as they could get there.

I figured about three hours.

I inched out to the perimeter of our position, laid a couple of banana clips out, put a couple of grenades where I could get to them fast, and then signaled the guys to start a counter-ambush drill.

"Whooooya!" I hollered. "Whoooya!"

I switched the M-14 to full automatic and started emptying clips. I threw the grenades, and shot some more. The rest of the team joined in.

The gooks opened up even harder for a short time, then the fire died down a little as they pulled back. I turned around to signal Billy, but he was already moving. He low-crawled just about to the open side of the ambush, and stood up and started working his way out at a low crouch.

The VC increased their shooting then and forced us down again. We seesawed back and forth that way for thirty minutes or better, banging away at each other, Charley trying to extend the horns of his ambush, and us trying to stop them. Both sides were getting low on ammunition, but the gooks knew they'd soon get help, so they settled into a snipe-and-move procedure. So did we. We'd snipe at them and fall back.

As we fell back, we set claymores. As they moved up, they set them off. Finally we got out of there and headed toward the canal and the pickup zone.

It was dusk by then, and I almost missed seeing the body. I thought at first it was the point man. It was Billy.

I don't remember what happened next.

Somehow, I got his body up over my shoulder and came out shooting. I wasn't going to leave him for them to cut on.

It was a long retreat back to the canal, and we fought a running fight all the way. Yancey took over the rear guard, and Chinese Lee took over the radio. I just carried Billy.

They were hot on our asses when we got to the canal, and I think they had reinforcements by then. They were shooting pretty hard, and we'd all taken minor wounds. We held them up for a while at the bank while Chinese Lee got on the radio and told the boats we were there. They were pressing us close by the time the PBRs came into sight.

We fired a flare, and Nigger pulled right in. The gooks opened up with machine guns and RPGs, but he held the boat's nose to the bank, and we ran out with lead flying overhead from both sides. Two PBRs swept up and down the bank and hosed the motherfuckers down as we pulled away.

I laid Billy down on the afterdeck. I was aware of the fifty calibers and the twenty and the forty all going off in one hell of a sustained roar. Incoming rounds made little geysers of water when they landed near us, and dull thuds when they hit the boat, but I just sat there and looked at

Billy. They'd shot him in the back of his head. The exit hole in his forehead had brains and little pieces of bone around it.

I was thinking about him being an Eagle Scout. He really was honest and loyal, and all that. . . . Hell, he was just an all-around good kid. And he was smart. He would've been a real asset to the country, and they should've kept him back in the States. He was wasted in Vietnam, literally wasted.

Down deep, I knew Billy was a volunteer from the word go. He believed in his country, in what we were trying to do over here, and he was in the SEALs because he believed the Special Forces were the only really effective way to fight a guerilla war. But it was so much easier to be bitter.

Somebody took me by the arm and tried to get me to stand up. I shook him off. I was going to stay down, keep down while the bullets were flying around.

"C'mon, let's go have a drink." It was the Lieutenant Commander. I wondered briefly what he was doing out here. But I didn't really give a shit right then. I was thinking about Billy's wife.

Somebody tried to pick Billy up, and I thought they were going to throw him overboard, and pushed them back.

"Let's get him on the barge, Tyler," somebody said. So we lifted him up and laid him on the deck, and I went with the Lieutenant Commander and had a drink.

I told the Lieutenant Commander that I wanted to work Sector Q14 as much as I could. I figured I had a score to settle with the VC in there. He said he would let me work in that area as much as he could.

He started smoking a marijuana cigarette. He had got to where he'd always carry one behind his ear, and he almost forgot once to take it out when some brass hats came out to the barge. Some sailor reminded him just in time. He claimed the marijuana was all that kept him from getting an ulcer, with all the increased activity, eight boats, and a hundred sailors or so to worry about. He worried about us SEALs, too. It got to him every time somebody came back shot up, and especially if they got killed. He'd drink a lot and smoke a lot, and then write the letters to their families. He'd let the letter lie there on his desk for a day or so while he sobered up, and then if it looked good to him sober, he'd send it out.

I thought about Billy. After a while, I took the Lieutenant Commander's bottle and a glass and went out onto the deck and waited for the sun to come up.

CHAPTER 17

We pulled away from the barge under a brooding cobalt-colored sky that constantly dripped rain. It was May, and the rainy season had come again. The river stretched out east and west, blank, featureless, gleaming dimly in the dusk like a sheet of steel. We turned east, toward the deepening night over the China Sea.

The jungle was a narrow black smudge at the edge of the river, but as we went downstream, it seemed to rise up and block the faint light in the west.

I was in the forward guntub, behind the twin fifty calibers. A couple of riverboat sailors squatted on the foredeck behind me, watching the shore. Brewster was crouching with his shotgun amidships, watching off to starboard. A man named Smith manned the twenty millimeter. He got to it first and wouldn't give it up. Brewster was still sulking about that. A cocky little black sumbitch we called Cowboy was at the helm, and the Lieutenant Commander sat behind him in the coxswain den.

We'd told the Lieutenant Commander, "Keep your ass on the barge, where it's safe. You're going home in a few days." He was already a week overdue, but his replacement hadn't shown up yet.

"I've been covered up with paperwork," he said. "Haven't been out for a month. And I've got to get all this shit ready for the guy that takes over from me. This will be the last chance for me to go out, my last trip on the river. Give me a break."

So he pulled patrol duty with the rest of us. We went down the river, turned into a narrow inlet, and followed this tributary stream that wandered out through the Delta. It took us to the canal. Down the canal a ways, we turned off into another channel that wandered down through Q14. Charley's country.

And it was Charley's weather. Drizzling, dark.

I could feel Charley out there, watching. I saw nothing, and could hear nothing over the mutter of the throttled-back engine, but I could feel eyes on me.

We came to a village on the bank, just three bamboo huts on stilts, standing partway over the water, and a few hooches, really just lean-tos made of branches and leaves, half-hidden by shadows back in the trees. There was a fire in the middle of the little clearing, and smoke hung low in the rainy night. There were no people. There were no dogs and no pigs. There was no movement whatsoever.

The word was passed forward: "Charley's village. Keep your eyes open."

Shit. That word came from a sailor with three weeks in-country. We'd been in Charley's backyard since we left the canal.

I glanced back. Over on the port side, a sailor was smoking. He was hunched over, but the flare when he lit up had caught my eye, and his posture and a wisp of white smoke gave him away. I passed the word back for him to put out the cigarette.

Instead, the word came back that he just *had* to have a smoke. The tension was killing him.

I yanked one of the sailors into the guntub, turned the fifties over to him, and took his M-16. Then I moved back toward the sailor who was smoking.

"Kill that damned cigarat, asshole!" I told him. I talked low, but right in his ear. "Charley can see it half a click away. You're makin' a target outta the whole fuckin' boat."

He objected. He was uptight. He needed his marijuana.

I laid the barrel of the M-16 up beside his ear. "Hey," I said, "put it out *now*. Ye don't smoke that shit on patrol with me! I don't give a damn if it's the best Saigon Gold money can buy—I ain't gettin' my ass blowed off jist because of yer habit. You put it out now or I'll waste ye myself!"

He put it out. I went back and took over the fifty.

The boat seemed motionless, like it was pinned to the river. The bow wave and wake could have been cast in concrete, for all the movement you could see. Even the jungle, towering up black on all sides, was featureless.

Then we were through the worst of it. The channel opened up, and the jungle pulled away.

Up ahead of us, a low headland jutted into the river. Even in the dark I recognized it. In the daylight, the jungle was a tangled mass of rotting deadfalls and vines and fungus. It reminded me of mold on a pork rind. At night, it sometimes glowed with foxfire.

I passed the word back to speed up. Cowboy inched the throttle open a little. I'm sure he felt the same uneasiness, but the Lieutenant Commander was thinking about the boat following us, and kept him from opening up all the way.

I heard the radio crackle with transmissions, but I couldn't make them out.

The rain washed oil and camo paint down my face into my eyes, which made them burn and water as I tried to keep a close watch on the headland. They were so tired and weak-feeling from not sleeping that they twitched, like an overworked muscle. I wished I'd been able to get another shot of oxygen before we pulled through this part of the channel.

There was a spark of light on the headland.

In the brief time it took me to cut my eyes to the spot and focus on the spark, it had grown into a hissing ball of fire.

I thought, what the shit? Then it dawned on me it was a rocket, coming right at us!

I tried to yell, "Rocket! Hit the throttle! Let's go!" Those words were in my mind, but it had already hit and my mouth was full of river water. There was a crack like the first crack of thunder when lightning hits close, and then there was just the faint patter of waves against the bank.

When I got my wits about me again I was treading water.

The night was pitch black. I'd lost my night vision in the flash, but slowly, I began to be able to see objects in the water. Flotsam. The PBR was gone. It must have broken in two and sunk like a rock.

A head bobbed in the water near me. One of the sailors. He seemed stunned. I swam over and got him started toward the nearest shore.

Another swimmer. Chinese Lee. We spread out, looking for others. I kept finding little odds and bits of floating debris, but no people. Finally I heard a voice calling softly, "Tyler . . . Tyler. Over here."

It was Chinese Lee, and he had Cowboy. Cowboy was

unconscious, but his life jacket had kept him floating. I tried slapping his face, but he didn't come around.

"He's hurt pretty bad," Lee said. "He's bleedin' and he's not talkin'. I felt him all over, and he's all there, but his leg seems to be messed up."

"Take him on over to th' bank," I told Lee, "and tie him to a bush so he won't float away. And gag him. When he comes to, he may start yellin'. Don't drag him out on the bank.... Charley'll be along soon."

Another swimmer. Brewster.

"Hell, I should a-knowed ye was too useless to git killed."

"Fuck you, too."

"Ye seen th' Lieutenant Commander?"

"Yeah—I got him."

"Is he okay?"

"Shit, no—he's dead."

"Dead? Where'd he get it?"

"Hell, I donno, I ain't found no wound."

We pulled the body over to the bank. I felt all over him, but I couldn't find anything wrong. His clothes were torn here and there, but his body was all intact. His head was intact. Could it have been concussion?

"I don't thank so," Brewster said. "The son of a bitch went over my head 'n' went off rat behind me. Blowed me halfway across th' damned river, an' I ain't dead."

We worked our way upstream until we were all together under the bank. Lee had rounded up one more sailor, unwounded. Two men were missing: Smith and another sailor. We took stock. Brewster and Lee and I had our .38s. We always carried them. We had our knives. We had a few grenades between us, but in the water they could be as dangerous to us as to the enemy. We were going to be in bad shape if we had to fight.

I expected Charley along any minute, so we pushed the Lieutenant Commander's body back under some brush hanging over the water, and we tied him to it so he wouldn't get carried away by the current. We did Cowboy the same way, but were more careful to tie him so his head stayed above the water. Then we pulled moss and crap down over both men to cover them, and we hid ourselves. There were no sounds except the lap-lap of little waves and a few strange bird calls, and the buzzing of cicadas.

We expected Charley to come along the bank.

He came by sampan.

Five VC sat in a little hollowed-out shell of a boat poled along by a sixth, who stood in the stern. They all had guns ready. One had a flashlight. They came down the river slowly, watching the bank carefully, sweeping their light along the water next to the shore. As they got closer, I could hear some rustling and crashing in the bush, and realized they were working their way along in coordination with a shore party.

They swept the light along toward the brush where Cowboy was tied, his face above the water. My asshole started to pucker. I waited for a burst of fire. I caught my breath and ducked under the water, holding myself down by gripping on to a root.

I decided that if they started shooting, I would swim out, tip the boat over, and knife as many as I could.

The pole made a dull "chunk" sound underwater as it was driven into the bottom. The light flickered briefly over the water above my head, and then passed on. I held my breath as long as I could and then slowly, slowly, let my head break the surface.

They were twenty meters downstream. Still poling. Watching the bank, mostly. One watched the river. They chattered back and forth to those on the shore, and moved on off.

Safe . . . for now, I thought. How the hell are we going to get out of here? We sure won't be safe come morning.

And we have to get help for Cowboy. The fish are probably eating on his leg right now.

I worked my way quietly over to him. He was awake. His eyes were extra large, it seemed. He was probably going into shock. They rolled over my way—we'd immobilized his head, and he couldn't turn it—and he couldn't talk or grin around the gag, so he raised a hand out of the water in a weak greeting. I grabbed his hand and squeezed it.

"I'm gonna leave you tied up," I whispered in his ear, "in case you pass out. So you won't drown. An' I'm a-gonna leave th' gag in, too, so you won't holler out if th' pain gets too bad." He managed to move his head up and down, and squeezed my hand in return. "Ye'd do th' same to me if ye had th' chance, wouldn't ye?"

He flipped me a finger. I knew he was going to be okay.

I moved up to where Brewster and Chinese Lee were crouched under the bank.

"What the fuck're we gonna do?"

"There'll be a boat along here in fifteen or twenty minutes."

"How are we a-gonna signal it? There's not a flare pistol or a flashlight in the bunch."

"Shoot our thirty-eights?"

"And be on th' receivin' end of the fifty caliber?"

"What else're we a-gonna do? Walk out?"

"Swim out?"

"I wish I coulda got that flashlight them gooks had."

"Maybe we could swim out into the channel, and they'd see us."

"Not much chance. We'd have to be almost in their path, and yell as they went by."

"Maybe that's th' best idea yet, though."

"Don't make a shitpot of difference now. Here comes another Cong patrol." We slipped back into the water.

This patrol had a flashlight, too, that they shined into the water and into the brush along the bank, and, of course, it ruined their night vision. Not only could they not see anything outside of the light, but they stumbled along and tripped over limbs and bushes.

After they passed, I started for the bank and glanced around at Brewster. He had the same idea.

"Them little fellers is jist about helpless, ain't they?"

"Let's go get us a light."

We took the last two out first, slashing their throats and dropping them beside the trail. Then we took the next two. One of them had the light. We figured he was the officer. At least three others had gone on out ahead, to get their night vision back as best they could. We took the light and the three AKs and went back to the guys by the bank. We took an AK-47 each, gave one to Chinese Lee, and gave the flashlight to a sailor.

"Now you put your T-shirt over that light," we told him, "and when that next boat comes along, you shine the light *straight at it*, and you signal in Morse Code. Signal SOS, BSU-One, PBR. Can you do that?" He said yes, he could.

"Okay. Don't shine that light nowhere else, understand?"

He said yes, he did.

We told him, "If you fuck up, you'll die."

Then the three of us with the AKs laagered up and waited for Charley to come back.

CHAPTER 18

Charley came back when he found the bodies, but he came back slowly and cautiously. He knew we were armed with AKs, and he knew we were dangerous.

We slipped down over the bank near the water and waited. The three survivors of the second patrol went on by. We watched them as they went by and figured they were more interested in getting back to camp without us finding them than they were in finding us.

But down the river, the sampan was working its way back upstream, still in coordination with the patrol on-shore.

I'd begun to think that other PBR had turned back when at last its engine's rumble became audible. In a matter of seconds it increased to a dull roar. The light on the sampan was turned out. Out in the channel, a bow wave gleamed dimly through the blackness.

"Now! Now!" we practically shouted at the sailor. The

light started flashing, aimed directly at the PBR but with its side glow muffled by the T-shirt. I wanted to turn and watch, as if somehow I could make the crew understand, to turn in and pick us up. But my job was to watch the bush and make sure that if Charley saw the light, he couldn't get there to hit us, or the boat, or both.

It seemed like hours before the pitch of the engine changed.

"He's coming in. . . . He's coming in!" the sailor hissed. If you can shout in a whisper, he was doing it.

"Jist hope he don't decide to shoot first an' ask questions later!" I told him.

"Signal the boat number! The boat number, God damn it!" I heard Chinese Lee telling him. Good idea.

I also heard some shouting out in the bush, and some crashing noises, like somebody running through the undergrowth.

"They're a-comin'," I told Lee. "Get ready!" I was afraid all his attention would be on the boat.

The engine noise changed again. They were definitely landing.

"Get the Cowboy cut loose!" I told the sailors. "Get th' Lieutenant Commander! Get ready to get 'em on th' boat!"

Shots from the bush. They were still too far out to see the boat, and they were firing blind as they ran. I started shooting, too, aiming at their muzzle flashes. I intended to keep them as far back as I could. I sort of cringed as I shot, expecting to be stitched up the back by fifty-caliber slugs from the boat.

There was shouting behind me, and splashing. Shouting in front of me, and shooting. I emptied the magazine of the AK. Brewster tugged at my sleeve.

"Let's go! Let's go!"

I turned and dived over the riverbank into the water just as an AK burst stitched the bank where I'd been sitting, and an answering burst of fifty-calibers sizzled by over my head.

I came up with one hand on the gunwale. I had the AK-47 in the other, but no ammunition for it. I tossed it out into the river beyond the stern of the PBR. Someone grabbed my hand and started pulling me on board. The boat was already backing away from the bank. I hooked one leg over the gunwale and rolled inside, and fell on something cold and wet: the Lieutenant Commander's body. Brewster came over the other gunwale.

"Is this everybody?" I tried to check and make sure that we were all there, but there was too much confusion. We turned broadside to the bank, about a hundred meters out, as we got ready to head downstream. The twenty millimeter and the fifty caliber were going full blast, and in the light from the spotlight and the tracers I could see figures running up the river bank, firing. They were firing RPG-7s, and someone on board was blasting back with an M-79. As we pulled away from there, the boat captain got the forty millimeter going, with flechette rounds. The running figures on the bank went down like quail in front of a shotgun. In the edge of the spotlight beam I saw the sampan and pointed. The forty millimeter swung around, and the water near the little boat erupted in geysers. Then we were gone.

When the shooting stopped and there was nothing but the roar of the engine, it was almost like sudden silence.

The boat captain was the big black son of a bitch that had decked me once in a bar in Vallejo. I went over and hugged him like a brother.

The Chief ran the outfit for a few days, until a replacement could be found for the Lieutenant Commander. The officer who was supposed to replace him hadn't shown up, for some reason. So they had to look around for someone else. The Chief ran things pretty well, but he wouldn't do the paperwork. Anyway, the brass thought they had to send an officer in.

The Chief and I packed up the Lieutenant Commander's things. We put his pictures of his wife and kids, and all his letters, and all his other personal stuff into a box—his seabag was already packed, he was so close to going home—and we sent the stuff out to the commander of the Coastal River Squadron. We kept his whiskey and his marijuana and passed it around.

The Navy came up with this real turd to replace him. The new commander's name was Morganti, and he was a full commander. He was a fleet officer bucking to make admiral. All the promotions were going to the riverboat sailors, because that's where all the fighting was going on, so he went to the Navy's School of Riverine Warfare at Vallejo and became an instant expert. He was just waiting for a command when Lieutenant Commander Gray got killed, and the damned vulture swooped right in. He had some kind of pull, I think. He knew somebody important or his family had lots of money, or something, because he wasn't qualified for command of BSU-One, not in a combat zone. Lieutenant Commander Gray was on his third tour; this bastard had never even been to 'Nam and had never commanded anything bigger than a PBR, and that in training. He was a staff officer. A pencil pusher.

Lieutenant Commander Gray had run things kind of unobtrusively. He didn't say much, and when he gave an order, he made it sound more like a request, but he always got things done his way. That's because he didn't try to be an expert on everything. He'd come to us and say, "Here's what we've got to do..." and he'd tell us, and then he'd say, "How do *you* think we ought to go about it?" If it was something to do with recon, he came to us. If it was something to do with the boats, he went to the coxswains. And we would've done goddamned near anything for him.

The new man didn't operate that way. Commander Morganti wanted us to salute him every damned time we saw him, on the barge and everywhere, and he chewed us all out for not being in uniform, insisting that we wear a full set of fatigues—bush greens—when we went on patrol. He made the boat crews wear hard hats and combat boots. The hard hats were also called "brain ovens," and the combat boots were dangerous if you went overboard. You could swim in tennies. It was a hell of a lot tougher in the boots.

When the chief and I tried to talk to the son of a bitch, he read us the riot act. He said he was responsible for us, and he'd make the decisions, and we would not question them. Regardless of the fact that we were SEALs, as long as we were attached to BSU-One, we were under his command. Then he called Lieutenant Commander Gray sloppy and irresponsible and said it was his fault BSU-One had such a high casualty rate.

I got all pissed off and wanted to drown the fucker right then, but the Chief said no, to wait. The Commander would either settle down or the Chief would talk to someone on the Admiral's staff and get the matter handled quietly. But when he tried to get through to the Admiral's office, he was told that there was to be no contact with higher echelon except with permission of Commander Morganti.

Our recon reports had indicated Charley was building up in Q14, particularly around the headland they'd fired the rocket from. There was a staging base in there for sappers, where they got organized and got the supplies together they needed to go out and hit firebases and such stuff. So someone in Operations decided they'd knock Charley out of there. They sent in a battalion of Air Cavalry. It was a full-scale operation, with gunship support and jet fighter-bombers.

They got their asses creamed.

Charley had SAMs in there, heat-seeking missiles, and they shot down three or four troop-carrying helicopters and a gunship or two, while the gunships couldn't do much against that tangle of brush and trees but defoliate the top few feet of the jungle.

Now Navy Intelligence wanted more recon information so they could plan another attack. They'd lost a lot of people and equipment in the first operation, and it had become a point of honor to get back in there and kick ass. They wanted us to slip in and find out just how many men and what kind of weapons the Viet Cong had in there.

We knew that it was going to be a hot LZ, and that anyone trying to go in by boat might be met at the bank by Charley, so we planned a diversion. We would go in with one boat and make out like we were going to land a patrol on the headland. While we had Charley's attention, the real recon patrol would come in on a fast boat and land in a cove about half a click upstream. Once they were landed, both boats would get the hell out of there. We couldn't get Morganti to agree to let us do it that way. He wanted the patrol to land right on the headland itself. Otherwise, he said, they might not get to where they were supposed to recon.

So we told him we would do it his way and planned among ourselves to do it ours once we got out on the river.

Of course, he decided to come along.

He wanted to see some action. He was Silver-Starry-eyed, already counting his metals.

At first, we welcomed the fucker along. We figured one trip would be enough for him, if he got shot at. We thought we had his number.

He started butting in right away, of course. He decided

who was going in on patrol and who was going on the diversion, and there wasn't any changing his mind. He picked the people with the most experience to be on the diversion boat with him: the Chief, Brewster, and me. Partly, I think he wanted to keep his damned eyes on us, look for some reason to dress us down. He picked Yancey and Virgil and two other SEALs, new guys, to make up the patrol. We tried to get him to let at least one of us experienced hands switch off, but no, fuck no, he wouldn't do it.

We went past the landing point at high speed, making a hell of a lot of noise, and there was no shooting. So we went on up the river—we'd come in from the downstream direction—and swung around and into a cove. There we throttled down. We coasted along the length of the cove with the engine throttled 'way back, and all of us alert. I was expecting another rocket at any minute, but nothing happened.

The radio crackled, and the other boat announced they were going in to insert the patrol.

We crept in toward the bank, like we were being real cautious. I don't need to tell you, I was tense. We had the boat with the quad-fifty, and I was sitting up there in the guntub, watching that shoreline get closer and closer, and expecting any minute to see tracers or RPGs coming out at us.

Nothing.

We got close enough to shore that the Commander had the coxswain reverse the engines. We backed away from the shore. Still no shooting. I kept listening for the radio, but it didn't make a sound. It was sure taking a long time for the other boat to insert the patrol.

We backed out near midchannel and started to circle. I looked around at the Chief, and he looked at me, and he was frowning. We were both feeling that something was wrong.

I got Brewster to take over the fifty caliber, and I went back to the coxswain's den.

"Somethin's gone wrong," I told the Commander. "They shoulda called an' said they'd pulled out by now."

"If anything's gone wrong, they'll let us know."

"We'd better go check it out," the Chief said. "They might be in trouble."

"Our job is to hold our station," he said. "We'll hold here until they notify us."

I looked at my watch.

"Time's up," I told him. "They should've dropped th' patrol an' been back by now. Somethin's wrong." The other boat had been a few minutes behind us, and they'd had twenty minutes to land the patrol.

"We'd better go check it out," the Chief insisted.

"God damn it, we'll leave this station when I give the order!" said Commander Morganti.

There was a flash of light behind the headland. The sound of a blast came a few seconds later.

"Hey, man, screw you, we're going!" the Chief yelled. He had to yell over the roar of the engines, because I'd already stepped past the coxswain and kicked the throttle wide open. The bow came up, and the stern just kind of dug down in the water like it was getting a better grip, and we went out of the cove, planing full bore. Commander Morganti didn't say anything to stop us. I guess he knew better.

When we came around the point, there wasn't anything to see but bodies in the water. The PBR had been blown to pieces, and the pieces sank right away. The bodies were all held up by their life jackets.

We went past once and raked the shore with the quad-fifty and the twenty and the forty millimeters, and after the first pass, we didn't draw any fire. Then we came back and slowed down and hooked the bodies on board while running about one-quarter throttle. It was pretty rough on the bodies, but they were past caring.

We laid them out on the afterdeck, and we could see two of the four SEALs had been shot, and two of the sailors. The other two SEALs were probably killed by the explosion. I looked down at Virgil, with a hole in his neck, and what we had been able to find of Yancey. They were just kids. They shouldn't have been put into that hellhole without some more-experienced hand along to guide them.

The water was choppy, because we were cutting back across our own wake, and the deck was heaving a little. I turned around, and the son of a bitch was standing there. I saw red. I threw a punch at him that should have knocked the walls off a brick shithouse, but the pitching of the boat ruined my aim. It caught him a glancing blow on the jaw, and he staggered back against the gunwale.

Oh shit, I thought, it's the stockade for me now.

Morganti got up madder than hell, of course, cursing me for insubordination and striking an officer, and telling me what all he was going to do to me. The Chief stepped forward and swung his gun butt. Morganti threw up his arm to block it, and the butt glanced off his shoulder and hit him behind his ear, and knocked him to his knees.

"Shut your fucking face," the Chief told him. "We'll just put your ass over the side right here."

The next morning, we got orders to report to the flagship. The signals man that took the message told them, "You can send a helicopter, but for God's sake don't send SPs. These guys are mad enough to declare war on the Navy."

We had to go up before the Admiral, on the flagship of the Coastal River Squadron, the U.S.S. *Eldorado*. I was all prepared for that son of a bitch Morganti to be sitting in the Admiral's office, smirking, but he wasn't there. We went in, and the Admiral had us sit down. He drummed his fingers on his desk a while and looked us over. He looked me in the eye for what seemed like a week.

"The last time I talked to you it was certainly under different circumstances," he said. I jumped. I didn't think he'd have any idea he'd ever seen me before.

"Do you still feel the same way about your medals?" he asked.

"I feel like I've earned one now," I told him.

"For what?"

"For knocking the shit out of that incompetent son of a bitch."

He read something on his desk for a few minutes.

"I've heard his side of the story. Why don't you tell me yours?" he said.

So we did. We told him how Morganti operated, how he dictated the way he wanted SEALs to run recon patrols, how he told the coxswains how to run their boats, despite his lack of experience in combat. We told how Morganti had insisted that the recon patrol go in on the headland and the diversion take place upstream, instead of the other way around. We told how he wouldn't leave the decoy site when there was ample reason to think something was wrong. And we told how we reacted to the sight of the bodies.

"If you send him back to that barge, he's dead," we told the Admiral. "You can lock us up in the brig right now, but there's others on that barge that feel just like we do. One night, he'll just disappear. He'll go for a long walk on a short barge, and there won't be anybody that'll tell you a goddamned thing about it."

He listened without saying a word or asking a question, until we were finished.

Then he asked, "Why didn't you just kill him then,

when there were no witnesses? Surely you realized he'd bring charges."

We thought about it for a while.

"I guess it was because he was wearing a Navy uniform," I said. "Because we're trained to respect officers, no matter what kind of turds they are. I don't really know why, unless it was just all that training."

"You'll be confined to the brig until I decide what to do about this matter," he said, and they took us away.

We were in the brig overnight. It wasn't the first time for any of us, but we'd always deserved it before. This time, we felt like we'd done the Navy a service. I suspected the Admiral felt the same way, but couldn't let it show. We didn't spend the night worrying about what was going to happen to us. We knew we were right, and damn the consequences.

The next morning, we went before the Old Man again.

"My aide talked to some of the sailors in BSU-One last night," he began. I got this sudden sinking feeling. "They were guarded, but what they had to say was very revealing." He sat and looked at us for several minutes.

"Commander Morganti has been transferred. There's not much likelihood that any of you will ever encounter him again." He paused for several minutes, as if thinking of the best way to go on. "You are going back to your unit. You will be reduced in rank one grade and fined six months' pay, and the reduction and fine are suspended . . ."

We looked around at one another and grinned.

". . . pending further disciplinary problems. In plain English: If you fuck up again, I'm going to throw the book at you.

"If you're planning a Navy career, this thing is going to come back to haunt you," he went on. "But right now, we need men with your experience and training to hold this operation together more than we need inept officers getting their tickets punched for promotion."

He sent a warrant officer to take over BSU-One until they could get someone to replace Morganti. The warrant officer was one of the Admiral's aides. He went out on the same helicopter that took us back.

"You guys are goddamned lucky," he told us. "Commander Morganti wanted to have you court martialed for mutiny. The Admiral told him that if he did, some of the things that came out would wreck Morganti's career. So they reduced the charges to striking an officer, and the Old Man told him you would be 'appropriately disciplined.' The Admiral may take some flak about it, if Morganti ever follows up, but he wanted to get that SOB off his back, and you back out in the bush. He just had to make it look like you were being disciplined."

I told him, "We are being punished. We're being sent back out here to die."

CHAPTER 19

I'd swim just about every chance I got, at night or early in the morning. Swimming during the day was impossible. There was too much going on. Too much boat traffic and air traffic. But at night, I'd swim underwater out into the river. I'd dive down as deep as I could go, and stay down as long as I could.... I even got to checking out the diving gear so I could stay under longer. Down there I was away from it all, all the killing and all the dying, all the tension and all the fear. I relaxed then, the only times that I'd let down since I'd been in Vietnam.

When it was time to come back, I could feel the tension mounting and the fear growing as I neared the surface.

Swimming didn't get rid of the nightmares and the flashbacks. It just pushed them away for a while.

The strain was showing up in all of us. Guys would have temper tantrums over the littlest things, throwing shit around and cursing and screaming, sometimes fighting. Somebody else might just hit the bottle, or get stoned out of his mind for a day or two, until he worked things out for himself. One guy blew his brains out—over what, we never figured out. Fighting was common, even among people that weren't especially known for their tempers. One guy got a letter from home and sat around with a long face, until one of his buddies came up and slapped him on the back, and said in a joking manner, "What's the matter? Somebody fucking your old lady?" The other guy just knocked the shit out of him. The letter was from his brother, and that's just what the brother had told him.

Brewster got in a fight with the big black boat captain that pulled us off the bank the night we were hit by the rocket. There was nothing unusual about Brewster fighting with blacks; it was a way of life with him. What was unusual was the black almost got the best of him. They went at it for a few minutes, and when the rest of us thought they'd be tired and quit, the black guy got Brewster pinned down. That was a mistake. The guy could knock the shit out of him, kick him around, as long as Brewster felt like he was winning, but pinning him was a mistake. Bob bit the son of a bitch on the lower lip...bit it *off*, and spit it overboard. He let Bob up then, of course. Bob got up and hit him up beside the head with a chair while the guy was holding his mouth. We pulled Bob off before he killed the guy.

Brewster was broken a couple of grades and fined. He didn't give a shit. The black guy went home. I hope they sent him to a plastic surgeon before his family saw him.

Then one morning I woke up and my rifle had been moved. Not much. But it wasn't where I had left it. I woke up everybody in the cots nearby. They hadn't moved it. They knew better.

"Look out, it may be booby-trapped," I told them. Then I spent half an hour on my goddamned hands and knees, looking for trip wires. Finally, I decided that it

wasn't going to blow up if I moved it, so I picked it up
and looked it over. I removed the clip, took the bullets
out, and threw them away. I stripped the weapon down
until I could look through the bore. Clean as a whistle.

I was putting it back together when this cocksucker
came in and wanted to know what the hell was going on.

"Tyler's rifle was moved last night," they told him,
"and he thought it might be booby-trapped."

"Oh, hell, I bumped into it on the way to the head,"
he said.

I lost it there for a minute. I slapped that little son of
a bitch around and cursed him and called him every filthy
name I could think of. The more I hit him, the madder I
got.

"I tried to put it back," he said.

He ran out onto the foredeck, and I chased him, kicking
his butt all the way. He fell down, and I kicked him in
the nuts and threw him in the river. I was going over the
side to make sure he drowned when the little warrant
officer that was running the show came out and stopped
me.

They launched a full-scale assault against that headland
down in Sector Q14. But they still couldn't get into the
place by air, and their attempted landing was beaten off.
It was obvious the VC and NVA were there in force, but
what the hell were they doing in there? Memories of
Tet were still strong in the minds of the generals and
admirals of MAC-V, and they feared the worst. They
didn't want any repetitions. Charley had to be driven out
of Q14.

They tried B-52 raids. They did a hell of a lot of damage
to the jungle, and killed a lot of fish in the river, but we
could tell that they hadn't had much effect on the VC.
Something else had to be done.

The Chief and I went into Saigon, met with some of

the Intelligence people, looked at some maps and photographs of the area, and made our suggestions. When we went back to the barge it was with a fresh supply of C-4 and claymore mines, and four Mark VI underwater breathing outfits. The plan was for four of us to swim ashore some dark night (they were all dark now, with the rains starting again) and set out the C-4 to destroy the communist bunkers. An assault force would land at dawn. The claymores would kill any Vietnamese who tried to move up to any remaining positions near the beach. If any made it, there would be a row of claymores set just beside the brushline, with trip wires in designated locations on the beach so that the troops could set them off if they got pinned down.

After two assaults, Charley *knew* we would be coming back. He'd have double the normal number of sentries out, if not triple. I figured they would be waiting for us as we came out of the water. We had two days to think about it. I was drunk all the first day, and got put on report.

The second day, we checked out our gear. We made sure the timers worked, by popping caps with them. We dived with the breathing apparatus. I cleaned my rifle and my .38 and loaded both with fresh ammunition. I sharpened my knife. I lay down and smoked a cigarette. I wrote my mother. I got up and checked to make sure I'd packed all my gear. I tore up the letter to my mother. I had a drink. I went out on deck and watched the sunset. I ate. I drank four cups of coffee. I wrote my brother. I tore up the letter to my brother. All the time, I had this picture in my mind: my head rising slowly out of the water until half the face mask was exposed, and then *zap*! the face mask caves in as an AK-47 round goes in.

I looked over at Brewster. He hadn't moved in two hours. He was sitting on his cot, reading some kind of fuck book. He only moved when he turned the pages, and that wasn't very often. I wished I could be that oblivious.

"Bob... I ain't comin' back from this one."

"Why not? Ye goin' over th' hill?"

"No... I got this feeling."

"Fuck it. I'm trying to read."

At last, it was time to go. I made one more check of my gear: regulator, tanks, mouthpiece, mask, fins. Tanks full. The .38 wrapped tightly in a plastic bag and taped. The knife by my left shoulder, where I could get to it with each hand. Diving watch with the diving compass attached to the band. Diving light. C-4. Timers. Claymore mines. Extra wire. Face blackened. Exposed skin blackened.

We went to get on the boat. The last thing I noticed as we left the crew's quarters was Bob's fuck book turned over on his bunk, carefully marking the place.

I took my M-14, in case something came down before we got there. I hoped something would.

Sometimes it seemed to take hours to get to Sector Q14. Tonight it seemed to only take minutes. The closer we got to the insert point, the stronger my premonition got. I would've prayed, except I felt like such a damned hypocrite doing it. It was a high-speed drop. We put on our gear, checked the tanks and regulator one more time, and leaned backwards off the boat. We rendezvoused in the blackness by swimming along the wake, two back and two forward, until we met. Then, after making sure there were no problems, we started in.

We staged ourselves. That is, one dived down to just about the bottom, one a few feet above him, then another a few feet above him, and so on. The uppermost swimmer had to be deep enough that his light wouldn't show through to the surface. We would swim a compass bearing in, and back out to the pickup spot. The watch, depth gauge, and compass all had luminous dials, but there was always the possibility of swimming into trouble if you tried going in blind.

I took the bottom going in, figuring I had the most experience and could avoid any obstacles such as trip wires for mines, or barbed wire thrown out to make an obstacle for swimmers. Brewster was the top man, and would be the first one on the beach.

It was a gently rolling, ripple-marked, silty bottom. Except for a few fish that came to investigate the light, I saw nothing. I stayed about five feet above the bottom as it started to shoal. I read the depth gauge and the compass at regular intervals. Finally, the right amount of time had elapsed, and I was only twenty feet down. I should be somewhere close to the beach.

I turned out the light and let myself rise to the surface. I was very near to neutral buoyancy, so I rose slowly. When the dark water grew noticeably lighter I knew I was almost to the surface. That murky water would let light penetrate only to very shallow depths during the day. I let my head break the surface, and I gritted my teeth, and I waited for the bullet.

It didn't come.

I was a good thirty meters out. Between me and the beach were two more swimmers—I could barely make out their black silhouettes against the gray beach.

I swam underwater for another twenty meters, then broke the surface again. There were now three patches of shadow on the beach, one very near the jungle edge. I turned off the regulator and spat out the mouthpiece. I had to save some air for the swim back out.

I moved in with a cautious breaststroke, careful not to splash, watching the line of the jungle beyond the beach. Where the water was too shallow to swim, I pulled myself along with my hands, then crawled out onto the sand.

One by one we crept into the brush.

"What kept ye so long?" Brewster hissed.

"I was sightseein'."

It was raining, and the constant murmur of the rain in the leaves and bamboo thickets hid the sounds of our movements. It also hid any sounds that the Viet Cong sentries might make.

We took off our diving gear, cached it, and got out our .38s and explosives. Then we crept in and watched Charley for a while and tried to decide where to set our charges. Once we made our decision, we split up, each one going to his assigned area. Brewster and I took out a sentry each.

I went back to the beach area and set out a row of claymores to hit Charley's positions just inside the tree-line. I unrolled the extra trip wire and fixed up two spots. All the claymores could be set off from any one of those two spots. Then I marked the spots so the troops could see them when they came off the landing boats.

There was a little pier that they had built there to unload heavy stuff off sampans. It wasn't much: bamboo and some boards. I set a little C-4 on that and set the timer to blow it just before the boats got there.

The other guys came down to the beach, and we waded out into the water and got the hell out. There was no shooting. Brewster swam fifteen feet down. I staged just below him at about thirty-five feet. Chinese Lee was twenty feet below me, and the other guy was down near the bottom.

We were forty or fifty meters offshore when I heard a distinct click that seemed to come from over on my right. My first thought was that someone had just cocked a spear gun, and I quickly looked that way.

CHAPTER 20

I don't know how they got it placed out there, but I know I was lucky it was just a concussion grenade, and not one or two hundred pounds of explosives.

As it was, it jarred the hell out of me.

It must have been right below me, because it knocked the breath out of me. It was like being hit by a club in the stomach and the head at the same time. I was stunned for a second or so, and when I started coming around, my face mask was gone. I couldn't breathe, even though I still had the regulator in my mouth. I'd dropped the light. I was only conscious of the darkness and a tremendous ringing in my ears, and the fact that I had the breath knocked out of me. The only thing in my mind was getting to the surface.

I reached down and dropped my weight belt, and my knife and .38, and tried to swim upward. I didn't seem to be getting anywhere, despite having dropped the weight.

I wasn't getting any breath, and I could feel myself blacking out. I reached up to check the regulator, thinking it might have been damaged, but it was there. I was afraid I'd black out before I reached the surface, and drown, so I took the mouthpiece out and stuck it into my wet suit, and made a bubble. Then I stuck it back in my mouth. With the air in my wet suit, I shot to the surface.

I started to get my breath back on the way up. Maybe the lessening pressure had something to do with it. But I started breathing too fast, really hyperventilating. Because of the fast breathing and the pressure drop, I got nitrogen bubbles in my lungs. At the depth I had been I really should not have had to decompress.

Brewster was about ten feet away when I popped to the surface, and he got right over to me.

I wasn't thinking clearly. The left side of my face was numb, and my ears were ringing, and my lungs ached.

"Am I hurt? Am I hurt?" I kept asking him.

"Yer askin' me?" he said. Then, "I donno...ye got blood comin' outta yer head. Yeah, ye got hit in th' head."

"Is it bad?"

"Shit, I cain't see.... Yer all there...."

I couldn't swim real well, my coordination was so shot, so Brewster started pulling me out toward the pickup point.

I heard some dull thudding noises faintly, over the ringing in my ears.

"What's that?"

"Claymores. The Viet Cong are a-comin' out to see what th' explosion was. They hit th' trip wires." He kept swimming.

After a few minutes, or maybe only seconds—I was pretty disoriented—I heard another noise.

"The boats are a-comin' in. They heard th' explosion, too," Brewster told me.

The Chief was captain on the pickup boat, and there

were some other PBRs and a hydrofoil close by to support the landing. They all came in, and their guns shot up the beach while the Chief pulled us on board.

They didn't make a high-speed pickup like they'd planned—there wasn't any point now. The Chief just brought the boat up to us, stopped, and had us pulled on board. Then we moved off at high speed.

I dropped down in the coxswain's den and leaned up against a gunwale. Some son of a bitch came along and pushed me over. I sat back up, and he pushed me over again. I had to talk to the Chief, about the other two guys. Brewster was sitting by the gunwale on the other side of the coxswain's den, covered up in a poncho. He looked awfully tired and pale. The Chief was looking back at something. We slowed down until the engine was just idling. Then I heard the whop-whop of a helicopter rotor.

The helicopter came in and hovered just over the stern of the PBR, and a bunch of guys picked me up and put me in there. I kept saying, shit, I can walk, but they wouldn't let me. Brewster climbed in with me. There was a corpsman in there, and he gave me a shot while the helicopter was still climbing away.

I kept trying to make them understand they had to get the other two guys, but Brewster just shook his head.

If I thought anything clearly, I thought, well, I'm going home.

I woke up in a hospital.

Something was attached to the side of my head, so I couldn't turn very well, especially not to the left. I could look around enough to see I was in a hospital ward. There was a long row of men in beds, their heads and arms and legs all in bandages or casts. There was nothing I could see to tell me where I was.

I wiggled. Everything moved. I raised my right hand. . . . It was all there. I raised my left hand, and saw it had an IV needle in it. I felt of the side of my head with it. There were some bandages there, and some tubes. I couldn't tell much about it, except that it hurt like hell, that it seemed to be all there, and that the left side of my head somehow had the sensation of being covered with a pillow.

I didn't know if I was in Saigon or in the States, or how long I'd been here, or even if the war was still going on.

An orderly came by a little later and told me I was in Manila. I'd been there two days, and he didn't know shit about what was wrong with me. I couldn't go to the head because of all the tubes. He went off to tell someone I was awake.

Later, some little Filipino nurses came and took all the tubes loose and changed the bandages. They told me that if I ate a good dinner, they'd take the IV loose, so I ordered a steak. They went off giggling.

I didn't get my steak, but by the next day I was up and walking around. The doctors came and looked at me, and decided I was fit for two weeks' R and R and told me I had a ruptured eardrum and some burst blood vessels in the side of my head. They weren't sure if I'd ever hear in that ear again, and I'd never dive again, they said.

"Hell, that mean I'm goin' home?" I asked, hoping it did. Believing it did.

"No . . . there's nothing in our guidelines that says you're unfit for combat duty."

"Fuck your guidelines! I'm a diver! A SEAL! You just said I'd never dive again! So why the fuck can't I go home?"

"You've got two weeks' R and R coming. Take your two weeks and then come back. . . . I'll contact your commander and see if he thinks you're fit for duty, and we'll let you know then."

"Hell, I was hurt in a diving action.... How the hell could I be fit for duty?"

"Check back in two weeks."

They couldn't tell me anything about Brewster or the other two guys.

"Nobody else from your outfit came in with you."

I remembered enough to know Brewster was okay. I was also pretty damned sure about Chinese Lee and the other diver.

They were dead.

I left the hospital with nothing more than some cotton in that ear, money in my pocket, and a fresh uniform, and I went out to enjoy two weeks in Manila. I wanted something to drink, a woman, and some good food, in that order. I checked into a hotel, went down to the bar for a drink, and got into a fight, in that order.

I was sitting there minding my business and my rum, feeling like the left side of my head was wrapped in a pillow, when I noticed this son of a bitch staring at me. A goddamned airman. So I stared back at him. He must not have liked it. He said something to me that I didn't hear—the music was too loud, I guess. So I just kept on looking at him, and sneered a little bit. The son of a bitch got up and came over. He was big: six feet four and two hundred and forty pounds at least. And he had a friend who just sat watching and grinning.

The son of a bitch came up from my left side and mumbled something that I still didn't hear. I just sat there and looked at him and didn't say anything; out of the corner of my eye, I could see the bartender watching. The airman said something else. Then he made a quick grab for my collar with his left hand and pulled his right fist back.

As I came off the barstool, I hit him in the eyes with my drink and in the nuts with my knee. Then I got him inside the knee with my heel and in the kidneys with my elbow as I came back around. He crashed into the bar and fell over on the floor, still holding his eyes with both hands.

His buddy took a running jump at me, so I stepped aside and grabbed his wrist and helped him along a little. He landed two tables over, on a bottle of bourbon, a Filipino whore, and an angry Marine.

Then the big asshole on the floor started to stand up, and I flashed back. All I could see was black cotton pajamas and a coolie hat. I didn't have a weapon in my hands, so I went after the son of a bitch barehanded. A couple of seconds more and I would've had him—I was going after his eyes first, then when he was blind, I was going to kill him at my leisure.

Then a bunch of guys jumped me and dragged me into an alley, where they stood me up against a wall and shook me for a while. All I could see of the nearest guy was his mouth: I looked at the cracks in his lips as he talked, watched the funny way his tongue moved, and noticed the yellow stains on his teeth. After a while, I realized he was speaking English. His words slowly cut through the buzzing in my head. I understood him to say something about snapping out of it. My eyes focused on him finally. He was a Marine.

"What the shit's goin' on?" I asked. There were sirens somewhere.

"You got in a fight and blacked out. Tried to kill a big dude," he told me.

"Did I make it?"

"No, we got to you first. C'mon, the SPs are on their way now. . . . Let's get the fuck out of here."

So I went down the street with these three Marines, and we had steak and potatoes, and bar hopped until early in the morning. Somehow I got back to my room. I woke up in the afternoon, feeling like shit warmed over, and swore I'd never do it again.

I rode around Manila on a rickshaw, bought some junk that was promptly ripped off, picked up a couple of whores, and spent the rest of my time either drinking or trying to sleep. If I did fall asleep, I had nightmares. There was no way to get rid of them except to wake up and drink myself into a stupor.

By the time that two weeks was over, I was all wrung out. I reported back to the hospital bored, sleepy, and hungover. The doctor looked at my ear and said it was okay. He gave me a piece of paper and sent me to the hospital administrator.

"I'm here to get my orders to go home," I said.

"I'm sorry, Mr. Tyler, but you're going back to 'Nam."

I couldn't believe it. I was half deaf, and I couldn't dive. The brass were stupid, but not *that* stupid.

"I still cain't hear in that ear," I pointed out.

"YOU'RE GOING BACK TO 'NAM," he shouted.

"God damn it, I heard ye. . . . I jist said my ear ain't recovered no hearing."

"You're not cleared to dive. You can't do any more underwater work. But they want you back with your outfit."

"Shit! How'm I gonna lead a goddamned patrol if I cain't hear what the fuck is happenin' over on that left side?" I slammed my fist down on the table.

I guess that was the last straw.

"Take your goddamned papers and get the hell out of here before we call the Shore Patrol and have them put you on the airplane."

They flew me into Tan Son Nhut. There were three other Navy men on the plane, all going to Cam Ranh Bay. I hustled a ride down to the dock and was picked up that afternoon with the rest of the supplies.

"Jesus, Tyler, I didn't expect to ever see you again," the coxswain said when I jumped on board the PBR.

"I was a-hopin' you wouldn't," I told him.

They had a new commander for BSU-One. He was an older man, a thirty-year man, in his late fifties, I'd judge, and a real nice fellow. He was one of those Navy officers who had a wartime commission, who hadn't gone to the Naval Academy, and who usually got passed over for promotions. He was a senior-grade Commander. Heyward was his name.

I went to him and told him who I was and where I'd been, and I showed him my papers. I told him that I couldn't hear a blessed thing out of my left ear, and that I shouldn't be in combat. At least, I shouldn't be on reconnaissance patrols. . . . I shouldn't be patrolling at all, except in a PBR.

He was real sympathetic and understanding. He looked at my medical records and the doctor's declaration that I shouldn't be allowed to dive, and then he went to his file and pulled out some other papers.

"God damn it, Tyler. . . . I'm in a bind. I agree with you all the way, but I've got this letter that says you're the best recon patrol leader in the outfit. That's why you were returned to active duty. It expressly *forbids* my using you just for boat patrols," he said.

"Let me see that goddamned letter!" I reached for it, and he handed it to me.

It was signed: N. N. Morganti, DEPCOMRECOPS, NAVIINTELGROUP, Saigon.

The Chief and Brewster were out on patrols. They wouldn't be in for two or three more days. Commander Heyward had a letter about them, too.

He thought it was highly unusual, but it was only after I told him the story, over a bottle of beer, that he understood.

"The Admiral's on R-and-R," he told me. "When he gets back, I'll take this up with him. I'll see if we can just disregard the letter. I'll even see if we can send you home."

I said, "Shit, you're senior to Morganti. . . . You out-rank him! Just disregard the letter yourself; you're in command here."

But he was looking out after his own ass. This was his last command, and he wanted one last promotion before he retired, so that he could retire with a big boost in retirement pay. He didn't want to do anything that might block that promotion.

Before either Brewster or the Chief got back, I was taking patrols out.

They were all people I didn't know, green SEALs, with no more than a week in-country, any of them. There was no choice for me except to take the point.

First I took them out on some overnight patrols near the barge in relatively "safe" areas. It was as bad as I expected. In the dark, I depended a lot more on my ears than on my eyes, and now I was "blind" on one side. The rain had a tendency to reduce your ability to discriminate sounds anyway, in addition to making the nights even darker. And it was July, when it rains twenty to twenty-five days and is overcast during the rest of the month; the undergrowth is naturally thicker then, too. Under those conditions, five meters is long range for a firefight, and you have to keep a patrol pretty close together to keep them together at all. The point man can't get too far out in front either.

The first couple of nights, we set a couple of ambushes that caught no one. I let different guys take the point going back in, because I felt pretty safe in those areas. After I'd judged the team a little better and got used to working with them, I took them up for a two-day patrol near the Xuyen Canal, where Charley usually infiltrated in small groups.

A good ambush site at night, especially a dark night in the monsoon season, can be drastically different from a good ambush site for a daylight ambush. I was the point man. We were still looking for a good site when I became aware that Charley was around. I could smell the stench of *nuoc-mam*.

I went into a crouch and started turning so as to look . . . and listen . . . all around.

The gook came from behind and to my left. I was just turning that way when he ran in toward me . . . out of the corner of my eye I saw a sudden movement and a dim glimmer of light. He had a knife. I whirled, hit him with the gun barrel, pushed him back, and shot him. I shot two others as they appeared. I wasn't trying to be quiet, because they were. That told me they were probably the only three around. They didn't want to attract the patrol. . . . They just wanted to get the point man and leave the others wondering what had happened.

There was a crashing in the brush. I turned quickly and almost shot a SEAL, but he called out my name, and I held up.

"I told ye to hold yer positions!" I hissed at him.

"We heard something going on, then we heard you shoot. We thought we'd better get up here to help out!"

"First of all, I might've shot ye, and second, ye might've run rat into an ambush! Next time, think before ye run up like that," I told them.

We booby-trapped one of the bodies, and then pulled out. We went back to the canal to call for a pickup. The shots had given our position away.

The gook almost got me. That worried me. A month earlier, I would've heard him before he could get close. . . . I might have spotted him before he moved, even.

There was no doubt about it now: I was over the hill as far as this job was concerned. The kids coming out of

BUDS could do just about as well as I could, and those who'd been in-country a few weeks could do better.

I began to appreciate how my daddy felt, when us wet-behind-the-ears teenage boys got to where we could run the pig farm just as well as he could. He used to hang around while we did the chores, just looking for something to pick at us about, but we'd learned our lessons well—he'd taught us—and he'd seldom find anything wrong with the way we cared for the hogs or worked in the hayfields. It seemed to depress him when he didn't find anything. If we'd been older, and wiser, we probably would've screwed up something just to give him something to find fault about, so he'd feel needed, so he'd feel like he still had to be around to keep things running right. But we weren't that smart. . . . We did everything the best we could, because we didn't want to be chewed out for something we did wrong. It made him feel useless. He'd get depressed, and that's when he'd start to fight with us about our going out drinking or running around. We didn't understand why we were always getting chewed out even when he couldn't find fault with our work. We'd get pissed off and say things we'd be ashamed of later. Then, one day, after a cussin' fight, he went in the house and blew his brains out.

Now I began to understand what it felt like to be in his shoes. These dumb, green kids, with good sets of ears, could be better point men than I could. I was really feeling useless.

By the time we got to the canal, we were all getting tired out, so we laagered up and checked in with the barge. I'd just started to sign off when the radioman on the barge said he had a message for me.

"Go ahead. Over," I said.

I heard Commander Heyward's voice. "We got your ticket home today. Do you still want it?"

"Say again? Over."

He repeated his message and elaborated: "The Admiral says to ship you home right away. Abort your patrol and come on in."

I felt like jumping up and whooya-ing my fool head off.

That morning when we got back, Brewster was already in from his patrol. He was still the same uncouth, insulting, dirty son of a bitch. He said they'd flown him out to a carrier and checked him over, but he had only been stunned a little, so they sent him right back. He was surprised that I'd showed up again.

"I thought we seen the last of ye," he said, "the way ye was a-bleedin'. How come they sent ye back?"

"Morganti," I told him. "Somehow, that sumbitch got transferred to Intelligence, an' he was the one decided."

"That figgers. The Navy *would* put him in Intelligence—he's got about as much intelligence as a fuckin' snake. We should've drowned him while we had the chance."

I agreed with him. Then I told him I was going home anyway.

We sat and drank whiskey and beer until dawn. It was my three hundredth day in Vietnam.

CHAPTER 21

I knew I was in for it when I got off the plane in San Diego and this little M.P. came strutting up to me and told me to take off my beret.

"What do ye mean? That's part of my uniform," I told him.

"Not over here it ain't. Offends the little old ladies. The new order of the day is that no elite outfit can display their berets," he told me. "So get it off, get it put away, or I'll have to take you in."

I looked him over, all five foot four of him, and started to tell him to go fuck himself, that I had earned that beret and was, by God, going to wear it. But, tired of fighting, tired of all this shit, I took my beret off and put it inside my shirt.

When I got back over here, I wanted to tell people how I felt, what was bothering me, but nobody wanted to talk about it. Friends, people I knew before I went over, they'd just sit there like they were embarrassed, or they'd avoid me altogether. If they did talk about it, they always wanted to know the same things.

"What was the use of it?" they'd ask. "Why were we over there in the first place?"

"Hell, I can't tell ye why the government wanted us over there," I'd tell them. "Johnson and Westmoreland didn't come down here and talk those things over with me, ye know. Maybe they believed in that Domino Theory. Maybe they didn't want the Communists to have Cam Ranh Bay—it's the best deep-water port in Southeast Asia. Maybe there was oil in the Mekong Delta. I don't know. But I *can* tell ye why *I* was over there, and most of the guys I knew. There were some there for the killin'—war attracts that kind. And I'll swear a lot of 'em were there to make their fortunes on the black market. But I was there, and my friends were there, to help those people keep their freedom, and to keep them from being butchered by the damned Communists. I know it sounds corny, but we really were. Hell, I wouldn't have gone over there to fight for no oil."

"Was it worth it?"

"Do ye think I'm goin' to sit here and tell ye it wasn't? After goin' through that hell over there, after seein' some good friends die, and losin' my hearing in one ear along with four years of my life? Hell, yes, it was worth it! We were fightin' for their freedom. No matter what Johnson's motives were, or Nixon's. Ours were right. Maybe we were propping up a two-bit dictator. . . . We were opposing a worse one. Hell, the Vietnamese just wanted to be rid of all of it: of Ho Chi Minh and Nixon, of the Viet Cong and the U.S. Army. They just wanted to grow rice and have kids."

Once in a while somebody would ask, "What does it make you feel like, knowing you lost the war?"

I would tell 'em, "I didn't lose any goddamned war.

We whupped Charley just about ever time we met him, even when he outnumbered us. It was you people over here that lost th' fuckin' war. The soldier with his butt out in the boondocks might not have won every fight, and we wasted all kinds of shit over there—bombs and planes and people—but we had Charley fought to a standstill. Then we pulled out—that's what we aimed to do all along. We should've gone back in when North Vietnam invaded. Russia was helping *them*. You people over here, you listened to the newsmen give their opinion, and to Jane Fonda, but you didn't listen to anybody that knew what was going on. You just pulled the goddamned plug and let it all go down the drain. Everything I fought for. Risked my life for. I didn't lose any war. You did.

"Now that that's clear, I'll answer your question: It makes me feel like shit."

I guess the bottom line is, if I could live those years over, would I go through it again, or would I go off to Canada, or to jail, or march around protesting?

I'd go through it again. This time, I wouldn't wait, though. I'd volunteer, before they tried to draft me.

I'd do it again.

The little Chinese girl at the counter of the liquor store looked at me as if she wasn't sure whether to sell me my bottle or call the cops. Where had I seen her before?

"Did you get your money?" she asked.

I said, "Yeah . . . I've got money. What the hell do ye mean?"

She said, "You were in here ten minutes ago, and you set that bottle down and looked at me funny and left." She pointed to a bottle of rum sitting on one corner of the counter, a bottle just like the one I'd just set down. "I thought you'd left your money in your car, or dropped your wallet, and you went out to get it."

Now, why would she make up a crazy story like that?

Where had I seen her, anyway? I'd never been in this
store before, but her face sure looked familiar.

"I wasn't in here ten minutes ago.... I just walked in
here now."

"Oh, I'm sure you're the one," she said. "Is this some
kind of a joke?" Her face started getting hard and drawn-
looking, like she was in pain.

"That's what *I* want to know," I told her. "What's that
burning smell? You cooking something?" It was a nau-
seating burned-meat smell. My hands suddenly felt very
empty and helpless.... They felt like they should be
wrapped around the stock of an M-14.

She just stood there and looked at me. Then I spotted
the bomb strapped to her back and started backing away.
She sort of bent to one side as if she was hurting.... I
kept on backing up until I was out the door, to make sure
she didn't come after me with that bomb....

I told my wife before we got married that I had this
problem. She didn't realize how bad it could be, I guess,
because she just said that compared to the ones her former
husband had, it was minor. That was before the first time
she saw it happen.

Even then, it wasn't so bad: She woke up in the middle
of the night with me sitting on her chest, my hands over
her mouth so she wouldn't yell out, whispering, "Shhh!
They'll hear ye! Don't say a word!" She whopped me up
beside the head and woke me up.

But the next time...

I woke up in midair, leaping at her. She'd got out of
bed to go to the bathroom, and when she came back to
bed, I didn't even wake up, I just reacted.... My hands
were closing on her throat by the time I was awake enough
to stop. That scared her. Me, too.

And, it didn't always happen at night.

One hot summer afternoon, she ran out to the store to

get the fixin's for a barbecue while I finished mowing the front lawn and sweeping grass clippings off the sidewalk. A thundershower came up before I got through, and it started booming, and big old drops of rain started splattering around, kicking up puffs of dust like bullets hitting. I went inside and got a beer and sat down with the broom across my knees to watch the baseball game on TV. It was hot and muggy, and I sort of dozed off.

I woke up squatting down in a hooch, searching it. I could hear artillery rumbling in the distance. Then a grenade went off with a sharp crack right behind me. The ambush was coming down! I jumped up and turned to run outside and met this gook woman coming in. I knocked her down with my gun butt and ran on outside. Two VC were running across the clearing, and I charged out and captured them.

Then my wife's voice cut through it all. The two businessmen I'd captured were looking at me like I'd just escaped from a loony farm. I sheepishly quit pointing the broom at them and started sweeping the sidewalk with it.

"What are ye a-lookin' at?" I asked. "Didn't ye ever see anybody sweep a sidewalk before?"

It takes a hell of a woman to live with shit like that.

The nightmares and the flashbacks kept bothering me.... The nightmares I could put up with, but the flashbacks scared me. I was afraid I'd flash back and kill somebody. Somebody I loved. After I married, I was even more afraid of it.

She's a good woman. She's put up with a lot of horseshit, stuff she shouldn't have had to put up with.

She would listen... some. She didn't really want to hear it, didn't want to know some of those things about me. She tried, but she really couldn't understand what I was trying to get across to her—what a godawful thing it was to kill somebody, to have ended the life of another human being and have that forever on your conscience

... what it was like to have the brains and guts of a friend—or even an enemy—splattered all over you ... what it was like to cut a man's throat and feel his hot blood spraying onto your hand and wrist, and smell it, like walking into a slaughterhouse ... what it was like to do a dirty job like that for your country, a dangerous job, and come back and be treated like a fool or a criminal.

When I got back to Arkansas, I went over to see my old uncle, the one that had been in World War Two.

"These flashbacks, these nightmares ... how long are they going to last?" I asked him.

He put down his jug and looked down toward old Dry Jordan, where the locusts were singing in the sycamores, and his eyes seemed to focus on something ten thousand miles away. He used to do that when he was telling us kids his war stories, and I knew he'd just sit and rock for a long time without saying anything. As a kid, I always got a little impatient with him, when he went away into his own mind like that, but I guess one thing you learn when you sit on ambush a lot is patience. I just sat down on the porch step, took a pull at the jug, and puffed my cigarette and waited.

I always wondered what was going on in his mind when he did that, and at the same time I was thinking about my flashbacks and nightmares. I guess something clicked, because I put it all together.

He was flashing back.

He was reliving a battle from thirty years past. He wasn't listening to the locusts on Dry Jordan; he was listening to the jungle sounds on some South Pacific island, or the rattle of machine guns and the crash of grenades on some bullet-swept beach.

A chill started crawling up my backbone like mist rising out of a swamp. I took a long pull of 'shine from the jug, but the chill didn't go away.

I knew what his answer would be.

Finally, they beat off that banzai attack, or whatever it was, and he sighed and took a swig from the jug.

"How long ye figger ye'll live, J.E.?"

ABOUT THE AUTHOR

James R. Reeves is a mineral exploration geologist. He lives in Spokane, Washington, with his wife, Leeann, a public school teacher and part-time college instructor, and his two children: son Tom Brian and daughter Shannon. Jim and Leeann are natives of West Texas. Jim began writing fiction in grade school, but this is his first effort at a novel.